The Litt in T

JULIE CAPLIN

O
OneMoreChapter

One More Chapter
a division of HarperCollins*Publishers*
The News Building
1 London Bridge Street
London SE1 9GF

www.harpercollins.co.uk

This paperback edition 2020

First published in Great Britain in ebook format by
HarperCollins*Publishers* 2020

A catalogue record for this book
is available from the British Library

Ebook ISBN: 978-0-00-839308-3
B Format Paperback ISBN: 978-0-00-839309-0

Set in Birka by Palimpsest Book Production Ltd, Falkirk
Stirlingshire

Printed and bound in Great Britain by
CPI Group (UK) Ltd, Croydon CR0 4YY

To Nick, Ellie and Matt, who thankfully are all brilliant at fending for themselves.

Chapter 1

Haneda International Airport, Tokyo

'Blend in, Fiona, blend in,' she told herself, the mantra an old and familiar one, while rubbing the back of one calf with her leg like an awkward stork and tugging at the tail of her long blonde plait. Which was totally ridiculous when she was surrounded by teeny tiny women scurrying about like super busy ants. Next to the petite, fey females with their delicate features and thick, lustrous, glossy hair, she felt like a woolly mammoth that had somehow lumbered onto a Paris catwalk. For a horrible moment it was like being back at school, surrounded by the cool girls and their scornful dismissal.

She sucked in what was supposed to be a calming breath but instead sounded more like a tortured wheeze. All around her people were being met, their names held up on little signs by slender men in immaculate suits. She was starting to remember what it was like never to be picked in PE, the duffer that no one wanted on their team.

Trying not to look as anxious as she felt, she peered again

1

at the white signs, praying she'd spot her name. Her ears were ringing with that big-airport echo and her spine tingled with an increasing sense of dislocation. The flight had landed an hour ago, her baggage disgorged with what she'd already realised was Japanese optimum efficiency and here she was still waiting. It was tempting to check the document stuffed in her bag with all the details but doing that, again, would feel too needy and nervous. *Trust the piece of paper and the promises made therein, Fiona*, she told herself. She was here. She was bold. It was no secret she was massively out of her comfort zone but she was going to do this. Despite her mother's reservations, this was the opportunity of a lifetime and one that she'd never believed would happen to her.

Winning the prize of an all-expenses-paid trip to Japan in conjunction with the Faculty of Arts at the Tokyo University Polytechnic was brilliant enough but the chance to exhibit her photographs at the Japan Centre in London was the icing on the cake. She was so thankful that she'd signed up for the evening course run by one of the London universities.

Digging her hand into her pocket, her fingers rubbed over the smooth ivory of the *netsuke*, the little carved figure that would once have been worn as part of traditional Japanese dress. The little rabbit carving travelled everywhere with her, the only thing she had from her father who died when she was a baby. It had inspired a vague, loose interest in Japan, so that when the competition had been announced, even without the prompting of her bossy friend Avril, she'd been tempted to enter. Avril had pushed temptation into action.

And now here she was for two weeks. Two weeks of experiencing everything Japan had to offer, including a mentoring programme with one of the best photographers in the world, Yutaka Araki. She'd worked hard on her application form and whether she believed it or not, she deserved to be here.

Her fingers itched to retrieve the carefully folded white piece of paper in her bag, for the reassurance of reading it just once more. Stop, she told herself, you know it quite clearly says that you'll be met at Haneda International Airport. Someone with one of those neat little whiteboards bearing your name will be here any minute. It might even be the famous Yutaka Araki, himself. Her hand closed over her phone, nestled next to the little rabbit in the deep pocket of her mohair coat. No, she wasn't going to get her phone out and check her messages. There was bound to be another text from her mother with an update on her blood pressure this morning. It regularly rose whenever Fiona did something her mother didn't quite approve of.

Focusing on the airy space surrounding her and gazing around the crowded arrivals hall, she tried to analyse what made it so different. Thankfully some of the signs were in English as well as the fascinating but baffling Japanese calligraphy. Not being able to read basic information had been one of her biggest worries, along with the fact that she had never mastered using chopsticks and had never even tried sushi before because she really didn't fancy raw fish. What on earth was she going to eat?

She swallowed hard. What if no one turned up? What would she do? A rising tide of despair began to take hold and she sighed and shifted to her other foot, gazing hopefully at approaching newcomers. Everything felt alien and uncomfortable. Although she could make out the Coca-Cola logo in the outsized vending machine opposite, the contents of all the other brightly coloured cans were utterly incomprehensible.

Her eyes lit on someone half running, half walking down the concourse towards her, his coat flapping. As he came closer, she narrowed her gaze. It couldn't be. She was imagining things.

Oh, flipping heck with multiple bells on it.

It was.

She almost did that comedic, exaggerated eye-rubbing but there was nothing wrong with her eyesight. Realising it was definitely him, she ducked down into her coat like a turtle.

Gabriel Burnett, *Times* Photographer of the Year, Portrait of Britain winner, Wordham-Smith winner, and recipient of a gazillion other awards for his amazing photographs. The man had talent in spades, not to mention charm, looks and charisma by the bucket load, and had once been quite the media darling.

What was he doing here? No. He couldn't be here for her. It had to be a complete coincidence. But things were adding up in her head. She'd won a photography competition. He was a photographer. She was supposed to be met. He was in the arrivals hall.

He. Could. Not. Be. Meeting. Her.

Despite expressly forbidding herself to feel anything at all, her heart stopped dead for at least ten seconds before erupting into action like a train bursting out of a tunnel at a thousand beats a minute. Gabe Burnett. Heading straight towards her.

Pushing his hand through dark hair that flopped forwards onto his forehead with those quick jerky movements she suddenly remembered so well.

If she could have turned and fled she might well have done, except her feet seemed to have turned into great lumps of clay that she didn't know what to do with. He drew alongside the barrier and pulled out a sheet of white paper with a series of bold slashes. FIONA H. Her name was written as if he'd been in too much of a rush to get the surname down but was at least concerned enough that there might be another Fiona that he'd added the H. Would he recognise the name? It had been ten years. Would he recognise *her*? Highly unlikely. He must have tutored hundreds of students since then. In those days, she'd been much more flamboyant and confident, with a predilection towards Bananarama dungarees, cropped T-shaped jumpers in primary colours and paisley scarves with which she bundled up her hair. Fiona could pinpoint the exact moment that her confidence had shrivelled like an aged walnut. It had a lot to do with the man now standing ten feet in front of her holding up the scruffy bit of paper with her name on it, glancing nonchalantly around the crowded terminal with the style and ease of someone who felt at home anywhere.

'That's me,' she said, putting up her hand like a school girl and nodding towards the piece of paper, 'Fiona. Fiona Hanning.'

'Great. Been waiting long?' He stuffed the makeshift sign into his pocket and, to her surprise, dropped his head and upper body in a quick fluid bow.

She stared at him, putting away the hand she'd held out for want of anything better to do, twisting her mouth slightly at the complete absence of an apology. He was half an hour late. But then, people like him didn't apologise to lesser mortals. They didn't need to.

'I'm Gabriel Burnett. Gabe to most people. Nice to meet you.' He bowed again but then did hold out his hand and she had to scrabble her hand out of her pocket to meet it. 'People bow in greeting here.'

She knew that because she had done some mugging up. She just hadn't expected it from him. 'You get used to it very quickly. They also love a business card. If you're offered one, make sure you take it with both hands and treat it like a revered object. Whatever you do don't stuff it into your pocket. Make sure you put it carefully in your purse, wallet or whatever. Treat it with respect. They're big on respect in Japan.'

'Right,' she said, bemused by his deluge of information. She remembered him as being rather reticent and a man of few words, although expansive when he was talking about his work. But then, she hadn't seen him for ten years. And she'd certainly changed – hugely – in that time. With a sudden smile, she remembered Avril's last words to her before she'd dropped her at the airport. 'Quit the wallflower act. No one knows you there, be who you want to be.' Which was great in theory, especially when you were a super-confident breakfast TV reporter married to the love of your life and had the most adorable two-year-old. Since their press trip to Copenhagen, Avril had become one of Fiona's closest friends.

'This your stuff?' asked Gabe interrupting her reverie.

She nodded lifting her chin slightly. She wasn't eighteen any more.

'You travel light.' He raised an eyebrow in question. 'This all you have?'

'Yes,' she said.

'That'll make it easier on the monorail.' And with that he took charge of what she thought was a huge case and led the way.

Packing for two weeks for a place you'd never been to before had been a minefield, saved only by Avril coming to the rescue with benign bullying. If Fiona had stuck to her original wardrobe plans of jeans and T-shirts her case would have been half the size.

Keeping up with Gabe, weaving through the crowds and taking in all the unfamiliar sights and sounds, took all of her concentration and it wasn't until they were waiting for the monorail, standing in the painted queue lines laid out on the platform, that she had time to catch up with herself.

'Erm … it's very nice of you to meet me.'

Gabe's face fell a little and his voice dropped so she could only just hear it. 'Ah, yes. There's been a slight hitch in the plans. Unfortunately, Yutaka Araki has had a family bereavement and had to return home to Niseko. I'm afraid you're going to have to make do with me.' There was a sardonic twist to his mouth before he added, 'I'm quite well qualified.'

Irritated by the sudden quickening of her pulse and that cocky confidence, she glared at him. 'And I'm well aware of who you are Mr Burnett,' she said, having to lean closer to hear him.

'Mr Burnett. Ouch. That's put me in my place and made me sound like I'm a hundred and three as well.' He laughed quietly

She gritted her teeth to stop herself from pointing out that she knew exactly how old he was.

'Anyway. I'm sorry about Yutaka but it really couldn't be helped. The university contacted me – I used to teach there – and they asked if I could step in. I know Professor Kobashi, who runs the programme here in Tokyo, and his wife; they're actually my landlords. I rent my apartment and studio from them. Anyway, if you're really desperate to meet Yutaka, he might be back at the end of your stay.'

'I'm sure you'll do fine,' said Fiona, surprising herself with her boldness but adopting his lowered tone as she hissed, 'As you said, you're *quite* well qualified.'

Instead of being offended, he grinned at her. 'Nothing like being put in my place, again.'

'I imagine it doesn't happen very often,' she said dryly before she could stop the words coming out of her mouth. Was she teasing Gabe Burnett?

With a wry smile, he turned and examined her face as if looking at her properly for the first time. It was impossible to hide or retreat, not when he was standing right beside her. 'I'm not that insufferable, you know. You shouldn't believe everything you read in the papers.' His eyes studied hers and for a moment she imagined there was more to what he was saying. There had been a period when his photo had appeared in the papers almost as much as his own photographs were featured. Young models had been his favourite props.

'I rarely read the papers. My friend Kate used to work in PR and she says most of it is made up, and my friend Avril works in breakfast TV and usually knows the truth behind the gossip.'

'Sensible,' he said. 'So why Japan?'

Maybe it was the approving look he gave her or the fact that he clearly had no recollection of her, but she drew out the little ivory *netsuke* from her pocket. 'This.'

He immediately put a finger out to stroke the smooth flank. 'May I?'

She handed it over. 'It was my father's. He died when I was a baby and I found it when I was six. I had no idea what it was until my granny told me. A *netsuke*. He bought it in an antique shop when he was a boy and had always wanted to go to Japan as a result. He never got there. When I heard about the competition ...' She shrugged as he gave it back to her. It settled with a reassuring thud in her pocket, a small lump nestled against her thigh.

'Sentimental but nice. You'll get a real flavour of the country in Tokyo.' For a moment, his smile was wistful. 'It's a country of contrasts: flash, modern, innovative, ridiculously neon and technological, all of which resides alongside a deep appreciation and respect for art, culture, and tradition. I've never lived anywhere quite like it before.'

'You live here?'

'Between here and London.' He paused. 'You'll be staying with the Kobashi family.' Again there was that wry smile. 'Professor Kobashi's wife Haruka is lovely and rather interesting. She's a master of tea.'

Fiona straightened with sudden interest. 'I love my tea. One of the things I really want to do is go to a tea ceremony, although I've no idea what it involves.'

'Well you'll be in the right place. She's the expert. She and her daughter own a teashop where she holds ceremonies. They live above it.'

'Really.' Fiona's eyes shone. One of her favourite possessions was a little pottery narrow-spouted teapot with a bamboo handle. She loved the delicacy and simplicity of the design that was as much functional as beautiful. Letting her guard down and forgetting that she wasn't supposed to have met him before, she smiled warmly at him, straight into his grey eyes. He was still a very handsome man.

'Hmm,' said Gabe, stiffening and turning his head away as if she'd got a bit too close or something. His jaw hardened as he stared across the crowded platform.

She pushed her hands into her pockets, one finger stroking the *netsuke*. His withdrawal had been subtle but definite. There was a hardness in her chest as if she'd swallowed a whole brick of wholemeal bread. Tall, gawky girls like her weren't Gabe Burnett's type but he didn't need to make it quite so obvious. She knew he went for glossy, glamorous, pint-size brunettes who exuded confidence from every last pore. Before his move to Japan a few years ago, his love-life had been well documented in the tabloids.

'If you like that sort of thing,' he said dismissively glancing down at his watch. 'All a bit tedious when you've seen it before. One for the tourists.'

'Just as well I *am* a tourist,' Fiona bit out, annoyed by his attitude.

'Which reminds me, have you got your Japan Rail pass?'

'Yes.' The little she had managed to read up on before she came had recommended buying one in advance, and hers had been sent through with her plane tickets.

Gabe didn't say anything as the monorail glided into the station. When they boarded, Fiona turned to say something to Gabe, but even before he put his finger to his lips the hush of the carriage registered. She peered around. It appeared that in Japan people didn't talk on the trains. Gabe had pulled out his phone and was scrolling through something, so she copied him and they spent the rest of the journey in rather convenient silence.

They got off the monorail and dived into the melee of people as Gabe led them across the concourse through to a platform where they changed onto a train line.

'This is the Yamanote line. You'll use it a lot, so it's worth familiarising yourself with it. It's a circular line that stops at all the major city stations. We're headed to Nippori. Professor Kobashi lives in a lovely traditional area called Yanaka.'

After a crowded but silent journey they emerged into the pale sunlight of late afternoon nearly an hour later. Now the initial excitement of being here had faded, exhaustion had crept in to every limb and Fiona found it an effort to put one foot in front of the other as Gabe set a cracking pace along the street without even checking to see if she was following. At least he'd taken charge of her suitcase and was pushing it ahead of him like a man on a mission. A mission to rid himself of her, she surmised, watching his broad shoulders as he marched a few steps in front of her giving her the distinct impression he did not want to be here.

She followed him, disliking the intense sensation of disorientation because she had absolutely no idea where they were in relation to the city. It gave her an uncomfortable and unnerving fear of having lost control. She was a very long way from home. The sixteen-hour flight cocooned in the close confines of the aircraft had cushioned her awareness of the true distance. Now the reality hit hard as she took in the unfamiliar architecture of the buildings, the strange roads signs, the huge multitude of overhead cables that you didn't see at home, and the lamp posts which looked more like ornate bird boxes. It was like nowhere she'd ever been before. Although the street was wide, the houses came right up to the edge of the road with pots of plants around the doors as if to compensate for the lack of front garden. Everything seemed to be made from wood apart from the dark green tiled roofs that sloped down sharply to create a slight overhang.

When she stopped to study the bamboo screens covering the windows, Gabe did pause and wait for her to catch up. 'This is quite a traditional area. These houses are a couple of hundred years old.'

'I love all the wood,' she said, fascinated by the buildings even though they symbolised how far from home she was.

'*Sugi*. Japanese cedar,' he replied as he kept moving, still a few steps ahead of her.

She glared at his back and picked up her stride to keep up with him as he veered off to the right, down another narrower street, and stopped to wait for her outside a shop front.

With a smile, she stared up at the big wood-framed square window, a cross between a bay window at home and a balcony. Trailing jasmine surrounded the window which had a gorgeous but minimalist display of elegantly spouted teapots and beautifully glazed traditional teacups. Underneath the window were several big pots with leafy camellias with deep pink buds about to burst into bloom.

'This is gorgeous,' she blurted out, wishing her camera was to hand.

'Be prepared to get used to it. This is Haruka's teashop; she and Professor Kobashi live upstairs, which is where you'll be staying.'

Fiona clapped her hands in delight. 'It's so lovely.' She took another moment to study the low tiled roof – curling up at the edges like sultan's slippers – that jutted out above the window with its glossy green tiles.

Inside the doorway, a flight of stairs led to the right into the teashop, while on the left was a wider porch area. Gabe immediately toed off his shoes and called out in Japanese. She caught the words '*Haruka san*'.

'You speak Japanese?'

He shook his head. 'Basic greetings. The odd word. That's all. You need to take your shoes off. The slippers there will be for you.' He'd already pushed his feet into a pair of larger slippers.

The door of what looked like paper and wood slid open

to reveal a tiny Japanese woman with her dark hair swept back from her face and piled in a lustrous bun which added at least two inches to her height.

'*Gabriel san.*' She greeted him with clear delight, bowing before kissing him on both cheeks, her dark button eyes shining before addressing him in a stream of low voiced Japanese and patting his arms.

Fiona studied the enthusiastic welcome with curiosity. She'd expected Japanese people to be formal and reserved. There was no sign of that here.

'*Haruka san*, this is Fiona.'

She stepped forward and put both hands together before nodding to Fiona with a polite little bow. 'Welcome, Fiona. It is very good to meet you.' Her smile, though friendly, wasn't quite as effusive as the one Gabe had received; he was obviously very popular round here.

'Come, come.' She led the way with small, neat steps, up a flight of stairs that turned right on itself on a small landing, so that Fiona guessed they were now above the teashop. She couldn't wait to go inside that, although her curiosity was piqued by the very different Japanese interior. The woman led them into a large living area. It was decidedly minimalist with very little furniture and wooden floors which were covered with large mats encompassing the entire central floor area. There were a few very low-level chairs with high upright backs and an odd-looking table that seemed to have its own futon mattress. Apart from a few pottery items on a low-level wooden sideboard and a couple of painted scrolls hanging on the walls, Fiona realised there were very few ornaments and none of the sort of clutter that characterised her mother's house. She smiled; she rather liked the clean lines and tidiness of the room.

Her hostess drew a few more of the sliding doors open and then led them up another wooden staircase to a series of rooms all divided by the same paper and wooden doors. Gabe carried Fiona's case for her and they finally came to a small square room containing a futon on the floor. Haruka raised the bamboo blinds to reveal a balcony that ran the full length of the back of the house, overlooking a very pretty zen-style garden.

'Oh, that's lovely,' exclaimed Fiona, clasping her hands together in delight and earning a warm smile from the Japanese woman.

'I'll show you later. Would you like something to drink?'

'I can't stay,' said Gabe hurriedly. 'I need to get back.' He turned to Fiona. 'For the first couple of days, I thought I could show you around Tokyo. Acclimatise yourself and then you can start thinking about the focus for your exhibition.'

Fiona nodded, pleased he knew that much. It was already causing her a fair amount of anxiety. Although she'd been drawn to the competition by the idea of a trip to Japan, the real prize was the guaranteed exhibition at the Japan Centre in Kensington in London two weeks after she returned home. It was a fantastic opportunity to gain some recognition and perhaps sell some work. She'd been looking forward to working with Yukata Araki, renowned for his beautiful land-scapes, and hoping to learn a lot from him as well as seek his advice on a theme for the exhibition.

But now she was stuck with Gabe. She wasn't sure he would be the right person to help her. He specialised in portraits, for a start.

'Acclimatisation sounds good,' she murmured, the punch-drunk reeling sensation of jet lag starting to make her feel dizzy. She swayed on the spot and Gabe caught her arm. Her eyes immediately shot to his and her breath caught in her chest, almost imagining a quick flare of something before he hurriedly dropped her arm again. Stiffening, she forced herself to focus. Gabe had nothing to fear from her. She'd made a complete dick of herself with him before with fanciful imaginings. She wasn't going to do it again, no matter how flipping attractive she found him.

Chapter 2

'Why? Why? Why?' he asked himself in the mirror as he ran the razor blade over his foaming chin. Going into Tokyo was a pain in the arse at the best of times. Having to take some wide-eyed girl, who really was wide-eyed and wobbly legged – she reminded him of Bambi with those long limbs – was doubly irritating.

Professor Kobashi's pleas hadn't moved him to volunteer to take over as mentor; no, it had been Haruka's distraught tears over her husband's potential humiliation that the plans he'd so carefully laid had collapsed. The Japanese didn't do failure and it would bring shame on the professor if the trip had to be cancelled and Gabe was all too aware of the debt he owed Haruka. Although now Gabe was regretting it. He glanced at his watch; he'd deliberately timed things to avoid travelling during the hideous rush hour that was unique to Tokyo and its eight million commuters. This deliberate ploy, thankfully, also reduced the number of babysitting hours duty required him to fulfil.

With an exaggerated sigh, he took one last look in the mirror and leaned closer to inspect the smooth skin, making sure he'd not missed a spot, although he couldn't have said why he cared. Normally he avoided shaving as often as possible; it was a mindless chore that bored the pants off him. A bit like most things these days. He had a couple of commissions lined up for the next month for Japanese magazines – film stars doing the usual promotional rounds being poked and prodded by their publicists for the right responses but not much else – unless he got a last minute call which did happen more often than not.

He grabbed his phone from the side of the washbasin and read for the third time the text from Yumi.

Meiko is away again. No one else understands me here. I'm so lonely. Come take me out to dinner. Y

On the Shinkansen, the bullet train, the trip to Osaka was only an hour and if he didn't have this babysitting job, he'd have gone like a shot but sadly he had obligations, even though they were weighty and unwelcome. Haruka would definitely disapprove of any dereliction of duty.

Reluctantly he texted back.

Sorry. I'm working today. Perhaps tomorrow.

He never added a kiss. Not anymore. She was a married woman now. The familiar feeling of despair hit and settled into place. For a moment he waited, one hand resting on the still damp sink but there was no response and he could picture her face. He laughed without mirth. Picture her face? He knew every line and plane of that beautiful face, the shape of each delicate feature and every shadow cast by her graceful, elegant bone structure.

In his mind's eye he could see the petulance of her bottom lip and the shadowed sad frown of disappointment. Poor Yumi, she was so desperately lonely and isolated out there in Osaka. She needed a friend. Her husband neglected her, but at the same time indulged her every wish and whim with his wealth.

He shook off the melancholy thoughts. Haruka always said to him Yumi had made her bed and must lie in it – or rather, the Japanese equivalent. Gabe stuffed his phone in his back pocket and left the house.

Fiona was ready, waiting, and bouncing; that was the only way he could describe it. Enthusiasm leaked from her and he almost took a step back as if it might be catching.

'Morning,' she called, kicking off her slippers and sliding her feet into a neat pair of Chelsea boots.

'You're very bright and cheerful. I take it you slept well.'

'I did. There's something different ... I think it's the smell of the tatami mats. It's like sleeping outdoors.'

He raised one sceptical eyebrow, having become accustomed to the fragrant, grassy smell over the years.

'Haruka been giving you a 101 in Japanese culture?'

'I asked her about the mats. And,' she added eagerly, 'the sliding doors. Made of paper and wood. They're rather beautiful.'

'*Shoji* screens.' He'd got used to them but he could remember a time when they'd been a novelty. 'Designed originally to create space for a *samurai* to swing his sword.' Okay, so he'd absorbed some information over the years and wasn't averse to trying to impress her a little.

'Yes, that's what Haruka told me.'

He smiled. 'The Japanese are very good at keeping their traditions alive while at the same time being one of the most innovative and technologically advanced societies. Talking of which, if you're ready, we'll take the train and then hit the subway system which should be a lot more civilised at this time of day.'

She stooped to pick up a padded camera bag.

'You're probably not going to need that today.'

'Really?' She clutched the strap as if he might have to wrest it away from her.

'I want you to look today, see things, feel the atmosphere. Be in the moment. Too many photographers hide behind their cameras and they end up with superficial, surface shots. A good photographer reveals the layers beneath.'

She blinked at him.

And well she might. Where had that come from? Bullshit 101. It was something he might have believed once but now … Now he didn't want her slowing down the day snapping at everything in sight; it would make an already tedious day even more unbearable.

Today was something to get through as smoothly as possible. He'd decided his strategy and he couldn't help but wish he was on the train to Osaka instead.

Once they left the train station, Fiona developed an ache in her neck, craning this way and that to take everything in.

Skyscrapers, neon lights flashing and, taking up every available bit of space, so many people. She'd never seen crowds like it. Gabe had said very little to her on the subway, although she realised that was probably due to local travel etiquette.

'Here we are,' said Gabe but she'd seen the sign from further down the road and had excitedly increased her pace. This had been one of the key priorities on her wish list when she'd been swotting up with her guide book on the long flight here. TOP Museum, the letters announced, which made her smile. The Tokyo Photographic Art Museum.

'Perfect.' She beamed at him. 'How did you know?'

'Know?' She almost laughed at his horrified uncertainty and the way he stepped back as if she'd handed him a grenade and was waving the pin at him.

'That this was my number one destination. The place I really wanted to visit.'

'You're a photographer?' He spread his hands wide, his face wreathed in a charmingly insincere smile.

'An amateur. I'm still learning. I'm actually a blogger and Instagrammer. Until I won this competition, I've never really thought of myself as a proper photographer but I'm really excited to see these pictures, although they'll probably depress the hell out of me. Looking at all that talent. Does it do that to you? Or does it inspire you to go and be better?'

Lines creased his brow and it struck her that he knew nothing about her. He certainly hadn't bothered asking her any questions about herself and yet had been arrogant enough to assume she knew who he was at the airport. The thought made her feel inconsequential and for a moment she shrivelled a little, but then a little line of anger trickled down her spine, like the flash fire along a fuse. She'd come all this way, taken a risk, been prepared to step away from the handrail and he didn't seem to know anything about her. Had he even taken the trouble to read her application to the competition or open up the file of photos that went with it? She was proud of those and, she acknowledged bitterly, she still wanted his approval. Craved his praise. Because he was a professional, she told herself, and not in the way she'd wanted it at eighteen when she'd been desperate for him to notice her. A touch of anger stirred in her twenty-eight-year-old self, older and a lot wiser. Surely looking at her application would have been a basic courtesy both to herself and to the person he'd taken over from. What was the point of half doing the job? Was he really that egotistical that he just didn't care?

'Have you even seen my portfolio?' she asked with sudden sarcasm. 'Read my entry?'

He held up his hands. 'I'm sorry. No. I didn't.'

You had to admire someone who didn't try to lie their way out of trouble and faced it head on but even so ... 'No surprise there. I had you down as a flake.' Oops, not quite the word she'd been aiming for and judging by his scandalised affront, completely the wrong thing to say. She had a habit of doing that.

'Excuse me? A flake? How on earth do you figure that? You don't even know me.'

'Yeah.' Except she did know him. 'You're the sort of guy that does what he wants.' She knew that from his perfunctory attempt at teaching a class when most of the students had been too dazzled by his celebrity status to complain and, truth be told, she had been one of the worst offenders. But no more. She was here to learn. Two short weeks were all she had to nail the exhibition which would give her a foot in the door of an exhaustingly competitive industry. 'How did they con you into taking over Araki's gig then?'

'There was no con involved.' He bristled and glared back at her. 'Now, if you want to maximise your time here, I suggest you make a start. I'll meet you back here in three hours.' Before he could say another word, he wheeled around and walked away, leaving her standing with her mouth open and doing a very passable impression of a goldfish.

The ... the ... had he just dumped her here? What sort of mentoring was that? With a huff she turned around and walked into the museum, grateful for the English signage everywhere. It would be better without him, she decided.

And it was. With five floors of galleries, there was so much to see and it felt positively self-indulgent to glide about at her own pace, skipping the things that didn't interest her and pondering for much longer the pictures that did. Recently, she'd decided that life was too short to spend time on things you didn't have to, like finishing books that didn't appeal, watching the end of a film that wasn't your thing, and studying every picture in an exhibit.

Enjoying the quiet, serene atmosphere with hushed whispers and soft footsteps, she turned a corner and walked into a new section where she came face to face with a Gabriel Burnett. It was the picture that caught her attention first rather than his name: an arresting image of a beautiful Japanese woman buried in cherry blossom petals, her limbs carefully arranged in a sea of the flowers with one graceful arm held out, the hand in supplication, catching a frothy pink, out-of-focus, falling blossom. At first when Fiona saw the picture she could admire the technique, the lighting and the way the edges of the flowers blurred, but as she studied the picture, so much more emerged creating a slight but definite unsettling awareness.

Exquisite eyebrows framed the woman's almond-shaped eyes and the camera highlighted her flawless magnolia skin, but when you examined that beautiful bow-shaped mouth for a second time, the smile held a knowing hint of provocation. Although the composition of the picture was fresh and wholesome – a pretty girl in the flowers – when you looked deeper there were hints of secrets and sexuality, mystery and suppressed desire. All was not what it seemed. Fiona could almost imagine the serpent writhing alongside in the blooms. Eve, the temptress.

The small label to the side of the print called it *Girl in Blossom* by Gabriel Burnett, 2016. Beside that was a small biography of Gabe which included the information that the model in the picture, Yumi Mimura, was his long-time muse and favourite subject.

Fiona moved around the room and came to a second picture. This time, the setting was a party and Yumi, wearing a deep blue, satin cocktail dress with a tiny nipped in waist and wide skirt, peeped out from behind two sober grey-suited men with their backs to the camera. Holding a martini glass, she possessed an Audrey Hepburn-esque elegance and sophistication combined with an elfin appearance and a sense that she was planning some mischief quite at odds with her glamorous appearance. Fiona smiled; the composition was quite enchanting and very different from the previous picture.

Intrigued now both by the subject and Gabe's undeniable skill, she focused on the pictures he'd taken of Yumi Mimura over the years. In some she wore western clothes, in others Japanese kimonos, and sometimes she was tastefully nude revealing nothing she shouldn't in terms of flesh, but in each picture there was always an additional, subtle depth that conveyed an untold story or an emotion. The pictures all highlighted Gabe's incredible skill. Coming at last to the final picture, Fiona examined the composition. In it Yumi wore a sophisticated white silk dress which hung beautifully, the folds draped over her exquisite body. The way it was lit made her appear as if she were glowing with angelic beauty but then Fiona paused and suppressed a sudden wince. Triumph. That was what she saw in the composition. Inviolate confidence and self-assurance. Sure of her beauty and her place in the world. Exactly the sort of person who made Fiona all too aware of her own short comings.

Gabe was, she realised, nothing short of a genius. Every bit as talented and celebrated as Yutaka Araki. What had she been thinking of, deliberately goading him earlier? He'd earned his arrogance. Now she felt humble. Who was she to question him? She could learn so much from him if she could keep a civil tongue in her head. If she were honest with herself, she was indulging in teenage sulks that she should have grown out of. When was she going to grow up and forget about that stupid class? He clearly had. In fact, she guessed now, with the sharpened vision of hindsight, that the episode had probably never registered with him. He didn't even remember her name.

With half an hour to kill before she was due to meet Gabe in the foyer downstairs, Fiona toyed with having lunch in the museum's restaurant, but the unfamiliar menu, with foods she'd never heard of, and the prospect of having to eat in public with chopsticks, put her off. She was going to have to ask Haruka, who had been kind enough to refrain from laughing at Fiona's ineptitude over dinner last night, to help her master chopsticks, otherwise she was going to have to get very used to cold food.

She took her time going down the stairs to meet Gabe. Having seen his work, she felt shy and uncertain ... but also inspired, and she couldn't wait to get started. For the first time, she acknowledged to herself that when she'd signed up for his class all those years ago, like every other student she'd been starstruck by his celebrity status rather than a real admirer of his talent.

Outside, she spotted him studying one of the huge pictures outside the museum – ironically, a scene of Paris.

'I love this picture,' he said idly as she drew alongside him, without so much as looking at her. 'It captures that *je ne sais quois* of the French perfectly. Are you all done?'

'Yes.'

'Enjoy it?'

'Yes.' She paused, waiting for him to ask more questions or solicit her opinion on what she'd seen.

'Good.' He turned and began to walk briskly, inviting no further conversation.

Realising he had no intention of waiting for her, she trotted after him, determined to engage with him. He'd had three hours to himself. He was supposed to be her mentor; he owed her

'I can't decide whether I feel inspired or depressed. I'm never going to be that good.'

'Probably not,' said Gabe equably.

For a moment it took a minute for his blunt words to sink in. 'Thanks for the encouragement.'

'I don't deal in dishonesty. You wouldn't come out of the Louvre and say I'm never going to be as good as Monet or Van Gogh. Because no one would be. They were geniuses of their age. Here you've had a snapshot of the very best of the very best.'

'I suppose so,' she said.

'If it's any consolation, from what I've seen you're a good, competent technician.'

She turned, a touch deflated. 'Damning with faint praise.'

'No, encouraging with honesty. Any idiot can take a once-in-a-lifetime photo through sheer luck. A good, competent technician can look for those perfect compositions, seek them out, know it when they see it, and take the shot.'

She could see what he meant but it still stung a little.

'You're here to find those compositions ... with my help.' He cocked his head. 'Have you eaten?'

27

'No, I was—' Thankfully he interrupted before she had to confess what a wuss she'd been.

'Good. There's a great tempura bar not far from here. We can grab a bite to eat there.' What was a tempura bar? She didn't like to ask but, given her stomach was rumbling like a volcano, at the moment she'd probably eat anything.

Gabe knew he'd been an arse; you couldn't miss the disappointment in that expressive face. The blue eyes damn well shimmered with it. She was a heart-on-her-sleeve girl but he couldn't bear to talk about photography, about the amazing, often gut-wrenching, pictures in that incredible collection. Pinching his lips tight as he noted the droop of her shoulders, he considered an apology; she deserved more but ... he couldn't do it. Like a snake gliding through his gut, his stomach tied in knots at the thought of it. She was bound to want to talk about the greats – he could already see the earnest enthusiasm that wanted to bubble out of her. She'd want to talk techniques, what she'd seen, what she loved ... and he didn't think he could bear it.

When was the last time he'd taken a decent shot? A truly memorable picture? Sure, he could take pictures that made people happy enough, like a performing bloody monkey, but he'd lost that ability to find and capture what was under the skin. Really lost it, and he missed it like a part of his body. Once it had been second nature, constantly lurking in his peripheral vision, an added sixth sense he could call upon at any moment. A has-been, that's what they called people like him.

'If you don't mind a bit of a walk, we'll go to the restaurant and then we could take in Shibuya Crossing,' he offered, taking her arm and steering her down the path. If they ate quickly, they could pick up the subway there and still be in plenty of time to avoid rush hour.

'What's that?' she asked as wary as a puppy that had been kicked once, making him feel even more of a shit. Yet he couldn't help the little prickle of anticipation at showing her one of Tokyo's iconic landmarks.

'Wait and see,' he said with a quick grin.

'That's mean,' she said, rolling her eyes. His heart gave a funny twist at her instant sunny acceptance. A point to her. She didn't seem to bear grudges.

'I know,' he waggled his eyebrows at her to make her laugh. 'But I want to see your face.' He fingered the small Lumix camera in his pocket which he carried out of habit rather than that previous obsessive desire that he should never miss out on a potential shot. He frowned, an elusive wisp of a memory sliding through his brain. For a moment as she laughed, he thought she looked familiar.

'Will I like it?' she asked.

'Hmm, I'm not sure *like* is the right word but it's got to be seen. There's quite a lot to see in Tokyo. Do you have anything you're desperate to see?'

'I'd like to see the cherry blossoms, Mount Fuji, although I know it's a way out, and some of the shrines.' She lifted her shoulders. 'I was quite busy before I came, so I didn't get a chance to do as much research as I'd have liked.'

'You said you're a blogger.' While he'd been waiting in a

coffee shop for her he'd dug out the emails, read her application, seen her photos, and visited her blog. He hadn't expected to be impressed, but he was. 'What does that entail, day to day? I took a peek at your site. You're a busy bee.'

She blushed but gave a little laugh. 'It grew ... like *Alice.* Originally it started as me visiting places I was interested in and taking photographs and blogging about my trips but then people began to follow me. And then PR companies started inviting me to places. I even went to Copenhagen once on a press trip and now I'm asked to do things which has expanded the focus of my articles. So really it's now more of a magazine site. Sometimes I have my readers vote on what I should do next – that was flipping Avril's idea, which means they're really invested.' Her mouth crimped in amusement. 'Sometimes I think they don't like me very much ... but it's ... really made me do things I'd never have done. Last month they had me abseiling down a church tower to raise money for charity and the month before I was driving around Silverstone in a Ferrari. Although, that turned out to be a lot of fun and not half as scary as I'd imagined. Then in the last few weeks I've been basket weaving, visited Castle Howard, and learned how to make sourdough bread.'

He nodded. 'And who's Avril? Your sister?'

Fiona snorted. 'Ha! No. She would be insulted by that. She's a very glamorous TV presenter that I met on that press trip in Copenhagen who, for some bizarre reason, has been determined to foster my career ever since. She's totally forceful and I have to meet her at least once a month. It's her fault I'm here. If there were an Olympic gold in nagging, she'd win it hands down. But,' she sobered, 'she, that trip, and my friends Kate and Eva, they really ... well, they helped me.'

'How?' Now he was interested. There was a story here. He kept up a brisk pace with the occasional glance her way, so as not to scare her off.

Her laugh was tinged with the high pitch of nerves. 'Before ... before that trip, I kind of hid from real life. Lived my life online rather than mixing with people.'

He deliberately didn't comment, waiting for her to continue to fill the silence in the natural way that people always did. The technique had served him well over the years when he was trying to get to the essence of someone when he had to photograph them. Those unguarded moments when they revealed truths about themselves were pure gold if he could press the shutter at exactly the right moment. Luckily for him he had excellent reflexes.

Unlike most people, Fiona didn't elaborate. Instead she closed in on herself, as if the introspection had brought with it unhappy memories.

'Sorry, I didn't mean to pry. It's part of my technique to get my portrait subjects to open up.'

'I'm not one of your subjects,' she said, her voice sharp. 'And I have no desire to be.'

A pangolin rather than a hedgehog, he mused, finding himself fascinated by the way she'd hunched into her coat – a hideous hairy thing that ought to be tossed in the nearest skip – and how her shoulders gained a stooped curve. Much as he wanted to take a photograph, he refrained.

'That's a refreshing change,' he said lightly. 'Most people

are desperate for me to take their picture and, more often than not, for free. And others fancy being my muse.' It was, he supposed, the photographer's equivalent of a groupie.

She unbent a little and one side of her mouth lifted. 'I definitely don't. It must be irritating though.'

'A touch. No one wants to pay for anything these days – music, books, art, films.'

'The downside of technology, but the upside is that it's given me a living.'

'I think more than technology has played a part. You must be good at what you do; there are thousands of people out there with blogs.'

Her response was a shrug that irritated him. 'There's nothing worse than false modesty,' he accused, and he was annoyed when she stared at him. 'What? I know my worth. You should too. Especially when it's how you earn your way.'

'I'm not trying to be modest, false or otherwise,' she retorted. 'I do what I do. I'm lucky that people like it and continue to follow and get involved.'

'But there must be a level of skill to garner that kind of engagement, in your writing, in posting the right pictures that will elicit people's interest.'

Again she shrugged.

'You need to have more self-confidence.'

'Sure, like it's something you can pick up off the shelf,' she said with a snap to her voice. 'Oh look, I'll have half a pound of belief, a pinch of arrogance, and a side serving of assurance. Because it's really that easy.' Her final words were spoken in a lower tone as if they were unwillingly dragged out of her and once again he felt that stab of guilt.

The restaurant was packed but Gabe led the way, worming his way through the crowd to snag the last two barstools facing the kitchen where a couple of chefs were working.

'Ever had tempura before?' he asked as she shed her coat and picked up a menu.

'No.' She glanced around the busy and very noisy restaurant. Over the chatter she could hear the swish of hot oil and the ting, ting of utensils scraping metal as the chefs worked at a furious pace in the kitchen in front of them.

'Then you're in for a treat, although this place will spoil you for ever after.'

'I don't even know tem ... temp ... what it is.'

'Tempura,' supplied Gabe. 'It's basically food deep fried in batter ... but nothing like the heavy batter you get on fish at home. You wait.'

She stared at the menu, her mind a little boggled. It was all in Japanese and completely unintelligible. Over in the kitchen one of the chefs was dipping something raw and almost translucent into a jug of white – what she now realised, must be – batter.

'Don't worry.' Gabe put out a hand and pushed her menu down. 'Do you like seafood?'

She nodded. 'Leave it to me. Japanese cuisine is all about the freshness and simplicity of the ingredients. They tend to shop daily for their food to make sure it's as fresh as it can be.'

Gabe ordered in Japanese and in seconds two steaming cups of green tea arrived. Fiona took a hesitant sip and sighed. 'Oh, I needed that.'

The clean, light flavour and burst of warmth down her throat revived her flagging spirits immediately. It was both refreshing and comforting at the same time, especially when she cupped both hands around the pottery cup the way Gabe had done.

The chef stopped in front of them and showed them a bamboo woven plate of raw prawns, scallops, tiny fillets of fish, squid, and some baby sweet corn, a slice of an odd-looking root vegetable, aubergine, and what she guessed were chestnut mushrooms.

She nodded and smiled at the chef, wondering if she was supposed to take the plate. Her stomach rolled a little at the thought of raw seafood but before she could do anything, Gabe spoke in Japanese and the man took the plate away.

'Your face,' teased Gabe as a waitress brought them a set of small pottery dishes each containing different sauces and seasonings.

'I thought he was giving it to us.'

'No, just showing us the quality. Did you notice it didn't smell at all fishy?'

'Yes.' Now he pointed it out, the lack of smell was noticeable.

'That's a mark of how fresh it is. And now he's going to cook it for us. Watch. See the batter in the jug there. It's very thin and almost translucent.'

Fiona watched as the chef dipped the scallops in the batter and then tossed them in a deep pan of oil that was so hot it was smoking. With quick, lithe movements, the chef lifted the scallops out of the oil and tossed them around the basket with a definite air of performance before sliding the crispy golden scallops onto small oval plates with a flick of the wrist and placing them on the counter in front of them. Talk about freshly cooked – this was instant.

Fiona inhaled deeply; she could see the fine sheen of oil still bubbling on the surface. The scallops smelled delicious and her mouth was already watering.

'Now you dip them in any of these.' He pointed to an herb-speckled sea salt, the coarse white crystals mixed with tiny crumbs of green, and several other condiments. 'This is seasoned salt, usually with bamboo greens, and this is grated *daikon*, a sort of radish, which you mix with the soy sauce to make a dipping sauce. Try it.'

She fumbled with her chopsticks and almost sent the little scallop flying.

'I'm not very good with these.'

Gabe smiled. 'It takes a while to master them. No ... not that like that. Here.'

He took the chopsticks from her hand and took it in his, his thumb brushing the tender skin on her palm. Intimate and unexpected, Fiona felt a rush of heat at the sensitive touch. She deliberately avoided looking at him and kept a fixed gaze on her fingers.

'Relax,' he said in a soothing voice which made her do anything but. It was just sensitive skin, that was all. Slightly ticklish. She straightened her back and concentrated on what he was saying.

'Right.' With his hand covering hers, he repositioned the top chopstick between her thumb and index and middle finger. 'Hold it like a pen but two thirds of the way up rather than down at the bottom. Now anchor the second one on your ring finger.'

Desperate to shake off his hand and stop the ridiculous awareness of him buzzing through her system, she moved her fingers and promptly dropped the lower chopstick. She blushed. Clumsy as ever.

'Have another go. It takes a while to master and luckily Japanese culture is all about enjoyment of food which means they don't get hung up on table manners.' He gave her an encouraging smile but it didn't stop her worrying about being a complete klutz.

'That's just as well, otherwise I might starve.'

'Not on my watch.' With a quick, fluid movement he scooped up one of the scallops and held it in front of her mouth. Obediently she opened up and took the dainty morsel, groaning as the flavours hit her tongue.

'Oh my goodness, that is ... mmm.' The amazing taste distracted her from the thought that being fed by Gabe was a little uncomfortable. A bit too up close and personal. The outside of the batter was so crisp and light while the scallop inside was tender and fleshy with a lovely, slightly sweet flavour. 'That's one of the best things I've ever tasted. I didn't think I liked scallops. Aren't they sometimes a bit chewy?'

In the meantime, Gabe had taken one himself. 'Not if they're cooked to perfection, like this. Now try one with the grated *daikon* and soy sauce. Just mix the two and then dip.'

She managed to catch a scallop after chasing it around the plate; she discovered, greed was a great incentive to improve a person's skills. Putting a mouthful between her lips, she found that the addition of salty soy and the fresh sharpness of the radish created an amazing burst of flavour in her mouth and she let out another involuntarily moan.

By this time, the chef had dished up a small plate of prawns, which were wonderfully juicy and tender and were definitely the best prawns she'd ever eaten. This was followed by the delicate fillet of fish encased in its light, crisp case, the textures complimenting each other perfectly. Over the next fifteen minutes they worked their way through vegetables which had just the right amount of crunch, melt-in-the-mouth squid and several types of mushrooms with meaty textures and rich juices.

'That was absolutely delicious,' sighed Fiona as she polished off the last mouthful of what had turned out to be lotus root. She felt comfortably full but not stuffed as if she'd eaten exactly the right amount. 'I thought it would be sushi everywhere.'

'That's a common misconception. Sushi is actually more for special occasions. A bit like we would have roast beef. And there's a lot more to sushi than those plastic trays in the lunch section of supermarkets in London.' As Gabe spoke, she was already busy thinking about writing a blog post describing her first experience of Japanese food.

Gabe guided her out of the restaurant and up the street which became noticeably busier as they neared the hub of Shibuya and the famous crossing.

'Oh!' exclaimed Fiona, and Gabe smiled. It was the Tokyo of so many pictures, the huge crossing of two-lane highways intersected by a series of zebra crossings surrounded by huge neon billboards flashing with adverts and brand names. It was brash, vibrant, bold and a little bit mind blowing, even to someone who'd seen it a hundred times before. The bemused shock on Fiona's face as she stared up at the electronic boards had him reaching for the Lumix in his pocket.

'I feel like I'm in *Blade Runner*.' She shot a quick frustrated glare at him. 'I wish I'd brought my camera now. This would be perfect for my blog.' She took out her phone instead and busied herself taking lots of snaps. 'And it's definitely an Instagram moment.'

Around them were lots of other spellbound tourists trying to capture the brightly coloured images which streamed across the giant screens mounted on every available surface of the buildings guarding the busy intersection. Gabe knew from experience they didn't photograph well without the right equipment but left Fiona to it, watching her expressive, mobile face, thoughtful and absorbed by degrees as she snapped away.

Intrigued and slightly bemused by the realisation, it occurred to him that for the first time in a very long time, he could feel that creative itch. He wanted to take her picture and capture all that wholesome enthusiasm.

'Come on, we haven't got much time. We ought to be thinking about getting back.' He took a few steps forward as she paused to take one last picture with her phone and then the lights changed and a surge of pedestrians came across the road, like a tidal flood with a fast-flowing stream coming the other way. One minute Fiona was by his side and the next she'd vanished.

Swept along by the rush of people, Fiona suddenly realised how crowded it was. This was worse than Oxford Street on Christmas Eve. Even though she was a little taller than the average person here, she couldn't see through the mass of people. Where was Gabe? She'd lost him. Trying to stand still and search for him was impossible; she was jostled and pushed in every direction like a piece of flotsam bobbing in the sea. Working her way through the crowd, she did her best to make it back to the place where she'd last seen Gabe but she couldn't seem to find it and realised she'd lost her bearings. With the changing images, she wasn't sure if this was the street they'd been on. There were several to choose from at the busy crossing.

Being among this many people was suffocating and her throat tightened. *Don't panic*, she told herself. *You'll find him.* But even as she eyed the masses of people, her stomach tightened into a hard knot. There was no sign of him and they hadn't exchanged mobile numbers – her own fault; she hadn't wanted to ask him. Hadn't wanted anything that would be too familiar. Foolish now, she thought. He hadn't even remembered her anyway.

A light sweat filtered its way down her back. Among all these people she was overheating and had to undo her coat. Did she even know how to get back to Haruka's house? Nippon, Nipple, something like that. Even though Gabe had told her the name of the station they'd used yesterday, the unfamiliar name hadn't sunk in. Nor the line they'd used. Yamaha? Yama something. Would she even be able to find it? This was worse than when she'd got lost on the beach in Scarborough on holiday with her mum. At least then she spoke the language and the nice lady that had found her had called the police. It had been terrifying but she'd known what to do. Pulling out of the crowd, she rested against one of the shop windows, her breath shallow. Tears filled her eyes and she wished she was back at home in safe and familiar surroundings. The environment here seemed so alien and different from anything she'd ever known. For a moment she wished she hadn't come and she pushed both her hands in her pockets, huddling into her coat in despair. Her fingers found her rail pass and the little *netsuke*. She rubbed its smooth surface trying to be brave. Her dad hadn't made it to her age – he'd died of some undiagnosed heart condition – and the thought of it made her remember that this was supposed to be an opportunity. A once-in-a-lifetime trip. She needed to pull herself together and ask for help.

No one gave her so much as a second look as they hurried by, heads down, with great purpose. There were quite a few Western tourists about but without knowing which station she needed to get to, she could hardly ask for help. Suddenly she remembered that Gabe had said it was a circular line. And she knew it began with Yama. That was a start. On shaky legs, she headed across the road to the station, buffeted by the growing tide of commuters who were starting to head home.

Above the ticket barriers were a plethora of signs, coloured lines and numbers. And then she spotted it. Green. Yamanote. That was it. Light-headed with relief, she wriggled her way through to the correct barrier with her rail pass. She had no idea which platform to choose but if the line was circular she would just stay on it and pray she recognised a station name. She gritted her teeth and made a choice wishing for the hundredth time that she'd never come here.

The platform she chose was already ten deep with everyone wedged up against each other in the neat lines. The pervading silence felt hostile as if everyone was gearing up to go into battle the minute train arrived. She'd barely been there thirty seconds before a train thundered in and everyone surged forward with death defying eagerness before it had even stopped. As soon as the doors opened her feet barely touched the floor – it was like crowd surfing at a gig and thoroughly unnerving. Even if she'd wanted to there was no way she could have changed direction. Somehow, she was carried forward onto the train and pinned between several people who held her upright. Close to tears again, she stared glassy eyed at the map on the carriage wall trying to make out the impossibly unpronounceable names. Shinjuku, Takadanobaba, Ikebukuro, all of which sounded as if they were places in a galaxy far, far away. Nishi Nippori. Nippori. That was it. Her heart sped up with sudden excitement. Nippori, she remembered. Thank God. The sudden relief kept her sane through the miserably overcrowded journey.

By the time the train pulled into Nippori, she didn't care if it was the wrong station or not, she was so desperate to escape the stifling crowd. Limp and exhausted, she staggered off the train, wishing she could catch the next flight home. This place was alien, inhospitable, and claustrophobic, and now, to cap it all off, it was pissing with rain. The only bright side was that at least she recognised the little parade of kiosks opposite the station and knew where to go. She hoped.

Chapter 3

There it was. Through the sheeting rain, the lamp burning in the window of the pretty little teahouse was a magical beacon and Fiona almost collapsed with relief. She'd made it.

Remembering that Gabe had told her the Japanese never locked their doors, she stepped inside the house, shivering slightly in the sudden warmth, kicked off her sopping shoes and slid her feet into the dry slippers.

Haruka came bustling to the door, concern etched into the worried frown on her face. 'Come, come. What happened?'

'I lost Gabe,' Fiona muttered, wrung out with emotion but also with a slight sense of triumph. Despite all her fears and the awful journey, she had found her way back.

Within minutes, Fiona was wrapped in a blanket and led into a room where two other women were seated at the funny table with its own duvet. 'Come, sit.' Haruka urged her towards one of the floor-level padded chairs with its high back and she crouched down into it. The chair was a foot off the floor but as soon as her legs were tucked under the table she felt a delicious heat. It was warm underneath the duvet and slowly the cold in her bones started to seep away.

She slumped in the chair, too drained to say anything, while Haruka called Gabe to let him know she was safe and sound. Apparently he was still at Shibuya looking for her. Fiona couldn't help but smile at the thought.

Gradually she began to revive, the warmth of the wonderful table bringing her back to life.

'Mmm,' she finally groaned, the numbness in her cold toes starting to recede. 'This is lovely. Is Gabe OK?'

'He was worried but ... I knew you were a sensible girl.' Haruka beamed at her. '*Fiona san*, this is my daughter Setsuko and my granddaughter, Mayu.'

'Hello,' said Fiona nodding shyly, slightly unnerved by being thrust into such close proximity to complete strangers but with goose bumps running riot over her skin there was no way she was retreating from the lovely comfort of this, her new favourite piece of furniture. 'What is this?' Would it be rude to lift the curtain of thick, heavy fabric to peer underneath?

'It's a *kotatsu*,' explained Haruka.

'There's a heater underneath,' said Mayu in flawless English. 'You don't have anything like it in England.'

Fiona smiled at her slightly boastful tone. 'We don't. Have you been to England?'

'I spent six months there at the language school in Winchester where Jane Austen is buried.'

'Did you enjoy it?'

'I love England. I can practise my English with you.'

'It sounds pretty good to me.'

'My dad is American. He's a pilot with JAL. Japanese Airlines.'

That explained a lot.

'Would you like some tea?' asked Haruka leaning forward to the centre of the table to pick up a ceramic teapot. She poured the tea into the small pottery cups and dispensed them with a slight bow. Fiona inhaled the fragrant brew and smiled to herself. After her hellish journey she already felt as if she were in another world. This was a lovely, cosy cocoon, like coming back to shore after being cast adrift in a storm.

'Green tea, a special mix of my own,' said Haruka. 'You must come into the teashop. I will show you around.'

'You'll enjoy that,' said Setsuko with a quiet smile. 'My *haha* is quite an expert. Unless you're a coffee addict.'

'No, I drink it but I prefer tea. Gabe told me that you are'—she turned to Haruka—'a master of tea.'

'She is,' said Setsuko proudly. 'And in the teashop there are many, many blends of tea. They can be bought. This is where we hold the tea ceremonies. You should come,' said Setsuko, checking in with her mother who seemed to have no problem following her daughter's English.

Haruka nodded. 'Yes. You must come.'

'Yes, please, I'd like that,' said Fiona taking a tiny sip, both hands cupped around the hot china. 'Mmm. That's good.'

Haruka nodded approvingly and sipped at her own tea. 'Apart from your journey home, did you have a good day?'

'Very interesting.' Fiona nodded, telling them where she'd been. Surprisingly, as the cosy warmth gradually permeated her chilly bones, she found herself abandoning her usual reticence and raving about the tempura bar and how Gabe had introduced her to the wonderful food.

'He is a good man,' observed Haruka.

'He's a very good photographer. I saw a few of his pictures in the museum. Of a woman called Yumi.'

'Pah!' said Haruka, turning away from the table. She let loose a volley of low-pitched Japanese. Fiona didn't need a translator to surmise that Yumi was not popular with the older woman. 'She is not a good woman.'

Setsuko patted her mother's hand with a chiding tut while her daughter, Mayu, rolled her eyes in a gesture that was entirely teenage. '*Okasaan*, you shouldn't say such things.'

'Yumi is very famous and very beautiful,' Mayu chipped in with teenage bluntness. '*Jiji* doesn't like her.'

Haruka said something else and Setsuko shook her head, ducking it slightly to hide a reluctant smile.

'What did she say?' asked Fiona.

'It's a phrase we use,' explained Setsuko, her eyes dancing although she tried to keep her face sombre. 'The literal translation is "Dumplings over flowers". It means you should value practical things, like dumplings, that will feed you, over things that are beautiful. Just as you might say something like all style and no substance.'

'And Yumi,' Setsuko smiled as Haruka nodded enthusiastically, 'beautiful as she is, has no substance. Or at least my mother doesn't think so.' Setsuko's gentle tone robbed her words of offence.

Mayu shook her head. 'But that contradicts *Jiji*'s other beliefs that we should find and respect beauty in nature.'

Setsuko frowned at her but this time Haruka shook her head before she could say anything.

46

'It's different,' said Haruka. '*Wabi Sabi*. I don't know. You young people don't understand.'

'No, *Jiji*,' said Mayu, with a resigned teasing lilt to her voice, but she leaned over and gave her grandmother a hug, while shooting a naughty wink Fiona's way.

'They just think they do,' said Haruka. Fiona had to take a hefty gulp of tea and do her best not to snort in laughter when, over Mayu's bent head, Haruka winked at her as well.

Setsuko, who saw all of this, sent her eyes heavenward before giving Fiona a warm smile.

'You all speak such good English.' Fiona was keen to divert a family row although, on reflection, there seemed to be so much warmth and genuine affection between the three generations, she thought perhaps her effort hadn't been required.

'My husband's job took us to America for many years. Setsuko grew up there and we spent fifteen years there.'

'It took me a long time to learn to speak Japanese,' admitted Setsuko. 'Growing up in America, I wanted to fit in. I didn't always want to keep the old ways. Of course, now I'm older, I'm very glad that my mother keeps the traditions alive, so I feel I'm a good balance between East and West.'

'She's training to be a master of tea, too,' announced Haruka, giving her daughter a proud glance.

'Yeah, it is kinda cool,' said Mayu, also sending her mother a cheeky grin. 'Especially when she gets all dressed up.'

'What, in a *kimono*? I wasn't sure if I'd see people wearing them or not? I was sort of hoping I might,' confessed Fiona. Maybe it was the warmth of the *kotatsu*, the calm acceptance of the three women or the bliss of feeling safe again but she felt unusually at ease.

'These days people tend to wear them for special events, like weddings, a traditional tea ceremony, or at coming of age ceremonies.'

'The one Grandma wears for the tea ceremony is really cool,' said Mayu.

Haruka bowed her head. 'It was my *soba's*, my grandmother's, and is very heavy silk, rich with gold threads. It is very beautiful.'

'I'd love to see that one day while I'm here,' said Fiona immediately thinking that she could write a really interesting blog post. 'And learn how you put them on and all the different components.'

Haruka clapped her hands. 'You can try one. I have several, including my cousin's. She was a tall woman. Tall for Japanese.'

'That would be wonderful.'

'Now.' Mayu clapped her hands. 'Let's do it now.'

'Oh, but I'm still wet ...' Fiona tried to refuse but Haruka had nimbly leapt to her feet and was whisking her way through the *shoji* screens. She returned in seconds, her arms billowing full of rich silk fabric, her dark head peeping over the top and her eyes twinkling full of mischief.

Setsuko jumped up and clapped her hands. 'Oh, yes.'

Fiona started to feel a little apprehensive as Mayu hauled her to her feet and, while she was still wobbling and trying to gain her balance, started plucking at her clothes like a determined bird pecking at seed. 'Take this off,' she tugged at Fiona's jumper.

Setsuko picked a garment from the pile in her mother's arms. 'First the under layer.' She held out a white cotton T-shaped piece of fabric. 'The *hadujaban*.'

The next thing Fiona knew was that Mayu had pulled off her jumper and Setsuko was guiding her arms into the wide square sleeves and threading the ties through holes under her arms while Haruka watched, her head bobbing up and down in approval.

Next came the sumptuous *kimono* which wasn't as flimsy and lightweight as it first appeared because the gorgeous bright red silk was lined with a slightly heavier fabric. Following more of Setsuko's gentle commands, she held out her arms on either side. With careful ceremony, Setsuko posted her arms through the voluminous sleeves as Haruka and May looked on, Haruka beaming with quiet pride.

'This is beautiful,' said Fiona, taking a quick moment to stroke one of the intricately embroidered motifs adorning the fabric: a black-headed, long-necked bird pictured in full flight with white frilled wings and long legs trailing gracefully beneath a black tail.

'A crane,' said Haruka.

'They are very lucky in Japanese culture; in folk tales they lived for a thousand years,' explained Setsuko, smoothing the fabric across Fiona's chest before taking the front edges of the robe and wrapping them tightly across her body. 'Always left to right,' she said tugging the fabric tighter. 'The other way for the dead.'

Haruka stepped forward with the wide cream band that Fiona recognised as the sash that went around the middle.

'What's it called?' she asked, reaching out a hand to touch the cream silk.

'It's an *obi*,' said Haruka handing it with both hands to her daughter.

For once Fiona didn't mind being the centre of attention as Setsuko smiled up at her, wrapping the wide bulky sash around her middle. The Japanese woman pointed out the little stiffening rods set into the fabric to give the large bow at the back its shape as she tied it in place.

Finally, a little like a princess, she waited as Setsuko fitted white socks on to each foot and helped her step into the *geta*, the traditional wooden sandals with their thick soles.

Mayu darted forward shaking her head. 'Your hair.'

Standing on one of the chairs and ignoring Haruka's quick frown, she swept Fiona's strawberry blonde hair back from her face and scooped her long plait up, coiling it into a bun. She then stuffed a bamboo comb into the hair with a sharp thrust which made Fiona wince as it scraped her scalp.

'That's better. There now.' Mayu jumped down.

The three ladies stepped back to admire the picture and Fiona took a few steps in the shoes which felt very odd, forcing her to take careful, tiny moves. Against her skin, the cotton *hadjuban* felt soft and light, while the heavy silk of the *kimono* and the tight *obi* made her feel cocooned and a little constricted, but that was more than made up for by the easy, happy acceptance of the three women and the delighted expressions on their faces. Haruka clapped her hands together, her serene, elegant face wreathed in a motherly smile and Setsuko beamed at her, while Mayu nodded, her head tilted and her arms folded, pulling her mouth in an approving teenage moue.

On the table, Fiona's phone began to ring with the Facetime tone. She winced and shook her head as Mayu went to pick it up and offer it to her.

'No, I'll call them later.' She spread out her arms and did a little twirl for her audience, not wanting the spell to be broken. Although a foot taller than the three diminutive women, for once being different didn't feel like being out of place or looking in from the outside.

'Would you like me to take some pictures?' asked Setsuko.

Fiona hesitated a moment; she didn't really like having her photo taken. The minute a lens was pointed her way, it made her stiff and self-conscious but the *kimono* pictures would be perfect for her blog and she wanted to capture this lovely moment. She also wanted pictures of the three generations of women together. 'Yes, please. With my camera. It's in my room.'

'I'll get it.' Mayu sprang up, hovered in the doorway for permission, and at Fiona's nod darted away.

Mayu was keen to take the pictures and was a very quick learner – as soon as Fiona had shown her the basic controls on her SLR camera, she snapped away, pretending to be a paparazzo, which soon had all the women laughing.

'Here, darling. Smile for me, Fiona. Give it to me baby. More. More.'

It was easy to relax with the enthusiastic teenager, laughing and joking and Fiona found herself loosening up, knowing she could easily delete most of the photos. She could always cut her own head off if her usual tortured grimaces were truly awful.

After a mixed day, including a low point where she'd really wanted to go home, Fiona reflected as she went to bed on how welcome the three women had made her feel. Maybe underneath it all, when you thought about what really mattered, Japan wasn't so very different. People still loved, laughed, and cared for each other and those were values that were shared the world over.

Chapter 4

$\mathbf{F}$aced with the slew of querulous texts that greeted her when she went to bed, relinquishing the warm company of the three women, Fiona couldn't face calling her mother knowing that it would be a combative conversation. Her mother really hadn't wanted her to come to Japan. Instead, she quickly worked out that if she called at seven the next morning, it would be ten at night in the UK. She sent a quick text, explaining it had been a long day and saying she'd call later.

The futon mattress was much more comfortable than she'd expected and with the thick padded covers, again so different from home, she found herself as snug as a bug and, despite the peaks and troughs of the day, she fell into a deep and dreamless sleep as soon as she switched off the light.

She woke to her phone bleeping and blearily accepted the facetime call.

'Fiona, I've been so worried about you.'

Fiona sighed. Her mother had got in first, before she could jump in with all the positives, like the *kotatsu* table, the *kimono*, the delicious breaded *katsu* chicken that Haruka had prepared for dinner, and the photographs she'd seen.

'Hello to you too.' She yawned and pushed her hair out of her face. 'And why are you worried?'

'Well the texts I was getting were very short. Anything could have happened and you didn't call this morning.'

'Mum.' Two seconds in and Fiona's patience had to be forced. 'Japan is one of the safest countries in the world.'

'Well, they might they say that but I don't know. And I hadn't heard from you and I've been feeling awful.'

Fiona ignored her latter comment. 'I called you as soon as I landed.' And messaged yesterday morning and evening. Luckily the nine-hour time difference meant that her mother would have been asleep during the middle of the day so she'd been able to avoid getting into a conversation with her, unlike now.

'I've got a terrible sense of foreboding, you know.'

Fiona's smile didn't reflect her internal sigh of frustration. 'Are you taking your tablets?'

'Yes,' her mother said with an indignant glare. 'Of course I'm taking my tablets. I'm not senile, you know. And Dr Smithson was so mean last time.'

'He wasn't mean, he was concerned and was trying to impress the importance of taking your blood-pressure tablets.'

'Well my blood pressure is bound to be through the roof with my only daughter so far away on her own in another country. Anything could happen to you.' Before her mother could launch into a litany of terrible things that had happened to lone women travellers over the years, Fiona reminded her she wasn't on her own.

'The family I'm staying with are very kind and all speak

excellent English.' Now would have been the time to tell her about trying on the *kimono* but she didn't want to spoil the memory of it, that lovely glow of belonging and warmth. Instead she chose, without thinking it through properly, safer ground. 'And I'll be with Gabe during the day.' Well, in as much as yesterday he'd delivered her to places and collected her later like an unwelcome parcel he'd rather return to sender.

'Gabe? Who's Gabe? I thought you were going to be with Yutaka Araki.'

Funny, when it suited her, her mother's vagueness vanished.

Fiona really did sigh this time. Rookie error. 'Unfortunately, Mr Araki has had a family bereavement, so he can't mentor me.'

Her mother seemed shocked and for a moment Fiona thought she might get away with it as she remained speechless for oh, at least five seconds. 'You mean you've gone all that way for nothing? I knew it was a mistake, didn't I tell you?'

'Mum, it's all fine. They've provided me with another mentor.'

'As well they might but it's hardly going to be comparable to Yutaka Araki, is it?' With time on her hands, of course her mother had Googled him. Now, after weeks of complaint, she chose to be impressed. 'I really do think you've made a terrible mistake.'

'He's a very good photographer. I'll learn plenty.'

'Who? Who is as good that they can find just like that? You're being fobbed off with someone who won't be anywhere near as good as Yutaka Araki. You do know his pictures are displayed in museums and galleries all around the world? New York, Boston, Tokyo'—at that Fiona really did roll her eyes; she'd seen several yesterday—'Sydney, Toronto. Who are they possibly going to find to replace him?'

Fiona weighed it up and the balance of the scales fell to the wrong side, but honesty was the best policy and it was better to get this over and done with. You never know, it might distract her mother from her health.

'My mentor is ...' Oh God, she was going to have to say it. She looked directly at the screen, at her mother's fluttering hands and her frail form sitting in the usual high-backed armchair that was more suited to an elderly, infirm person rather than a woman of not quite fifty.

'Who?'

'It's Gabriel Burnett.'

That really did shock her into silence and then her mother clutched her throat with melodramatic horror. 'Gabriel Burnett! The man who ruined your life!' Her mother's face contorted. 'I think I'm having a spasm.'

'Mother you're not flaming Mrs Bennet in *Pride and Prejudice*. People don't have spasms. And he didn't *ruin* my life.' Just changed its course a little.

'Gabriel Burnett.' Her mother shook her head. 'Gabriel Burnett. What did he say? I hope he apologised.'

'He didn't recognise me and he hasn't got anything to apologise for.'

'Oh. Well I still think it's a mistake.'

'He's a very good photographer and someone I can learn from.'

'Well you learned plenty from him last time, didn't you? I'd have thought once bitten and all that.'

'Mum, that was a long time ago.' She shifted her gaze towards the window where the bright sunshine was peeping around the edges of the blind, as if trying to entice her outside. 'I was eighteen and very young for my age at that.' Fiona felt the flush of embarrassment stain her cheek. God, she had been incredibly young for her age. Naïve and clumsy. And yes, she'd beaten herself up about it for years, supported admirably by her mother's melodramatics, until she'd confessed what she'd done to Avril who'd laughed her head off and told her it was perfectly normal deluded teenage behaviour and to stop being such a wally about it. Everyone did stupid things when they were young. Her precise words had been, 'Get over yourself already.'

In hindsight, Fiona wondered whether, had her mother had taken a more rational, balanced approach at the time, she could have been reconciled to the whole silly episode far sooner and been more practical about sorting out the bullying at school that had followed.

'Well just watch yourself with him. Men like him don't change their spots.'

'Like I said, he doesn't even remember me. Anyway, I need to go. Gabe is picking me up to go to the Tokyo Skytree.' Actually, he wasn't coming until lunchtime but her mother didn't need to know that and it looked like a gorgeous morning. Fiona was itching to do some exploring; she hadn't seen anything of the garden or the teashop.

'You're actually going to go with him? Do you think that's a good idea? You're not going to fall in love with him all over again, are you?'

'No, Mum. I'm not a silly, impressionable teenager anymore. I'm not the least bit attracted to him.'

'Well, I'm not happy.' Her hand clapped to her chest. 'I think I can feel palpitations.'

'Mum, you'll be fine. Make yourself a nice cup of tea. Did I tell you the lady I'm staying with is a master of tea? It's a really big deal in Japan. And she runs a teashop. And conducts tea ceremonies. I think that will be fascinating to see, don't you?'

Her mother sniffed. 'It does sound interesting. Perhaps you can bring me some tea back. The Japanese are an incredibly healthy nation, after all.'

Fiona bit back a smile, grateful she'd successfully diverted her mother.

They talked tea for the final few minutes of the conversation, before Fiona gratefully said goodbye to her mother and plugged in her phone to charge.

It irked that her mother thought she might fall for Gabe again. She was nearly thirty, not an impressionable eighteen-year-old. Gabe Burnett did nothing for her now. She was far too sensible and grown-up to fall for his looks or his charm, which was in decided short supply these days.

Wide awake now and thoroughly irritated by her mother, Fiona got up and dressed quickly. Fresh air and sunshine called.

There was no sign of life when she crept down the stairs and went out into the street with her camera. Stepping back to the other side of the street, she took a couple of quick shots of the pretty scene before realising that Setsuko was in the window of the teahouse beckoning her over.

In the next minute she was at the door.

'Good morning, *Fiona san*. Did you sleep well?'

'I did ... until my mother called.' She tried to hide the irritation which had left her raw and chafed inside. Setsuko might not approve. Japanese families were renowned for looking after their elders and she seemed very close to her own mother.

Setsuko's clear, dark eyes surveyed her face. 'Is everything all right?' she asked in her gentle way.

'It's fine,' said Fiona, guilty now. Her mother wasn't so bad, just lonely and bored, which made her focus most of her attention on her health and her only daughter.

Setsuko raised one elegant eyebrow. 'I think you need a cup of tea. Come on.' She turned and led the way into the shop.

Without stopping to make sure Fiona was following her, Setsuko hurried into the shop and through an open doorway. Fiona stopped to take stock and was immediately transfixed by the quaint interior. It was like stepping back in time and there was a hushed air of calm in the small but perfectly formed shop. What struck her the most was that all the materials were natural, from the wood panelled walls and bamboo stools, to the cotton-padded dark wood benches and the linen hangings next to the now familiar *shoji* screens. Gentle light filtered in through the big bay window, highlighting dust motes dancing like tiny fairies. One wall of the shop was shelved from floor to ceiling, the shelves containing big black lacquered canisters, each with elegant Japanese script in golden ink on the front, promising secrets and magic. On the small counter opposite were little open hessian sacks full of different teas, curled like tiny caterpillar husks, pieces of bark and dried grasses, the scents of jasmine, smoke and grass spilling from them. It was like a magician's cave where blends of sorcery and magic were served up in the delicate tea pots, glazed in pale blues, greens and bronzes and the solid china cups that would fit perfectly in your hands.

Beyond the room, Setsuko was standing in a tiny, almost primitive kitchen, with a large frying-pan-sized ring full of glowing coals, atop which was a big copper kettle. Fiona had never seen anything like it and couldn't imagine how Setsuko could work in such a tiny space although it was beautifully organised with everything in its place on the bamboo shelves. There wasn't a single electric appliance apart from a rice steamer and the only other modern thing was a calculator next to a pot of bamboo and wood utensils.

Setsuko had laid a red lacquer tray with a matt black teapot with a curved bamboo handle and two cups glazed with turquoise around the rims fading to darker blue at the bottom, and once she'd poured boiling water into the teapot from the big copper kettle, she motioned for Fiona to follow her to one of the tables which looked out to the other side of the building and to a secret garden hidden by a canopy of green shrubbery.

As soon as she sat down, the weight seemed to lift from her shoulders and that abraded rawness inside that her mother always managed to stir up eased. Being here was like being in a private den, closed off from the rest of the world and the worries it carried with it. 'This is lovely. It's so ...' she couldn't quite put it into words. Romantic, otherworldly, traditional.

Setsuko poured them each a cup of tea and handed one to Fiona.

'It's a place to think and to be. Or to talk and share.'

Fiona studied the pale green liquid, the steam bringing the scent of grass and pine. Share. That wasn't something she did very much of.

'One of my own blends,' said Setsuko holding her cup in both hands and bowing to Fiona. 'It contains *kanayamidori* and *sayamakaori* green teas.'

'I love these ... what do you call them?' she indicated the handleless cups.

'*Chawan*. Or *matcha* bowl.'

Setsuko stared down into her own tea, the picture of humility and respect, leaving the silence to stretch out between them. The peace of the room brought a mesmerising sense of calm. A smile crossed Fiona's face.

'It makes me want to tell you things.'

'You do not have to tell me anything. I wanted to bring you peace.'

Fiona studied her demure hostess. 'You've done that. Thank you.'

'I know how it is to feel ... troubled.'

'You do?' Fiona was surprised. Setsuko seemed to epitomise serenity.

With a gracious incline of her head, she smiled at Fiona's disbelief.

'When we first came back to Japan, I was a teenager. An American teenager. I hated my parents for taking me away from everything I knew. Japan was alien and different, although in some ways familiar. It confused me but rather than learn, I fought. I fought against everything. You think

Mayu is rebellious ...' she laughed. 'She is easy. It took me a long time to settle. To learn that this is home. To learn that the traditional ways bring their own peace and harmony. I made life very difficult for my mother.'

Fiona raised her eyebrows. Setsuko seemed so calm and gentle it was difficult to believe.

'My mother is a remarkable woman. And very wise. She didn't fight back. Not in obvious ways. She allowed herself to find her way back into the traditions and to share them with me. She never forced me to do anything or insist I followed the old ways and gradually I saw for myself that there was beauty and peace in them. Mayu complains that we make her go to the *sakura*, the cherry blossom, every year ... but we never insist she comes. It is always her choice. And she always chooses to come. She pretends family is not so important but she loves her *Jiji*.'

Fiona took a sip of the fragrant tea. 'Teenage years are difficult in every culture.'

'I think so. We know so little of ourselves, we're not yet us. But we think we are.'

'That's a good way of putting it.' Fiona was struck by the thought. She'd placed far too much emphasis on a youthful mistake that should have been laughed off as exactly that.

They drank the rest of the tea in silence and a couple of times, Fiona wondered about telling Setsuko what had happened but the other woman didn't prod her or have a hungry, expectant look on her face; she seemed as if her own thoughts had taken her elsewhere, so Fiona leaned back against the wall in the cosy confines of the room, sipped her tea, and let the memories wash over her.

She'd been eighteen. She and Evie Blundell, a friend – not a best friend but they'd shared a passion for photography – had both been nominated by their art teacher to spend half term at an art camp in London, the October prior to A levels. Fiona brought the cup up to her nose, inhaling the fragrant smell of the tea, recalling that youthful fizz of excitement as the two of them boarded the train for their first day. An autumn day of russet colours where sunshine dappled the trees, heralding a morning full of the promise of what might be.

Day one had exceeded expectation as they'd found themselves in a college environment where they were treated like young adults on first-name terms with their tutors rather than the formal distance of school. Fiona smiled to herself. By the end of the first week, she and Evie had imagined themselves quite grown up with a gloss of sophistication acquired through regular commuting into London and mixing with slightly older students, although everyone in the class had been equally star struck when it was announced that the following week Gabriel Burnett would be tutoring them. Gabriel Burnett. Even the cool kids were impressed.

Even now, Fiona remembered the first time she'd met him.

Gabriel Burnett had the bluest eyes Fiona had ever seen. He turned up slightly late on the first morning and apologised with charm and a laid-back approach that immediately set the over-excited class at ease. He might be used to mixing with models and celebrities, but he treated them as equals.

'Isn't he gorgeous?' Fiona had sighed, gazing at him from the second row back.

'Utterly, but way out of our league,' agreed Evie, settling her chin into her hand and studying him with a happy groan.

'Those eyes,' Fiona whispered and as she did he glanced up sharply and stared right at her as if he'd heard her. A fizz bounced around her stomach as he'd held her gaze for ... well, for ages – or at least it had felt like ages.

'Contacts. They must be,' said Evie, breaking the spell. 'But he's seriously fit. Check out that arse.'

Fiona was too busy checking out the high cheekbones and longish hair swept off his face, tied with a leather strap which had seemed desperately glamorous and strikingly bohemian at the same time. Inside her chest her heart fluttered like a butterfly flitting from flower to flower.

And he was so nice. So friendly. He chatted to everyone. She'd thought he might be arrogant and full of himself but he wasn't at all. He was lovely.

The highlight of the week came on Wednesday when he singled out one of her pictures, leaning over her, so close that she could see the tiny pinpricks of stubble on his skin and smell his aftershave – some woodsy, sophisticated scent that had made her breath shudder in appreciation.

'This is a great composition, Fiona.' Her heart had thundered in her chest. He. Knew. Her. Name. 'I love what you've done bringing the background into focus here.' He laid a hand on her shoulder as he leaned even closer to point to something on the picture. 'And that little plane of light. This is excellent work.' She swallowed and turned her head, meeting his eyes, and she saw them suddenly flare. A hot sweat seared through her. He felt it too.

He smiled at her. 'Very good work, Fiona.' And then as if nothing had happened, he stood up and walked to the next student. But she hadn't imagined it. Gabriel Burnett liked her.

'It was the way he looked at me,' she had said to Evie on the way home that evening.

'He looks at everyone that way,' said Evie, who was clearly jealous that Gabe hadn't singled her work out. 'It's a bit cheesy to be honest.'

She didn't agree; when he talked to her, she really felt like he knew her and understood her.

Fiona shuddered at the vivid memories and Setsuko turned her gentle doe eyes towards her.

'I kissed him,' Fiona announced rather baldly.

Setsuko raised one delicately arched eyebrow in silent query.

'Gabe Burnett. When I was eighteen. He was my teacher.' She let out a half sob, half giggle. 'Like the Abba song, "When I kissed the teacher".'

Both of Setsuko's eyebrows rose, startled.

'I know.' Fiona took in a deep breath, horrified that she'd blurted it out like that. 'I don't know why I told you that.'

'Perhaps because you needed to.'

'I kissed him. He was standing in front of me, in the corridor. It was the end of the week and I knew I might never see him again. And I was mad about him. And stupidly I'd convinced myself that he might feel the same. So I stood on tip toe. Kissed him. Right on the mouth.' She paused watching Setsuko's reaction carefully.

Now Setsuko began to smile. 'You kissed *Gabe san*.' Her mouth curved, shy dimples appearing.

65

Fiona nodded.

Setsuko sniggered, an unladylike snuffly snorting noise that was most unlike her usual graceful demeanour. 'You kissed Gabe.' She clapped her hands over her mouth, her eyes dancing with mirth.

Fiona, remembering the moment, suddenly saw the ridiculousness of it. That quick, hasty bob up to peck at his mouth and she smiled back at Setsuko, a giggle escaping.

'I know. Crazy teenage hormones.' And as she relaxed and saw the funny side of it, escaping the band of shame that had dogged her for so many years, a memory tumbled loose – his hands, warm and firm, coming to rest on her hips, steadying them. Her pulse missed a beat. And with a heart-jolting shock, she remembered his lips moving under hers. He. Had. Kissed. Her. Back.

She sat up straight and had to put a hand over her heart to steady the ridiculous rollicking beat that it had taken up. Gabe had kissed her back ... and she'd completely forgotten. It had been buried in everything that came after. Not that it meant anything now but it kind of made up for all that embarrassment. The humiliation ... well, that had come later.

'What happened after that?' asked Setsuko, her almond eyes wide and for once her reserve cast aside.

'I don't know who was more shocked, him or me. And then,' she sobered, 'my friend, my so-called friend, Evie, came round the corner. Gabe was already pushing me away. He must have been horrified that this girl was throwing herself at him. I mean, he dated sophisticated models, famous actors ... people like Yumi. But Evie saw enough. And later I told her what I'd done. Well it was pretty obvious.' Fiona's face crumpled, the pain still as sharp as ever.

Setsuko winced. 'Something bad.'

'Evie told everyone at school what I'd done and that Gabe had rejected me. It was awful. Everyone laughed at me. A couple of the teachers were really disapproving. And for a few weeks I kept my head down hoping it would blow over, but then at the end of term, in the annual talent show, Evie with a couple of other girls sang the Abba song. This time everyone in the whole school knew.'

'Oh no.' Setsuko laid a cool hand on hers.

'Instead of getting better, the girls just got worse. I couldn't face going to school. I felt sick every day. Eventually I told my mum what had happened and ... she was great.' Except she hadn't been, not really. No, her mum had made a melodrama out of her. Caused a fuss and said no daughter of hers was going back to that school. She could stay at home. And that had been the worst thing Fiona could have done. Isolated herself.

'I didn't go back to school. Didn't take my exams. Didn't go to university. Started spending more time online and blogging. And ... well, that has been good.' She shrugged her shoulders; it had taken a long time to be good. 'And then a couple of years ago, my Instagram posts started to take off and I started going out and meeting people in real life instead of just online. I made some friends who are quite bossy and inspirational, who chivvy me into doing things, and it was my friend Avril who suggested I enter the competition to come here.'

Setsuko's mouth dropped open into a pretty little 'o'. 'And you had no idea that you would meet *Gabe san*.'

'No,' said Fiona. 'Although he doesn't recognise me.'

'Are you going to tell him?'

'God no! That would be so embarrassing.'

'He might have been flattered.'

'Look at me. He associates with people like Yumi.'

'But she is not very beautiful on the inside,' said Setsuko with unexpected severity. 'You have what we call *shibui*.'

'What's that?' Fiona leaned forward, keen to learn more about Japanese culture.

'*Shibui* is simplicity, modesty, naturalness, everydayness ... you are you. You don't try to be something that you're not. Subdued in some ways but not others.' She smiled. 'Today when you were talking I saw the flash of fire in your eyes, especially when you talked about Gabe. You are understated but your hair has subtle beauty. You are very well mannered. *Shibui* is all of these things.'

Fiona smiled. 'Well, I'm glad about that. My mother would be pleased to hear that I'm well mannered.'

'That is why my mother liked you straight away. You are refined. You listen and accord respect. You are interested.'

'Who wouldn't be? Your country is fascinating. This ...' she waved her hand, indicating the teashop, 'it's such a contrast to the Tokyo I saw yesterday.'

Setsuko smiled. 'And there is so much more to see.'

Fiona felt her heart suddenly blossom, like a flower blooming from bud. 'There is.' She beamed at the other woman realising that she wanted to know more, more about the city, the culture, the art ... God, there was just so much. 'Thank you, Setsuko. You've opened my eyes this morning.'

Chapter 5

Haruka fussed over her when she returned to the house, leaving Setsuko in the teashop laying out an exquisitely presented breakfast of tiny square dishes filled with pickled vegetables and salad vegetables, along with a small bowl of steaming miso soup and a little bowl of steamed rice.

For a moment, Fiona examined the perfect presentation and the attention to detail, amazed by the work that had gone into breakfast. This wasn't 'grab a bowl of cereal by the sink in the morning'. With all the little bowls and dishes on the red, black, and gold lacquer tray, she could have been in a restaurant and Haruka had clearly made a huge effort.

'Thank you,' she said to her hostess, biting her lip, a little uncertain where to start. Immediately Haruka patted her on the arm and stepped forward, sitting down opposite her, as ever a generous and kind hostess.

'This is miso soup. Very good for starting the day. Gentle on your stomach. Warming for the body. This is pickled ginger and here is a salad.'

'It smells good,' said Fiona a little reluctantly. Soup for breakfast, that was a new one, but it was well known that the

Japanese were a long-lived nation and all the women Fiona had seen were exceptionally trim. The diet here was famed for being healthy and nutritionally well balanced, so who was she to argue. Copying her hostess, she picked up the bowl and took a careful sip of the hot soup as Haruka watched her like a mother anticipating her child's first steps.

'Mmm,' she said, surprised by the clean, bright flavour. 'This is delicious.' She took another eager mouthful of the fragrant soup, thinking that she could get used to eating like this. Picking up the chopsticks, she attempted to dig into the bowl of rice to take a scoop and Haruka tsked as she dropped half of it on the table.

'Sorry,' said Fiona.

'Like this.' Once again Haruka showed her, guiding her fingers and thumb onto the wooden sticks, showing Fiona how to hold them properly and pushed the bowl into her hands and towards her mouth. It reminded her of Gabe yesterday and that unwelcome flutter of sensation when he'd held her hand.

'Ah, that's much easier,' said Fiona, pushing Gabe out of her head and taking a mouthful of the cool sticky rice. The consistency was slightly different to that at home but it had a freshness and a nuttier flavour. The combination of the rice, the soup, and the pickled ginger was a marriage of light, sharp and clean and as unfamiliar as it was, Fiona enjoyed every mouthful. Perhaps, thanks to her early morning tea with Setsuko, she was far more open to trying new things.

To finish, Haruka brought out a mouth-watering shallow

plate of beautifully arranged fruit. There were slices of juicy mandarin, carefully peeled so there wasn't a speck of white pith, sliced love hearts of bright red strawberries, which looked too good to eat, and translucent thin sections of honeydew melon. 'This looks too good to disturb.'

'No, no. You must. It is fresh from the market today.'

Haruka beamed at her as she sighed over the sweetness of the strawberries and the tang of the mandarins.

'Thank you, that was a lovely breakfast. I usually just have toast and cereal, neither of which I think are very good for you.'

'There is very little bread in our diet.' Haruka explained. 'In the West you eat too much bread. It is not good for ...' she patted her stomach.

'No, this is lovely and light.' She didn't feel the least bit bloated or over full.

As Haruka cleared away the dishes, insisting that she didn't need any help despite the offer, Fiona checked her watch. Gabe was due to collect her in under an hour. She was all set, her camera at her side as well as a notebook. She wanted to do a tourist's guide to Tokyo on her blog and planned to write down station names, because she'd never remember them, and directions to key tourist landmarks. Today Gabe was taking her to the Skytree, the tallest building in Japan and, Mayu had told her proudly the night before, the tallest tower in the world. Fiona had smiled. It was all about definitions, she thought.

'Would you mind if I took some pictures of the house?'

she asked Haruka. 'I'd like to put them on my Instagram page and write about what it's like to live in a Japanese house; it's so different to houses at home. Especially the toilet.'

She hadn't had the courage to ask her hostess about all the buttons and symbols on the toilet. It all looked rather high tech and complicated, although she was taken with the nifty tap-sink arrangement on top of the toilet cistern where you washed your hands and the water was used to flush the toilet. Completely ingenious.

As she rose to her feet, her phone beeped.

I'm afraid an unexpected job has come up and I shall be tied up in the studio all day today. We shall have to postpone our trip. Pick you up at the same time tomorrow?

Fiona dropped her phone on the table. 'I don't believe it,' she said letting out a heartfelt groan. 'Gabe has called today off.'

Haruka frowned. 'That is very bad mannered. Is he unwell?'

'No, he says he has to work.'

Her mouth folded into a disapproving line and Haruka looked positively cross – well, as cross as was possible on her lovely serene face. 'You could go to work with him. That would be mentoring. I am very sorry.'

'It's fine.' Fiona winced. It wasn't fine at all. She was eager to get started today and take some pictures for her exhibition.

'No, it is not,' said Haruka, blinking furiously, her hands fidgeting on the table

Fiona's voice softened and she reached out to touch the agitated woman. 'It's not your fault.'

'You are a guest in our country. It is most impolite and very unlike Gabriel. I am disappointed in him.'

'It's okay. I'll do something else. At least I know how to find my way on the trains.'

Haruka ignored the feeble joke and patted her hand. 'Green tea. I'll make some tea and then we will decide what to do.'

Fiona almost smiled at the very Englishness of it, tea and sympathy, and watched as Haruka rolled up her sleeves and bustled busily back to the kitchen, her slippers whispering over the *tatami* mats.

She followed her and was gestured into a seat as Haruka warmed the water on one of the gas rings. The kitchen was very spare and compact compared to her mother's cluttered farmhouse style and it took her a moment to work out what was missing. There was no oven. The only way of cooking seemed to be the gas rings on a small hob, not that it seemed to hold Haruka back, but it was still positively modern compared to the cubby hole in the teashop.

As soon as she set the blackened pot on one of the rings, the older woman began to stab furiously at her phone.

'You're not texting Gabe, are you?' asked Fiona a shade anxiously.

'No.' Haruka's crisp reply stopped her asking any more questions and she sat in silence, wondering what next, until Haruka poured tea into two porcelain pots and held one out with both hands to Fiona with one of her small, neat bows.

'Thank you.'

Haruka kept glancing down at her phone.

73

'How do you know Gabe?' asked Fiona, a question that had piqued her since yesterday.

'He came to teach at the university for six months and my husband invited him to stay here. Then he got lots of work and decided to stay. He moved into the apartment we own when it became free and made some rooms into a studio.' She smiled fondly. 'He was like a son.' The smile slipped into a scowl. 'And then he met Yumi.'

'You don't like her.'

'She's bad news,' she said, sounding very American, but to Fiona's disappointment didn't elaborate further, perhaps because her phone suddenly sprang into life with a strident ring. She seized it and began to speak at speed. Fiona listened, amused by the unfamiliar language, Haruka's intent expression and the very different inflexions. Her hostess sounded like an angry warlord barking instructions to a subordinate.

When she put down the phone, the beam was back in place. The general had laid out her battle plans. 'Mayu will take you this morning but then we will go to Ueno Park. It is only a short walk and a good time for *Hanami*.'

'Cherry-blossom viewing season,' said Fiona, remembering the term from one of the guide books.

Haruka nodded with her wise-owl expression, clearly pleased. 'This afternoon Setsuko and I will take you to visit *sakura*.'

'The cherry blossom,' said Fiona feeling like an A-star pupil when Haruka gave another slight bob of her head.

'But first Mayu will take you. She is not at class today. She will take you into Tokyo.'

'Oh, she doesn't need to do that,' said Fiona. 'I'll be fine on my own. And you don't have to take me anywhere.'

'It is all agreed. Mayu will take you and then you both join us.' Just one look at Haruka's implacable and slightly triumphant expression told Fiona that she'd have more chance taking on the famed might of the Japanese Imperial Army than the kind but steely woman. 'We will have a picnic.'

'That's very kind of you.' Fiona wondered if poor Mayu had had much say about it. Taking an older tourist around the city probably wasn't high on the teenager's agenda.

A scant ten minutes later, dressed in an eye-watering neon-blue wig, knee-high white socks, a short pleated skirt, platform sneakers and a bright yellow puffer jacket, Mayu appeared at the door to the kitchen, her face full of mischief and excitement.

'*Fiona san*. We're going to Tokyo. Come. Come. Are you ready?' She shot her grandmother a quick glance, assuming an innocent air. 'This morning we will do fun, exciting things.'

Haruka folded her arms and studied her granddaughter with an implacable expression but made no comment about either the clothes or the provocative line.

'I'll grab a coat,' said Fiona, wondering what on earth she was letting herself in for.

No one batted an eyelid at Mayu's outlandish outfit on the train journey into the city centre. Like most of the other passengers on the train, as soon as she sat down she pulled out her phone and was soon absorbed in the screen. Following Mayu's lead, Fiona scrolled through her WhatsApp group with

Avril, Sophie, Kate, Eva and David, the dear friends she'd made on that life-changing trip to Copenhagen.

Who'd have thought she'd end up being friends with someone like Avril? Fiona rubbed at a patch on her jeans above her knee, already slightly worn. Kind, scary, bossy Avril had promised – some people might say threatened – to promote Fiona's photo exhibition and Fiona knew she would. Avril was nothing if not totally loyal and also rather blunt. She spent the journey mulling over possible ideas for the exhibition. If Avril hadn't made such a big deal of it and she could have got away with being a bit anonymous, she wouldn't have to worry quite so much. But Avril had outed her on the group and now they were all rooting for her; they'd all promised, apart from Sophie who lived in the States, that they would be there for the official opening in a few weeks' time.

When the train drew in to their final destination, as if they were best friends for ever – a term that Fiona felt Mayu was very familiar with – the teenager linked her arm through Fiona's and led her out through the busy station into the life force of Tokyo – bright, vibrant and throbbing with life, colour and neon. Above them lights flashed, the traffic crept along and the smell of soy and noodles from a nearby kiosk teased her senses. Fiona liked the immediate sense that she knew exactly which country she was in. Already in a few days it had become unmistakable.

'Where are we going?' asked Fiona, half running to keep up with Mayu's frantic pace. She was the polar opposite to her serene, quiet mother. Living life at four hundred miles an hour. A Shinkansen train next to a steam locomotive.

'It's a surprise.' Mayu's voice sang with excitement. 'And you are going to love it. It's the best. Better than boring old cherry blossom. Every year *Jiji* and *Haha* want to go.' She rolled her eyes in true teenage fashion. 'Boring, but don't worry, where we're going first is banging.'

Hmm. Fiona glanced at the anime school-girl outfit and wondered what cultural experience constituted banging while she tried to keep up with the enthusiastic teen. She managed to slow Mayu down enough to take a few pictures en route. She tried to capture the busyness of the city, but the elusive essence of Japan evaded her and when she looked at the digital view finder she was disappointed. There was something 'other' about the streets that she couldn't quite capture. Frustration bubbled like an itch below the surface of her skin. What was missing? Why couldn't she get it? The pictures seemed pedestrian and dull. God, she'd better up her game and pronto if she wanted to get enough material for an exhibition. This was where she could do with a proper mentor, someone who would actually take an interest.

'We're nearly there,' said Mayu, the pitch in her voice rising, and then she threw an arm forward. 'Borderless, Team Lab, digital art museum.'

Fiona nodded, having absolutely no idea what a digital art museum was.

They walked into the crowded foyer, paid their entrance fee and filed in with crowds of Japanese and Western tourists.

'It's the best place on earth,' declared Mayu. 'And we have to, *have* to, go to the Butterfly House, first. It's major.' And like a frantic butterfly herself, Mayu darted forward into a dark corridor following the signs. Fiona followed more slowly; she wasn't very keen on flappy things and tended to avoid getting too close to birds, butterflies and moths.

Stepping inside the first room she realised her fears were unfounded as gentle music played and her eyes widened at the spectacle before her. The room was full of light and sound, butterflies growing and morphing before her eyes, projected onto a series of black screens that filled the room, dividing it into smaller spaces. Everywhere she looked a different scene was projected onto the walls. Colour and movement. Shapes and shades. A visual feast for the eyes. For a moment she stood trying to take it all in and then focused on one scene where hundreds of butterflies took flight, dappling a would-be sky.

It was impossible not to smile. Not to feel joyous as the magical sights and constant movement flooded the senses. Like a child, Mayu had darted away chasing a cloud of butterflies. Entranced, Fiona touched a flower which immediately wilted under her fingers before springing up and blooming again a few feet away. The floor and walls were alive with light and images that changed constantly as people interacted with them. Fiona had never seen anything like it before. It was impossible to take photos in here, she thought, not with the constantly changing light and besides, you'd lose the sense of immersing yourself in the scenes and images. Liberating, that was how she'd describe it. You had the freedom to wander, to watch, and to touch and see the constant changes. No scene was the same and your actions could change things. It was both fascinating and mesmerising. No wonder Mayu had been so excited.

And she was good company – enthusiastic, knowledgeable and desperate to show Fiona every last exciting gallery and section of the museum.

'Here. Here. The waterfall, this is my favourite.' With the sound of the rush of water and the detailed graphics, it was easy to believe you were standing underneath a waterfall and when Fiona touched the wall, to her amazement and delight, a cherry blossom began to bloom beneath her fingers, as flower after flower burst into life.

'Cool, eh?' asked Mayu

Fiona shook her head. 'Way better than cool. It's magical.' The whole place was joyous, crazy, and utterly inspiring. While slightly frenetic and stimulating to the brain, to put it mildly, it was also in a weird and completely counter-intuitive way rather relaxing. The digital explosion of sight and sound was so absorbing, it left no room for anything else, which meant she could switch off from worrying about photography. You could only truly appreciate the magic by throwing yourself wholeheartedly into the interactive elements, take part in the magic, and be in the moment. Hadn't Gabe said something about that yesterday?

You had to focus on the here and now. People, mused Fiona at one point stepping back and seeing the wonder and enjoyment on the faces around her, had fallen out of the habit of living in the moment. Enjoying what they could see rather than trying to capture it to show other people. It was like putting a butterfly in a jar: the short term gain fizzled out very quickly when it died. People should be immersing themselves in the moment.

The revelation hit her with surprising weight, it wasn't something she'd ever thought about properly before. She wanted her pictures to be more, to tell a story, to make people look deeper, to see more than a picture. Rather like Gabe's pictures of Yumi. He would understand, she thought. Tomorrow she wouldn't be so easily fobbed off. If he had work, she would go to his studio and watch him. Learn from him.

But in the meantime, she was going to enjoy Mayu's company and this afternoon the famous cherry blossom was bound to provide plenty of material.

Chapter 6

The trees were dripping with blossom, fat, fistfuls of pink petals lining the starkly contrasting dark branches and Fiona couldn't help but reach out to touch the pink pom-poms and feel the velvet softness against the tips of her fingers. Ueno Park was more spectacular than she could possibly have imagined.

'This is ...' Her eyes shone as she tried to take it all in.

Mayu rolled her eyes. 'Lame but kinda cool too. My mom and *Jiji* come here every year.'

'With you?'

'Yeah.' Her round face creased into a sudden naughty grin. 'Don't tell them, but I like it really. It's a family tradition. We come again at the weekend with Dad and *Ojōchan*. But I like it when it's the three of us ... and you of course,' she added quickly. 'Come this way; we have a favourite place.' She linked her arm through Fiona's and led the way along the path.

The trees that lined the avenue next to the lake ranged as far as the eye could see, along with vast numbers of people who had come out to see them. Fiona was astounded by the positively festive atmosphere and the tangible excitement that buzzed in the air. The noise of people chattering and exclaiming was louder than a flock of geese and the paths were so crowded it was difficult to find room to raise her arms to take any pictures until Haruka and Setsuko led her off the path under the branches. Underneath the trees, small family groups sat on blankets enjoying picnics, their hair dappled with the odd falling petal.

'This is ...'

'Cherry blossom,' said Mayu with a deliberate yawn but her eyes glinted with mischief.

'Once a year,' scolded Hakura. 'Once a year. And every year different. If the wind comes too soon ...' She waved her hand to indicate that the petals would be wafted into the sky. 'It is the cycle of life.'

'That is what makes it special,' explained Setsuko. 'That it is here for such a short time and we must make the most of it. There are blossom reports telling people when are the best times to come so you can see the trees at their best. They also warn if a storm is coming. That is beautiful too but signals the end of the *sakura*. It is nature, birth, beauty and death.'

'Ephemeral,' said Fiona, immediately understanding what she was getting at.

'Yes.' Setsuko's gentle smile was full of approval while Haruka was giving her granddaughter a telling glare.

'It is beautiful, *Jiji*,' said Mayu dutifully, with a wink at Fiona, bringing back a memory of the cherry blossom appearing and fading in the digital museum. Haruka's face softened and she patted Mayu on the arm and said something that Fiona guessed was along the lines of, 'you're a good girl really.'

Setsuko unrolled a blanket that she'd had tucked under her arm and Mayu took it from her without being asked, spreading it under the nearest cherry tree. Haruka produced a rectangular, two-tiered bamboo box, held together with a grey strap, and placed it in the centre of the heavy cotton blanket before inviting everyone to come and sit. Undoing the strap and taking off the top lid, Setsuko offered the box to Fiona. '*Onigiri.*'

Inside were two rows of small, triangular-shaped rice balls. She took one and bit into it and found that the centre was both sharp and sweet and absolutely delicious.

'Mm, that's good,' she said pointing to the middle. 'What's this?'

'That one is filled with pickled plum.'

'Oh my, I love it.' The sweet-sour flavour burst on her tongue, tempered perfectly by the simple taste of the rice.

'This is a very traditional snack. Some have salted salmon and others tuna and Japanese mayonnaise,' explained Setsuko, offering the box to Mayu.

'*Jiji* makes the best *onigiri*,' said the girl, giving her grandmother a warm smile. 'When I take them to school in my bento box, everyone wants to try them.'

Haruka nodded and her eyes wrinkled with satisfaction.

'You make these,' said Fiona looking at the rest of the rice ball in her hand.

'I can teach you, *Fiona san.*'

'That would be great. It would make a nice piece for my

blog post and I could impress my friend Sophie who's a cookery writer.'

'You're honoured,' said Mayu. 'This is a very old family recipe. *Jiji* never tells anyone.'

Haruka let out a chuckle and said something in rapid Japanese before turning to Fiona. 'I will show you but the recipe ... that stays in the family.'

Setsuko groaned. 'She never shares it with anyone. Not even me.'

'Traditions are best held by those who honour them,' said Haruka with a mysterious wave of her hand.

After lunch, Setsuko and Haruka decided to take a stroll, while Fiona busied herself taking lots of photos of the trees, the picnicking families, and a pretty girl in a pale blue kimono holding a silk parasol. When she made her way back to the picnic rug, Mayu was absorbed in a video game on her phone and Fiona wasn't sure she'd even noticed her absence. Loathe to sit down again, she took a couple of close ups of the blowsy pink flowers, tight shots of the frilly stamens inside and the love heart edges of the petals. Then she wandered to the edge of the path to try and get a picture of the trees lining the avenue like romantic sentries. She crouched, trying to get the long shot and all the jostling bodies and then spotted Haruka and Setsuko, arm in arm, their heads turned towards each other deep in conversation. The sight of the two of them in such harmony tugged hard at her heart strings. Mother and daughter. Setsuko was laughing and her mother was patting the forearm linked through hers. Fiona raised her camera and took the shot, a ping of regret making a little hole in heart. She couldn't imagine ever strolling arm in arm with her mother. They walked at such different paces for a starter, her mother always walked with quick, angry bird hops, fierce but not really gaining ground. And conversation was never easy – her mother had too much to say about very little, to which, Fiona acknowledged with a wince, she often didn't listen. Maybe she ought to make a bit more effort. Her mum was lonely and scared of what would happen when Fiona finally moved out. Her hypochondria was a symptom of her need to hang on to her daughter.

Fiona wondered what the two Japanese women were talking about, both of them absorbed in each other and seemingly oblivious of their beautiful surroundings, as she took another shot of Setsuko's graceful hands describing something to her mother, noting the way the two of them walked hip to hip with careful matching steps. Celestial harmony, that's what she should call the picture. The backdrop of a pink so pale it was almost white framed the two women perfectly, making it appear as if they'd emerged from a cloud.

'*Fiona san*,' Haruka bowed when the women returned. 'What do you think of the *sakura*?'

'It's beautiful.'

'Have you taken lots of pictures?' asked Setsuko nodding her head towards the camera.

Before Fiona could answer, Haruka interrupted. 'I should like to have one with Mayu and Setsuko. The three generations with the *sakura*.' She nodded towards the picnic blanket. 'There.'

'Yes mother,' said Setsuko, sending a quick smile of apology to Fiona.

'It's fine,' she said, smiling back and following Haruka who was bustling forward and haranguing Mayu, clearly about being on her phone. Fiona bit back her amusement as the older woman shooed and bullied her granddaughter into position before demanding Setsuko come and sit with them.

'This. Take it like this.' Haruka waved her hand to indicate that this was the desired pose. Even though it was stilted and wooden, with Mayu's barely contained disgust and Setsuko's silent apology, Fiona snapped away and was rewarded by Haruka's regal nod at the end. She showed the women the series of shots through the viewfinder. Haruka harrumphed her approval, Mayu made a few groaning noises, and Setsuko thanked Fiona in her quiet, gentle voice.

Fiona scrolled back through the shots she'd taken. Plenty of cherry blossom. That's what people would expect to see in an exhibition on Japan. Stuff Gabe Burnett! It was a good job she'd come today. Like Setsuko said, an overnight storm could rip the blossom away from the trees and she might not get the chance again. And at least she knew she could manage by herself if he continued to be elusive. She didn't need Gabe.

Chapter 7

Gabe woke solo in bed with a hangover and the taste of regret in his mouth. All of which was bad enough without an ultra-polite text from Haruka requesting a phone call that pinged onto his mobile the moment he opened bleary eyes. Polite was not good. Polite meant restrained anger. Disapproval. Disappointment. She couldn't possibly know he'd played hooky yesterday. Or maybe she could. She seemed to have a sixth sense about these things and she'd never approved of Yumi, even less so since she'd got married.

He shook his head and cleared away the empty bottle and wine glasses from the table in the lounge. The view from the balcony in the kitchen out over the city was blurred this morning and his head hurt like it should. He deserved it. Haruka was right; he should ignore Yumi's texts. And yesterday he shouldn't have called her. And he shouldn't have offered to take her to dinner when he heard she was in Tokyo shopping, and he definitely shouldn't have brought her here for a night cap.

He closed his eyes picturing her slim body, draped in the jade-green silk dress, curled up on his sofa, her clever cat eyes watching him over the wine glass like prey. Except at the end of the evening she hadn't pounced; a text had brought her back into line and with a satisfied smile and a feline sway of hips she turned her tail on him, pecked him on the cheek, before sauntering to the lift and to the waiting cab below without a backward glance while on the phone to her husband. Why did he keep doing this? Habit? When he'd first met Yumi, it had been her vulnerability and an overriding desire to protect her that had drawn him to her. It had made him feel that he could be a better person. He'd had too many fleeting relationships in London that meant nothing, and with Yumi he'd felt that she needed him and that he could look after her. It had also helped that out of a score of suitors, she'd chosen him. Together their careers had blossomed and they'd become the golden couple of both London and Tokyo media circles. He picked up his ringing phone, his arm heavy with a bone-deep weariness that seemed a constant companion.

'*Haruka san*,' he tried to sound cheerful. 'You wanted me.'

She let loose a torrent of Japanese; he might not have understood it all but he got the gist. She was furious with him. He was letting everyone down. He was supposed to be mentoring Fiona – he noticed with a sinking heart that she was no longer 'the English girl'. Haruka had taken her under her wing. Now there was no getting out of his duties.

'I'll be there within the hour. Yes, I'll take her to the studio today. Yes, Haruka. And tomorrow I will take her into Tokyo.'

Fiona didn't seem particularly pleased to see him. In fact, she looked a little embarrassed and resigned, as if she knew she was the consolation prize, and when they arrived at the studio door, her shoulders were so hunched her neck had disappeared. For the second time, she reminded him of a turtle seeking refuge in its shell.

The studio and his apartment he rented from the Kobashis was only a few streets away from the teashop. Haruka owned this building and tended to things when he was away, including the dust and the bills. When he was here, she rarely intruded and never without a specific invitation, for which he was very grateful. This was his private space. A place where he could brood and take refuge from the rest of the world.

He bristled slightly as Fiona followed him up the stairs, irritated that he would have to share the space today. Then, mindful of Haruka's scold and her husband's honour, he forced himself to at least try and be pleasant to the poor girl. It was one day, for goodness' sake. Had he really turned into that much of a misery? He led the way into the main room, a deliberately minimalist, wide-open, airy space so that visitors, when there were any, focused on the handful of pictures on the wall. Five in total. Two on two walls and one, in all its solitary glory, on the third wall. The last wall was taken up by a set of the traditional *shoji* doors leading through to his photo lab, as he liked to call it.

Fiona's attention was immediately drawn to the single picture on the far wall and without saying a word, she walked forward to stand ten paces in front of it. A wry smile touched his mouth. He'd taken that picture over seven years ago – an elfin Yumi with big dark eyes, dressed in gossamer silk, blowing a dandelion clock, as if she held the mystery of time in her hand. The picture had gained him international acclaim and won numerous awards. It had also earned him a fortune and continued to do so, thanks to the numerous prints and posters that were sold around the world but particularly in Asia.

And now she was married. To someone else. And he felt empty inside.

'It's bigger than I thought it would be,' Fiona said. 'This is the original?'

'Sure is,' he drawled.

'I thought it would be surrounded by infra-red beams and heavy-duty alarms,' she said, turning her head as if she expected to find some hidden, hi-tech security.

He shrugged, eying the glossy black and white print in the simple black frame. 'People can buy it for a couple hundred yen. It's not worth stealing.'

Fiona turned sharp eyes his way and saw too much.

He hated that the image could be bought so cheaply. A popular image, it earned the cash. He shouldn't complain since it enabled him to do pretty much as he pleased these days. Well, most of the time. He gave his watch a surreptitious check. A couple of hours, that was all he had to give up.

Fiona turned and surveyed the other pictures, taking her time, stalking around the room with those long-legged strides, visiting and studying each picture like the perfect student. Although, he had to give her some credit. She wasn't fawning over him or pandering to his ego. He left her to her silent, careful contemplation and pulled open the doors to fire up the computer and monitors in the other room.

'When you're done, come through and we'll take a look at what you've got,' he called as he switched on the coffee machine. 'You want a drink?'

'I'd love a coffee,' she said, appearing in the doorway, examining the space with interest and checking out all the equipment spread across one large bench at the back of the room: scanner, two twenty-four-inch screens and a high-definition printer.

'Do you ever develop film?'

'Not for a while but I've got a developing room,' he jerked his head towards the little doorway tucked in the corner and the square shape that bit into the room.

'There?' she pointed.

He nodded, realising that he'd got out of the habit of pointing to things, instead using his head to indicate things more often than not. 'That's considered very rude in Japan.'

She pulled her hand back. 'What, pointing?'

'Yes, and blowing your nose. Japanese people think using a tissue is pretty disgusting.'

'I'll remember that. Good job I don't get hayfever.'

'Haruka took you to her beloved *sakura* yesterday, I gather.'

'Yes.' Her lips compressed and he read in them the silent condemnation; guilt paid another unwanted visit.

'Sorry I let you down yesterday. But you must have got some great pictures. The blossom is spectacular.' Although he couldn't remember the last time he'd made a conscious effort to seek it out, to take part in the Japanese ritual of *hanami*.

'I didn't say anything.'

'You didn't need to,' he said dryly. 'And Haruka made her views quite clear this morning.'

Anger flashed in Fiona's eyes. 'That's nothing to do with me. I never said a word. I was quite happy to spend the day with her and her family. They're lovely people.' He could see from the wistful smile that lightened her face that she genuinely liked them. For some reason it pleased him that she could appreciate what special people they were.

In a softer voice he said, 'Let's see what you've got then.'

He held out his hand to take her camera from her. 'Nice job. I had one of these once. Now I use a Canon. I find it's better for still life but this is good for outdoor work. Landscapes and the like.'

'You don't like landscapes?'

'Not my bag. I find there's too much tweaking, making the sky bluer, the grass greener. It's not real. It feels like people are cheating. It's not true to the image.'

Fiona tilted her head as if considering his words, her mouth twisting slightly to one side. He could almost see her running through the concept and turning it over in her head to examine the different permutations. It had been a long time since anyone had paid this much attention to what he said. There was a lot of nodding and yessing but now he'd reached a certain level of success, there were very few people that actually ever challenged or thought about what he said. When he'd taught many years ago, students had been keen to discuss and dissect his ideas and views; it had been refreshing being surrounded by all that youthful enthusiasm. Fiona was like that, he realised, although she had the sort of maturity that made her think carefully before she spoke. He watched her with unexpected anticipation as to what her verdict would be.

'I think you're right. I was at Borderless yesterday, the digital lab, with Mayu.'

'Ah, the *enfant terrible*,' he said with a wry smile. Mayu was an endless source of fun and entertainment, so steadfast in her rebellion, so sure she was doing things differently and challenging the world but also just like every other teenager the world over.

'She's fun.'

'She certainly is,' he agreed. 'What did you think of the place?'

'Fascinating and a bit mind blowing. Clever, and I'm glad I went but it's not really my bag. A bit too show-offy and look-at-me.'

He raised an eyebrow.

'What?' she asked, her tone a shade defensive.

'That's exactly what I think about the place. I prefer understated.'

'Oh.' Her face resumed its gravity.

'You were going to say something?' For once he was interested. 'About Borderless?'

'No, it was a thought I had there. You were talking about landscapes being doctored and while I was at Borderless, everyone was desperately trying to take pictures rather than live in the moment. It made me think that the perfect photograph should be the capture of a moment.' She frowned. 'Does that sound pretentious?'

'No,' he stepped back, unnerved by how closely her words echoed his own philosophy, and again how long it had been since he'd consciously thought about this sort of thing. 'No, not all.

'Did you capture many moments yesterday?'

Her face turned gloomy and she sighed, her cheeks puffing out. 'No, turns out I'm not that inspired by cherry blossom.'

He let out a gasp and a theatrical clutch at his throat. 'Sacrilege. Don't let Haruka hear you say that.'

She batted his arm, suddenly relaxing. 'I loved the blossom, it was beautiful. The park was lovely but ... I don't know. I took loads of photos but nothing I'm really proud of. There was one ... possibly.' She lifted her shoulders in a defeated shrug.

Now it was Gabe's turn to tilt his head and study her. He'd heard plenty of students and fellow photographers declaring with false modesty that their work wasn't very good, wanting someone to soothe their ego and tell them that on the contrary it was excellent, but Fiona's honesty resonated in her words.

'Well let's take a look and let me be the judge.'

With sure, steady fingers Fiona removed the SD card from her camera but then he saw her stiffen, seeming awkward as she held it out to him, as if she didn't want to touch him.

'Let's go through them,' he said, resigning himself to a couple of hours of sheer boredom.

'They're really not very good,' she said.

He gave her a narrow-eyed stare and his best teacher frown. 'Perhaps you'll be good enough to let me be the judge of that.'

She lapsed into silence, fidgeting with her hands in her lap and he immediately felt like an overbearing twat. He hadn't needed to do that.

'And beauty is in the eye of the beholder,' he added.

He scanned through the shots, making a note of the numbers of some of them but he could see that they were just pictures of cherry blossom. Well enough executed if you liked that sort of thing, which he absolutely didn't. Dull. Dull. Dull.

'Make a note of the ones you like,' he said, his mind wandering elsewhere. Pulling himself together, he invited her to share the screen and yanked a pen out of the pot on the desk then offered it to her. 'We'll compare notes. Then we'll scroll through to the next page and repeat the exercise.'

Uncertainty marred her face and she leaned forward towards the screen. He examined her profile as she studied the shots, chin tilted forward, careful concentration stilling her apart from her mobile mouth moving constantly as if she were talking to herself. It was rather endearing.

'Ok, how are we doing?' He tried to sound enthusiastic even though he hadn't seen a single thing that was worth his attention.

She gave him a miserable frown. 'They're all a bit ...'

'A bit what?' he prompted, a little kernel of hope kindled by her honesty. He wasn't being unkind but he always thought it was wrong to give false praise. She was smart enough to realise that.

'Dull. Nothingy. They're just pictures.'

He leaned back in his chair. 'Yup.'

She turned, her eyes widening. 'Sorry.'

'You're right. They're nothing special,' he said.

'Thanks.'

'Well, you said it first.'

'Yes, but you're not supposed to—'

'Agree? But if that's the truth ...?'

'Yes, well aren't you supposed to give me pointers or suggestions?'

'I can help you improve, but not if the original composition has nothing to recommend it.'

'So you're saying I don't have an eye for a composition?'

'Not exactly. Just not in this case. Anyone could have taken these pictures with a bit of know-how and a camera as good as you've got.'

'Great.'

'On the plus side, technically they're very competent.' He could see her deflating in front of him. He hadn't meant to dent her confidence; he'd wanted to stir her up.

'It's a question of what you want to take pictures of.'

'I don't know yet. That's what I'm here to find out.'

'No, I don't mean that.' He paused. 'What made you take these pictures?'

She stared at him, and for a moment he felt exposed as those blue eyes roved over his face, a slight frown and a not entirely pleasant twist to her mouth. If he'd captured a picture of that expression now, he'd call the portrait disgust. 'What drove you each time you clicked the shutter? What were you hoping to take? Why did you take them?'

He could almost see the comprehension click as her back

straightened and her hand reached for the mouse, running the cursor over several of the pictures.

'They were there.' He heard the raw honesty and disillusionment in her voice. 'I felt obliged. *Hanami* is a big deal. Especially to Haruka, and I thought it would be good for the exhibition. Japan is famous for *sakura*.'

'And now what do you think of them?'

Her mouth pressed tight in mutinous defiance. 'They're not very good.'

'They're fine. Technically they're good enough. You could sell them as stock shots.'

'But they're not very interesting,' she sighed, and her shoulders drooped.

'I think your heart wasn't in it.'

She stared at the screen but he didn't miss the tell-tale swallow.

'I'm not trying to upset you.'

'Who said I was upset?' Her quick denial was high and tight.

God, he hated mentoring. He wasn't cut out to deal with emotional women – emotional men either. Emotional anything. Life was easier when it was kept on a nice, even keel.

'Let's have a look at the next page.'

'What's the point? You've already told me I'm ... technically competent.' He winced as she sat ramrod straight in her chair, stiffness in her limbs.

'Because I'm your mentor and it's my job.'

He heard the mutter under her breath and the drawn out, 'Riiiight.'

It irritated him. Did she know he was doing her a huge favour? This was not his idea of a fun way to spend a Saturday morning. If he'd had his way, he'd have taken his black coffee back to bed and stayed there for the rest of the morning.

With a glare, he picked up the mouse and leaned forward, irked even more when she deliberately moved backward out of range as if he were a leper or something. 'I don't have anything contagious, you know.'

She ignored him, her focus on the screen.

'And I don't hit on women unless they want me to.'

The glare she shot him would have shrivelled most men at thirty paces. Blimey, she really didn't like him, he thought as he scrolled through the new page of pictures. Normally women flirted with him. Fiona seemed to find him repulsive and was impervious, except he hadn't missed those quick, curious glances she sent his way when she thought he couldn't see, as if she were searching for some kind of answer. Again it crossed his mind that he'd met her before. Each time she secretly glanced at him, an uncanny prickle ran down his spine.

'Haruka wanted me to take that one.' Fiona blurted out as he clicked on a shot of the three generations of women. 'Do you think I could print a copy out today? I'd like to give it to her.'

'Yeah, sure. It's a nice shot.'

'Nice,' she said.

'She'll be thrilled with it.' It was a nice family shot. The three woman sitting together, their likeness to each other captured perfectly as well as their individual personalities. 'Good job. If we crop it like this.'

They spent the next half hour working on the picture, enhancing and cropping it before printing it and putting it into one of the photo frames that he kept in stock. He was grateful that it used up a good portion of time and meant that there was less time to work through the next batch of shots.

After a second coffee, they returned to the remainder of Fiona's pictures and he checked his watch. Almost two. He felt that he could respectably call it a day quite soon and hopefully he'd spent enough time with Fiona to appease Haruka.

With a weary internal sigh he returned to the screen and began to scroll through the images again. His fingers froze, hovering over the mouse, and then he leaned forward. Double clicking, he opened the picture up, watching as it enlarged on the screen. It was a shot of Haruka and Setsuko sharing an intimate smile as they walked arm in arm, their heads haloed with clouds of palest pink blossom. Love, it said. Pure mother-daughter love. His own heart clenched at the sight of it. Pure love. A distillation of something so special, and caught in the scant second it took to press the shutter. Had he ever loved Yumi with that much purity? Like his parents loved each other? The question shocked him. He'd never considered it before.

'This is ...' He cast a quick glance at Fiona, seeing her profile suddenly lift with the alertness of the scent of something. Ah, she saw it too. 'This is good. Very good. Brilliant.'

His finger traced the image, unable to determine quite what it was about the picture that made it what it was. It just was, and that was its perfection.

He turned to Fiona. 'This is beautiful.'

A slow smile transformed her face, her eyes luminous with delight and ... *oh my God*, he thought as it hit him. He *had* met her before.

Bloody hell.

It was her.

Chapter 8

'We're going to the Tokyo Skytree today,' said Gabe to Haruka who, despite yesterday's displeasure towards him, insisted he came in for tea before they headed off, offering him breakfast and asking if his coat was warm enough and whether he'd like to borrow one of her husband's scarves.

Gabe lapped it up, patting her hand and putting his arm around her to give her a quick squeeze.

'What would I do without you? Yes, I'd love a cup of your green tea. Do you have any of the *gyokuro* jade?'

Her beaming look his way was positively dazzling, as if he'd performed the best parlour trick in the book. 'Especially for you.' She turned to Fiona. 'It is one of the finest green teas. Gabe has very excellent taste.'

Fiona refrained from rolling her eyes at this blatant sucking up, even if it was rather sweet to see Gabe enfolding the tiny woman in his arms.

'Skytree will be good,' said Haurka. 'Cold, but good.'

Gabe nodded, turning to Fiona. 'It's a clear day, so there'll be some great views from up there. You get a real idea of the size and scale of the city.'

Fiona scowled to herself. He sounded as if he was quoting a guidebook. She didn't want to sound like a petulant school-girl but she didn't want to go sightseeing, she wanted ... That was the problem – she wasn't sure what she wanted. She needed to find a theme for her exhibition. To start taking some proper photographs. Much as she'd enjoyed the museum in Mayu's company, and the cherry blossom, apart from the one shot of Haruka and Setsuko, which she wasn't sure she wanted to exhibit, she didn't feel like she'd achieved very much. That one photo didn't give her a starting point for an exhibition. Frustration made her fingertips itch and she tossed her heavy plait over her shoulder, slightly embarrassed when she realised Gabriel was watching her, a thoughtful expression on his face as he studied her braided hair. For some reason, the attention made her heart trip slightly, which made her even crosser. A couple of times yesterday in the studio, she'd been horribly aware of his closeness and had developed a fascination for the dark hairs on his wrists as he manipulated the mouse. She was not eighteen any more. Gabe was an attractive man, there was no denying that, but she did not have feelings for him. Never had, really. Raging teenage hormones had brainwashed her into believing something which was complete fantasy. With the memory swept a blush that burned her face and she had to turn away and bend down, pretending to fuss with one of her socks.

She drank calming green tea as Gabe talked to Haruka and she watched as he gradually relaxed, his smiles less guarded and his eyes starting to dance with amusement and animation.

By the time a second cup of tea had been drunk, Gabe was teasing Haruka with a warm, gentle affection that surprised Fiona. If she hadn't seen it with her own eyes, she wouldn't have believed this softer side to him existed.

'*Haruka san*, you make the best tea in Japan.' He raised the tiny china bowl, dwarfed in his large hands, and bowed to her.

'And you, *Gabriel san*, are full of bull.'

Fiona almost snorted her tea out of her nose while Gabriel roared with laughter.

Haruka smiled serenely at the pair of them and dusted an invisible crumb from the table.

'I'd forgotten how long you lived in America, *Haruka san*.'

She pressed her hands together and bowed, that irrepressible twinkle lighting her dark eyes.

Despite the visible softening of his character, he turned taciturn as soon as they left the house. When they emerged from the busy station at the other end, she was too busy concentrating on following him as he weaved the crowded streets at top speed to attempt to talk to him again, something she thought was deliberate on his part.

'Here you go. The Skytree. Officially the tallest tower in the world, although not the tallest building. There's a definite distinction of which locals are very proud.' He handed over a sheet of paper. 'I booked online. Here's your ticket.' He flicked his watch out from his sleeve. 'I'll meet you back here in two hours. It takes a while to get up there and I'm sure you'll want to take lots of pictures. Visibility should be good.'

Too gobsmacked to say a word, Fiona took the proffered ticket.

'See you later,' he said, adding flippantly, 'Have fun,' and before she could collect her somewhat scattered wits, he'd wheeled around and disappeared into the flow of people passing by. She didn't even have a chance to frame the words, 'But, but ...'

By the time she'd built a head of steam and hit fuming, ready to give him a piece of her mind, he was long gone. Had he really dumped her again?

'Why the arrogant pr—!' she muttered under her breath, clenching her fingers into tight fists. She'd never hit anyone or wanted to, in her life but Gabe was bidding to be the very first candidate. How dare he leave with such obvious haste, as if she were a nasty virus he was trying to avoid catching? It was hardly flattering.

And she was assailed by memories, not for the first time. Sick embarrassment coiled in her stomach. He'd given no sign that he remembered or recognised her. Surely it wasn't anything to do with that. No, he was a rude, uncommunicative git who wasn't even attempting to play mentor. Still boiling mad, she was drawn forward into the hordes of tourists all pushing their way into the lift heading to the first viewing level, the Tembo Deck. Despite her anger, she couldn't fail to admire the technology and design mastery that had gone into the tower. It had all mod cons with additional bells and whistles. Built a few years ago, this tower had been designed to entertain and enthral its visitors, as well as make sure they didn't have to actually climb the stairs to any of the mind-boggling four-hundred-and-fifty floors.

The first viewing platform on the mere three-hundred-and-fortieth floor offered an incredible view of the city, including a glass floor where you could see all the way down to the ground.

Fiona hesitated on the threshold of the glass.

'Safe as houses, honey,' said a friendly American man with an encouraging smile. *Hmm*, she thought, thinking of the three little pigs' houses. 'Thanks,' she said and stepped gingerly onto the glass, shuffling across the glossy surface, which was quite busy with everyone gazing downwards. If she had a stool, that might make a cool shot, standing slightly higher than everyone else, looking down at everyone with their necks bent. Then she could juxtapose the shot with another one, perhaps at the Shibuya Crossing with everyone peering up.

The more she thought about it, the more she liked the idea. Bloody Gabe. If he'd been here, she might have asked him what he thought.

Looking down, she was relieved to see that there was a secondary framework of steel and glass less than a foot below, but even so, she felt a slight touch of disorientation. It really was a long way down. But at least it felt totally safe and, with a smile, she realised it reminded her of the Round Tower in Copenhagen and the tiny circle of old, thick glass that provided a view all the way to the bottom.

All thoughts of feeling safe were brushed away on the next portion of the climb to the top of the tower when she was swept along by the crowd of enthusiastic tourists, both Japanese and Western, into the lift which was on the outside of the building. Standing pressed against the glass, she held her breath during the rapid climb over the next hundred floors. Around her were excited cries and gasps of awe, some smiling faces, some apprehensive and others wide eyed with wonder, and for a moment she wished there were someone with her to share the heart-whooshing sensation as the lift glided upwards leaving little goose bumps of not-quite fear and not-quite excitement. Being on the outside of the building was both disconcerting and exhilarating and thankfully lasted a matter of seconds before the doors opened and they were disgorged onto the Tembo Gallery with its 360-degree view of the city.

Touching one of the huge curved glass panels, Fiona stopped, stunned by the sheer size of the city spread out below and the engineering feat that had built this extraordinary tower so high up in the sky. The sheer ingenuity of man never ceased to amaze her.

The view was truly spectacular, the city spread far below and stretching out towards the horizon. For a moment, she considered trying to take a series of panoramic pictures that she could match up at a later date to create the full 360-degree view as one. It was tempting but also a bit dull and technical. The idea didn't grab her by the scruff of the neck and make her want to seize her camera with that adrenaline-junkie hope that this might be the big one.

She watched as a young boy reached out as if he could touch one of the skyscrapers in the distance, his face wide with wonder. And the idea clicked. She could take photos of the responses of other people up here and their reactions to the views and the sights. This was where a mentor would come in really handy. There was still over an hour before she was due to meet Gabe.

Irritated by his absence, she abandoned the views and took the lift back down to ground level in search of a coffee shop.

Having scanned the street at the bottom, in case he was anywhere in sight, she resigned herself to drinking coffee and brooding for the next hour until it was time to meet him. Foolishly, she still hadn't asked to swap mobile numbers. As she went to open the door of the nearest coffee shop, she spotted Gabe, sitting three tables ahead with a cup in one hand, pushing an empty sachet of sugar around the table with the other.

She watched him, his finger toying with the white packet. Bored, was he? Good. He deserved to be. She'd assumed he had better things to do and that was why he hadn't accompanied her. It stung that he clearly couldn't be bothered. With a grim face she ordered a cup of coffee at the counter using a combination of sign language and nodding and made her way over to his table.

Without saying a word, she took his empty cup from him, not quite slamming hers down but making sure she had his full attention. Then she pulled out a chair and sat opposite him.

She was pleased to see that he seemed startled and then wary.

'Afternoon,' she said with icy calm.

'How was it?'

'Fine.' She took a sip of the coffee, grateful for the fierce hit of caffeine.

He raised his eyebrows.

'Problem?'

'No. Not at all,' she said with blithe insincerity.

With a wince he held his hand out for his coffee cup and then realising that it was empty put his hand back down again. 'Is there something wrong?'

'Now, why would you think that?' Hiding a smile of satisfaction, she saw it register, a slight wariness denting that bored and indifferent facade.

'You seem ...' He paused but she didn't rush to fill the silence. Instead she left it hanging there and saw him groping for words.

Now it was her turn to raise an eyebrow.

With a shrug of his shoulders, he met her angry gaze: 'I'm not into crowds and tourist places. I thought you'd be better off on your own.'

'Perhaps. But just when does this mentoring kick in? Or do you plan to dump me at the key tourist attractions and hide out at the nearest coffee bar for the next two weeks?'

'I'm not hiding out,' he said, snapping upright with an indignant glare.

'No?' she asked. 'Looks that way to me. I've been here for four days now and you've not exactly been very helpful.'

'We went to the studio yesterday and the day before I was busy. Work.'

'I'm not denying that ... but I'd have thought your work would have provided a mentoring opportunity. I need to come up with an exhibition and a portfolio of pictures in the next two weeks. You're supposed to be helping.'

Gabe didn't quite go as far as looking ashamed but he pursed his lips and dropped his folded arms. His fingers worried at the sugar sachet again.

'Have you had any ideas?' he asked lightly, his gaze skimming beyond her as if the answer was of no real interest.

'A few,' she snapped. 'It would have been helpful to discuss them with my mentor at the time.'

'Well, now's your chance,' he said with a sudden smirk that she wanted to punch off his face. 'I'm all ears.'

Now it was her turn to purse her lips. How had he done that? Turned the tables and made her feel like a needy child wanting attention? She didn't like it. Not one bit. Because she wasn't that child any more.

'Do you know what, Gabe? I've flown over nine thousand miles for this trip, to be mentored by one of the best photographers in the world.' She gave him a fierce stare. 'And instead I get a second-rate replacement who can't even be bothered with me.' She felt a thrill of bitchiness when his eyes widened at the, 'second rate replacement' line. Good, she wanted him to feel bad. And if insulting him worked, she'd happily do it again. 'Haruka has been nothing but kind to me and she seems to think you're the bee's knees. I've no idea why. I'm not asking for much but if you can't be bothered then perhaps you can put me in touch with someone who can. Or I can ask Haruka's husband for an alternative.'

'You can't do that,' said Gabe and she saw him brace the table suddenly as if stopping himself from rising to his feet. 'You know you can't.'

Guilt pricked at her; no, she couldn't. The family had been

nothing but kind to her and she would do anything to avoid upsetting Haruka but Gabe didn't know that. She shrugged. 'I don't see that I have much choice. You're not interested. I came here to learn. Why would it bother you? It would let you off the hook. You can spend all day lazing around in coffee shops.'

Gabe glared at her. 'I won't have you upsetting Haruka. She's been very good to me.' His mouth crumpled mutinously before he asked. 'What is it you want from me?'

Fiona felt the tension ease in her shoulders as triumph streamed through, at the same time as a little bump of disappointment that he so readily believed she was prepared to be that ruthless. She never would have done something like that. But then Gabe had never known her; she'd just been one of a multitude of students and the impact he'd made on her far eclipsed hers on him. Her overheated hormones and imagination had created a magical, romantic connection between them which had all been in her silly head. The familiar shame threatened to derail her thoughts and she reined them back.

'To teach me. To mentor me. To listen to my ideas. Would any of that really kill you?'

'No. I guess not,' he said quietly, pausing to snatch at the sugar sachet, scrunching it up in his palm and staring beyond her through the window before saying with candid honesty, 'I'm used to doing my own thing. It's years since I taught and my commissions tend to be commercial these days rather than private. They don't require much of me.' The face he pulled suggested that he was disappointed with the latter.

'Is that by choice?' she asked, her tone much gentler.

He focused on her face, sudden light in his eyes as if he'd woken up and was now not just awake but wide awake. With a shrug, he took another sugar sachet out of the pot on the table and tapped on the surface. She imagined the grains inside tumbling over themselves in a rush to greet gravity and recognised it as a delaying tactic. She didn't fill the silence.

Instead she leaned back in her chair and surveyed his handsome face and the lines around his mouth that deepened as he talked.

'Yes.' He rubbed at one eyebrow. 'Commercial commissions usually have very fixed ideas about what they want. The piper plays the tune and I don't enjoy that. And teaching ... I find all that energy and enthusiasm exhausting. Always thinking they've invented a new wheel. Does that answer your question?' She felt a rush of disappointment in him which must have showed because he adopted a mocking smile and asked, 'Nothing to say?'

She shook her head. What had changed? What had changed him from the vibrant, excitable man overflowing with enthusiasm and seize-the-moment drive that she remembered. There had been a time when you could feel the fizz of his energy, when he could barely keep still because he was bursting with ideas and impatient to move on to the next thing.

For a moment the silence between them hung heavy as they were both lost in their own thoughts.

Finally, Gabe tossed the sugar sachet aside. 'Tomorrow we'll start again. Have you any idea where you'd like to go?'

This was as much of an olive branch as she was going to get.

'I'd like to see something a bit more traditional.'

'Okay.' He nodded and then unexpectedly, as if he wanted a real answer and not a general platitude, asked, 'Any particular reason why?'

She narrowed her eyes, considering for a second. 'I'm thinking about the photographer as a voyeur of tourists. So rather than taking pictures of the tourist places, I'm taking pictures of the tourists' reaction to them.'

'Go on.' He sounded bored but those blue eyes met hers in a shrewd, assessing examination, as if he was reluctantly interested. She ducked hers as her pulse picked up. His eyes had always fascinated her. Fringed with dark lashes, bright and attentive – or rather they had been, once. Then they had missed nothing, constantly roving as if on the lookout for the perfect shot and then they would suddenly stop as if arrested by something. Her teenage hormones had supplied plenty of examples of his eyes resting on her face, softening with admiration, interest, even passion. Those teenage hormones had been fanciful, duplicitous and unreliable.

Ignoring her dry mouth, she forced herself to speak. 'For example, when we were at Shibuya. Everyone was looking up. Today at the tower on the glass floor. Everyone was looking down.'

'A contrast.' He nodded approvingly.

Her face lit up with a sudden smile, thrilled that he'd immediately connected with her idea. She hadn't even had to explain. And then caution told her to temper her enthusiasm. *You made a fool of yourself once before.*

In a calmer, more professional voice, she explained her idea in more detail.

'Clever,' observed Gabe. 'Watching the watchers. But you might find voyeurism has been done to death.'

His laconic shrug infuriated her.

'So you don't think it's a good idea,' she said, deflating faster than a punctured balloon.

'I didn't say that, exactly. Just that it's been done before. Like I said, that's why I don't like teaching. I've done enough soul searching for one day. If you want any more culture, the Edo Tokyo museum is nearby. I can drop you there if you want.'

'No, it's fine,' she muttered, tucking her hands beneath her thighs. The urge to strangle him was almost too much to resist. He was the most infuriating man on the planet. He hadn't heard a word she'd said and had damned her big idea with faint praise. She was so disappointed she could cry.

'Tomorrow you can decide where you want to go.' And with that he stood, indicating the day was over.

Chapter 9

'How was the Skytree?' asked Setsuko with one of her gentle smiles when Fiona returned late in the afternoon. She was seated at the table in the centre of the room, her dainty figure coiled around a seat and her legs tucked underneath. 'And where is *Gabriel san?*'

'He had things to do,' said Fiona flatly, following Setsuko's beckoning to take a seat at the table, immediately grateful for the lovely warmth. 'It was very ... interesting.' There was something about the calm, serenity of Setsuko that encouraged her to tell the truth rather than offer the expected conventional tourist praise. 'Busy.'

'Hmph,' said Haruka, making no pains to hide her disapproval as she bustled in, laden down with a large tray. Fiona wasn't sure if the derisive snort was aimed at the tower or at Gabe. Setsuko jumped up and tried to take it from her mother who responded with a harsh clicking of her tongue and said something in Japanese. Giving her daughter a tart look and whirling out of reach, she placed it on the *kotatsu* table.

'And did you take some photos?' asked Setsuko, rearranging

herself at the table as if the exchange with her mother hadn't happened.

'Some,' said Fiona, sensing, despite the placid enquiry, more than polite interest from Setsuko. 'Would you like to see?' At least someone was interested in her work. Her fingers clenched under the table, the only indication she allowed herself of how annoyed she was with Gabe.

The other woman nodded and while Haruka arranged the tea things to her satisfaction, Fiona showed her the pictures she'd taken.

'Better places to go,' said Haruka as she poured the tea. She smiled at the framed photo Fiona had taken of her, Setsuko and Mayu under the cherry blossom. Fiona had decided to keep the picture of her and Setsuko under wraps for the time being. She hoped they would be happy for her to exhibit it.

Setsuko hid a smile. 'My mother doesn't approve of the modern eyesores in Tokyo.'

'Where is the grace and beauty in a big modern tower? The *wabi sabi*? There is no dignity, no humility in this. It is all man-made.'

Haruka laid a warm hand on hers. 'Come, drink tea, and I will tell you much more about nature and Japanese culture.'

Haruka took her time fussing with the delicate porcelain cups until they were arranged to her satisfaction before pouring the very pale-green-tinged tea. 'This is *genmaicha*.' She pushed one of the steaming tea cups towards Fiona, with a dip of her head towards her daughter.

'*Genmaicha* tea is a blend of *sencha* green tea with roasted rice and popcorn,' explained Setsuko with a wry smile. 'It is also known as peasant's tea because in the old days, rice was added to make the green tea go further.'

'Hmph,' sniffed Haruka. 'It has a good flavour and has many health benefits. Good for you and'—she dipped her head and inhaled the fragrance—'for a foreigner is a good tea. It is mild in flavour and not too intense.'

They all sipped the tea, Fiona copying the way the other two women clasped the porcelain bowls between both hands. She felt the clean freshness of the flavour as the hot liquid slipped down her throat. There was a soothing quiet as all three women savoured their tea, and the comforting warmth of the china clasped between her hands made her feel grounded and somehow connected to the other two women.

They sat in peaceful silence for ten minutes and Fiona let the cleansing tea wash away the ups and downs of the day, although disappointment and frustration sat heavy on her shoulders. Gabe just didn't seem to understand how important this exhibition was.

Then Haruka sat up abruptly. '*Wabi Sabi.*' With that she rose from the table, said something in Japanese to Setsuko, and disappeared through the shoji doors.

'She'd like to take you to the garden.' Setsuko's face filled with fond affection. 'She's very proud of her gardens. When we first came here from America, there was nothing and she made the garden herself. I think it was hard for her at first there because it was so different, and although she adapted, when she came back she embraced the things she'd really missed, like the tea and nature.'

Dressed warmly in a borrowed, padded down coat, Fiona

followed Setsuko downstairs and through the teashop to a wooden veranda in dark wood running the whole way across the back of the building. With the grace of a deer, Setsuko walked swiftly around the balcony, which she explained was called an *engawa*, to where Haruka sat on a cushion looking out over a lush green garden. Next to her, two more cushions were lined up, ready and waiting. Fiona hid a smile at the sight; Haruka did like things done properly. She followed suit as Setsuko sank down onto one of the cushions beside her mother, although perhaps not quite as gracefully.

Haruka didn't acknowledge them; instead she remained focused on the garden in front of her, her legs curled to one side breathing slow deep breaths. Setsuko immediately took up a similar pose. There was a stillness to the early evening and Fiona could smell the scent of pine and cedar in the quiet air. Copying her hosts, she began to take slow deep breaths, drawing in all the different elements of the beautifully planned garden. It was a landscape in miniature, she realised, studying the neatly trimmed and shaped shrubs that formed the core of the garden which was then enhanced by a series of bonsai trees in pots providing striking, elegant profiles. In the background, a pair of weeping cherries, just coming into bloom, swept their willowy branches to the floor like the limbs of ballerinas while in the foreground a gravel path wove in and out of the many burnished copper pots curving around a tiny pond, which reflected the deep green of the shrubs around and was fed by a tiny fall of water coming from a terracotta pot on its side.

You could sit here for hours, thought Fiona, absorbing the

incredible detail of the garden. It was a living work of art and she realised that was the intent behind the garden. Her fingers itched for her camera to take a close up of a nearby bonsai spruce. It looked as if it had been honed by a windswept moor, leaning slightly to one side with its ancient, thick, gnarled trunk and tiny, dark green needles. She focussed on the detail of the bark and let the rich green of the needles blur slightly. A light wind rustled at the weeping cherries and the ripple of movement made her think of the corps de ballet dancing in perfect unison.

She felt Haruka's warm hand come to rest on top of hers, a light, careful touch, her breath still deep and steady, but on her face there was an expression of utter peace.

Fiona turned back to the garden and took her own deep breaths, aware of the anchor of Haruka's hand on hers.

She could hear the gentle flow of the fountain, water on water, could see the outward ripples of circles as though an insect had landed on the surface, the dappled shade on the path as the sun peeped through the trees. Her shoulders lifted as if a weight had been pulled away and she felt it, a magical lightness, the sensation that she could float away, yet at the same time she felt rooted and connected. This was tranquillity. It seeped into her bones, a lovely sense of peace and calm. She was aware of the scent of the trees, the touch of the breeze caressing her face, the colours and shapes of nature. When she closed her eyes briefly and then opened them, she was struck by the vividness of the greens, the delicate prettiness of the pale pink blossom and the contrast of the dark wood of the balcony. In a sudden moment of understanding she was glad she didn't have her camera and the obligation to capture the scene. When was the last time she'd felt such ease with herself, or this floaty sense of contentment, or that all her senses had been unlocked and left to do their own thing?

'*Wabi Sabi*,' murmured Haruka. 'It is part of Japanese culture. It is an appreciation of things that aren't perfect or finished, and that is their attraction. It's accepting the value of things – an old pot, an old person – and understanding that those things have wisdom, that they have seen things. They have a value in being.' From underneath her navy tunic she pulled out a small pot and held it up. It was pretty but had been broken – at some point a large triangular piece had broken away – but it had been repaired. The repair was very obvious, outlined in a vein of gold which highlighted the defect rather than hiding it. 'This is old; it was my grand-mother's grandmother's.' With a slender finger she pointed to the golden seam. 'We value the old, so we repair things, but we embrace the repair. This is *kintsugi*; it celebrates the imper-fection. The blemish is celebrated, made in gold because beauty is found in the uniqueness of its imperfection. An old face is lined with years of happiness, sorrow, and achievement but those lines have been earned. *Wabi Sabi* is to value the imperfections because they are a reflection of our reality.'

Fiona's gaze traced the golden vein outlining the jagged edge of the repair against the pale blue china and took it from Haruka's outstretched hand. 'It's lovely.'

'*Wabi Sabi* is also a recognition that nothing is permanent and we must appreciate things for the here and now. The cherry blossoms are celebrated as much for their beauty as for their transience; tomorrow they may be gone and the beauty is in the moment of seeing them. That is why in Japan the seasons are so important, because nature is beautiful but you can never capture it forever.'

Fiona nodded. These were lovely sentiments and she was charmed by them.

Haruka spread out a hand towards the garden. 'Taking time to be with nature is vital. It is our lifeforce. It recharges the batteries and it grounds us. It takes us back to the simplicity of life and away from the stresses of modern life. In Japan, work can be stressful. People work very long hours and have very little holiday, so taking this time to find oneself and appreciate nature is something important.'

'That's a lovely philosophy,' said Fiona gently, 'and I can feel the calming influence of the garden. It's very beautiful.' The seething irritation and annoyance that had festered under her skin earlier had been soothed away by the quiet, beautiful garden and the gentle philosophy that Haruka had expounded.

'Thank you. Now I must go and cook dinner but Setsuko will show you around the garden.' With that she rose with ease whereas Fiona knew that she would be a little stiff when she uncurled her legs to stand.

Setsuko led Fiona along the little gravel path to stand by one of the weeping cherries and they looked back at the teashop.

'It is beautiful, especially the bonsai trees; they fascinate me. Do they need an incredible amount of work?'

'Yes, and I would be terrified to touch one. They are my mother's babies.' Setsuko's dramatic shudder made Fiona laugh. 'One leaf trimmed that should have been left and I would be in so much trouble. *Haha* designed and created the garden herself,' said Setsuko. 'It is a real labour of love. She wanted the perfect setting for her tea ceremonies. Those are her real passion.'

'And something I want to learn more about.'

Setsuko let out a light tinkling laugh. 'Don't you worry, she is dying to show you but ... the moment has to be right and the ceremonies are not held every day, but perhaps tomorrow you'd like to come and visit the shop again.'

'I'd like that. Although I will be going out with Gabe.' She scowled.

'You like him again.' Setsuko gave Fiona an uncharacteristic nudge in the ribs and for a moment it was as if they were two teenagers.

'I-I ...' The blush deepened and she tucked her hands into her pockets and hunched into the coat, hoping to hide the flare of colour.

'He's very attractive. I didn't tell you before but I had a terrible crush on him when I first met him.' Setsuko giggled. 'I don't think I ate anything the first week he stayed with us. Then my mother told me off for being a silly girl. And I realised, when I got used to him, that he's just a man. When I met my Miro, I knew what ...' It was Setsuko's turn to blush. 'I couldn't even speak to Miro. Luckily, he felt the same way. It was ...' There was her quiet smile again. 'The way he looked at me, the very first time ...'

Fiona swallowed. 'Yes. Well, Gabe's very attractive. But he's not my type,' she said hurriedly. 'We have nothing in common.

He seems ... quite bored with life. Not very interested in things. And certainly not interesting in being a mentor.' She pursed her lips thinking of their conversation earlier in the day.

'He's changed,' observed Setsuko with a wistful sigh. 'It is very sad. He used to be ... quite charming. Arrogant as well.' Fiona nodded. She knew that side of Gabe. But then, he'd been at the top of his profession and he'd earned the right.

Tightening her mouth, Setsuko added, 'But he has been troubled for a long time. Mother says he is blind to the beauty of the world. He has lost his way.'

It sounded a little fanciful to Fiona. Gabe had become jaded and cynical. Too much success too early on.

'Yumi. She was bad news.'

'Why?' Fiona asked out of politeness rather than real interest.

Setsuko's lips twisted. 'She's a very famous model in Japan and she was Gabe's muse for a long time. They had a very passionate affair and it was a little bit infamous. She was a Japanese treasure, everyone loved her and she was an icon ... but to be with a foreigner ... it is not always seen as a good thing by the more traditional people. My grandmother was horrified that I married an American even though his parents are Japanese. Our culture was very isolated for many years. I think Yumi liked that she shocked people, perhaps more than she liked Gabe. But he was very much in love.' She clasped her hands behind her back and continued to walk through the garden. 'When she suddenly married Meiko Mitoki, it was a great shock to everyone ... especially Gabe. He took it badly.'

'I can imagine,' said Fiona, trying not to show too much prurient interest.

'He is a flawed man but he has a good heart.'

'Mmm, I'm not sure even he'd believe that.'

'He feels deeply but he hides it well. When Yumi ran away to get married, she didn't tell him. He was in love with her and he didn't know anything about Meiko until after the wedding. It was on the news. He is very wealthy. An important businessman. It was a big story.'

'Oh.' Her heart clenched at the betrayal. 'That must have been awful. Especially when it was so public. I didn't know.'

'He was in a very bad way for a little while. Drinking too much whisky and sake. My mother saved him.'

Fiona whipped her head around.

'He didn't eat. He didn't take care of himself. Mother left him to feel sorry for himself for a while but he stayed sad for too long. She bullied him into eating. To coming to the house for meals.' She chuckled. 'She raised his rent so high that he had to go out and work. She stole his clothes at night so he had to put clean ones on. She filled his bottles of whisky with tea.'

Fiona laughed. 'She sounds evil.'

'That's what Gabe thought; they had many big fights but he didn't leave. I think he likes fighting. And then one day he came into the garden with her. I don't what she said to him but after that he started living again. Going out, not getting drunk all the time, taking pictures again. That was three years ago.'

'But he's still in love with Yumi.'

'He thinks he is. It's a habit. That's what my mother says. She never liked Yumi. My mother tries to look after him.' Setsuko smiled. 'She loves to take care of people. Take them under her wing. You are her new project.'

'Don't you mind?' asked Fiona, thinking her own mother would be quite jealous if she heard that. Judy Hanning was very possessive of her daughter and liked to think that they were very close.

'No, not at all. We have always had a good, strong bond,' Setsuko sighed. 'I wish it was like that with Mayu. She's very ... modern and outspoken. She never listens to me.' She spread her hands out in bewildered disapproval.

'She's a teenager,' said Fiona with a reassuring smile. 'It will change. And she's a good kid. I enjoyed her company the other day and you'd never have known that her grandmother had coerced her into taking me out for the day.'

Setsuko laughed. 'She took you to her favourite place. I don't think it was a particular hardship.'

'Maybe not.' Fiona grinned. 'But all the same, she was good company and wouldn't you rather she was confident and independent?'

'I guess so. The American part of me, yes. But everything is so loud. The music, the clothes, the films. I don't understand any of it.'

'I'm not sure you're supposed to. Mums and teenagers never see eye to eye. It comes later,' said Fiona as if she knew what she was talking about. She was the last person who should be dispensing any advice on mother-daughter relationships. With a wince she crossed her fingers in her pockets. Her mother had been a nightmare when she was a teenager, even bigger on melodrama than Fiona herself had been. Fiona couldn't remember her ever dispensing sensible guidance and advice.

'So Gabe. Tomorrow. Where is he taking you?'

'I have to tell him where I want to go. I have no idea what to choose but it needs to be somewhere traditional, somewhere Japanese people go.'

Setsuko gave one of her gentle smiles. 'We shall decide over dinner.'

Chapter 10

'You take Fiona to Meji Shrine today,' said Haruka in a scolding voice to Gabe as he arrived the next morning for breakfast, at the same time as giving him a welcoming hug. 'And you look like hell. You drink too much.'

He ignored the latter comment – he was a big boy, after all – instead shooting Fiona an accusing 'what have you been saying?' glower. Haruka was very good at making him feel like he was in the doghouse but she was the one person he couldn't bring himself to be rude to. Or Setsuko for that matter. The latter was far too gentle and the former had a backbone of steel that he wouldn't want to mess with, plus the fact that this had become his second home and, despite the admonishments he received from Haruka on a regular basis about the way he lived his life, he knew it was well meant and that she cared.

Fiona's eyes widened and she held up her hands in innocence. 'I haven't said a word.'

No, she probably hadn't, not intentionally, but Haruka had a way of winkling information out of you without you realising it. The woman had an uncanny talent for listening to what *was* said, and hearing what *wasn't* said.

127

'Is that where Fiona would like to go, or where you've decided she should go?' he asked, knowing the tiny woman's bossiness outweighed her stature.

Haruka smiled, serene, confident, and a trifle smug. 'It is a very beautiful, peaceful place and I think *Fiona san* will enjoy it very much.'

'We talked over dinner last night and I think it will be perfect for what I want,' snapped Fiona and he had to bite back a smile at her quickness to defend her host and herself. Looked like someone else had fallen slave to Haruka's indomitable will.

'Okay, the Meji Shrine it is. Certainly a gorgeous day for it.' The chill of early spring had receded today and the promise of summer shimmered in the warm morning air, along with bright sunshine and a clear blue sky.

Putting his shoulders back, he gave Fiona a discreetly assessing glance as she busied herself checking everything was in her camera bag. Today he was going to try to be on his best behaviour, even though a trip to the shrine was right up there on the tedious list. Seen one, seen a dozen. But he owed Haruka and while guilt wasn't entirely the right word for how Fiona's challenge had impacted him yesterday, he did feel a sense of obligation. In his defence, he felt it was hardly shirking his duties to take her to the top tourist spots. That was definitely part of the deal ... and it wasn't his fault he'd seen them all before a dozen times and couldn't bear to go again. Okay, so he might have been a tad selfish in dumping her and running – he was man enough to admit that.

What he'd found more difficult to swallow and had brooded

about last night over the better part of a very nice and very expensive bottle of red wine, was her apparent disappointment in him. The watchful waiting while she drank her tea, as though she expected a better version of him to appear.

Well, she was in for a long wait. This was as good as it got these days. But her disappointment had chafed at him, like a burr under his skin, and all evening her words had kept coming back to him.

Her phone beeped – a text notification, he guessed – the sound loud and discordant in the kitchen. Fiona glanced at the screen and then at her watch, frowning before shoving the phone into her back pocket.

'Right,' he said. 'We'd better be off. Make hay while the sun shines and all that. Got everything?'

'Yes,' said Fiona, brushing the end of her thick plait over her palm, as he'd seen her do a couple of times. Her eyes were a little unfocused as if she were elsewhere and he took the moment to study the unusual colour of her hair – real strawberry blonde. It fascinated him, and his photographer's eye imagined it in different lights, turning burnished gold in some and dark bronze in others.

'Everything okay?'

'Hmm,' she said and a few lines appeared on her forehead. 'Yes. Just ...' she continued absently, still playing with her hair. 'Sorry, I was thinking about the light today. It's very bright.'

He took her words at face value, even though he thought her distraction had a lot to do with the text. 'Don't worry, there are plenty of trees; you'll be able to get lots of light and shade to take some interesting shots. Come on then, let's do this.' He ushered her towards the door after giving Haruka a quick hug.

'Take care of her,' said Haruka, a touch mysteriously.

'I think she'll be safe at the shrine.'

As Fiona opened the door, the sun burst in, turning her hair into the exact shade of burnished gold he'd imagined. Struck by the colour, he stopped and for an uncharacteristic moment was almost tempted to ask her to undo her braid and let it ripple down over her shoulders so he could get the full effect. Just then, she glanced back over her shoulder and the juxtaposition of an innocent goddess framed by the halo of gold almost punched him in the gut. It was the first time in a very long time that he felt a burning need to take a picture. It would be a near impossible shot to capture, with the full sun behind her but his mind was already darting off in a different direction as to how it might be achieved.

'Gabe?' Fiona was staring at him. 'Are you okay?'

'Fine. Why?'

'You looked a little ...' She lifted her shoulders in a shrug and then gave him an unexpected, cheeky smile. 'Away with the fairies. If there are such things in Gabe Burnett's world. I suspect fairies are too prosaic.'

Being away with the fairies was better than being struck dumb, he mused as he followed her down the stairs. Now that he remembered her, things kept coming back to him. Like being fascinated by her hair and those bright, roving, questing blue eyes.

'What do you know about the Meji Shrine?' he asked,

shoving the thoughts back in the box they belonged to, the one marked ancient history.

'Not a lot, but I have this.' She waved a guide book. 'I can read it on the train.'

'Or I could tell you a little about it on the way there. There's quite a walk up to the main gate through Yoyogi Park and it's such a lovely day that it would be a shame not to make the most of it.'

He laughed at the suspicion on her face. 'Who are you and what have you done with crotchety Gabe Burnett?'

'Let's say my mood has improved with the sunshine. And being shown the error of my ways.' Her smug smile almost rivalled Haruka's. 'And I'm terrified of Haruka.'

'Oh please. She adores you.'

'It's mutual. She's been a very good friend.'

'She's lovely.'

'Hmm ... not so sure lovely is quite the word I'd use. There's an iron fist in that velvet glove. You do know that.'

'I'd guessed, but she has a very good heart.'

'That she does. And she's a very canny business woman. Although not as shrewd as Setsuko; that one is a fox among hens. Watch out for her.'

'Setsuko!' Fiona gave a disbelieving laugh.

'Just don't say I didn't warn you. The woman makes Alan Sugar look like a pussycat.' He had an entire cupboard of tea to prove it.

Fiona rolled her eyes.

'On your head be it. Now, are you going to listen to me or not? I can tell you about the shrine because I did a two-day shoot there a long time ago, for Burberry actually, when I was going through my David Bailey phase and I was escorted by a very chatty Japanese PR girl who insisted I know all about it. Some of it stuck. It's actually quite interesting.'

'Quite interesting,' teased Fiona. 'Now you're really selling it.'

He paused, remembering the very first time he'd seen the shrine and how struck he'd been by the huge wooden *torii*, the main gate. The immense structure that left such a lasting impression with its simple beauty. Gosh, he'd forgotten that wonderful sense of otherness, of being somewhere so different from home. The feelings rushed back into a space that he'd thought was empty. The magic of seeing through a visitor's eyes, for the very first time. When had he lost that wonder?

'Do you know what, I think I'll let you see it for yourself.'

A fizz of excitement bellied its way up from his stomach and he suddenly felt ten years younger, remembering that indeterminate sensation of always being on the cusp of discovering some amazing shot, the belief that possibility was always waiting around the next corner.

With a sudden jolt, he realised that he had taken the germ of her idea, pictures of tourists discovering the sights, but he was interested in her response. Yesterday he'd been reluctantly impressed by her ideas for the exhibition, even though he wasn't convinced they were new ideas, but then it did depend on the interpretation of them. She'd talked intelligently about bringing them to life. As she'd talked, her slender butterfly hands had caught his attention, those long, slim fingers that conveyed everything with great animation. She had a habit of lifting her chin, almost as if she were daring the world to challenge her, a habit that exposed her long neck and the smooth expanse of throat. Not that he was thinking about her pale skin or the soft peach bloom on her cheeks, which in this morning's sunshine appeared luminous and dewy fresh. It was the portrait photographer in him, he told himself.

Taking another look, he mentally framed her face; she'd make a good subject, when she wasn't aware of the camera. There was a self-consciousness about her that he'd noticed the first time he'd seen her at the airport. It intrigued him and he'd almost considered photographing her then. Almost. He wasn't in the market for a new subject or a muse. He didn't do that sort of thing any more. He did the jobs he was asked to do. Earned the big bucks thanks to his reputation. If anyone guessed that he was just going through the motions these days, they were far too polite to say so. It was too much effort putting himself out there these days.

They walked through the heavily wooded park in silence accompanied by the trill of birdsong and the heavy scent of the trees. Sunlight stole through the leaves leaving intricate dappled patterns on the broad paths.

'This is so peaceful,' Fiona finally said. 'Almost spiritual.'

'Wait until you get to the shrine. It was erected as a memorial to the Emperor Meji who died in 1912.'

'So not that old?'

'Not old at all. It was destroyed in air raids during World War Two and completely rebuilt in 1958.'

The path meandered through the trees and then he paused,

taking out his camera, before they rounded the corner of the path that would give them the first sight of the *torii*.

'Wow,' said Fiona, her face lighting up with simple wonder, and with the press of a button he was able to capture the stars in her eyes and the perfect 'o' of her mouth as she gazed up at the huge wooden uprights that held the cross bars.

'The *torii* is a gateway marking the transition from the mundane world to the sacred,' he explained and watched as she absorbed the information with a gentle smile that touched her almost-too-wide mouth.

She gazed up with awestruck silence as they passed between the two uprights and under the gate. 'This is it. This is where I want to get pictures of people seeing it for the first time. It will be the perfect spot.'

'Don't you want to see the rest of the shrine before you make up your mind?'

'No, this is it. It's awe inspiring. Unique. I've never seen anything like it before. It says Japan. Although getting the scale and size of it will be tricky.' She tilted her head further back. 'I want that sky as well. And I want quite a few people, all looking up.'

She crouched down on the ground, the bottom of her jeans trailing in the still damp grass and angled her camera up. His mouth twitched, remembering himself years ago, contorting himself at strange angles, hanging off trees, perching on the top of fences trying to get the right picture in his viewfinder.

'Don't lie down,' he warned as she began to lean forward. 'You'll get soaked.'

She grimaced up at him, 'But ...'

With a laugh that felt sort of rusty, he held up his hands, recalling the fervour that had once gripped him. 'I know, I know. It's the shot. But you'll be sopping wet all morning. And it's still early. There aren't that many people about. It'll get busier.'

'I want to get the shot lined up; it'll be dry later.' Her pout amused him – not easy with that mouth – and he laughed again.

'Here, give me your camera.' He held out a hand. 'Do a handstand, hook your legs over my shoulders and I'll hold you and you can take some practice shots ... see if the angles work.'

'What?' She stared at him. 'I'm not doing that.'

'Live a little,' he teased. 'You never know you might snag an award winner.'

'You might drop me.'

He shrugged. 'Where's the pleasure in an easy shot? You've got to suffer for your art.'

She raised one of those delicate golden eyebrows.

'Go on, I dare you.'

'How are old you?'

'Old enough to know better.' He grinned at her; she was weakening.

'No,' she shook her head. 'It's far too crazy. Besides, I haven't done a handstand since I was at school. I'd probably kick you in the face or knock you over.'

'But I bet you do Pilates or yoga or something.' With those long limbs and that slim athletic build, she had to do something.

'Haven't you noticed how clumsy I am?'

'No. Are you? I hadn't noticed it.'

She stared at him, genuine confusion on her face. 'What?'

'Nothing.' She lifted her shoulders. 'I feel clumsy. I was always the tallest at school. Always out of place. I tower over the women here.'

'That doesn't make you clumsy.'

'I never know what to do with my legs.' She shrugged again. 'My ... my mum says I'm ungainly. I always feel ... out of place, clumsy.'

Now it was his turn to stare at her. 'Well don't.' The words came out a little more forcefully than he meant them to and he added more softly, 'You're actually rather graceful.' As soon as he said it, he realised that it was true and was also something he'd unconsciously noticed about her – that long-legged, smooth stride and the elegant way she used her arms when she was talking or gesticulating. Her hands often did the talking for her, punctuating her speech and extending her ideas.

She laughed at that. 'As Haruka would say, you're full of bull.'

A Japanese family came into view, a man and a woman with an elderly woman and a toddler who was bundled up in a red anorak, his dark hair shining in the sunshine. The small boy hadn't spotted the *torii* gate yet and as the thought popped into Gabe's head, from the sudden gasp below him he knew it had occurred to Fiona. Heedless of the wet grass, she threw herself forward onto the ground, turned onto her side and raised the camera in anticipation, preparing herself for the ground level shot.

He heard the whirr of the shutter at the very moment the little boy stopped and craned his head backwards, the tiny figure dwarfed by the structure towering over him. Gabe grinned.

Something made him raise his own camera as Fiona rolled over and sat up, beaming up at him. He took the shot, a split-second decision, homing on in her face which contained the most delightful combination of smugness and elation.

'You got it.'

With a nod, she held out her camera. Instead, he grasped her wrist, tutted at the dark blue patches on her jeans where the dew had well and truly soaked in, and hauled her to her feet.

'Look,' she said, ignoring him, the fizz of excitement almost radiating from her as she cradled the camera in both hands to frame the viewfinder.

Although the digital image was tiny, the composition was spot on. The tiny boy, dwarfed by one of the timber posts of the *torii* gate, was spot lit by a slanting sunbeam. It was one of those shots of a lifetime and he felt … he felt happy. Really happy. Quite ecstatic on her behalf.

Tamping down the unfamiliar emotion, he tapped the viewfinder with his index finger. 'I think you might have the makings of a great shot, here. Well done, you.'

Turning her head, scant inches from him, she gave him an unreservedly impish, excited grin as if she'd forgotten who he was and then … it happened – a funny flipping sensation in his chest, like a landed salmon flopping about. In the morning sunshine she glowed with happiness and it ... it made him want to scoop her up, hug her, and spin her around. Which was not a Gabe Burnett thing to do.

'You're going to catch your death of cold,' he said brusquely.

'Please! Whose granny are you? Check out this shot. Worth a cold at the very least.'

'Hmm,' he said. 'Well don't come complaining to me.'

But he knew she wouldn't; she was still buzzing with that amazing high when you know you've nailed it. There was nothing quite like the rush – it made you feel invincible, as if anything were possible. Once, he'd been on top of the world. Where had it all gone? When had taking pictures become a job? When had he lost the thrill of knowing that the next shot was out there just waiting to be caught?

'I can't wait until I can get these onto my laptop and see them in full size.'

He knew the feeling; there were a couple of shots he'd taken this morning that he was itching to get into the studio to see himself.

'Come to the studio this evening before dinner and we'll go through them,' he suggested before adding, 'Shall we move on?'

Fiona nodded, camera in hand, scrolling through the series of pictures she'd taken of the boy. Unable to resist, he lifted his own camera and took a quick shot, the sun glistening on her hair, the absorption in her face, the curve of her neck revealing the creamy skin.

She glanced up sharply. 'What are you doing?'

'Squirrel.' He pointed beyond her to the trees on the other side of the path. 'But I don't think I was quick enough.'

Suspicion darkened her eyes for a second before she turned away and squinted at the trees.

'I don't see it.'

'No, it moved fast. It'll probably be a blur. Come on, let's keep moving. You need to keep warm.'

It was a while since he'd been to the shrine or anywhere like it, to be honest. He'd stopped playing the tourist in Japan a long time ago and now regret niggled at him like a splinter just burrowed under the skin. There was something about the hushed appreciation of the other visitors, both tourists and those who'd come to pay their respects, that made his senses kick into gear almost as if they'd been dozing. The Japanese were big on respect and honouring people, something he'd admired when he'd first lived here. Even a hardened cynic like him couldn't fail to be moved by the prayer boards, small rectangles of wood inscribed with the prayers of visitors that hung on a wall. When he'd first come to the country he'd been fascinated by the spiritual side of the Japanese. Haruka had brought him here and it had been such a balm after the frenetic pace of London, where he'd lived life too fast. Japan had brought him peace and also a new sense of purpose for his photography. The memories of those early days tumbled through his mind like an avalanche, bringing with it small pinpricks of pleasure.

Fiona was soaking it all in, in her quiet measured way, studying things carefully before she picked up her camera. She stopped in front of the prayer wall, watching as a young woman bowed before hanging one of the wooden prayer boards onto a hook in front of her. Fiona bowed to her when they caught each other's eye and lowered her camera, waiting until the other woman had moved away and then she hesitated and stepped back, a thoughtful frown on her face.

'Don't you want a picture of the prayer wall?' he asked.

'No. Having seen that woman, it seems a bit of an invasion of privacy.' She laughed at herself. 'Even though they're in plain view. It doesn't feel right. Not very respectful. A prayer is a private thing ... even if it is in plain sight. Does that sound silly?'

'No. It sounds very Japanese and I think Haruka would be very proud of you.'

Fiona beamed.

'I see she's got you under her spell too,' he grumbled, steering her towards the main shrine area.

'She's ... something else,' said Fiona. 'She showed me her garden last night. It's beautiful.' Her mouth bunched into a wrinkled prune as her phone buzzed and she rolled her eyes.

'Anxious suitor?' he asked, intrigued. She'd pulled her phone out a handful of times on the walk up to the shrine from the *torii* gate and pushed it back into her pocket.

'Ha!' She said with a scowl. 'It's my mother.'

'I guess she's worried about you. Mothers do that. You're a long way from home.' With a smile, he thought of his own parents. Thank goodness for FaceTime. It was rare for him not to speak to them at least once a week, even though his dad insisted on updating him on Plymouth Argyle's latest dismal performance at Home Park every single time.

'Hmm, it's not me she's worrying about. She thinks she's having a stroke.'

There was a silence while he tried to connect the alarming words with the curious mix of mutinous resignation on her face.

'A stroke!' That was serious. Fiona seemed remarkably calm. 'Don't you want to call her or something? Make sure she's all right?' His dad had had a minor heart attack last year and even though the doctors had assured his mother he was fine, Gabe had been on the next flight home.

Staring down at her hands, she exhaled with a small sigh. 'She's fine.'

'You don't sound completely sure.'

'It's a regular occurrence ... usually when I'm doing something she doesn't want me to.'

'Oh ... but what ...?'

'If you're worrying about the old "cry wolf" scenario, don't. Been there, done that.'

'What? She really did have a stroke?'

'No, but she had some kind of funny turn. She hadn't been taking her medication. She has high blood pressure. The doctor had warned her. All I can do is make sure she takes her tablets. I remind her every day. Sorry, I must sound cold-hearted. It's been a regular pattern for a long time. My mother's a bit of a hypochondriac. I should be more sympathetic really because it's born of loneliness and too much time on her hands.'

'Do you still live at home?'

'For the time being, yes. Until I can afford to move out. I feel guilty thinking about it because then she'll be on her own.'

'Heavy responsibility. She must have had you quite late.'

Fiona let out a mirthless laugh. 'My mother's only forty-eight.'

He raised an eyebrow at that. 'That's young.'

'I know, but she's dissatisfied with the way her life turned out. My dad died when I was a baby. He was supposed to take care of her.'

'And now you have to,' he said, joining the dots.

She shrugged. 'Something like that.'

'You could switch your phone off.'

'What if there were a real emergency?' She was tugging at her braid again, flicking the tufted end between her fingers.

'There's not a lot you can do from here.' He gave her a reassuring smile but she stared beyond him, her eyes clouded. 'If she can contact you, she can call 999.'

Fiona pursed her lips and focused back on his face. 'Shall we go and see the shrine?'

Sublime to the ridiculous, he thought, several hours later as they crossed the road while Fiona scouted the views trying to work out where she could take the best picture. After the quiet peace of the shrine, the madness of the traffic and the rush of people brushing by, Shibuya crossing was a salutary reminder of why he loved this crazy country. He enjoyed the contrasts.

When he'd asked, 'Where to next?' he'd been slightly taken aback when she said, 'I'd like to go back to Shibuya.'

Apart from the texts which Fiona was more surreptitious about checking, the day was far better than he'd expected. For some reason they irritated him, but the sudden change of pace and scene had staved off the inevitable boredom he'd anticipated and now he was enjoying the intense concentration on Fiona's face as she strode from street corner to street corner, taking her life in her hands as she stopped mid-stream among the flow of pedestrians to try and take her pictures.

Any moment now she was liable to be taken out by a swinging laptop case or a tourist's backpack. It was both comical and slightly terrifying but it didn't seem to faze her – in fact, she seemed oblivious, so intent was she on getting the picture that she'd envisioned. And there it was, as he'd foreseen, a man hurrying by caught her. She span, buffeted by the passing man, and he took the shot just as she twirled out of range, her skirt whipping up to expose long, slender legs. His heart caught in his mouth and he wasn't sure if it was the sight of the elegant limbs or the elation of nailing the picture. It was one of those moments when everything dropped into place with the sort of serendipitous perfection that he no longer believed in.

When he finally took a good long look at the digital image, his mouth quirked at the sight of her lemon skirt a blur, her plait flying out behind her and her wide mouth open. That was what he'd call it: 'Surprise on Shibuya'.

When he lifted his head, Fiona had gone and he peered through the crowd trying to spot her. Not again!

Then he spotted the golden hair towering above everyone, literally a good foot above and he realised as he wove his way closer through the busy street that she was standing on top of one of the street vendors' carts, the owner gleefully admiring her legs while he held the cart steady for her. Quite a crowd had drawn to watch her, which was hardly surprising because it wasn't something you saw every day on a Japanese street. Fiona was happily snapping away, throwing the odd word down to the vendor, without a care in the world. Gabe stopped dead with horrified admiration. You didn't make a spectacle of yourself in Japan; you were quiet and respectful in public but … he grinned. By God, she looked amazing. A warrior princess on a mission. For someone who on the surface seemed quite shy and retiring, it appeared in reality she was a Valkyrie. Widening the angle to include the onlookers, he took a couple of landscape shots before swapping to portrait. It was certainly a one-off composition.

'Hey up there,' he called as he approached, weaving his way through the gathered crowd.

'Hello, I wondered where you'd got to,' she said, glancing down, barely registering his arrival as she raised her camera to her eye, her brow wrinkling with concentration. She fired off another volley of quick snaps, her mouth moving in tandem, as if emoting with her subjects. He shook his head at her absorption and waited, folding his arms and leaning against the nearby wall, although he did give the vendor a warning nod of the head. The man gave him an indefatigable grin and said something in quick Japanese to the effect of 'she's quite something'. Gabe rolled his eyes and agreed. She'd surprised him today.

Finally, she jumped down, offered the vendor some money which he declined, shaking his head furiously and bowing to her several times. A couple of people in the audience clapped and she grinned at them.

'He says it was an honour,' drawled Gabe, a little irritated.

'Oh, that's sweet of him.'

'Should I even ask how you came to be standing up there?'

'I was trying to get the shots of people tilting their heads backwards and I realised I wanted to be higher than them, so I found a box but as soon as I stood on it, it collapsed. Yuto, who used to live in London, asked me what I was doing and when I explained, he said I could stand on the cart. Wasn't that nice of him?'

'Yes, very nice. I don't suppose it had anything to do with the fact he had a bird's eye view of your legs.'

Fiona tutted. 'Don't be ridiculous. He's interested in photography. We had a very nice chat about the museum. He's a big fan of Araki's so he was very excited when I told him that he was supposed to be mentoring me.'

'I'll just bet he was.'

'Are you cross with me?' asked Fiona.

'No, what gives you that impression?'

'Your voice goes all drawly and disinterested, as if you can't be bothered with anything.'

How astute, he thought. 'I'm fine. Just slightly appalled by you almost causing a riot in the street. Haruka would be horrified, although I think young Mayu would be thrilled by your behaviour.'

'I didn't think. I ... got a bit carried away. I could see the picture in my head. I needed to get a bit of height and when he ...'

'Hey, don't beat yourself up. I was teasing. You don't remember lamppost-gate then?'

Her worry slid away as awareness dawned on her face. 'You were arrested. I do remember; it made the front page of most of the newspapers.'

'That's because Dolly Fitzsimmons belted the policeman that helped me down from the lamppost. She was the one who was arrested.' In fact, if the lanky model hadn't been so handy with her right hook, he might have got away with a simple warning, instead of which the pair of them were marched off to the nearest police station.

'Why were you up there?'

He grinned at her. 'Like you, I wanted to get the perfect shot and it seemed the logical thing to do at the time.'

For a moment she stared owlishly at him before her face broke into a smile of understanding. 'So it's not just me then.'

He'd timed it badly for the journey back as the rush hour had begun and the subway train they needed to catch for the main line was already rammed. Despite the orderly queue adhering to the white lines on the platform, there was a territorial rush and push when the train pulled into the station and he and Fiona were swept forward into the tightly packed crush. They ended up almost nose to nose in the carriage as she hung onto the pole that was all that separated them. On autopilot, as he always did, his eyes scanned her face, the cool inventory-taking of a portrait photographer identifying the quirks and anomalies that made her face different. He catalogued the light dusting of freckles over her nose and cheekbones, noted that the hairs at her temple were even fairer, one arched eyebrow was infinitesimally higher than the other, and the wide mouth that made her face different became lit up with her smile, when it came, making it even more rewarding.

She looked up sharply and he saw her body stiffen as if she were straining to put distance between them.

'You okay?' He mouthed.

Her mobile mouth tightened and she nodded, the tendons in her neck belying her meaning. With deliberate coolness that didn't fool him, she lifted her chin and gazed beyond him.

Was she embarrassed by their proximity because of what had happened all those years ago? He hated to think that was the case. He gripped the pole tighter and deliberately went back to studying her face. That mouth drew his attention again and he examined the tiny lines at the corners, the little dip under her nose. It crimped tightly closed with displeasure and although she refused acknowledge him, her chin lifted another centimetre higher.

Just then the train jolted in an archetypal cliched moment that threw them together, his hands grabbing her waist as she catapulted into him. His face brushed hers and he caught the faint scent of freesia as he tried to steady her.

She recoiled sharply, pulling her face away with a gasp which punched right to his stomach. Now he felt awful. He should have told her before that he recognised her. Although, he was puzzled as to why she was so skittish around him.

From what he remembered that kiss had been consensual. In fact, he was sure he'd pulled away first because sense had knocked its way through the haze of desire, reminding him that as her teacher his behaviour was totally inappropriate.

A crowded train carriage was probably not the place to have that conversation though. He'd have to wait until she came to the studio that evening to go through the day's pictures.

Chapter 11

S he really wanted to see how the pictures of the little boy at Meji had come out and Gabe had said to come over any time before dinner – he was invited to Haruka's that evening – so she was taking him at his word. He'd given her a few searching looks on the train, probably because she'd overreacted. For some bizarre reason, being in such close proximity had stirred her up and the urge to kiss him had resurrected itself with alarming urgency. The thought of him seeing that while he was so intently studying her face had been terrifying. She really ought to come clean, make a joke of it. Ha, ha, isn't it funny we've ended up working together. What a small world.

The main light of the studio was off but she could see the glow of light in the other room. It lit the shadowed figure of Gabe standing in front of the picture of Yumi. She paused and unanticipated pity swelled in her chest at the sight of the disconsolate figure that he posed. One side of his face was illuminated by the sliver of light that came through the doors and she could see the slash of his mouth, grim and brooding. With his hunched shoulders, hands stuffed in his pockets, he seemed a little lost. The dejected posture made her stop rather than disturb him. If she'd had her camera and it wasn't such an invasion of privacy, it would have made a perfect shot. A picture of demoralised solitude.

Carefully and quietly she backed down the stairs, her palms sweaty. She'd geared herself up for this. For a moment she stood at the bottom of the stairs waiting for her pulse to regain its equilibrium and then she took a breath. She needed to be brave; it was past time to put this stupid episode behind her. It had happened ten years ago and for too long it had influenced her life. It hadn't ruined her life, as her mother liked to say, but it had impacted it. For a while it had held her back, stopped her doing the things she should have been doing at her age, but it had been a sliding-doors moment and if it hadn't happened, she wouldn't be where she was today and she was quite proud of what she'd achieved in the last couple of years. Gabe didn't need to know about the heartache caused by her momentary madness.

'Gabe? Are you up there?' she called. 'It's Fiona.' She did her best with the soft slippers to make a sound on the steps to make it clear she was headed on up.

She heard him clear his throat. 'Yes, up here.'

By the time she reached the top, he'd moved into the other room, now fully lit, and had perched himself on one edge of the desk.

She gave him a perfunctory smile, the knots in her stomach as taut as macramé. 'Gabe—'

'Fiona,' he interrupted. 'There's something I should have said before. I didn't recognise you at first but ...'

'You remember me.' She froze, a flush of heat racing up to the tips of her ears. Oh God, let the ground swallow her now. She couldn't look at him. Just couldn't.

When he spoke again, she was grateful for his gentle tone. 'I realised the other day.'

'Oh.' The word dropped out of her mouth because she couldn't think of anything else to say.

'Sorry, I ... Perhaps should have said something before but ... well, you hadn't said anything so I wasn't sure if you ...'

She lifted her shoulders and ducked her head, her toes curling with shame. 'All a bit embarrassing.' With a swallow she raised her head to sneak a peep at him.

There was a quiet frown of concern marring his face.

'Don't worry,' her tone brittle, 'I won't do it again.'

His frown deepened. 'I—'

'I owe you an apology really. Ten years late. But I'm sorry. I behaved like an idiot. I don't know what came over me.' She ground to halt and hauled in a shaky breath.

'Well that's kind of disappointing.' Her head shot up and she met his gaze. He was smiling, amusement dancing in his eyes. 'There was me hoping it was my irresistible good looks.'

He was joking about this? Now her breath whooshed out in a rush.

'You mean ... you didn't mind?'

'Mind? Why would I mind being kissed by a gorgeous, leggy blonde?'

'I ...' She lifted her palms with a hopeless shrug.

'Fi, you were young.' His face softened and he lifted a hand as if he were going to touch her face but then he dropped it, a touch awkwardly. 'It was flattering. Made me feel like a rock star or something.'

'You were in those days. All the girls had a crush on you.' She blushed and forced herself to go on. It would have been so much easier if she'd said something at the airport and got it out of the way, instead of behaving like a virgin bride with him. 'I made a right tit of myself. I'm sorry.'

Gabe laughed. 'Funny how we come at it from different angles ... like pictures. I recall this gorgeous young girl who kissed me. Spontaneously. Seizing the moment. Grabbing life by both hands. I loved your attitude then. You were fearless and inquisitive. And that kiss ... what's not to like, except I was six years older and your teacher, so it was inappropriate. But like I said, it was flattering.'

'Really?' Fiona stared at him. That had not occurred to her. And the things he said about her ... She didn't remember being fearless. Ever. That final term had school had crumpled her confidence like a used tissue.

'Hell, yes. I'm a bloke. It's not every day a stunning, blue-eyed blonde with legs up to her armpits plants one on me. But like I said, cute as you were, I was your teacher. The college tends to frown on that sort of thing. And I knew it didn't mean anything. Hell, you were eighteen. Just a kid. So don't get hung up on it. To be honest, I'd forgotten all about it ... until you said something in the studio the other day and it popped back into my head.'

Fiona was still trying to process 'fearless and gorgeous', not to mention 'blue-eyed blonde with legs up to her armpits'. He made her sound ... well *gorgeous* instead of awkward and clumsy and ... well, *not* gorgeous. People like Avril with their perfect make-up and immaculate clothes were gorgeous. Fiona with her charity-shop buys and arty style ... well, no one had ever called her gorgeous. Slightly bemused, all she could do was nod but Gabe was talking again so he didn't seem to notice her stupefied silence.

'Now it's out in the open, we can laugh about it. I'll never forget your friend's face when she came round the corner and caught us!'

Fiona winced.

'Hopefully, kissing the teacher did your street cred some good.'

'Something like that,' she muttered through stiff lips.

'But we've got an exhibition to sort for you, so we need to crack on with some work. I'm sorry I've not been that helpful. I realised today at Meji and Shibuya ... well, you remind me of myself when I first started out. Today reminded me of what it's all about. That magic when the reality of the shot mirrors what you'd hoped it would be.' He wrinkled his face. 'Do you think you can forgive me?' He suddenly grinned. 'I know you think I'm an arse.'

'I ...'

With a laugh he pushed his hands through his hair. 'Don't deny it. You have one of the most expressive faces I've ever seen. And I've been thinking ... your idea ... I think it has real potential but we need to visit a few famous sights to make it work. Mount Fuji is a definite, it's so iconic. But Haruka's the one for that. Let's talk with her over dinner. Truce?' He held out a hand.

153

She took it and ignored the tiny spark of something at the brief touch. 'Truce, unless you start being an arse again. All bets are off then.'

This time his laugh was rich and deep and did something very strange to her. She found herself grinning back at him, as if they'd been friends for years.

'I promise I'll be on my best behaviour.'

'Hmm.' Fiona peered at him from under her lashes.

'Let's go and see Haruka and do some planning.'

'Well, as you say, Fuji is a must.' Fiona amazed herself with her even tone. 'And I really want to see a tea ceremony.'

'Well if we can't fix that up with Haruka, we're doomed. Now, while you're here, why don't we take a quick look at those shots at the *torii* gate and your mountaineering shots at Shibuya?'

Fiona nodded shyly, not quite able to believe the transformation in Gabe and the huge weight that had suddenly lifted off her shoulders. It felt weird and yet wonderful at the same time. She turned all the words he used – leggy, gorgeous, stunning – over in her mind. They were so far from the image she'd had of herself that it was as if the fairy godmother had waved a magic wand. The boulder of shame, mortification, and embarrassment that had dogged her had been dislodged and she could almost believe the things he'd said about her. For a vain, stupid moment, she wanted to find a mirror and study herself, this new version of Fiona Hanning, to see if she could determine any difference.

Chapter 12

Kaito, Haruka's husband, worked long hours and it was rare to see him in the evenings but tonight he was present for dinner, along with Setsuko's husband, Mayu, and Gabe. It was quite the party and they ate in a larger room seated on cushions around a long table loaded with an array of small, beautifully presented dishes ranging from colourful salads, bright green wasabi, rich brown, salty soy, the fiery orange chilli dipping sauce through to glistening slivers of raw fish and neatly packed rice parcels of sushi. Haruka had gone to a lot of effort and seemed to be in her absolute element, tweaking and arranging the dishes.

With a low bow of greeting, Kaito asked Fiona in perfect English – albeit with a slight American accent – how she was finding her trip and how the photography was coming along.

It was with some relief that she was able to answer honestly as Haruka and Setsuko handed out white china plates with a small lip for dinner.

'Gabe and I have been discussing an idea for the exhibition. We're looking for recommendations of where to visit.'

'Ah. That will cause a heated family debate,' said Kaito with a wry smile at his wife and daughter.

'I will tell you the best places,' said Mayu stoutly. 'Interesting places. Not boring old places. You should go to Disneyland and you must go to the Robot Restaurant.'

Haruka let out a little moan of distress which Mayu chose not to hear. 'The robots are awesome.' She pulled out her phone and showed Fiona a picture full of colour and weirdness with girls dressed up in outlandish clothes riding giant robotic figures. 'It's seriously cool.'

Fiona studied the picture. Not her cup of tea but she could see that it would enchant younger visitors and she had said she wanted her pictures to show all sides of Japan.

She looked up in time to catch Gabe winking at Mayu. 'What sort of places do you want to visit?' asked Haruka serenely, as if oblivious to her granddaughter's healthy disdain. She invited Fiona to take some of the thinly sliced raw fish laid out the long narrow dish in front of her. 'This is *sashimi*, *ahi* tuna. You take it like this.' With expert fingers, she used her chopsticks to dip the slice of fish into bright green wasabi.

Fiona followed suit, with a little less grace, and popped the sliver of fish into her mouth. Wow. Her eyes watered and her mouth stung at the fiery burst of heat from the wasabi. 'Gosh,' she said blinking. Everyone very politely pretended not to notice her streaming eyes; even Mayu managed to duck her head to hide a smirk.

'If you dilute it with the soy, it takes the fire out,' said Gabe kindly, pouring a small dish of soy from the large bottle of Kikkoman on the table and pushing it towards her. Haruka gave him a regally approving nod and in response he grinned.

'You have not tried wasabi before?' asked Haruka.

Fiona shook her head, still trying to catch her breath and get the fiery taste off her tongue. 'It's powerful stuff. A bit like horseradish or mustard, I guess.' And to be fair she liked both of them. Desperate to reassure her hostess, she added. 'I like it a lot, it was just ... unexpected.'

'Try some sushi,' said Setsuko. 'Dip it into the soy. This is *maki*, and the rice is rolled in *nori*, which is a seaweed wrap, and there are different fillings in the rice. Shrimp, avocado and cucumber. And this,' she nudged a plate of pink slices, 'is pickled ginger. Good to eat between to cleanse your palate.'

'Right,' said Fiona grateful for the explanations. A little clumsily she picked up one of the delicate parcels, marvelling at the patience it must have taken to create each tiny one; they were little works of art. Managing to hang on to it and dip it into the soy, she was rewarded with a bite of savoury bliss; inside the salty wrap of seaweed, the milder rice offset the sweet, meatier flavour of a large piece of prawn to perfection.

'Did you make these?' she asked Haruka. 'They're wonderful.'

Haruka nodded and the faintest of pleased smiles touched the corners of her mouth.

Not wanting to appear too greedy, Fiona held back for a moment before selecting her next one, desperate to try the sushi with the roll of cured salmon. It tasted every bit as good as it looked and before long she'd worked her way through several more under the approving eye of her hostess.

'You were talking about places you'd like to visit,' encouraged Kaito, clearly keen to hear the details.

'I'd like to go to a variety of different places. Places that epitomise Japan but also that draw tourists, both local and international,' she explained as she chose what Setsuko told her was a *maki* roll filled with rice and pickled cucumber.

With the aid of Gabe, she tried to explain her idea as everyone ate.

'You want to take pictures of tourists?' Mayu waved her chopstick in slight disbelief and from the expression on her face, Fiona got the impression she thought it was lame.

Haruka, after an initial nod of reproof about the chopstick waving, pushed another dish towards Fiona. 'Eat. Eat.'

'Sounds ...' Mayu pulled a face.

'I want to illustrate their response to the place. Why they're drawn to it.'

'I think it's a great idea,' said Gabe, expertly picking up a piece of sushi flecked with tiny bits of green with one hand and nudging Mayu with his elbow. She nudged him back. They were like a pair of school children and although Haruka ignored the two of them, there was a faint smile on her face. It was clear that Gabe was very much one of the family. She was surprised to see this lighter side of him.

'Mount Fuji is a must,' said Setsuko, neatly popping a piece of sushi dipped in the fiery wasabi into her mouth. 'It is iconic and most people recognise it.'

'But boring,' protested Mayu looking towards Gabe to back her up.

He held his hands up in surrender. 'Your mum is right. It's a symbol of the country.'

She rolled her eyes at him.

Fuji was a definite but Fiona wanted something a little closer to home. She turned to Setsuko. 'I'd like to take some pictures of the teashop and you serving in there, if I may.'

Setsuko smiled both, pleased and modest. 'I'd be most honoured.'

'And I'd very much like to see a tea ceremony.' Fiona turned to Haruka, not sure if it was appropriate to take photos during such a ceremony. There seemed to be a lot of importance placed on the ceremony and she didn't want to cause offence.

'One day this week,' said Haruka. 'I have a few small groups coming. You may join us the day after tomorrow if you would like. I have a group booked in for the afternoon.'

'Thank you.' Fiona felt that she'd been accorded a huge honour and from the solemn expression on Setsuko's face, it would appear she had. Even Mayu looked quite impressed.

'If you go to Fuji,' said Kaito, 'you will need accommodation. When would you like to go?' He encompassed Gabe in his calm bow.

'I have a day's work in Kyoto tomorrow. A previous commitment.' Gabe nodded at Kaito as if reminding him. 'I'm taking pictures of Ken Akito. But after that I'm free,' said Gabe easily, turning to Fiona.

There was a stunned silence around the table as the family

all stared at Gabe before Mayu launched into enthusiastic Japanese and Fiona picked out a couple of 'cools' which, along with the bounce in her seat and beseeching expression, suggested that this Ken person was a very big deal.

'Sorry, pipsqueak. No can do. This is work. And definitely no autographs; it's not professional.'

Mayu tried again with a new bid, putting a hand on Gabe's arm and even in Japanese, Fiona could discern the wheedling tone. Gabe shook his head and grinned at her. 'Sorry, kid.'

Mayu pouted and Setsuko smiled, explaining to Fiona, 'Ken is a very popular film star. Mayu is a big fan and she wants to go with Gabe. Says she'll be his assistant. Or she'll do anything.'

Gabe grinned. 'What, clean my studio for the next year?'

At Mayu's eager response, Setsuko and her husband exchanged knowing smiles. 'She doesn't like chores,' whispered Setsuko to Fiona as Mayu continued to beg and plead with Gabe.

Haruka shook her head, her dark eyes sharp, flicking from Mayu to Setsuko to Gabe before she suddenly said, 'Fiona could be your assistant.'

The words silenced the whole table and everyone turned to look at her, even Gabe.

'Oh, no. I couldn't do that. I'm sure Gabe can't take anyone with him. I'll be quite happy here. I can ... well, I can find things to do.'

'Actually, why not?' said Gabe, his forehead furrowed as if giving the idea serious consideration. 'It would be a good opportunity to see me at work. Proper mentoring.' The latter was said with a quick smile and without rancour. 'It's an overnight trip but we'll be back in time for = Haruka's tea ceremony.'

'Don't be silly. The publicity people aren't going to want a hanger-on,' said Fiona, a blush staining her face. Observing Gabe at work would be fascinating and suddenly she wanted it more than anything else. To see how he approached his work. Just watching Gabe was ... inspiring. Those long, strong fingers handling his camera. For some reason, her pulse began to skitter about like a colt on ice at the very thought of it. 'You can't take me with you.'

Gabe grinned, his face lighting up with sudden devilish charm. 'I'm Gabe Burnett, babe.' He raised both eyebrows and his eyes glinted with arrogant merriment. 'They want me. I'm the best at what I do. My terms.'

Haruka's head shot up like the lioness of a pride and her eyes narrowed as they rested with disapproval on Gabe.

To Fiona's astonishment, Gabe ducked his head and bowed as if in apology. It seemed that he really cared what Haruka thought. The revelation made Fiona study him with new eyes. She'd seen a much softer and more carefree side to him during dinner, as if he'd dropped his usual cynical barriers and allowed himself to be one of the family.

'Even so,' said Fiona, doing her best to tamp down the fizz of excitement dancing low in her stomach, 'I can't come with you.'

'I'm staying at the Four Seasons in Kyoto. I can arrange another room easily.'

Mayu muttered under her breath, very disgruntled. It didn't

take much to imagine that the words 'it's not fair' had been voiced. Setsuko placed a placating hand on her daughter's forearm and Mayu lapsed into sulky silence, shooting her grandmother a glowering death stare.

'Maybe you could take me to this Robot Restaurant when I'm back,' suggested Fiona. 'I could take some shots of you there, maybe in your blue wig.'

'Cool. You're gonna love it. We could get you a costume too.' She eyed Fiona a little sceptically. 'My friend is tall but she's not as tall as you. She has a Princess Gothic outfit.'

From the corner of her eye, Fiona saw both Haruka and Setsuko quash almost identical shudders of horror.

'The restaurant sounds perfect, although I'm not sure about the dressing up,' said Fiona, wondering what on earth she'd let herself in for.

'Rather you than me,' said Gabe, pulling a *yeugh* face at Mayu, who stuck her tongue out at him. 'Your eyeballs will be burnt out.'

Mayu contented herself with yet another roll of her eyes and went back to her phone, busy tapping out a text with one hand while using her chopsticks with consummate ease to select another piece of sushi which Gabe equally deftly wrestled away from her.

In seconds he was teasing her again while she laughed and complained to her mother and Haruka looked on with fond indulgence.

Chapter 13

'Now at least I feel like a proper photographer's assistant,' said Fiona attempting to sound cheery as she picked up one of the black cases and followed Gabe with his little portable trolley down to the platform. She'd had four messages from her mother already this morning. It was going to be a long journey if she continued in the same vein, which Fiona had a horrible feeling she would.

'Don't get carried away. I don't need an assistant. I prefer working alone.' Although Gabe said this with a smile, there was an uncompromising firmness to his words as he set off across the hexagonal concourse following the signs to the Kyoto line.

'Don't worry,' said Fiona with a quick roll of her eyes, 'I know the great Gabe Burnett is according me a huge honour.'

'And don't you forget it,' he threw over his shoulder, this time the tone a little lighter, as he weaved through the station which buzzed with people all intent on getting to where they needed to be.

A few steps along, he stopped at one of the many kiosks.

'We might as well get lunch here and eat early on the train.

We'll need to go straight to the hotel when we get to Kyoto. I'll get us a couple of bento boxes.'

Fiona nodded even though he'd turned his back on her and was talking to the young man behind the counter.

'Fancy a Kit-Kat?'

'Yes,' said Fiona, startled by the question. She'd got used to everything being very Japanese.

Gabe's face held a hint of mischief. 'What flavour would you like?'

'Sorry?'

He nodded towards a display on the front shelf of the kiosk. Fiona stared at the familiar, and yet totally unfamiliar, display of at least ten different Kit-Kat bars. She could see the familiar logo but that was where all similarity with what she was used to parted company with what she saw. These bars were wrapped in colourful packaging – green, pale blue, pink, orange, black – but also featured pictures indicating different flavours. There were lemons, peaches, nuts, even cherry blossom on the front.

'I don't even know what they are.'

'*Kit-Kat Matcha* is green-tea flavour, *Kit-Kat Tirol* is apple flavour, *Kit-Kat Sakura* is green-tea and cherry blossom. Then there's salt and caramel, soy sauce, wasabi.'

'Soy?' She pulled a *yeuch* face in disbelief. 'You're having me on.'

'I'm not.' He picked up a bar with purple and cream packaging which had a little bottle of soy sauce pictured in the left-hand corner and then nudged the bright green wasabi flavour with his thumb.

164

'No, that's so wrong! Although I guess I could be enticed by the salt and caramel. That sounds good.' But she was hesitant. 'But I'm not sure they needed to mess with a good thing.'

'It's a case of what you're used to, but I have to confess I still prefer the classic. Want to try the salt and caramel?'

'Hmm ...' She dithered for a moment.

'Go on, live dangerously.' Although he was teasing, there was a slight challenge in the words. Fiona wasn't one for living dangerously. She had once. Before she kissed Gabe Burnett. Now she played safe. Always.

Suddenly she said, 'I'll have the salt and caramel,' and ignored Gabe's triumphant grin.

Down on the platform there was a hushed stillness as though they were in the presence of a great beast which was what the large white train put Fiona in mind of. Alongside each carriage doorway, painted lines on the platform made it clear where people were expected to queue. But Fiona was busy checking out the length of the train and all the carriages as the long white line stretched way down the platform. The sleek train had acquired almost mythical status in her head. With the promised magical speeds, it was going to be nothing like the little train that trundled into London from her Surrey village at home, which still had level crossings en route.

'Do you mind if I go and take a few pictures?'

'No, go ahead. We're in carriage nine. I'll get loaded up and you can come and find me.'

Fiona walked quickly as there was quite a distance to cover.

She studied the smooth, aerodynamic lines of the carriages. The unusual, long, flat-nosed front of the train, so different from the ones at home – which, to be perfectly honest, she had zero interest in – reminded her of a snake, lethal and silent, lying in the grass, waiting to be fired up. She stared at the storm-trooper-like, glossy white finish, the distinctive shape jangling a memory. Kaa, that was it, the sneaky mesmerising snake in the original *Jungle Book*. Amused by her thoughts, she lifted her camera and took a few quick, basic shots, aware of a couple of other tourists around her snapping away with their phones, posing and taking selfies. In her pocket, her bloody phone buzzed again. She ignored it. She was working. Instead, she took note of a couple of serious trainspotters with serious cameras taking serious pictures. One of them, a middle-aged man with a baseball cap and a huge messenger bag, had delight written all over his face. He caught Fiona's eye. 'Isn't she a beauty?' he breathed, awe struck, in an American accent.

'Yes, I guess she is,' replied Fiona.

'You know she can get up to speeds of 186 mph.'

Fiona nodded, watching his beaming face as he paused in silent, happy contemplation of the miracle before him.

'Would you ... would you mind if I took a couple of photos of you and ...' she nodded her head towards the train.

'Me?'

'Yes, act natural.' She prayed he wouldn't stiffen up and lose the unaffected joy that shone in his face. 'Just take a couple of photos and write whatever you were writing. And keep seeing the magic,' she added with a wink.

'It is magic, isn't it. What mankind can achieve?' He beamed at her again. 'And I'll happily do that, if you'll take a couple of pictures of me with my camera.'

'Deal,' said Fiona. 'Pretend I'm not here.' That, it appeared, as he went back to studying the train with the same previous passion, wasn't very difficult. And there it was, the perfect shot, his head tilted, his whole body almost leaning forward as if he were drawn magnetically to the train. She crouched down, one knee brushing the dusty platform floor, to take the shot. That was it. Her heart did a little flip of delight. His dark tracksuit trousers with white stripes contrasted nicely with the white finish of the train. She fired off several shots, pleased with the way that the overhead lights bounced off the glossy surface. For a fanciful moment, she could almost imagine it rearing its head and taking a bite of any of the pesky tourists who didn't keep a respectful distance.

'Thank you, thank you,' she said, unable to stop herself grinning at him. 'Safe travels and thank you, again.'

There was a definite bounce in her own stride as she made her way to back along the platform to find Gabe.

'You're pleased with yourself,' he said when she found him in the carriage, sitting in a big, wide seat like on airline ... except for the fact there was plenty of legroom. She still couldn't quite believe the change in him since they'd declared their truce; it was like being with a different man.

'I got ... well I think it's going to be a good shot. Want to see?' She was dying to show him, although nervous at the same time. He'd been so complimentary about her shot of

Haruka and Setsuko, hopefully he'd see something in this one too.

She slid into the seat next to him and handed her camera over, as her phone buzzed in her pocket again. As he examined the picture, she checked the message, let out a barely stifled groan of irritation and shoved the phone back in her pocket.

Gabe lifted one brow in silent question.

'My mother.' She nodded to the camera.

He went back to studying the view finder and then glanced at her, his face serious.

'It's good. Very good.' He handed back the camera and Fiona tried not to feel too crestfallen at his delivery. She'd been so pleased with the picture.

'Thanks,' she said, matching his business-like tone. 'I'm beginning to think I might actually have the makings of an exhibition.'

'Of course you will. Don't be so faint hearted. Besides, most of the punters that come to these things wouldn't know a good photograph if it bit them.'

Fiona clasped her camera to her chest and shot him a glare. '*I'd* know.'

'Fair enough.' Gabe shrugged.

'How come you're so cynical these days?' she asked, taking another quick peek at the American man's expression as he beheld his beloved train.

'I'm not.'

Now it was her turn to raise an eyebrow. 'Well that sounded pretty cynical to me.'

'I was being honest. There's a difference. I don't believe in sugar coating things. Or saying things to make people feel better.'

'I had noticed that,' she said with feeling. She'd been so pleased with her shot of the trainspotter.

'What's the point? Prolonging the agony. Making difficulties.'

'Or perhaps it's smoothing the path sometimes. Making life a bit easier. Brutal honesty can be quite hurtful.'

Gabe shrugged again as, with very little ceremony, the train pulled away from the station, the motion so smooth that Fiona thought if she closed her eyes she wouldn't know she was moving. He leaned back into his chair and closed his eyes, a resigned twist to his mouth.

'Have you done this journey a lot?' asked Fiona

'Just a few times. At the end of the day, it's a train, albeit a very fast train.'

She thought of the picture and her American friend, who no doubt would be enjoying his journey with all the enthusiastic delight of a puppy. A joy clearly lost on some people. She still got a kick out of going into an airport terminal; she wondered if the American man's pleasure would ever fade, and she was grateful that she'd been able to capture that moment of delightful anticipation.

What had Pepys famously said? 'When a man is tired of London, he is tired of life.' Gabe seemed to be tired of everything.

They quickly slid out of Tokyo and before long the train was hurtling through the open countryside. The Shinkansen wasn't called a bullet train for nothing.

Now they were speeding through brilliant green countryside, paddy fields laid out in squares, the curved roof temples dotted here and there and in the distance, tree-covered hills and mountains.

As usual, there was near silence in the carriage and with an apologetic gesture, waving his earphones to indicate the silent carriage, Gabe plugged them in and began to listen to something on his phone. Fiona followed suit by listening to a downloaded BBC Radio 4 *News Quiz* podcast and doing her best to ignore the incoming bombardment of messages from her mother.

'She still having a stroke?' asked Gabe in a low whisper, nudging her with his elbow after she'd been exchanging messages for a good twenty minutes.

'No ... she thinks she's got an upper respiratory infection,' Fiona whispered back.

'And is it serious?'

'No, with mum that's long hand for a common cold.' Fiona had done her best to send sympathetic but firm no-nonsense messages with advice that her mother clearly had no intention of following. 'I told her to stay in bed for the day, take a Lemsip and go back to sleep.'

'Sage advice.' He frowned. 'Isn't it one o'clock in the morning there?'

'It is but she can't sleep.' Fiona sighed because apparently that was her fault too. 'She doesn't like being alone in the house.' Fiona let out a despairing sigh as another message popped up on the screen.

There was no doubt that Gabe could easily see the pathetic first line of the message.

I feel so poorly, I really wish you were …

It didn't take any prizes to guess the rest. Fiona turned the phone over on her knee and put her hand over it, both helpless and irritated. There was nothing she could do from here.

'You could switch it off,' he suggested in another one of those low, intimate whispers, laying an unexpected hand over hers guarding the phone.

'I could,' she replied, conscious of the warm touch of his fingers lightly settled on hers. He regarded her with a steady gaze and she felt her rib cage lift and tighten as she held her breath. God, he was still as gorgeous as ever. Those eyes. So blue. She sucked in the breath, giving herself a stern talking to. *Stop imagining things again, Fiona.* With a calm smile she said, 'But all those messages would still be there when I switched it on. It's better to keep responding. If I ignore her she'll work herself up into an even bigger state. It's easier to keep pace with them.'

'How about trying to distract her?' Gabe's mouth quirked with sympathy. 'That's always a good technique.' He tapped his index finger on her hand on the phone. 'Send her pictures of the view.'

Relieved to slide her hand out from under his before she did something silly and misinterpret his touch, she picked up her camera and took a couple of shots from the window. 'Good idea.'

She forgot to whisper and the man in the row next to them turned their way and gave them a fierce, disapproving stare.

'I don't suppose you can block your own mother,' Gabe leaned in and whispered in her ear. Even at this low tone his words resonated with mischief and his warm breath brushed a little too close to her skin.

'Don't tempt me,' she whispered back, horribly aware of how close their faces were. She could see the little dark flecks around the iris of those almost navy-blue eyes as they danced with wicked amusement as if daring her to go right ahead.

'Tell her that the train goes so fast it doesn't get a signal so you'll be offline for the next couple of hours.' The fine lines around his eyes crinkled in naughty challenge.

She stared up at him with reluctant admiration and as they stared at each other, again something tightened in her stomach. 'That's a terribly good idea,' she whispered in an over jolly way, trying to compensate for the rush of something inappropriate currently coursing through her body. *Don't make that mistake again, Fiona.* Quickly she looked away and busied herself sending another message to her mother. She noticed Gabe stuffing his earphones back in and closing his eyes. *See? It didn't mean anything to him.*

Thankfully that last message gave her a reprieve for the rest of the journey. Following Gabe's example, she plugged her own earphones in and began to listen to Miles Jupp and the team, every now and then breaking into silent laughter before her eyelids drooped. It had been an early start and she gave in, switching off her phone and nestling into the seat.

Just as she'd settled into a light doze she jerked awake at the familiar, irritating, silent buzz but realised it was Gabe's phone. He stared down at the screen and hesitated as if he wasn't sure he wanted to pick it up. She saw the name Yumi flashing on the screen, along with a tiny avatar of a close up of her gorgeous face. Gabe turned the phone over and tapped his fingers on his jean-clad thigh. A few seconds later the phone rang again. His mouth tightened.

When the phone rang for the third time, Fiona lifted her face to his.

'Aren't you going to answer that?' she whispered, aware that the carriage was still silent and her words were pretty redundant. 'Or switch your phone off?'

She regretted her words when she met his steady, unapproachable stare and her stomach flipped again, this time with a touch of nerves. He seemed so cold and unapproachable. Where was the earlier teasing warmth?

She dropped her gaze to his fingers tap-tap-tapping with a slow drumbeat on his leg. It felt as if she were sitting next to a tiger who might lash out at any moment. Each time he examined the screen there was a little frown of frustration etching a deep furrow in his forehead. The phone rang again and this time he snatched it up and rose from his seat, walking in quick jerky strides down the carriage. Fiona had noticed quite a few people walking up and down and realised that they were going to make calls in the deck area between the carriages.

When Gabe came back he seemed distracted and didn't

say anything. He put his earphones in and closed his eyes but Fiona got the impression he was deep in thought.

When they finally drew in to their destination after a half hour during which they'd not spoken at all, Gabe was cool and distracted as Fiona tried to help him get the bags down from the overhead luggage racks. She was tempted to ask him what had got into him but she had a pretty good idea what it was ... or rather *whom*.

Chapter 14

By the time they arrived at the hotel – a beautiful compromise between Japanese and Western design – a touch of anxiety plagued Fiona. As the lift doors closed taking them up to their respective rooms, she sneaked a quick sideways peep at Gabe's stern profile, dismay making her swallow hard. She had that definite surplus-to-requirement feeling and suddenly regretted coming. But, bugger it, he had invited her. If he'd changed his mind, why didn't he say so?

'Are you okay?' asked Fiona shocked by her boldness as the lift pulled away.

'Fine.'

Fiona grimaced. 'You've gone very quiet.'

Gabe didn't even turn her way as he said, 'Just focused.'

The lift arrived at the second floor and thankfully their rooms were in opposite directions.

'I'll see you on the top floor in the suite whenever you're ready,' said Gabe and strode off down the corridor.

'Right,' said Fiona, more to herself than him, as he might as well be leaving roadrunner tracks in the carpet behind him the speed he was going.

She tugged her bag behind her and followed the room numbers to the right door and pushed it open.

'Nice,' she breathed as she walked into the luxurious room. 'Oh, yes, this will do nicely.'

Knowing that her mother would get a kick out of being able to boast about her daughter staying in five-star luxury, she took a couple of pictures quickly and WhatsApped them to her.

A huge bed dressed with white cotton bedding embroidered with a pale green bamboo motif dominated the room. It had to be bigger than a king-size. What was that? Emperor? Rather fitting for Japan, she guessed. She smoothed her fingers over the crisp duvet, too intimidated to bounce on it or throw herself onto it *Pretty Woman*-style; instead she dropped her squashy handbag onto one of the stylish grey button-backed chairs with its splayed-out beech legs.

Crossing to the sliding doors, she opened them and stepped out into the warm spring air. Sunlight poured over her and automatically she lifted her face to it, closing her eyes and taking in a few easy breaths. Oh, this was heaven. Finally opening her eyes, she stepped to the edge of the balcony and took in the view. Below her, stretching the entire length of the hotel, was a very pretty garden. From here she could identify a selection of acers with their delicately shaped leaves in varying shades of greens and yellows as well as several cherry trees which had yet to blossom and her favourites, the frothy blue-green fronds of the Japanese red cedar. Her eyes tracked the pale grey gravel paths threading through the trees with sure purpose, bordered here and there with big, sturdy, dark glazed pots, each one holding a bonsai. She could make out the low gurgle of water and followed the sound to a water feature, a small waterfall tumbling down over rocks that then flowed through the garden ending in a small pond overlooked by a red wooden bench.

She took in a deep breath and focused on one of the nearby cedars, remembering her visit to Haruka's beautiful garden. Already her mood had lifted and, now she thought about it, she realised that the pinching tension in her shoulders had floated away. With a smile she relaxed and let herself breathe in the fresh air as she leant against the balcony railing. The scent of cedar filled her nose. It was green and fresh and bright and as she took in another few deep breaths, remembering what Haruka had said, she wondered if perhaps she should send a quick text to Gabe and tell him to take some time out with nature. In the meantime, she wasn't going to hurry; she was going take her time and smell the proverbial roses for a while. She pulled up one of the chairs on the balcony and settled into it. Sod Gabe Burnett and his mercurial moods.

A zen-like calm carried her up to the top floor in the lift and down the corridor to the suite. It even survived the first few seconds of Gabe pacing like a tiger around the enormous room, which was something else. It was vast – her whole house could have fit in here. The three enormous sofas didn't even make a dent in the bright airy space.

Gabe was surveying the room with hooded eyes in a business-like manner, swivelling around to assess each corner of the room. He squinted at the light pouring in through the window and without acknowledging her arrival, suddenly stalked forward to toy with the blinds, his brow crinkling in thoughtful contemplation. He paced a few steps back and then turned and began to tug one of the three huge sofas to a different angle. Fiona stood like a spare part, her arms limply by her sides, and then, spurred on by instinct alone, she strode over to him, grabbed his shoulders and frog marched him over to the glass doors leading out onto the balcony.

'Go and stand out there and take a couple of deep breaths,' she commanded, sliding the balcony doors open and shoving him through. She'd clearly caught him on the hop because he stood there totally bemused for a second. 'Breathe.'

With a puzzled frown, he walked over to the balcony railing and looked out over the garden.

'Give yourself a few minutes.' Behind his back she pulled a face, pleased with her uncharacteristic assertiveness.

They stood in silence and she watched him as he leaned on the top rail, both elbows resting on the black metal.

Presently he straightened and uttered a brief, 'Thanks,' then walked back into the hotel room.

'Is there anything I can do?' she asked.

It took a moment for him to respond, almost as if he hadn't heard. 'Sorry?'

'Can I do anything?'

He frowned as if she'd asked a tricky question before saying with sudden animation, 'Yes, come and sit here.'

As she approached the sofa, he grasped her shoulders and

firmly guided her into position, so that she sat at a slight right-angle.

'Turn your face towards the window. No, not so far.' He stood back and then stepped forward again, his hands taking her chin and moving it a touch back. She lifted her eyes, careful to stay still and not flinch from the tingle his touch left.

'No, don't look up at me.' His hand took her chin again turning it just so. 'There. Now lean back against the seat and drape your arm along the back, bend your knees and turn your legs to your left. That's it. Now don't move.'

At first she'd been too bemused to realise what he was doing but as soon as he picked up his camera, every tendon went into defence mode, tensing up and tugging at her muscles. Despite the desperate urge to escape, paralysis had set in and she couldn't move.

Gabe began rummaging through his camera bag as she sat in the plume of light coming in through the window, consumed by how much she hated this. She watched as he muttered to himself, pulling faces as he set up his camera, dreading the moment he'd start taking pictures.

When he finally swung round, he scowled. 'Relax,' he snapped certainly not practising what he preached. 'I'm not interested in taking pictures of you. It's for the light and you're probably about the same build as Ken. It will save some time when he gets here. I want to try out a few positions.'

Fiona flinched and swallowed hard. *Bastard.* It was one thing knowing you were statuesque – that was the kind way of saying it, although her mother tended to use the phrase 'big and broad of beam' – but she didn't need Gabe pointing it out. She had enough of that at home. It was crap when your mother was half the size of one of your thighs and delighted in clinking her gold bracelets on her teeny tiny wrists and comparing them to Fiona's tree trunk arms. And she was fed up with feeling crap. She was doing Gabe a favour here.

'How the hell am I supposed to relax with you glaring at me like that? I don't have to do this, you know.' Angrily, she rearranged her limbs, glaring back at him, and eased her body back into the sofa.

Gabe didn't pay the slightest bit of attention to her hissy fit, instead he ran his eyes over her body as impassively as if she were a piece of furniture.

'Right, think about the shot you took this morning. The man in black next to the train.'

Seriously? Fiona's anger seeped away at his total indifference. Being angry with him was pointless; he was in work mode. She huffed out a sigh and focused on the moment she'd taken the picture. Unconsciously, her mouth curved as she recalled the intense pleasure when she'd seen the shot in the viewfinder. Without thinking, she lifted her chin slightly. It was a damn good shot, although she was nonplussed by Gabe mentioning it; at the time he hadn't seemed to register it or even been that impressed. He was a conundrum but fascinating to watch working. She really was nothing but a job to him.

Click, click. Gabe snapped away, hidden behind his camera before finally saying.

'Good. Right, now could you turn and face me, put both elbows on your knees and support your chin in your hands and look straight at the camera. I want to see where the shadows will fall.'

Pursing her lips with resignation, she changed her pose, tempted to point out that the sun would have moved by the time the actor arrived but Gabe was in the zone. She didn't need to feel self-conscious any more – he was oblivious to her. For the next few minutes, he tweaked and changed her sitting position, not saying a word to her apart from the brusque instructions.

Then he came out from behind the camera and studied her impassively, his lips twitching and his eyes sharp and completely focused on her. She wanted to shrink away from the intense gaze; it was as if he could see all the way through her but at the same time didn't see her at all.

With narrowed eyes, holding the camera in one hand, he nodded with his head to the opposite end of the sofa. 'I want you to lie full length on the sofa. Your head that end.'

She glanced uncertainly to where he indicated but he gave an impatient nod. 'Stretch out and undo your hair.'

'My hair?'

He nodded, lowered the camera, and before she could lift a hand to her plait, he had already tugged the elastic tie from the tufted end. With one hand he began to snag his fingers through the braid, loosening and freeing her hair. Impatiently, he suddenly dropped the camera on the sofa beside her and used both hands to push her hair away from her face, his fingers sliding into her scalp and his thumbs smoothing across her cheekbones. The touch ignited a shower of fireworks in her chest and she took in a sharp breath. It sounded horribly loud in the quiet hum of the room. The hands on her face stilled, although one thumb continued to graze her cheek bone as he stared down into her startled eyes, holding her gaze. His mouth softened into a gentle smile. 'You have beautiful hair, Fi.' His husky tone stirred a kick to her heart. 'Beautiful.'

For a crazy moment – crazy given she'd been here once before and got it oh so wrong – she honestly thought he was going to kiss her. And dumb as it was, she couldn't help parting her lips in hopeless, helpless anticipation.

Then as if he'd pulled himself together, he pushed the heavy weight of her hair over her shoulders and took a step back, all business again. 'I want you to lie back, your head resting on the arm, so that your hair drapes over the arm and down. Like a waterfall.'

The moment evaporated and she blinked, taking a second to process his words.

'Why?'

'Because I want to see what it looks like,' he said, as if it were totally obvious and she was being obtuse.

As she started to move he snatched the camera back up.

'Okay,' she said, still slightly dazed and lifted her arms to push up her hair. Even before she moved into position he was snapping away.

'Right. Lie down. That's it.'

'Lie down?'

At his emphatic nod, as if it were the most obvious thing in the world, she did as she was told, even though she felt a bit silly lying full length on the sofa and a lot puzzled. What was this in aid of? Did the film star have particularly long hair? Had he grown it for a role? She arranged her hair over the arm and Gabe danced forwarded, smoothing it one handed into place.

'That's lovely. Now lift one leg, bend it at the knee and use the other foot to tease off your shoe.' She raised her head in protest.

'No. No. Stay there. Now close your eyes and dream of something nice.'

Closing her eyes made her feel vulnerable and she could feel herself stiffening up again.

'Or wasabi Kit-Kats.'

She laughed, relaxing as she did. 'That isn't something nice.'

'Made you smile though.'

'Mmm.'

'Think about your favourite thing since you've come to Japan.'

With her eyes closed it was simple to sift through the memories of the last few days and easy to settle upon the memory of sitting in the garden with Haruka and Setsuko.

'Now, I'm going to have to ask, you look very happy—No, don't open your eyes. Stay there, wherever you're thinking of. That's perfect.'

'Haruka's garden. Tree bathing.' She shot him a smug grin. 'Be honest, you felt better after I took you out on the balcony. After you communed with nature for a few minutes.' She thought he might deny it but instead he tilted his head to one side and nodded.

183

'Point taken. Thank you. I was a bit wound up. This is an important job. Have you taken any pictures of Haruka's garden yet?'

'Funnily enough, no.' It was something she ought to rectify.

'Now lift a hand behind your head and stroke along the length of your hair. Feel the silkiness of it.'

Busy thinking about how she might approach taking pictures of the garden, Fiona complied, remembering the acer leaves dancing in the slight breeze and the soft sway of the cherry tree branches.

'Excellent. That's it. Thank you, that's really helpful.'

She came to with a start and sat up hurriedly, frowning. Gabe had his back to her and was fiddling about with a different camera. 'Are you really going to get him to lie down like that?'

Gabe turned around, his eyes sliding to the window, a rather too innocent smile on his face. It was the sort of expression you'd find on the face of a boy caught with his hand in the biscuit jar.

'No. Sorry. As soon as you lay down, I realised the light was all wrong.'

'You could have said something earlier.' Fiona now felt a little foolish.

'You know photographers. Keep flogging a dead horse. I thought if I changed angles ... it might ... but nothing worked. Thanks for your help though.'

She eyed him suspiciously. 'You are going to delete all those shots ... aren't you?'

'Of course,' he said airily and a shade too quickly before

he went back to flicking through the shots he'd taken, nodding and running a hand over his mouth at periodic intervals as he weighed up the pictures.

'Promise?' Was she being ridiculously being paranoid? After all, why would Gabe want to keep pictures of her?

When the actor and a huge entourage arrived, the room suddenly filled up and there was an awful lot of bowing. Thankfully everyone spoke English and there was a flurry of introductions from the publicity girl from the film company, an uber-fashionable, strident young woman in cream, wide-legged culottes, blood-red loafers, ankle socks and a deconstructed square T-shirt. Fiona nodded and bowed as she was introduced to the make-up artist, her assistant, Ken's agent, the agent's assistant and a stylist along with her assistant pulling a wardrobe rail holding at least six suits and an extensive selection of casual wear.

Fiona widened her eyes at the sight of all the extra people and turned to Gabe who simply rolled his eyes, ignored everyone and strode straight over to Ken.

'Hi Ken. Good to see you again.'

'Gabriel. Good to be here.' After a quick bow, they shook hands, firm and manly with a definite touch of familiarity. It was easy to see that the two men liked and respected each other.

Ken was wearing a mid-blue suit which had that sort of fluidity and silkiness that suggested it was extremely expensive and, as Gabe had predicted, he was a man completely at home in his own skin.

'Right, let's get started,' said Gabe while the entourage was still fussing and arranging themselves – the make-up girl setting up her brushes and various pots on the console table on the side, the stylists flicking through the hangers on the rail while the agent and his assistant whispered to each other.

'I'd like you to sit here.' Gabe led him over to the sofa.

One of the stylists darted forward, holding a suit on a hanger in each hand, and spoke in a torrent of Japanese. Ken shook his head, stroked his fingers down at his own suit and shook his head again. Her face crumpled in disappointment but Ken smiled.

Ken spoke, calm and unhurried, and Fiona guessed that he was saying he was fine. With a mutinous expression on her face, the stylist and her assistant returned the suits to the rail.

With a brush full of powder, one of the make-up artists advanced and Fiona winced, seeing the implacable glint in the actor's eye.

Gabe held up his hand. 'We're taking a few test shots,' he said placatingly. 'Getting the positions set up and the light and then we'll see how we get on.' Fiona caught the wink he sent to Ken.

Ken nodded and spoke to the entourage who all stopped twittering and flapping. Whatever he said had clearly eased their minds.

'Tell you what,' said Gabe 'why doesn't everyone take a break, while we get set up?'

Ken translated and ushered everyone to the door.

Fiona's mouth twitched as she realised that the two men had cleared the room with the minimum of fuss.

'Phew, that's better,' said Gabe. 'I can hear myself think. We might be able to get done in half an hour, Ken.'

'Good. Very good.' His eyes twinkled. 'And who is this?'

'This is my new assistant, Fiona. And she'll be no trouble.'

'I didn't think she would be, Gabe.' He turned to Fiona, with a polite nod. 'He wouldn't allow it. Now, where do you want me?'

Following Gabe's instructions, Ken reclined back against the sofa in exactly the same position that Fiona had been just forty minutes ago. But when it came to the shot with him leaning forward, elbows on his knees looking directly into the camera, Fiona could feel Gabe's sudden excitement; it was as if a creative buzz fluttered across his skin.

Gabe moved the light reflector to a new position and asked Fiona to hold it up a fraction, pushing the light onto the actor's very handsome face. Ken flashed a warm smile at her and she smiled shyly back. Gabe was right – he had presence and that indefinable charisma.

'Nice. Keep smiling at Fi. Pretend she's one of your legion of fans. Even though she'd never heard of you before today.'

'Gabe!' Fi protested but Ken leant back and roared with laughter, easy and unaffected as the camera clicked and whirred, capturing the shot.

For the next twenty minutes, Gabe teased and taunted the actor who responded with good humour – clearly self-depre-cation was his middle name – and all the while, Gabe moved quickly and calmly snapping landscape and portrait shots, turning the camera this way and that. Crouching, leaning and stretching in a series of ninja moves like an elegant ballet dancer despite his rugby-player frame. Fiona watched. No wonder he was a legend. There was something indefinable about his total control and sense of purpose throughout. He knew exactly what he was doing and oozed self-confidence.

He shook his hair out of his face, the blue eyes glowing with excitement and enthusiasm and she froze, as something grabbed her heart and squeezed it. Her eighteen-year-old self hadn't known the half of it. Her mouth dried as she took in his lean hips while he crouched to take another shot, the nimble fingers holding the camera. *Bloody, bloody, bloody, hell.*

No. She didn't want to feel like this. This tumultuous rush of emotion. The warmth burning in her chest at the sight of him. Broad shoulders. Wide chest. Muscle-man thighs. Didn't want to imagine what it would be like to be held in those arms up against that chest. Did not want to be in love, smitten, or intoxicated with Gabe bloody Burnett. He was too far out of her league. He was too sophisticated. Too bored with life. Too cynical. Too arrogant. Too bloody talented. Too bloody gorgeous. Too everything.

But it was too late, whatever her head was telling her; that stupid organ which was supposed to be responsible for pumping blood around her body had other flaming ideas.

Mortified, she stood as a flush of heat raced through her body, staining her cheeks, leaving her hot and very bothered. She moved towards the balcony and laid a cheek against the cold glass. What the hell was she going to do? She'd made a complete fool of herself over Gabe Burnett once before; she absolutely *could not* do it again.

And as if it wasn't bad enough that she was as punch drunk as if a thunderbolt had come back for a second hit, Gabe swung his camera her way and took a shot.

'What are you doing?' her voice came out screechy and panicky.

'Sorry, I thought the shutter was sticking a bit; I wanted a test shot. Don't worry it's completely out of focus and there's too much light behind you.'

Relief almost made her knees buckle. God knows what might have shown on her face. From now on she was going to have to be very careful around Gabe, so she didn't give anything away. This wasn't love, just infatuation, and it would go as soon as she could get away from him. She only had to survive the next week. And surely she could come up with plenty of strategies to avoid him. Spend a day in the teashop with Setsuko. And she had the tea ceremony with Haruka. That left the trip to Mount Fuji, but hopefully now she knew what she was up against she could erect some barriers and keep her guard up, maintain a healthy distance etc. etc.

'Fi, are you listening?'

She blushed again, realising that both Gabe and Ken were staring at her.

'Sorry, I'm a bit light headed.' Which actually was the truth. Her pulse was just returning to normal.

Ken jumped up from the sofa and Gabe took her elbow and guided her to sit down. Seconds later the actor was pushing a glass of water into her hand and Gabe was crouched in front of her, holding one of her hands. 'You're a little flushed, are you okay?'

Oh heck. Her throat was so tight with embarrassment she couldn't say a word. Gratefully she took the glass and tried to shake her other hand free from Gabe's. The warm touch of his skin and the concern in his eyes wasn't doing her any good at all. He squeezed her hand, not letting go. 'Have some water. There, that's it.' Even his voice sounded worried.

Taking a sip, she managed to say, 'I'm fine.' Now she was even more mortified with both men staring anxiously at her. 'Honestly I'm fine.'

'Sit there for a moment.'

'But I'm holding you—'

'I'm pretty much all done.'

'That's what I like about working with you, Gabe. Quick and dirty, get the job done.'

'It's not always that easy,' said Gabe with feeling. 'Thanks for the support.'

Fiona was aware of a presence in the doorway and she turned to see a beautiful, slight woman, standing with an amused smile on her face, poised and waiting to be spotted. 'They're good people,' said Ken, unaware of the woman behind them. 'a bit ... how do you say it?' He lifted his palms upwards.

'Keen,' said Gabe with another roll of his eyes. He hadn't seen her either.

'But doing their jobs, like you and me.'

The woman's eyes had now narrowed and her lips had flattened, the expectant smile dimming. Fiona could see her displeasure in the way her hand slid to her hip and in the petulant tilt of head.

'You're a better man than I am,' said Gabe.

'I've got too many people ready to run me down if I'm not,' replied Ken, with weary grin.

'That's the price of being in the public eye.' Gabe raised both eyebrows.

Ouch, she really did not look happy. Fiona tried to catch Gabe's eye but he was now showing Ken the shots and with their heads together they were murmuring and discussing the pictures Gabe had taken.

The woman had taken a couple of steps forwards and had paused, posing again. Fiona tried to smile at her but the woman wasn't interested in her – all her attention, sharp and eerily focused, was on Gabe. She watched him with possessive hunger, her mouth pinched now. Her pose, initially relaxed with feline assurance, had stiffened with anger and irritation.

'Er ... Gabe,' said Fiona, fidgeting in her seat, loathe to stand up. Next to this tiny slender fairy creature, she was like a towering colossus and, as she acknowledged the thought, her heart plummeted to the bottom of the ocean with a total sense of hopelessness. Gabe was totally out of reach, she knew that. This was the sort of woman he went for.

'Mmm?' he said, still absorbed in his camera.

'You've got a visitor.'

'What?' He finally lifted his head. Yumi glowered at him.

'Yumi! What are you doing here?'

Suddenly she was all gracious smiles. 'You said you were

doing the shoot with Ken. And I finished earlier than I expected so I thought I'd come over and say hi.'

'Hi,' he said, clearly a little bemused. 'Ken, this is Yumi Mimura.'

'We've met before. Her smile was sultry as he bowed to her. 'And it's Yumi Mitoki now. I'm married to Meiko Mitoki.'

'Forgive me,' said Ken with practised ease, as if he was used to people claiming they knew him. 'Of course, and I do know your husband.'

'We met at the studios. I had a screen test. For your last film. But the producer and I agreed it wasn't quite the right role for my career. *Gabe san*, we can go to dinner earlier. As I finished quicker than I thought I've changed the reservation.'

Gabe rubbed the back of his neck. 'Er ... well, I need to get tidied up here. And ... oh, this is Fiona, remember I told you about her?'

Yumi didn't bother slinking over to make her acquaintance, Fiona noted. Instead she cast her a sidelong look and gave her a quick bow before moving with tiny steps to take her place next to Gabe, staking her claim.

'Fiona, this is Yumi. She's ... er ... she's ...'

Fiona took pity on him and despite Yumi's frigid indifference, she said in a friendly voice, 'Hi, I've seen your pictures. They're very beautiful.'

For a moment, the other woman preened at the compliment and then, as if a thought had struck her, she narrowed her eyes. 'In Gabe's studio?' she snapped, shooting a glare Gabe's way.

'In the Photography Museum in Toyko.'

'Ah, yes.' Placated, she gave Fiona a benevolent nod, like a queen accepting her due. Then she turned to Gabe, laying a hand on his arm, the pale slim fingers contrasting with his blue chambray shirt and the facets of the fine-cut Tiffany diamond of her engagement ring catching the light and sparkling like stars.

'I've made reservations at Kikunoi. Ken, perhaps you'd like to join us? I'm sure they could squeeze *you* in.'

'Unfortunately, I have a prior engagement, but thank you for the invitation.'

Gabe's mouth tightened and he busied himself with packing his cameras away in the foam-padded boxes. Now that her legs were steadier, Fiona stood up and began to fold the light reflector back into the big nylon bag.

Ken said his goodbyes and Gabe wished him luck with facing his entourage.

'I hope they forgive you,' he teased. Ken smiled and bowed, backing out of the room.

'Well, that went well,' said Gabe to Fiona. 'The feature's appearing in *The Sunday Times* in about six weeks. We'll work on the pictures in the studio when we get back tomorrow and you can tell me which ones you'd pick.'

'I think I know,' said Fiona, thinking of the shots Gabe had taken when Ken had burst out laughing.

'We'll see,' Gabe teased.

'Gabe,' Yumi slid a tiny arm through his. 'You're ignoring me.' She added a coy pout, like a little girl.

'I'm still working.' He gently disengaged her hand and bent down to pack away an unused tripod. 'And I did say I'd let you know about dinner.'

She gave him a beguiling smile as he straightened again, her face tilted up to his. 'You've got to eat and what else are you going to do? Meiko's away *again* and I'm all on my own. I'm always on my own.' Sadness filled her pretty face and even Fiona had to admit she felt sorry for the woman.

'Well …' Gabe's face filled with uncertainty. 'I …'

'Don't mind me,' Fiona said, seeing that he was torn. 'I'm quite happy to get room service. They've got really good Wi-Fi here; I can do a few bits on my blog and catch up.'

'I'm sure Kikunoi could … um … stretch to a table for three,' said Gabe.

Fiona just about managed to stop herself from rolling her eyes. Duh! Why the hell would she want to tag along and invite comparisons between her and Yumi? And why would he want her to when he could have the beautiful Japanese woman all to himself?'

'You go ahead.'

'Are you sure? It's a great restaurant.'

'The table is for two. It will be very difficult to change the reservation.' Yumi had completely forgotten that not even ten minutes ago she'd extended an invitation to Ken, which made Fiona bite her lips in amusement.

'I really don't mind.' She quite fancied getting some fresh air and going for a stroll. She might even be really brave and challenge herself to check out a local restaurant.

'See, she doesn't mind.' Yumi shrugged as if there'd never been any other outcome.

Still, thought Fiona, it might have been nice if Gabe had put a bit more effort into at least trying to be polite about it.

Chapter 15

Thoughts of Gabe buzzed around her head and it was a relief to get out of the hotel and breathe in some fresh air. Staying in her room for the evening would have driven her even more crazy. The determination to maximise her time, almost as much as not wanting to be left alone with her turbulent thoughts, had driven her out to eat by herself, instead of taking the easy option of ordering room service or going down to the hotel restaurant. She wanted an authentic experience and it would make the subject of a good blog post, one that she could write up on her phone during the experience.

How the hell could she have fallen in love with him? It was just lust, wasn't it? Over excited hormones, she tried to persuade herself. He was gorgeous. It was a given. But Fiona knew with a leaden, sinking sensation that what she felt for Gabe went deeper than that. It eclipsed anything she'd ever felt before and put her youthful crush on him into the shade.

Oh God, what had she done? And what was she going to do about it? A wry smile touched her lips. Maybe she should go for the kiss-first-ask-questions-later strategy again but sadly that impetuosity and daring no longer resided within her.

Striding along the street, reliving every moment of his hands delving into her hair, she tried to take note of the landmarks so that she could find her way back rather than dwell on the moment when she'd thought he might kiss her. *Keep your mind on the street, Fiona.* She glanced at the map the kind receptionist at the hotel had marked with a few suggested places to eat.

What would Gabe say if she kissed him now? Today he'd been so approachable until bloody Yumi had appeared on the scene. She was so lost in thought she realised she'd missed the street she was aiming for and cannoned into someone when she turned to retrace her steps. The man bowed good naturedly and she held up her hands in apology.

Gosh, what a contrast to the way she'd felt when she'd been on her own after losing Gabe at Shibuya and the fear that she'd always feel hopelessly lost and out of place. Japan would always feel very different but she was enjoying and embracing the differences now, even as she looked ahead at the unfamiliar street scene. One of the best things about the country was how incredibly safe it felt and although not many people spoke English there seemed to be a willingness to help.

She stopped to stare in a window full of plastic models of the dishes, including a very authentic-looking bowl of soup and noodles. It wasn't the first time she'd seen such a display; it seemed quite a common thing in Japan and quite handy given the language barrier. When she checked the name of the restaurant she realised she'd stumbled upon the very place she'd been trying to find, and when Fiona peered in through the door, it was busy but not too crowded, with a mix of

Japanese and Western tourists, which gave her hope that the menu might be in English. She wished Gabe was with her; he knew his way around Japanese food.

She was greeted with a bow by a very young man who didn't bat an eyelid at her solitary status when she asked for a table for one by holding up an index finger. He replied in English with a mischievous smile, 'Follow me,' leading her to a corner booth where she could look out and people watch but she wasn't completely conspicuous. He was rewarded for his thoughtfulness with a warm smile and she ordered an Asahi beer. Already her stomach was turning over at the smells. It had been a long time since the bento box and Kit-Kat on the train.

Her drink, when it arrived, hit the spot and she savoured the first malty mouthful of the pale golden beer. Just what the doctor ordered. She looked at the menu, none of which meant very much to her. With a decisive flick of her wrist, she put her menu down and caught the eye of the waiter.

'Excuse me. What's the best thing on the menu?'

He beamed with pleasure. '*Tonkotsu* ramen. Very good.'

'Can you tell me what's in it?' She didn't want any nasty surprises.

'Finest noodles. Made with best quality flour, fresh every day. Noodles rinsed five times.' She assumed that was to keep the water fresh and starch free.

'Noodles are served in natural pork bone soup. Bones are simmered for six hours for best flavour and skimmed for exquisite clarity. Then we add *dashi*.' At her frown of incomprehension, he explained, 'A very special recipe, only two people in kitchen know this. Super special fish stock which is added to broth. Then noodles, pork slices and the red sauce. Red sauce is unique to restaurant, blend of thirty spices and red pepper, mixed and aged for days and nights. Very secret recipe. Very spicy. Very good.' He finished with a proud bow.

'That sounds perfect.' Fiona smiled at him, impressed by his enthusiasm and delight in the food. When she looked around the restaurant, it did seem that most people were pulling noodles from large bowls with their chopsticks so she guessed *tonkotsu* ramen was the house speciality.

Before her meal arrived, the waiter brought a ceramic candle holder with a small tea light which was placed in front of her with careful, attentive ceremony and a characteristic bow. Immediately afterwards, the steaming broth arrived and was placed over the candle with more solicitude; she got the impression that it was really important to the waiter that she enjoyed this meal as he bowed once again and left her to it. Even in a restaurant, she felt like an honoured guest. It heightened the experience and made her aware of the need to appreciate the food in a way that she wouldn't have at home. Before she started, she took a moment to inhale the delicate fragrance of meat and the mix of spices. Her mouth watered as she admired the solid, glazed earthenware bowl in rich russets which seemed to enhance the appearance of the food. So much thought and care were always taken, she realised. There was a real respect for ingredients and the way food was prepared and presented.

Although it would have been nice to have Gabe with her, there was something rather comforting about a piping hot bowl of soup and noodles – or rather ramen as she ought to call it. Gripping her chopsticks, which she had become a little more adept with, she took a healthy pinch of ramen and with more appetite than grace slurped them up. They were soft but not soggy and had a very slight bite to them, and they had absorbed the light flavour of the meaty broth. With a little greedy moan she picked up another chopstick full and gulped down a mouthful. Then she took some from the middle where the red sauce had been added – although she'd have called it more of a deep auburn – prepared for it to be hot. To her relief, the spicy combination didn't burn her tongue or shoot her socks off; it was indeed very spicy – hotter than she was used to, causing a sheen of sweat to break out on her forehead – but it was the kind of spice that warmed and heated gradually with an expansion of flavours that swirled around the mouth – a touch of chilli, a smattering of cinnamon, a punch of ginger and lots of black pepper. She closed her eyes, savouring the delicious warming sensation spreading through her. Heaven in a bowl, she decided.

There was something rather decadent and indulgent about enjoying food on your own, she decided, as she finished the last dregs of the broth, tipping the bowl up a little self-consciously but copying the other diners. She felt nourished, fortified, and full of wellbeing but above all, proud of herself for going out by herself and not staying in and indulging in self-pity. Perhaps ramen was the answer. Special insulation for the heart. A bowl of that every day and she could cope with seeing Gabe for the next week.

A week wasn't so very long, was it?

Chapter 16

Gabe met her in reception the following morning ready for the journey back, crumpled and worn as if he'd not had much sleep.

In contrast, she felt fresh and bright, her night out having given her a boost of confidence. Going out to eat by herself was not something she'd have ever thought she could do. And not only had she got through it, she'd genuinely enjoyed the experience. She'd also had an early night and after returning from the restaurant had updated her blog, posting some of the tourist pictures she'd taken and a write up about the amazing digital museum. She'd also pondered writing a piece about meeting one of Japan's most famous film stars and how down-to-earth and normal he'd been, but she wasn't sure if that might get Gabe into trouble.

Now she wished she had as she examined his slightly dishevelled appearance.

'Good night?' she asked with a hint of acid. She was allowed to disapprove, she told herself, unable to keep at bay the slick eel of jealousy that wormed around in her stomach. Yumi was a married woman.

He winced. 'Not really.'

'Good,' she said, pleased at his quick flicker of surprise but he didn't say anything. Instead he hauled up his baggage, leaving the black reflector bag for her to carry, and headed out of the hotel.

For most of the journey, he worked through his email on his phone catching up with correspondence. Fiona tried to listen to her podcast but couldn't concentrate; she could smell the faint traces of Yumi's perfume on Gabe's shirt – the same one from yesterday. Why was it that the walk of shame left a man looking rumpled and sexy? And how could she possibly think he was sexy when he'd come from another woman's bed? That horrible jealousy coiled and slithered inside her and she steadfastly stared out of the window, horrified to find that a lone traitorous tear had escaped and was sliding down her face. Angrily, she dashed it away and sniffed, wishing she had the nerve to blow her nose but knowing from Gabe's warning it was considered extremely rude.

'You all right?' mouthed Gabe glancing up from his emails.

'Fine,' Fiona mouthed back.

He leaned closer and mercifully the tang of his aftershave overpowered the light perfume but nothing could dilute the sudden longing that tripped her pulse as he murmured in her ear.

'I'm sorry about last night. I shouldn't have ditched you. It was rude. But ... Yumi's quite fragile just now. She doesn't have many friends. We've known each other for a long time. I feel desperately sorry for her. Her husband's away all the time, doesn't pay her much attention. She's on her own a lot.'

'You don't need to justify it to me, Gabe,' she whispered back fiercely, unable to hide her anger at his excuses. 'It's nothing to do with me.'

His eyes narrowed as he grasped her meaning. 'I'm not sleeping with her,' he growled.

'You're a grown man.' Her whisper sounded accusing but the thought of him and Yumi together was more painful than she could have imagined. 'Like I said, it's nothing to do with me.'

'I. Am. Not. Sleeping with her.'

She shrugged and his blue eyes blazed.

He held her gaze and she had to drop her eyes.

Throwing himself back into his seat, he went back to his phone and she checked her watch. They were cutting it fine for her to get back in time for the tea ceremony. Suddenly she longed for the quiet calm of the older woman's house.

Setsuko's solemn attention as she folded Fiona into the *kimono* and her gentle chatter was calming in a way she wouldn't have believed possible. Her anger at Gabe had lasted the whole way back from the station. Couldn't the stupid man see how Yumi manipulated him? Her fingers clenched, but then softened. There was something about the steady ritual and the order as each garment went on. Something about being in the pared-down room with the sun pouring in and the sound of birdsong outside. Focusing on each element of the costume and Setsuko's gentle chatter, she ran a finger over one of the embroidered cranes on the fabric of the kimono.

Finally dressed, her hair piled in a lose bun secured by

ornate bamboo slides, Fiona and Setsuko took their *kimono*-constricted steps down to the teashop. Elegant though it was, the restrictive dress ensured a leisurely and measured journey along the *engawa*, the wooden veranda, skirting the garden and into Haruka's *chashitsu*. Fiona wondered if this, like so much else in Japanese culture, was deliberate and another form of mindfulness Slowing the pace, taking your time. You couldn't hurry in a *kimono*, that was for sure, and the slow steps as they'd walked down through the garden had brought a sense of peace. She was glad she'd agreed to wear the *kimono* at Setsuko's suggestion on her return. Had the other woman guessed how cross and upset she was?

There was a Western couple and another woman in the room and, to her astonishment, Gabe. What was he doing here? He hadn't mentioned anything about coming along. The last thing he'd said was 'Why don't you come over to the studio later to see the pictures of Ken?'

And that created its own dilemma. Part of her longed to see them and enjoy again that professional intimacy that they'd shared before Yumi had turned up, the other – the sensible – part knew it would be a terrible mistake. It would exacerbate that sense of hopelessness and heartache. Gabe was as far from reach as he had been when she was eighteen, except then, at least it had been just a silly crush. Not like this depth of emotion where the thoughts of what it would be like to kiss him kept creeping into her head like spidery cracks intent on forcing their way through. She was also terrified she might give herself away – on the train she'd had to limit herself to sneaking periodic peeps his way, scared she might get caught studying those cheekbones or staring hungrily at his lips. Yesterday, in the blink of an eye, she'd turned into some crazy person, desperate to capture his attention. Wanting him to notice her.

Despite the turmoil of her thoughts, she stared at him, and he responded with a nod. Haruka acknowledged her with a simple bow and if Fiona had to label it, the faintest smirk of triumph, as Setsuko escorted her into the room and guided her to one of the *tatami* mats. Fiona bowed to the other occupants of the room and lowered herself into a sitting position; she'd been warned not to attempt the kneeling position that Haruka had adopted as apparently that took years of practice to sustain.

Ignoring Gabe, who was unfortunately positioned opposite her, she sat down on her mat and concentrated on Haruka kneeling behind a small tea station which was surprising in its simplicity, although by now, Fiona thought, she ought to have been used to the streamlined Japanese approach where less was definitely more. She felt able to breathe more deeply in the uncluttered, pared-back room, as if her emotions had room to expand into the space. The steaming black pot positioned on a small gas ring drew her attention and she studied the neat arrangement of several assorted pots of differing sizes.

There was a quiet hush of almost breathless anticipation in the room and Fiona settled more comfortably, looking out beyond Haruka through the wide-open window to the greens, pinks, and reds of the garden which made the perfect backdrop. With a rush of happiness, Fiona smoothed down the soft silk, doubly glad she'd worn the *kimono* when she caught a quick approving gleam from the otherwise impassive Haruka. Now she'd started, it was very serious business. From what she'd picked up from Mayu, who was clearly very proud of both her grandmother and mother, it took years of study and practice to become a master of tea.

Inadvertently she caught Gabe's eye and prayed the rush of heat wasn't obvious to him. It was as if every sense were suddenly tuned into him even though she was still fuming at him. He was studying her face with quiet intensity which made her nerve endings tingle, almost as if he were touching her. *Breathe*, she told herself, focusing on Haruka, relieved when all the earlier agitation she'd felt began to dissipate.

Haruka took a little red napkin that had been tucked into her *obi* and flicked it out with a no-nonsense, audible click that signalled the ceremony had begun. With long, elegant fingers she smoothed down its length before folding it with careful exact movements. It was quickly apparent that every last part of the ceremony had been judiciously choreographed and that precision dominated each fluid transition.

Fiona watched, totally absorbed in the painstaking details as the ritual unfolded. The silence in the room made her aware of her own blood pumping around her body, the weight of her limbs pressed into the floor, and the rhythm of her breath.

Everyone's attention was on Haruka as she scooped up steaming water in the long-handled bamboo cup, which, once the water was poured into the *chawan*, was put down at a very precise angle. Next, she carefully wiped the long stick that was used to scoop out the *matcha* powder into the *chawan*. Once hot water was tipped into the cup and whisked with the delicate, spidery bamboo whisk, Haruka turned the cup several times before offering it up to Setsuko who took it to the woman nearest her. Before it was handed over, the bowl was turned several times and the woman accepted it with a bow.

There was a universal intake of breath as the woman took the bowl and lifted it to her mouth, sipping the liquid, and then a collective exhale when she nodded appreciatively.

Then Haruka began the whole painstaking process all over again. Fiona watched each regimented move, marvelling at Haruka's stolid patience and assiduous attention to every last detail. There was an almost balletic discipline and rigour to her movements and Fiona found her thoughts were not drifting so much as concentrating in one place. Where earlier her brain had been full of resignation, anger and despair, now she could see things more clearly, as if the calm environment allowed her thoughts to be filtered and rationalised.

The boiling water steamed gently into the air and Fiona imagined her pain dissipating like water vapour. She couldn't change the way she felt about Gabe but the feelings were something that should be cherished. She should enjoy the brief time she had with him and make the most of it, celebrate the things she loved about him: his gentle respect for Haruka and her family, the care he'd taken with her at the tempura bar, the way he'd treated her like an equal at the shoot, his passion for photography which, although well-hidden, was still there. The way he made her senses sing when he touched her and how he'd championed her so quickly against her mother. How he'd made her feel beautiful that night in the studio. How he'd given her back some self-esteem. If he couldn't see how Yumi's manipulation for what it was, that was his problem.

The quick shushing of the whisk in the tea brought Fiona's attention back as Haruka fluffed up the water into a deep, dark green, foamy froth with quick, firm strokes. Agitation, she thought. Sometimes you needed to shake things up. She had another week here and she was going to embrace every moment.

Setsuko approached with her small slow steps, turned the bowl, and with a bow offered it to Fiona – and with it came an insight. By taking the bowl, she was accepting what was offered and although she felt a little crack in her heart – it was going to take more than golden glue to mend it – she smiled to herself. She knew herself now. Knew who she was and what she was capable of. At eighteen she'd thought she was in love but it was only a facsimile of love. At eighteen she'd lost her self-esteem and sense of self-worth; now it was gradually coming back and that was something to celebrate.

She took a sip of the tea and nodded, making a silent toast inside to herself; a sense of wellbeing flooded her as if she'd completed a circle. This evening she would go over to Gabe's studio.

Gabe was fascinated by the play of emotions that danced across Fiona's face as she sat in a shaft of sunlight, so regal and elegant in the sumptuous *kimono*. That glorious hair ...

he remembered the silkiness of it sliding through his fingers and the clutch of his stomach when he'd nearly kissed her. God, he wished he had his camera. He could have taken a dozen shots, each seconds apart, and every one would have been different. Regret chafed at him. For not kissing her, as much as for not having his camera. It was a long time since he'd felt like that.

It was also a long time since he'd been to a tea ceremony, his overriding memory being boredom. He'd gone with Yumi and a couple of other people – he couldn't even remember their names now, even though he'd partied regularly with them – and they'd fidgeted, tugging at their clothes, whispering in undertones the whole way through. Today he'd come on a whim, wanting perhaps to show Fiona that there was more to him than she thought. That he wasn't the sort of shallow guy that slept with other people's wives.

With a touch of shame at his previous behaviour, he watched Haruka carefully placing the bamboo cup back at exactly the same angle. She took great pride in what she did; there were centuries of learning here and it deserved respect. The person he'd been, when he was with Yumi back then, wasn't someone he was particularly proud of. His mum and dad wouldn't be particularly proud of him either if they knew what his life was really like. Suburban Sally and Jim in Esher with a marriage as durable and reliable as Tupperware. Unlike them, he'd been going places with a heady, exciting, glamorous career. It had been easy to impress them with his success, his early achievements, but somewhere along the way he'd lost sight of the values he'd grown up with. He downplayed things in his regular calls, talked about work and the latest movie star he'd photographed, instead of that he'd lost his passion for photography and how tired and bored of life he was. They were sad for him when he split up with Yumi and he didn't reveal how low he'd sunk in that time. Upbeat, endlessly cheerful Sally and pragmatic Jim didn't have much truck with self-pity. They'd never met her and he knew in his heart of hearts that although they never would have breathed a word to him, they wouldn't have approved of his choice. And until now he'd never really understood just how great Tupperware was.

Haruka polished the wooden bamboo stick, spooning out a perfectly level serving of *matcha* tea. With every movement, there was clear purpose in what she was doing. She had trained for this for years and was totally in control. Absolutely assured in every element of the ceremony. She knew with bone-deep certainty exactly what came next. A certainty, he reflected that was rather reassuring.

And it made him question what his purpose was.

What was he doing with his life? Dinner with Yumi had been a disaster. She'd been cross that Ken hadn't joined them and he'd quickly realised that had been the real reason for her trip to Kyoto. When was he going to stop chasing after her? Did he even love her anymore? He cared about her and he worried about her. Despite her marriage, she was so unhappy. She put on a brave face in public but in private to him, she let the truth spill out. How lonely she was, how Meiko never had any time for her, how mean with money he was.

Across the room, Fiona accepted her tea from Setsuko, a sweet smile transforming the solemn concentration on her face. It pierced him with sudden awareness. In the last couple of days with Fiona he'd been ... more human. Like he was coming back to life. She challenged him, made him angry, made him laugh, made him think. He knew with certainty that the pictures he'd taken of Ken Akito were the best he'd taken in over a year. Was that down to her? And he'd taken some great shots of her which he was dying to take a closer look at. There was something about her expressive face that called to him.

Right now there was a look of unbearable sadness on her face, quickly followed by resignation. What had caused them? What on earth would she say if she knew about the unaccountable urge he had to put his arms around her and reassure her that everything would be all right?

'Hi, come on in.' He jumped up, eager to please and relieved to see her when Fiona tentatively rapped on the rice-paper screen of the *shoji* door to his studio workroom. He realised he'd been checking the clock rather a lot in the last hour, worried she might not turn up.

'I wanted to see Ken's pictures,' she said, surprising him slightly by sliding into the seat next to him. On the train she'd given him the impression she'd rather sit with a skunk than with him, staring out of the window for most of the journey.

'We've got some good ones,' he leaned towards the screen and, clicking away on the mouse, brought up a selection.

'We?'

His hand froze over the mouse. We. He'd said it without thinking. 'Yes. Teamwork. I've not had an assistant before. You were a big help.' Not wanting to analyse the slip, he covered it quickly. 'What do you think?'

She scanned the images and he watched her face, strangely anxious to hear her opinion. In his mind there was no doubt about it that the standout shot was the one of Ken, elbows on his knees, hands on his face, his mouth wide open with an unselfconscious laugh. It had been one of those rare unguarded moments that Gabe would have kicked himself forever if he'd missed.

'That one.' She pointed and immediately lowered her finger. 'Rude to point but definitely that one,' she added with uncharacteristic self-confidence. A bubble of pride swelled under his sternum. She had a very good eye and she understood what made a picture, what made it something above the ordinary.

'I think so too. And I think Ken will love it. I'm also thinking about sending these ones.' He clicked through a couple more pictures, one of Ken smiling at the camera in the same position, a little more sober than the laughing shot but still full of personality, kind, knowing eyes looking right into the lens, and one of Ken leaning back with his arm draped across the back of the sofa, relaxed and comfortable, as if he were waiting for a friend to join him at any minute.

'They're very good.'

'I think so. You must have inspired me.' Although he said it with a teasing smile, he realised he meant it. Her steady interest in the process as they set up in the suite and her easy compliance when he'd asked her to pose had given him new impetus. He'd actually wanted to do more than a good job. Yeah, it helped that Ken was a stand-up guy but Fiona's bright-eyed interest had made him care that little bit more. With a jolt he realised he hadn't cared about work properly for a long time – he was lucky enough to have the talent to get away with faking it. Was that shame curling around the edges of his thoughts?

'Yeah, right.' Fiona's voice rang with scepticism.

'No, seriously.' He reached out and laid a hand on her forearm, for some reason needing the contact, unsure whether he was reassuring her or himself. 'These are the best portrait shots I've taken for a while.' Clicking on the programme, he enlarged the picture so it filled the screen. 'There. Isn't Ken a man you'd want to be friends with?'

Fiona nodded.

'Which is exactly what I wanted. They've come out far better than I'd hoped. Look at that one. The way he's looking right at us. Open, warm, friendly.'

'Probably because all those people weren't hanging around,' said Fiona, pulling her arm away and cradling it to her chest as if his touch were dangerous.

'I always try to get rid of them,' said Gabe, swallowing down his odd sense of disappointment. 'Otherwise it destroys the intimacy.' He thought back to the brief half hour they'd shared in the suite before everyone had arrived, when there'd been that easy camaraderie between them. When she'd posed for him and when he'd had that urge to kiss her. Things were different now – what would she say if he did kiss her? Would she be as horrified as she was last time? He glanced at her face. The blue eyes were guarded and distant. If he kissed her would they soften and smile at him as they had done in the suite? A strange sense of longing like an ache coiled in his gut and he had to fight the urge to put a hand up to her face and trace that oddly attractive wide mouth. Fiona was avoiding his gaze and he realised he was in danger of doing something stupid.

What had he been saying? Ken's hangers-on, that was it.

'Nine times out of ten, the PR will rush over to remind us it's all about the film.' He scrolled through a few more pictures and ... oh shit. Please don't let her have seen that one. He thought he'd got rid of them all but no, like a hound dog following a scent, she spotted it.

'You are going to delete that, aren't you?'

'What?' His airy tone didn't fool her and she wasn't buying his attempt at nonchalance.

'That picture. Of me.'

'If you really want me to.'

'I do.' Surprised at her implacable tone, he turned to face her.

'It's a good shot.'

She snorted. 'Don't be—'

'Don't be what?'

'You're being ...'

He frowned down at the picture. It wasn't one of the best; he'd taken far better ones but there was nothing wrong with it.

'Come on, out with it. Let me guess, you think your nose

214

is a bit wonky or one eye is bigger than the other, or there's a tiny pimple on your cheek?'

Her mouth crimped shut and she'd done her usual warrior-princess, proud lift of her chin, refusing to look at him. He almost laughed while at the same time he was tempted to run a finger along the exposed skin on her throat. He felt the tightening in his groin. There was something about her, always had been, but clearly from her rigid pose and the body language screaming *don't come near me*, he was top of her hate list at the moment.

'You do realise every person I take pictures of wants me to allow for some imagined defect. Even Ken wanted me to make sure he didn't have a double chin in any of his shots.'

Puzzled, Gabe watched the convulsive swallow as her throat dipped. With a couple of mouse clicks he enlarged the image of her.

'What's wrong with this?' The sun lit her glorious hair, her eyes were closed, those long limbs sprawled and elegant, and there was a faint smile on her face. A goddess guarding a secret, the keys of knowledge. In fact, 'Goddess with a Secret' is what he'd have called it.

She turned tortured eyes to him.

'I look ridiculous and I think you're being mean.'

'What? How?' Was she even seeing the same picture?

'I'm enormous, clumsy, and stupid. Bloody dwarfing the sofa.'

'No, you aren't.' What the hell was she talking about? She was taller than the average woman but she certainly wasn't big. She looked perfectly proportioned to him.

'Statuesque, Amazonian ... I've heard it all.'

'More of a Viking with that hair, I'd say,' he drawled, not wanting to give himself away.

'What?' She rounded on him, her eyes flashing, reminding him of exactly that. 'So you do think I'm big.'

'No, I think you're perfect. I think you're absolutely gorgeous in that picture and I think you've got a hang up that really isn't merited.' Unnecessarily harsh, but he was worried he might say something he ought not to.

'A hang up,' she said scornfully. 'Easy for you to say.'

Flummoxed, he didn't know what to say next. The taut silence stretched out between them and he reached out a tentative hand to touch her shoulder. She didn't move. The word 'stoic' came to mind when he examined her rigid profile.

'I didn't mean to upset you. I'll delete it now, if it means that much. Watch.' He picked the image up and put it into the recycling bin, noting that she was carefully scanning the rest of the thumbnails.

'There, done.'

'Thank you.' Her voice was tight and her fingers were clenched in a fist on her thigh. 'I suppose you think I'm silly.'

'I don't think you're silly at all. I think it's a shame that you can't see what I see.'

'You're in the minority, there.' There was bitterness in her voice. 'Ironic.'

'Why?'

'It was always a thing at school. Fe-fi-fo-fum. Giant. It got worse after ...'

He waited, seeing that she was battling her emotions.

'After I kissed you.'

'God, I'm sorry,' he said, although he wasn't even sure what he was apologising for.

'It wasn't your fault, was it? Evie saw us. Told everyone at school. And after that Fe-fi-fo-fum was a complete laughing stock. I left not long after.'

'Oh my God, Fiona. I'm so—'

She wheeled round, a flush of anger in her cheeks. 'Why are you apologising? *I* kissed *you*. You didn't ask me to. You seemed horrified.'

The words sank in, along with an ocean of regret. At the sight of her pale, pinched face, he felt he owed her the truth.

'I wasn't horrified,' he said slowly. 'Well, I was, but only because I was your teacher and it was inappropriate. I was horrified at what I'd done.'

'What *you'd* done?' She screwed her face up in confusion.

'Fi ...' He owed her the truth. 'I flirted with you. All week. You were gorgeous. I was ... girls were always interested. It was easy and you were ... naïve. But I was your teacher, six years older. It was inappropriate and I shouldn't have ...' Should he confess that he'd felt a connection? That even then her youthful enthusiasm had made him see things differently?

Almost absently she touched her lips. 'You mean ... I didn't imagine it?'

He bit his lip and summoned up the courage to look her in the eye. 'No. And if Evie hadn't come around the corner, who knows where that kiss might have ended up?'

Her eyes widened as the words hit. 'You ... you mean you really did ...'

217

'I kissed you back.'

'Oh.' Her mouth parted and for a second he couldn't take his eyes from her lips. He'd kissed a lot of women but he still remembered that kiss, not just because of the shock factor – it had come out of nowhere, an enthusiastic, if amateur, faceplant – but underneath it all there'd been the fizz of attraction. And now he wanted to kiss her again, to slant his lips over that wide mouth ... and he couldn't because she deserved so much better.

Chapter 17

Gabe's surprising revelation had shocked Fiona to the core and radically rewritten her historical foundations. She lay in bed reliving the moment, ten years falling away. Gabe had confirmed he *had* kissed her back. She *hadn't* imagine those brief touches, the husky tone when he spoke to her or those meaningful eye meets. Although, it had been a game to him ... But she could be excused for her naivety. He was so handsome, a hero in her eyes ... and considerably more experienced. Even though it hadn't meant much to him, she felt a thousand times lighter. He had kissed her back. He hadn't been horrified.

What would have happened if Evie hadn't come careering around the corner?

Nothing, she told herself, firmly imagining the embarrassment when they pulled apart. But he might have invited her out for a drink ...

And this way lies madness, she told herself. It was ancient history. A sliding-doors moment that was best left shut. Gabe was in love with Yumi, anyone could see that, and despite his nice comments about her, who would seriously choose big-boned Fiona over a tiny, delicate waif like that?

Eventually she slept, grateful to wake to a sunny spring morning, although not to the three texts from her mother which she wearily responded to. Today she was going to the teashop to take some photos of Setsuko at work.

Fiona stared at herself in the mirror as she brushed out the night's tangles. She'd been in too much of a tizz to re-plait it before bed or to pay much attention to her usual routine which was why her mouth felt so fuzzy this morning; she hadn't even cleaned her teeth. She examined her hair in her reflection. She had her dad's colouring, although apparently he'd been more of a redhead with Irish ancestors. Her mother had commented many a time that she should be grateful she wasn't a proper ginger but no one had ever said it was beautiful before. She tossed it over her shoulder and glared at herself, snatching up the brush to part it into its usual three strands. She studied herself again in the mirror and dropped the skein of hair in her hand. It wouldn't hurt to wear it loose, just for one day, and before she could change her mind, she hurried down to breakfast following the familiar smell of miso soup.

'I'm going to miss this when I go home,' she said to Haruka as she sat down for breakfast, inhaling the simple broth that she'd quickly become used to.

'You take some back. Very easy to make.' She grinned, suddenly mischievous. 'Comes in packet.'

Fiona laughed. 'Even I can manage a packet, although I might stick to my toast and Marmite.'

'Marmite?'

'It's a savoury spread that we put on bread. It's very unique to Britain. I'll send you some.' Fiona realised as she said it that she was going to miss Haruka and Setsuko and their calm, quiet ways. She fingered her phone in her pocket which had been vibrating with new text messages since she sat down.

'Thank you.' Haruka bowed and Fiona bowed back, realising that too had become an automatic response, along with not pointing at things.

'I would like to take some pictures of the garden.' Maybe she should build a garden like Haruka's at home, get her mother involved. It could be a joint project; it would bring them both solace.

'I would be most honoured.'

'Perhaps a few with you and Setsuko.' She didn't think she'd ever recapture the mother-daughter warmth of the picture she'd taken in the cherry blossom, but she'd like to take a picture of Haruka in her *kimono* in the dappled shade of the acers. A woman of mystery and wisdom. Fiona smiled at the image. 'Yes, one of you in your *kimono*.' She nodded to the traditional dress that Haruka was wearing in preparation for another tea ceremony later that morning.

'Now?'

'Yes. That would be great,' said Fiona surprised by Haruka's alacrity. Setsuko hadn't been keen on having her picture taken until Fiona had explained that they would be working shots rather than posed. The light today would be perfect and she could fit it in before the minibus arrived with the tourists. 'I'll grab my camera.'

Haruka was the perfect model, pottering about in the garden, trimming the bonsai, sweeping up leaves, totally indifferent to Fiona's camera and the frequent buzz of her phone. The shot of her, her slender slight frame bent over as she tended to one of her bonsai, mirrored by the bend in the trunk of the delicate acer beside her was perfect. Rather than fearing the exhibition, Fiona realised that she was now looking forward to it. She wanted people to see these pictures and share the joy she'd found in the immense variety of the country. She had a title in mind. *People of Japan.*

'I must go prepare for the tea ceremony,' said Haruka with one of her small neat bows.

She paused, 'Today ... your hair, it is very beautiful in the sunshine.' She leaned forward and stroked it with a fond smile. 'You should wear it down more often. It brightens your eyes. Lifts the soul. It is the *kintsugi* of your soul, the golden glue that brings a pot back to its whole.'

Fiona stared after her, a little spooked by the woman's insight. Gabe's revelation last night had mended something. A little part of her that had festered for far too long. She swung her long hair back off her shoulder. *Kintsugi*, golden glue. She liked that.

Rather than return to the house, she stayed in the garden, sitting on the *engawa*, dangling her feet over the edge and listening to the water and the strains of music drifting over from the teashop.

Which was where Gabe found her half an hour later. Without a word he sat down next to her, their legs dangling companionably together.

'How are you today?'

'Fine,' she said warily, hoping he wasn't going to bring things up again.

'I got the pictures of Ken off and the picture desk is delighted with them. I thought you might want to know.'

'That's good.'

'They're interested in me going to LA to take pictures of David Beckham.' He actually sounded excited.

'Wow.'

'Yeah. I've not had a really big commission like that for a while. Thanks.'

'Why are you thanking me?'

'You made a difference.'

'What, holding the light reflector at the right angle?'

'Exactly.'

She rolled her eyes at his silliness, relaxing a little. Friends would be good. If she could be friends with Gabe. She liked him a lot more now than she had when she arrived.

'And I also came to tell you that Kaito has fixed up a trip to Mount Fuji for us. The day after tomorrow, which is good because the forecast for the next few days is sunny and bright. Otherwise the view of the peak can be shrouded in cloud. We're going to stay near Lake Kawaguchiko, which is very scenic anyway, so you'll get lots of shots there.' Gabe was gabbling which was not a Gabe thing to do. It was rather endearing.

'Brilliant. I don't think I could get away with not having Fuji in the exhibition. It's such an iconic landmark.'

'And many times photographed. I'll be interested to see the Hanning take on it.'

She gave him a suspicious look.

'I'm serious. You've got a good eye. You've always had good eye.'

'Thank you.' She rubbed at the knee of her jeans, knowing there was a subtext here and he was referring to last night's conversation. A truce. And she was grateful for his subtle permission for the two of them to move on without having to say anything more.

'I'll pick you up the day after tomorrow. I've got stuff to do tomorrow. You don't mind, do you?'

Pleased that he'd bothered to ask, she shook her head.

'No, I promised Mayu I'd go to her Robot Restaurant and I want to take pictures of Setsuko in the shop. I've got plenty to do.'

'Great. I'll come here at nine; it's about a two-hour train journey and you'll need an overnight bag as Kaito's arranged for us to stay for two nights in a hotel in Fujiyoshida, near the lake. It's been a while since I've been out there. I'm quite looking forward to it. And now I've surprised myself by saying that.'

'Goodness, are you ill?' she asked, still getting used to the idea of a truce. Of moving on.

'I think I might be,' he grinned at her and she couldn't help smiling back at him. 'Don't get used to it.'

'I'm not planning to. I'm sure you'll be back to your usual old curmudgeonly self very soon.'

'Old? Less of the old. I'm only thirty-four, you know. Do you really think of me as that much older?'

'No, not really. I feel older than my own mother and she can give you a good ten years.'

'How is she?'

'Complaining of chest pains today. Eventually I told her to take some indigestion tablets.'

'Harsh.'

'She had an Indian takeaway last night. They never agree with her. She's been texting me since seven o'clock this morning. I only twigged a little while ago.'

She took her phone out of her pocket and sure enough there were two new texts. 'What is she like?'

'Persistent. You should ignore her.'

'It's not that easy. I'm her daughter.'

'Yes, but it's not as if she's particularly old or infirm.'

'Gabe, I don't want to get into that now.'

'Okay. You left your hair loose. It's lovely.' Surprised by the abrupt comment, she blushed to the very roots of said lovely hair as he picked up a strand and rubbed it between his fingers and thumb. 'In this light it's like burnished bronze.'

'Haruka said it was like gold. *Kintsugi*, she said.'

Gabe raised an eyebrow and his eyes travelled over her face, a gentle smile touching his lips. 'She has a way of saying things, knowing things. She's ... very special. Even though she's a bossy old bat, I'm very fond of her. She ... she saved me. Saved my body at least. My soul still needs work, according to her.'

'When you broke up with Yumi.'

He winced. 'Not my finest hour. But then, how many people

deal well with public humiliation and absolute betrayal. By rights I should tell her she's made her bed but I think she's lonely and ... I feel sorry for her. She's so vulnerable. People think she's a lot tougher than she really is. She says I'm the only one who really understands her. I guess I still feel responsible for her.'

But that's her husband's job, thought Fiona, but as he stared off into the distance, her heart went out to him. He was the one who seemed lost and lonely. For some reason she put her hand down on his, instinctively wanting to offer comfort and her heart was gladdened when he turned his palm up and linked his fingers with hers.

She didn't know why he was holding her hand or why she was letting him but it felt nice. Part of her, broken for so long, had mended overnight.

'I didn't sleep with her,' he said in a low voice infused with desperate urgency.

'I know.' She swallowed hard, shocked by the sudden hot, sweet release of relief.

'She blows hot and cold but I know if I did ... I'd hate myself even more.'

At the pain in his voice, she squeezed his hand, feeling a lot older than him and wanting to put her arms around him. To tell him he deserved to be loved. But somehow she didn't think he'd believe her.

Chapter 18

'God, I'm knackered,' muttered Gabe with a huge yawn as they settled into their seats on the train to Fujiyoshida. 'I was up half the night negotiating with *The Sunday Times* and organising the Beckham shoot. It's a definite.' He picked up his camera and removed it from the case, fiddling with a few buttons before setting it down on the seat beside him.

'That's amazing,' she whispered. 'Well done. And don't keep yawning, you'll set me off; I'm a shadow of my former self after yesterday.'

He grinned at her. 'How was the Robot Restaurant?'

'Mayu had the time of her life,' she murmured and then pulled a face. 'My eyeballs were burnt out. All that neon and flashing lights. My poor retinas could be scarred for life. Have you seen those things? Some of them are downright terrifying.'

He laughed. 'Why do you think I didn't take you?'

The visit to the restaurant had definitely been one of the more bizarre experiences of Fiona's life. Huge *samurai* warrior robots riding glass horses. An enormous tyrannosaurus rex with Barbarella-style dancers in silver and turquoise lamé dancing on its back or at one point in its mouth. People riding

Pokémon-style monsters shooting laser canon streams of neon light. It wasn't something she was going to forget in a hurry.

'I'll probably include a shot for the exhibition ... to show the contrasts between the modern and the traditional and I got some great shots of Mayu for Setsuko and Haruka. She's quite a wild child, that one. I always thought Japanese children were supposed to be well behaved.'

'I think Mayu lets her hair down when her folks aren't around but like most Japanese kids, she's very respectful and deferential to her parents.'

'Well, I got some pictures of her that aren't quite so wild as well. If you don't mind, I'd like to work in the studio to create an album of pictures as a thank you when I leave.'

'Creep,' said Gabe, stifling another yawn. 'They'll bloody love that. No wonder Haruka thinks you're the bee's knees ...'

'I think you're still her favourite.'

'I don't know why,' he slumped into his seat, rubbing at the pale shadows underneath his eye.

'Because you adore her.'

'She's a grumpy, demanding old woman.'

'Gabe!' protested Fiona, her voice rising, and immediately she lowered it, glancing around at the other passengers. Luckily no one seemed to have noticed her quiet-carriage faux pas. 'She's not at all.'

'You've only seen her good side.' But despite his quiet harrumph and fierce whisper, she could see the gleam in his eye.

'That's because I'm the perfect guest.' Fiona grinned at him.

'Who told you that?'

'Setsuko.'

'See, I said you were a creep.' He folded his arms and leant his head back against the headrest.

She rolled her eyes at him and pulled out a guide book.

'And a swot,' he whispered, his eyes closed as he nudged her arm.

'I like to know where I'm going, don't you?'

'No, I like it to be an adventure. Besides I've been before.'

'To Lake Kawaguichiko?'

'Not there. I've actually walked up Mount Fuji. But you can only do that in July and August. You'll have to come back.'

'You know ... I might do that. I feel like I've barely scratched the surface. Every time I talk to Setsuko or Haruka they tell me something fascinating about the philosophy or the culture of the country. There's so much ... it's an amazing place.'

Gabe opened his eyes and turned his head against the headrest, studying her face, a slow smile spreading over his, as if sleepiness had dulled his senses. Her heart turned over at the drowsy warmth of his expression.

Then he reached for the camera on his knee and before she could protest took a couple of quick shots.

'Gabe!'

'Sorry, just had an idea for a shot ... on a train. Wanted to see if it would work. The blur in the background, you know. Arty sort of picture.'

'Oh,' she leaned back into her seat, eyeing him warily. He smiled at her, still sleepy and a touch dopey.

'What?'

'You're something else.' He continued to give her that gentle smile which made her heart miss a beat. 'Very good at reminding me of things that I'd forgotten. Stuff that I take for granted.' He closed his eyes again and for a moment she thought he was going to sleep.

There was a touch on her hand and she looked down to see him threading his fingers through hers. 'I'd forgotten what a special place this country is,' he murmured. 'Haruka. She's been trying to ... to remind me for a while. I wasn't paying attention. When I first came I was fascinated by those contrasts, by that spirituality. I lost my way for a while.'

'And now?' Fiona watched his face, saw the regret lining his mouth.

'Tupperware,' he murmured, or at least it sounded like that. It was obviously some Japanese word.

She waited for him to explain but all he did was smile that gentle smile at her, squeeze her hand, and then he leaned his head back against the headrest and went to sleep.

Watching someone sleep was supposed to be creepy and she knew it was an invasion of privacy, although she was pretty sure Gabe wouldn't have any such reserve. He'd probably be taking photos. It didn't excuse it ... but she couldn't help herself savouring the rare moment of unadulterated pleasure. He was, and always had been, a beautiful man with that thick, dark wavy hair swept back from his forehead. It brushed his collar but she'd never seem him fuss or fiddle with it. His eyebrows were slightly paler, untamed, over that strong brow. It was a masculine face rescued from harshness by those deep, intense eyes. Fiona sighed. He was gorgeous even despite the slight purple bruises shadowing his eyes which were fringed by the thick resting-spider-leg lashes. This close she could see the liquorice-black bristles breaking out over his chin and very faint freckles on his tanned skin, one in the corner of his mouth that for an uninhibited moment she wanted to lick ... which was so not standard Fiona behaviour. Gabe brought out something in her. A yearning which was nothing like that desperate infatuation before.

And what was with the hand-holding? She wasn't complaining ... but what did it mean? God, she was out of her depth. She'd had a couple of dates with people ... lost her virginity on one because she felt obliged to go through with it and had wanted rid of it. Went out with a guy called Olly who'd wanted her to move in with him but it had felt like settling for second best. Since then, she hadn't even been friends with a man – well, apart from her friends from Copenhagen but they didn't really count as one had a girl-friend, one was gay, and one was old enough to be her father. Her life had always been singularly lacking in male influences. Perhaps that was why she'd fallen so hard for Gabe the first time. He was the first man who'd ever shown any interest in her. If her father hadn't died, maybe things would have been different, or if her mother had remarried. Automatically, her hand slipped into her pocket to toy with the little *netsuke*.

Oh hell, her mother. Abandoning the tiny figure to the depths of her pocket, she began to dig in her bag for her phone. This morning had been such a rush, she hadn't sent her usual morning WhatsApp. No doubt there'd be a dozen messages by now. Damn. The inside pocket of her rucksack, where she normally kept her phone was empty. Rifling through the bag, she checked the other pockets. What had she done with it? She could have sworn she'd zipped it in there this morning. It must be back at Haruka's because she hadn't taken it out or used it on the journey.

Despite worrying about it, she quickly realised there was nothing she could actually do, not while Gabe was sleeping. Once he was awake, she'd ask if she could borrow his phone to text her mum and explain that she'd left her phone behind.

Somehow she dozed off, and when she woke she blinked furiously. The sunlight streamed in through the windows and she turned away, about to dig into her bag for her sunglasses when Gabe suddenly picked up his camera and stepped out of his seat into the aisle.

'There, like that. Don't move.'

Before she could even think about moving she heard the tell-tale click, click, whirr of the shutter.

'What are you doing?' she asked, horrified and glancing around the carriage. Luckily it seemed to have emptied at the last station.

'Taking pictures,' he grinned, the very devil of mischief peeping out of his eyes.

Lifting her chin slightly, she rolled her eyes. 'I can see that. But ...'

'Yes. Yes. Perfect.' And once again she heard the electronic purr of the camera.

'Gabe, stop it.' She reached out towards the camera.

'Why?'

'You know I don't like having my picture taken. I look hideous in—'

'I thought we'd cleared all that up, my lovely Valkyrie.'

Spluttering would have been undignified, so Fiona just stared at him.

'That's better.' He grinned, raising his camera again, talking while he snapped. 'I've decided to ignore you. You won't look hideous in my pictures,' he said with an arrogant tilt of his head.

She winced. Maybe not to him who was more interested in lines and planes, angles and shadows. She wasn't unrealistic enough to aspire to being a great beauty or anything, but seeing her own face always reminded her that she wasn't anything special. Online she might have thousands of followers, and post interesting blogs, but the reality was that behind *Hanning's Half Hour* was a very dull, ordinary person.

She realised Gabe was studying her through half-lidded eyes with the intensity that made her imagine he could see all the way through to her soul and the wretched lack of self-confidence writhing away in there. It was as much as she could do not to clench her stomach and tuck into herself like a turtle.

'Turn your head again and lift your chin an inch.'

'No, please don't take photos of me.'

'Do as you're told,' snapped Gabe.

'Why?' she turned back to him with a flash of anger.

'Because this shot could be a masterpiece and we'll never know, if you don't.'

And because it had been ingrained in her that photography

was capturing that one moment in time that might never happen again, she turned her head and lifted her chin as everything inside shrank with dismay.

'Fiona,' said Gabe gently and she turned her eyes towards him, touched by the understanding in his voice. For a moment she could have sworn his face softened before he lifted the camera and took a succession of quick shots.

'Look away for me.' With a disdainful, resigned sigh, she did as she was told. 'There's my Valkyrie.'

'Will you stop calling me that,' she spluttered, the unexpected term bringing a snort of denial. 'No one's ever called me that before.'

'No one else can see it,' said Gabe, lowering the camera, his voice silken. 'Pull your top down a little.'

'What?'

He took no notice of her horrified tone and leaned forward, doing it for her, tugging the off-the-shoulder top a little lower, but still within the bounds of modesty with a capital M.

'Gabe!'

Too late, her collar bone was exposed.

'That's better, it frames your shoulders.'

'My neck's too long. I'm too big, remember,' she blurted out, her skin prickling in sudden awareness. 'Mum calls me a giraffe.'

Gabe lowered his camera and with careful, deliberate moves laid it on the seat beside him. She felt the icy anger in the careful controlled movements. He leaned forward, his eyes meeting hers and she almost flinched from the storm of anger in them.

'She's wrong. You're ...' Lifting a hand, he ran a finger along the length of her collar bone, the calloused pad a sandpaper brush that coaxed all her nerve endings into life. She raised her chin and swallowed as she met his gaze, uncertain but unable to stop herself.

He smiled, 'Perfect. The other day I regretted not taking pictures of you at the tea ceremony.' Those blue eyes bored into her, so close now she could see the striations of blue were flecked with navy. 'And I regretted ... not kissing you.' She caught her breath as his fingers slid up her neck with infinitesimal slowness, a reverent exploration of the landscape of her skin and tendons, a determined pressure against her throat as if he wanted to catalogue every cell, sinew, and muscle. Unable to help herself, she tilted her head offering him a longer line, letting the breath slip out as his fingers stroked the underside of her chin. Her mouth parted in longing and invitation as one knuckle skirted her mouth. It sent blood coursing down between her legs, the touch far more sexually explicit than a mere kiss. The hoarse intake of his breath as his eyes maintained their hold told her that he was as affected as she was. Satisfaction warmed her as she wondered whether he would kiss her. Hope and trepidation warred. Now his hand cupped her chin and he rubbed a thumb across her lower lip. Instinct and desire brought the tip of her tongue to touch and taste his salty skin.

Every part of her ached. Ached to be kissed, to be held, to be held close, to be held against Gabe's chest. And she'd felt this before. The sharp dig of passion and longing brought memories tumbling and ploughing like an avalanche spilling down a mountain. Oh yes, she'd felt this before. But this time came the freedom, the knowledge, that she hadn't made a fool of herself. Gabe had kissed her back. Had *wanted* to kiss her.

'Fi?' Gabe's voice came from far away and she saw the concern in the lines crinkling around his eyes, his fingers tracing her mouth.

'Yes,' she said, lifting her chin, channelling warrior-princess vibes for all she was worth.

He stared at her, hunger in those beautiful blue eyes.

'I can't remember … but I think it's my turn to kiss you.'

One finger brushed her lower lip and then he leaned in, his breath carrying the faint tang of coffee. Her heart hammered against her ribs as, with a feather-light touch, his lips skimmed over hers. This was really happening and she could scarcely breathe as hope and anticipation bubbled up. Frozen into her seat, she felt his lips settle, pressing against her mouth, and heard his tiny huff of satisfaction. Her mouth opened under his with a small sigh.

It felt as if she'd been waiting for this for the last ten years. Warm and firm, his lips explored hers, teasing and coaxing. She wasn't sure who moaned – possibly her – but this was quite the most delicious thing and she wasn't backing away from it. Not this time. Boldly she kissed him back, sliding an arm around his neck. The rest of the world receded and there was only his mouth on hers. When he finally pulled away, he rested his forehead against hers, his fingers gliding over her cheekbone.

'Valkyrie,' he murmured. 'It was worth waiting for.'

'I'm not sure this is entirely appropriate,' she said, dazed and trying to grab on to normality instead of drifting off into this lovely fairy tale. 'If the Japanese don't like people talking on the train, I'm not sure kissing is going to go down terribly well.'

'Good job this bit of the carriage is empty then,' said Gabe, stealing another kiss. 'Because this is the best train journey I've had for quite a while.'

'We can't kiss for the whole journey; it's still another half hour to Fujiyoshida.'

'Why not? I haven't kissed you for ten years, that's a lot of kisses to catch up on.'

And when he put it like that, Fiona couldn't think of a single reason why not.

In fact, all she could think was that Gabe Burnett was kissing her and that the butterflies in her stomach had dived, soared, and jumped right out of her stomach and were now swirling around her head making everything spin in a dream-like way. Flushed and heated, she also felt relief. No pulling away in disgust at her inexperience. Kissing Gabe was every bit as wonderful as she could possibly have imagined. Her insides seem to have liquified with pure delight, leaving her molten and pliable. She, Fiona Hanning, was kissing Gabe Burnett! Pressing her lips to his, silken, soft, firm and oh so delicious ... Then her heart almost burst when he cupped her face with all the tenderness of a thousand rom-coms.

They didn't quite kiss all the way to the next stop but it was a close thing.

When the train slowed to pull in to the station, they hastily gathered their bags with surreptitious grins and made their way to the doors. It was as they stood in front of them that Fiona gave a guilty start.

'Gabe, I've left my phone behind.' Now it sounded as if she meant she'd lost it but before she could clarify her meaning, the doors opened and Gabe took her bag from her and helped her down without even acknowledging her comment.

'I think I've left it at Haruka's.' Peering up and down the platform he sought out the exit.

'Well at least you know you haven't lost it,' he said. 'Ah, this way.' He led the way to the right, obviously more cognisant with the Japanese than she'd realised as the English translation was in a much smaller and harder-to-read font.

He didn't seem the least bit bothered by the information.

'Would you mind if I borrowed your phone to text my mother?'

Gabe strode on as if he hadn't heard. 'Let's find a taxi.'

Once in the back of the cab, with her bag on her lap, she asked again. 'Your phone. Please can I borrow it?'

'No,' said Gabe.

'What?' His implacable answer shocked her. 'I'll give you the money,' she said with a touch of indignation.

'No,' he said mildly. 'I don't care about the money.'

'Then why not?'

He turned to her. 'Because then your mum will have my number and she'll be texting me every five minutes instead of you and that's the last thing I want.'

'She wouldn't.' Even as she said it, Fiona knew she would. Even so ... he could have been a bit more helpful. Well, if he was going to be like that ... It took a lot for her not to fold her arms and pout. Instead she lifted her head, pursed her lips, and stared out of the window.

'The warrior princess is back.' His fingers stroked the underside of her chin. 'Don't sulk. If she's worried about you, she can phone Haruka. And Haruka can phone me.'

From under her lashes she peeped up at him and read intractability all over his face. 'Come on, Fi. You said yourself she cries wolf all the time. This will give you a proper break. Two whole days away from the tyranny of the text.'

With a sigh, she glared at him but there wasn't much heat behind it. 'I guess you're right.'

He winked at her. 'I have ways of taking your mind off it.'

Her wretched body responded to that by warming up in places that had no place warming, kickstarting the gentle hum of desire that had never really gone away since that initial kiss on the train. It also ignited a debate that had begun to rage as soon as they'd gathered their bags: should she sleep with him ...

Not that he'd asked or anything.

Chapter 19

'Well, this is me.' Fiona dropped her bag and fumbled with the key card as Gabe waited politely.

The door swung open and she stood there wondering whether to invite him in or watch him walk up the corridor to his room, which by her calculation was another seven doors down.

A hotel room was a hotel room, wasn't it?

'Want to see?'

'I'm sure mine will probably be the same,' he drawled with a knowing smirk on his face.

'Yes,' she said. 'Right. Well then.'

As if he knew what was going through her mind, he just stood there.

She glared at him, snatched up her bag and marched three steps into the room before she heard the door shut. She turned around and there was Gabe who must have moved with some kind of preternatural vampire hero speed because he was right in front of her, his hand reaching to cup her face.

'You're adorable. Confused and dorky. I like it.'

And with that series of charming compliments, he laid his lips on hers and kissed her soundly until her knees started to wobble and the bag slid out of her hands with a thud that echoed the kick to her heart.

'Oh my.' She finally managed to breathe when they both pulled away.

'Oh my indeed. Kissing you is becoming kind of addictive.'

'Mmm,' she said, her eyes immediately going to his lips.

'And you're going to have to stop doing that.'

'Doing what?' Her eyes lifted to his, full of innocence even though inside she savoured a distinct thrill of feminine satisfaction and she deliberately dropped them again.

'That. When you look at me as if … It turns me on.'

Eek. Straight talking. Warrior-princess time. She lifted her chin and stared straight into his eyes. 'Me too.'

There. The gloves were off and she couldn't help a sultry smile.

Gabe lifted an eyebrow. The charged silence hummed through the room. They were still standing in the corridor area next to a run of wardrobes.

'You haven't even seen the view yet,' he said, gazing over her shoulder.

An imp of mischief took up residence. 'I'm quite happy with this one,' she said suddenly empowered, all female and, for the first time in her life, sexy. She lifted up on her tiptoes and gently kissed him back.

'You're killing me here. I was giving you the chance to go slow.'

'Who says I want to go slow? Ten years, remember?'

'Sometimes there's a lot of pleasure in the build-up,' he raised those sinfully sexy eyebrows and her insides turned to mush. How the hell could eyebrows be sexy? But they were.

He grasped her shoulders and gently spun her round.

'Oh!' she said. 'Oh. Wow. That's ...'

He stepped behind her and put his arms around her, pulling her back against his chest, and then propelled her forward to the huge plate-glass doors leading out to a balcony. 'Some view, eh?' He nuzzled her neck, before sliding his way up until they stood cheek to cheek, and for once she was glad she was tall and could stand like this with him. Okay, he had to duck a little but it felt solid and nice standing there together gazing at the perfect snow-capped mountain.

'I guess that's part of its allure,' said Fiona after they'd been standing in silent contemplation for a while. 'It's the exact pointy peak a child would draw of a mountain. You know, like how houses are always square with a door in the middle. It's a proper mountain shape. With the snow cap on the top.'

Gabe pulled her tighter against him and let out a light laugh. 'You have the most wonderful habit of making me see things differently. I've seen Fuji hundreds of times and I've never seen it in that way.'

'I think I'm going to have to settle for a fairly unoriginal shot of the mountain,' sighed Fiona. That was the problem with iconic landscapes; it was hard to find a new angle.

'Don't give up yet. We've got a couple of days here. What

do you fancy doing? I thought this evening we could for dinner in an *izakaya*.'

'What's an izzy ...?'

'*Izakaya*,' he said slowly. 'It's basically a Japanese pub where they serve food, a bit like a tapas bar.'

'Okay. That sounds good.'

'Why don't I go and unpack and then we could go out, stretch our legs, do a bit of exploring?'

'Sounds like a plan,' she agreed, a touch relieved that they could be normal with each other and that the sexual heat had tamped down.

He kissed her and headed for the door. 'And tomorrow I think I'll arrange a surprise for you.' Those beautiful eyes darkened with mischief and something else that made her heart clench.

'Oh, will I like it?'

'Definitely.' He smiled and left.

Once the door had closed behind him, she sank onto the bed. She brushed the end of her plait across her palm, relishing the flutter of excitement that danced low in her belly.

Crossing to the window she stared out at the sleeping volcano. It had been there for thousands of years while puny humans came and went. Life was ephemeral and there was beauty in that transience, as Haruka had taught her.

She tilted her head, stretching out the knot at the back of her neck. *In for a penny, in for a pound.* Being in Japan, being with Gabe. This was a once-in-a-lifetime experience. She didn't expect him to fall in love with her or anything and she was going in with her eyes wide open. After this week, she'd probably never see him again. If she went in prepared, he was hardly going to break her heart, was he?

The paths and steps, all three hundred and ninety-eight of them on the way up to the Chureito Pagoda, wound through cherry blossom just coming into bud and their perfume filled the air which was some distraction from the ache in her thighs … and in other places. Every now and then nerves would start jangling at the thought of *later*. It was a relief to be outside in the fresh air even if Gabe did keep taking her hand and rubbing his thumb over hers.

'That's some climb,' said Gabe as they stopped in front of the pagoda. Around them, birdsong filled the spring air.

'But worth it.' She must have taken nearly fifty photos on the walk up here. It was the archetypal view of Mount Fuji through the cherry blossoms and the clear blue sky dappled with a few picturesquely pure white clouds was absolutely perfect. There were a dozen pictures she could use, although none of them were particularly original. She'd snapped a sneaky one of him, arms aloft as he shucked out of his sweater. It was a sudden instinct spurred on by the thought that in another week she would be back at home and this might be all she had to remember him by.

She turned to take in the five-tiered pagoda painted in red with its green tiled roofs tilted up at north, south, east, and west. It was like an elaborate Christmas decoration and the bells on each corner tinkled rhythmically in the wind. 'Isn't it pretty?'

Gabe wrinkled his nose.

'Come on. It's beautiful.'

'Very Japanese.'

'That's why I'm here. Look at those bells, how cute are they? And the spire on the top.'

'Hmm.'

She nudged him with her arm. 'Admit it, it's beautiful up here. I'm not moving until you do.'

A wry smile twisted his lips and he leaned forward and tugged at her plait. 'You should have this loose; it would be beautiful in this sunshine. The light picks up all the nuances of the colours: amber, gold, umber, ochre, sienna.'

'There speaks a photographer,' she said batting his hand away. 'And it would be full of tangles in no time.' Despite her pragmatism, she couldn't help a little sigh inside at the words.

'Want some water?' He unscrewed the cap and handed it to her. When she dribbled, before she could swipe away the cool track of water, he'd lifted his thumb and wiped the drip upwards to her mouth, his thumb grazing her lips, holding her gaze the whole time. She felt the heat gather again and pushed his hand away. Was he doing this on purpose? The constant small touches? Spontaneous combustion was definitely an option if he kept this up. Deliberately, she wiped her mouth with a firm hand to remove his lingering touch.

'Come on, let's go up to the top.'

'Yes, boss,' he teased, taking her hand again and slowing her down by pulling her against him and sneaking another kiss.

With unaccustomed boldness, she lifted her chin and turned to him. 'What's changed?'

'The Haruka effect I think. And you. At the tea ceremony

I realised I've been treading water for too long and being with you has made me remember why I love photography. It's like I've woken up and life is worth living again. I've been a self-pitying bastard for too long. That answer the question?'

She tilted her head to one side considering him. 'It'll do.'

At the top there was a magnificent photo opportunity of both the pagoda and the mountain which acted as a bit of a distraction but she was very aware that Gabe was never far from her side as she took lots of shots. A great many of them were simply an excuse to try and keep her mind on the job and not on what might happen tonight. Despite the plethora of pictures of Mount Fuji's snow-capped top resplendent in a clear blue sky with one picturesque white puff of cloud floating on the horizon beyond, none of them made her particularly happy as she sat down on a nearby bench, positioned to take in the view, in order to review her shots.

'They're too postcardy,' she muttered, flicking through the viewfinder, pulling face after disgruntled face.

'You're worrying too much.' Gabe sat down on the bench next to her, his arm casually draped along the wooden back, denim-clad legs crossed and his face tilted up to the sun. 'Why not just enjoy being here?'

'I know,' she sighed, intoxicated by the glorious view, 'you're right.'

Enjoy being here. He *was* right. She should grab every opportunity with both hands, because at the end of the trip she'd have to go back to reality.

'I am right. I'm your mentor, remember?' Devilment danced in his eyes. She pushed her hands into her pockets, clenching

247

her fingers tight. Oh God, he was so much more experienced than her. She was playing with fire. He was way out of her league.

'You ...' her words dried and she turned away, a fierce blush fire flaring across her cheeks.

Gentle hands cupped her chin.

'Fi?'

She swallowed.

His blue eyes had darkened. 'I'm sorry. I didn't mean to tease.' He dropped a soft kiss on her mouth. 'You're such a breath of fresh air.'

She almost sobbed. 'Exactly. I'm hopelessly inexperienced. I bet you've had loads of ... of ... of lovers.'

Had she really blurted that out? She sounded even more gauche than normal. It didn't seem to faze him, of course it didn't. Lovers. Sparks showered inside her at the very thought of it. But why not? Enjoy being here. Take everything that was offered. Live while she was here. With a smile, she promised herself she would do exactly that from here on in.

With a rueful grin he shook his head. 'I'm not sure about the loads. You're making me feel old. The last few years, I've been quite discerning. After ... after Yumi, there really hasn't been anyone that I ... that I wanted to be with. Not like this. A few hook-ups. Nothing serious.' He winced. 'And Yumi kind of puts people off; she's still quite proprietary but she doesn't mean it. I think it's just habit. She was used to thinking of me as hers and I haven't felt the urge to kiss someone every five minutes ... well ... not since a blue-eyed warrior princess appeared on the scene.'

He lifted a hand and smoothed away the wisps of hair dancing around her forehead in the light breeze. 'Although I wasn't keen on you at first.'

'I know,' said Fiona with a wicked grin. 'You made it quite clear.'

'Nothing personal. I just didn't want to mentor anyone ... It was a chore and a drag. I was completely absorbed in my own little world ... until you challenged me, told me I was second rate and starting flashing your legs at impressionable young Japanese men and, worst of all, threatened to set Haruka on me.'

She giggled, light hearted and carefree.

'Should I even be kissing you, I wonder. Once again, I'm your mentor. In a position of responsibility.'

'Bollocks,' said Fiona rudely, although inside her heart was dancing, an energetic earth-shaking little jig, making the rest of her a little jittery and off kilter. 'I'm an adult now.'

Gabe laughed. 'You know how to spoil a romantic moment. Bollocks, she says while I'm trying to tell her that she's the first person I've wanted to ... to kiss,' he amended with a look that brought a searing blush to her cheeks, 'in over a year.'

'Oh. Right. Yes.' She thunked herself on the forehead with the heel of her hand. 'See, I told you. I'm not very good at this stuff.'

'You're fine. It's one of the things I most like about you. Your honesty. Life is too short for playing games. And for worrying about those photos. We've got the whole of tomorrow and part of the day afterif need be, we can always extend our stay. It's a very nice hotel.'

Her lips curved in a smile at the loaded meaning in his words.

'Okay.'

'I thought tomorrow we could go up the ropeway to Kawaguchiko Tenjozan Park. That's an excellent viewing spot and then in the afternoon we can take a bus or a train out to Lake Kawaguchiko. Maybe take a boat out.'

'A boat sounds lovely. The lake sounds perfect. Ropeway. Hmm, that sounds adventurous.'

'It's a cable car. That's what the Japanese call them.'

'Ah, I see. I guess that makes sense.'

'If you think of dirty great steel cables as ropes, yes.'

'Maybe I can get a shot of industry and nature,' mused Fiona and Gabe kissed her.

'Stop thinking about it. A picture will come. And there'll be plenty of opportunities. Now, did I tell you I've managed to book a surprise tomorrow evening? You're going to love it.' Again, those eyes danced wickedly.

Her eyes widened.

'Yes. Nine o'clock. Tomorrow evening.'

'That's ...' her voice was still strangled. He kissed her again.

'I'll be gentle with you. I promise.'

She lifted her chin. He wasn't having this all his own way. She might be inexperienced but she wasn't without guts. Gabe had called her a Valkyrie after all. 'The thing is ... will I be gentle with you?'

Chapter 20

Fiona had never been a clothes person and now she was panicking about what to wear this evening. Gabe had her dropped at the door to her room at five o'clock with another of those long lingering sexy kisses that promised so much before he withdrew with another smouldering smile and sauntered off to his room.

She deliberately didn't watch him go; he was too damn sure of himself. The bugger knew he was gorgeous. And in big demand. He had a conference call booked with a magazine in Tokyo to discuss a few upcoming shoots and some work to do, all of which reminded her that he was a hugely successful photographer and in some ways a minor celebrity in his own right. He was used to mixing with the rich, famous and super glamorous.

Oh heck, what was she going to wear? She stared at her hopelessly inadequate wardrobe lying pathetically in front of her in her case, as if mere staring might magic up a new addition.

She rummaged through it trying to remember everything she'd packed and dislodged a pale blue camisole vest. Avril.

She grinned. Avril had insisted on a shopping expedition and she'd put the new items at the bottom of her case and completely forgotten about them, perhaps because they weren't the sort of things she'd normally wear.

There was the navy-blue linen jumpsuit, belted at the waist, which she thought made her look like a plumber's assistant but Avril had insisted if she wore it with a cami underneath and a few buttons left open, would look like a sexy ninja girl along with a butter-soft khaki leather jacket, which Fiona secretly adored but she'd never dared wear because it was the sort of thing that other girls, with hot dates like Gabe, wore.

She shook out the jumpsuit and hung it on a hanger in the bathroom. It wasn't too badly creased and a steamy shower should help. Next she reviewed the leather jacket, trying it on and peering over her shoulder at her reflection in the mirror trying to channel sexy vibes. The jacket was great, but she wasn't sure about herself, though she really wanted to look like the sort of girl Gabe would be seen with.

A quick shower revived her and she focused on drying her hair, before changing into the new outfit. The butterflies were gathering in her chest like swallows at sunset and when she finally dared look in the mirror they took off with a great rush. With a smile she nodded at herself; for once she did look like the sort of girl who wore leather jackets. Through judicious wielding of her brush and the hairdryer, she'd managed to achieve curls in her hair and the touch of mascara, smoky eye shadow, and rose-pink lipstick – the sum total of her limited make-up arsenal – made her seem … well, quite striking really. Those butterflies were going berserk now. Was she really doing this?

Gabe's sharp knock at the door made her jump. She gave herself one last check in the mirror. 'You're doing this. Warrior Princess. Valkyrie,' she mouthed at her own image, lifting her chin before she turned and snatched up her bag and the new leather jacket.

Dealing with publicists and their neurotic clients was enough to wind anyone up and Gabe had just finished the last phone call of the day. Despite being a good size, this hotel room felt small and claustrophobic and he was about ready to punch someone. He'd left himself ten minutes to shower which he desperately needed to wash away some of the frustration. Why did publicists think that bloody hotel rooms or suites were the only place for a photo shoot? Didn't anyone want originality these days? He'd spent the last half hour trying to persuade the PR girl at the studios that were producing the umpteenth version of *Wolverine* that a shoot at London Zoo would make a dramatic backdrop. It wasn't as if he were proposing that the sodding actor got into the lion enclosure or posed with a tiger.

All the lovely anticipation that had built up over a morning of fresh air and mountain views had been wiped away and now he was irritable and cross. Hardly fair on Fiona. He paused, picturing her earlier today. She was lovely and she didn't deserve him in a cranky mood. In fact, she didn't deserve him full stop. Far too lovely, innocent and full of life. She deserved someone decent who still saw things through rosy lenses.

And he ought to be taking her to a nice restaurant, wining and dining her in style, but he was sick of those kinds of places. Of polite conversation and careful manners. Dinner with Yumi at Kikunoi had been dull, if he was honest. The food had been divine, no denying that. It was a fabulous restaurant. But it hadn't been fun. It had been grown up and stilted. Well mannered. Tonight he wanted the loud, raucousness of an *izakaya* – loud music, beer, and small bites. Casual and informal. In fact, he couldn't imagine Fiona in a posh restaurant. He mentally reviewed what he knew of her and what he'd observed of her – which was rather a lot, he realised –over the last ten days. Taking her to a restaurant like that would make her awkward and uncomfortable; he'd seen the way she hunkered down into herself sometimes when she wasn't sure about things or stood on one leg abstractedly rubbing the other behind it when she was a little lost or vulnerable. Or lifted her chin when she was being brave, which was more often than not. In fact, he realised, there were so many things he'd noticed about her, almost as if he'd been cataloguing her with the numerous photos he'd managed to take of her when she wasn't aware.

Suddenly he was keen to get going, to see Fiona. He smiled at himself in the mirror. Fiona. Oh, God, he looked positively goofy. Thinking about her seemed to have miraculously cleared his bad mood and turned him into a lovesick idiot. He glared at himself and picked up his card key. Lovesick idiot indeed. Men his age did not get lovesick, although the jury was probably out as to whether he was an idiot. Haruka often told him he was.

He knocked on Fiona's door with a pleasant buzz of anticipation. He was looking forward to spending the evening with
her ... bloody hell! His heart almost leapt out of his mouth
when the door opened. The golden hair rippled down over
her shoulders and her blue eyes popped, her pink lips mysteriously plumped. She was gorgeous, an earthy sex goddess
rolled into one.

And like an idiot – see, Haruka was right – all he could
do was stare at her as if he'd swallowed his tongue, which he
damn well nearly had done.

'You l-look ...' he swallowed.

She smiled. 'Thank you.'

He was truly grateful that she simply pulled her door to
and fell into step beside him because he had as much aplomb
as a sixteen-year-old on his first date.

By the time they reached the lift he'd recovered a little. No,
he hadn't. All he'd managed to do was pick up a skein of
golden hair and rub its softness between his fingers, inhaling
the apple-scented shampoo.

He took a deep breath and caught her smiling at her reflection in the mirror, both bemused and amused. There was no
doubt about it; he must seem like a complete idiot. He rolled
his eyes.

'Sorry, my usual *sang froid* has left the building. I like to
think I'm a bit smoother than this but ... you're gorgeous. I
like your hair down. It kind of took my breath away back
there.'

She laughed. 'It did ... I thought you were in pain at first.'

Gabe groaned and slapped his forehead. 'Great, spare

me my ego, why don't you? You're not supposed to tell me that.'

'Sorry,' her eyes sparkled with mischief and he wanted to kiss her. Since when had his heart taken up junior acrobatics?

'You will be, young lady. Teasing your olders and betters.'

'Sorry, old man.'

'Less of the old,' he growled and tugged at her hair. The lift stopped and a middle-aged Japanese couple stepped in. Gabe moved closer to Fiona to make room, his hand sliding up the inside of her wrist to let her know he was there. For some reason, he couldn't stop touching her or wanting to be near enough to smell that fresh apple scent. This is what happened, he told himself sternly, when you let yourself be led by less intelligent parts of your body.

Thankfully although the *izakaya* was buzzing when they arrived they managed to snag two seats opposite each other on the end of a crowded bench. He could finally stop thinking indecent thoughts about unpeeling Fiona out of the jumpsuit, the buttons of which were extremely tempting, as was the hint of blue lace underneath it.

'I like it here,' said Fiona, taking a sip of the Sapporo he'd fought his way through the bar to buy. The place was certainly lively and exactly what the doctor ordered. 'Reminds me of a cross between a Wagamama and a London pub.'

Gabe took a long cooling slug of the cold beer and it hit the spot. He let out a satisfied sigh and Fiona grinned at him.

'Difficult afternoon?' she asked.

For a moment he stared at her, impressed by her intuition. 'How did you guess?'

'You're all frowny. This afternoon when we were at the lookout spot at the pagoda, you seemed so much lighter.'

'Just boring conversations on the phone with unenlightened people who have no artistic vision.'

She gave him a sympathetic smile. 'I guess when they're paying, they get to call the shots.'

'Yes, but why pay for the best and not listen to advice? Pay for monkeys, get monkeys. Everyone's so goddamned entitled these days.'

'At least they're paying you and you have work. I'm hoping I might get some work as a result of the exhibition but it's a long shot. I'll still be unknown.'

'Basically, "Gabe stop moaning, you don't know you're born".'

Fiona slapped a hand over her mouth and he laughed at her horror-struck face.

'I didn't mean that at all.'

'I know,' he said, 'I was teasing but you ...' He shook his head. 'You do have a point. I should suck it up.'

She dragged a fingertip through the condensation on her glass focusing all her attention on the golden liquid.

'You have a delightful way of making me reassess things. Making me realise what a dick I am sometimes.'

'I don't mean to,' she said with widened eyes.

He laughed again. 'I know, that makes it doubly refreshing.'

'You keep using those words,' she said, frowning and

sticking her chin up in that familiar pose, 'refreshing, breath of fresh air ... as if I'm some country bumpkin.'

'Sorry. I don't mean it like that. You have an amazing habit of making me look at things differently. In a good way. No one's challenged me in a long time.' He shot her a rueful smile. 'I've been like a spoiled brat ... a bit too used to getting my own way all the time. Or being able to throw my weight around.' Both he and the publicist this afternoon had known that if he really wanted to get the actor to the zoo he could have won that battle but he hadn't cared enough one way or another to really push for it.

'I'll take that.' She gave him a sunny smile, as usual taking his words at face value. He was loathe to say it out loud again but she was so easy to be with, uncomplicated and honest.

'What do you fancy eating?' He'd picked up a couple of English menus from the bar.

They debated the pros and cons of varying dishes as it was tapas and they'd be sharing.

'That sounds lovely and I know what it is,' said Fiona pointing to the teriyaki beef. 'And I've got to have the tempura-battered prawns. The ones in Tokyo were so amazing.'

It was nice to be with someone who was enthusiastic about food and wanted to try new things. Japanese food had stopped being a novelty a long time ago but he would always remember his first taste of crisp tempura batter and the sensation of it melting on his tongue, and now he'd always remember taking Fiona to the same place.

'And I'm tempted by the *yakitori* skewers of chicken, even

though I have no idea what *yakitori* is or what *yuzu* mayonnaise will taste like.'

'*Yakitori* is a sweet, salty sauce, with soy sauce, sugar, ginger and *mirin*, which is a tangy rice wine. It's absolutely delicious.'

'I'm sold. And *yuzu*?'

'Yuzu is a citrus fruit. The flavour's unique. Some say a cross between a grapefruit and a lime.'

'Oh yes. Now I remember. It's one of those trendy flavours you see on cookery programmes like *Bake Off* and *Masterchef*.'

'I can't say I watch either.'

'You haven't watched *Bake Off*?' Fiona shook her head. 'You haven't lived.'

'Too busy, I'm afraid. When I'm in London, I'm usually there for work.'

He caught the eye of one of the busy waitresses and placed their order with Fiona exclaiming suddenly that they just had to have some ramen and telling him all about the meal she'd had in Kyoto. He smiled at her shining enthusiasm, recalling that he'd been in one of the finest restaurants in the city and had barely enjoyed a single mouthful.

'Do you go to London often?' asked Fiona, suddenly shy.

'I still have a flat there. My brother uses it quite a lot. He keeps an eye on it for me.'

'I didn't know you had a brother.'

'Fraser. He's a lot younger than me. I tease him and my mum that he was an after-thought. He's a good guy. He's been out to see me a couple of times. Haruka adores him.' His smile dimmed.

'She adores you,' said Fiona.

'She thinks Fraser is more discerning.'

'Why?' Fiona frowned, intuitive as ever, scenting a story, perhaps because he was giving enough away to want to tell it.

'He doesn't like Yumi.'

'Oh.'

'Doesn't understand that we're friends. He doesn't approve of us staying in touch. He thinks I'm ... well, I'm not. We're friends.'

Fiona nodded and in her usual quiet way didn't say anything, just absorbed the information.

'Is everything okay with your brother now?'

How did she do that? Home in on the nub of the matter straight away?

'He pissed me off a bit but we're still speaking. I'd say we're at the stage of warily circling round each other at the moment.'

'I always wanted a brother. Hoped he'd have been my champion at school. Seen off the mean girls.' She stared away over his shoulder for a moment before giving him a half-hearted smile.

He reached over and put a hand on her wrist, stroking the soft skin on her inner arm, wanting to take away the pain of the memories. 'I'm in London quite often. Perhaps we could meet up.'

At that moment he was interrupted by a waitress bringing plates and white packets of chopsticks to place on the table before them.

'I'd like to come to your exhibition.'

'You'll have seen it all before.'

'That's not the same ... and you know it. There'll be an official opening. It'll be a big deal for you.'

She pulled a face. 'Now you're making me nervous.'

'The Japanese Centre will want to have some kind of launch event.'

'Oh God. Really?'

He laughed. 'They want to get something out of this. No such thing as a free lunch or a free trip to Japan.'

'I know but ... well I thought it would be.' She rolled her eyes. 'Who am I kidding? My friend, Avril, remember I told you about her? Well, I know she's going to make a big thing of it. If she doesn't turn up with a film crew she'll get one of her friends to feature it in a newspaper or magazine or something.'

'Sounds like a good sort of friend to have.'

'Mmm,' said Fiona and looked down at her clothes. 'She is. I shouldn't complain. Most people probably think she's a bit flighty and spoiled. She's very glamorous and always immaculate but she's incredibly kind. If she can help she always will. She's very loyal.'

Gabe smiled.

'What?'

'I suspect you are too. I think Fiona Hanning, you would be a very good friend to have.'

'It's not hard.'

He raised an eyebrow. He didn't want to think too hard about friendship and what it entailed. The direction of those thoughts was not something he had much faith in.

Right on cue, Fiona blushed and it made him forget all his earlier resolutions.

The first dish arrived, steaming hot and even in the less formal surroundings, still with the usual impeccable presentation on beautiful small blue and white oval dishes.

'Oh God, I'm still rubbish with chopsticks,' said Fiona, eying the plump pink prawns with their fine coating of crisp batter hungrily.

'Here,' Gabe took pity on her, wrestled his chopsticks out of their wrapping and picked up a prawn, lifting it to her lips and offering it to her. Like a baby bird she opened her mouth and took a small crisp bite. He watched her and then wished he hadn't.

'Mmm, these prawns are to die for,' said Fiona with a throaty groan, closing her eyes in a blissed-out way that was probably unconscious but did serious damage to his self-control.

'Mmm,' he muttered, shifting uncomfortably in his seat. Forget sleeves, Fiona had a lovely habit of wearing her emotions right there on her face and, cliché or not, it was a refreshing change.

'Here, you try,' she said, picking up one of the tempura prawns with her fingers and grazing his lips as she held it up to his mouth. She watched him wide-eyed and innocent, waiting for his response. Her touch and that guileless gaze sent a tremor of awareness through his body. It was far too much like temptation and he couldn't help himself. He licked the knuckle of her thumb, grazing it quickly with his teeth before he bit into the prawn. It was worth it to see her eyes widen and hear her gasp as she snatched back her hand. He grinned at her. 'Delicious.'

It was a shame the waitress arrived at that moment with the *yakitori* and the glossy beef *teriyaki*.

'Thank you,' said Fiona to the waitress as if she'd personally sailed in to rescue her.

The waitress thanked her back.

'Try the chicken,' Fiona said, almost poking him in the face with the skewer.

He closed his hand over hers to steady the skewer and smiled at her.

'Will you stop doing that,' she said.

'Doing what?'

'You know.'

Her fierce stare made him feel a touch of chagrin.

'Sorry.' He let go of her hand.

'It's just, I'm nervous enough as it is.'

'Shit, Fi. I don't want to make you feel nervous. There's no pressure here.'

'I know, but you're all ... sophisticated and used to playing games and I'm just me.'

'And just you ... is'—he took in her worried blue eyes, the golden curtain of hair, and the hint of pale skin at her neck and throat—'is absolutely perfect.'

'Oh,' she said, even more flustered. 'Maybe we should ... go back to the hotel and ...'

'Fiona Hanning. Whatever happened to romance? I'm trying to seduce you and you want to go straight back to the hotel and get it over with.' He sent her a look of mock outrage and she winced. Then she slapped her hand over her mouth and ducked her head, hiding behind the screen of her hair. Her body shook slightly and at first he thought he'd made her cry.

'Hey Fi. I'm sorry.'

She glanced up from underneath her lashes and instead of tears, he saw blue eyes brimming with mirth. And then a giggle burst out and another.

'I'm s-sorry,' she laughed again. 'I'm rubbish at this.'

'I thought you were doing fine. Tell me more about your writing.'

They chatted easily and ordered another beer, and for the first time in a long time Gabe felt completely at ease.

Chapter 21

The spring night was decidedly chilly when they left the bar but the clear sky, lit by a half moon, gave Mount Fuji a ghostly air, a few silvery wisps of clouds surrounding the snow-capped peak.

'Nice jacket,' commented Gabe as she slipped her arms into the supple leather.

'Yes, but not very warm,' said Fiona. 'Though apparently nicer than my other coat.'

He laughed. 'The hairy number.'

'Don't you start.'

'Sorry.' He put an arm around her and pulled her close as they began to walk back to the hotel. 'Who else has been giving you grief about it?'

'Avril, of course. She says it's like a monkey.'

'I can't wait to meet her.' Avril had a point but he decided to keep quiet.

'Hmm, that will be interesting. You'll meet your match there.'

'And I haven't here? I'm still banking on you being gentle with me.'

She gave him a shy nudge with her elbow, a faint smile hovering on her lips, but didn't say anything as they walked along a brightly light strip of restaurants and bars, all of which were packed with people. Cherry blossom season had brought all the tourists out. It was only half past eight. Still early.

'Want to try another Japanese institution?'

'Like what?' she asked, suspicion coating the word.

'Karaoke. There's a bar along here.' He nodded towards the neon sign. 'We can have a night cap in there, if you don't fancy joining in, or we can go back to the hotel bar.'

He felt Fiona straighten and to his astonishment she said without hesitation. 'Yes.'

'Yes?'

'Karaoke bar.' Gabe almost laughed at her unexpectedly enthusiastic response.

'OK. Karaoke bar it is. Have you been to one before?'

'No. Never. Have you?'

'I live in Japan. Somehow it seems inevitable to end up in one, especially after a heavy night out. The Japanese really do love them. You should see Haruka go.'

'Haruka! No, you're having me on.'

'Swear to God and cross my heart.' He held his hand up boy-scout style. 'It was Mayu's birthday treat.' He shuddered. 'And she sang "Like a Virgin". Mayu that is, not Haruka.'

Fiona giggled. 'I'd like to have seen that. What did Haruka sing?'

He laughed. 'She sang Whitney's "I Will Always Love You".'

'Interesting,'

'It certainly was.' He grimaced.

266

'Can you? Sing, that is?'

'I can hold a tune. And when I've had a few I'm the next best thing to Robbie Williams.' He grinned at her. 'How about you?'

She shrugged. 'I'm okay.'

They pushed their way into the bar, through a crowd of very happy Japanese youngsters who were just leaving. The place was packed with plenty of people and there was a group of German tourists on stage, gleefully murdering a Mariah Carey song much to the evident enjoyment of the assembled crowd of mainly tourists.

'What would you like to drink?' Gabe had to shout in her ear over the noise of the clapping and cheering.

Fiona, who was taking everything in with interest, pulled a face. 'I've no idea. I usually drink wine but I'm not sure ... what do people drink here?'

'Highballs, mainly, or beer.'

'I've had enough beer. What's in a highball?'

'It's a long drink of Japanese whisky and soda although some people drink it with Coke or lemonade.'

'I'll try one of those. With lemonade please.'

He muscled his way to the front of the bar and caught the eye of the waitress who was singing along to the song at a decibel level that might burst an ear drum. Carrying the drinks, he wriggled his way through the chairs and tables to where Fiona had found two spare seats at the end of a long table that was occupied by two other parties.

'*Kanpai*,' he said, raising his glass to chink against hers.

'*Kanpai*,' she said back. 'I guess that means cheers.'

'Sort of. The direct translation is "empty your glass".'

Fiona took a couple of sips and then tipped her neck back and drained the glass in one.

'Whoa. You were thirsty. I didn't mean you to take it literally. Do you want another?'

'Yes please,' she said as sweetly and placidly as a nun, as if she hadn't just necked a double whisky.

'Okay. You're sure?'

'Yes.'

When he brought back the second drink, he said, 'Go slowly with this one. That whisky can pack quite a punch.'

'OK,' she said, tossing her hair over her shoulder and watching the proceedings avidly as the German singers left the stage and another couple took to the mic.

'This is quite a traditional karaoke bar. These days the big chains in Tokyo and big cities tend to have different sized private rooms that you can hire by the hour. A lot of them are themed and some even have costumes for a bit of cosplay.'

'Wow. That sounds ... hideous. Oh,' her eyes darted to the stage, 'I love this song.'

'It's a karaoke classic isn't?' Gabe teased as the strains of 'Islands in the Stream' began to play.

'So what song would you choose for us to sing together?' he asked.

'"Don't Go Breaking My Heart".' She winced. 'That came out ... wrong. It was the first duet that I could think of.' Her eyes were suddenly a little grave. 'But you probably could.'

The words punched him in the throat and he swallowed,

the sudden sense of responsibility weighing heavy and making him feel a little panic stricken.

Her lip curled, as if she could hear the thoughts running through his head.

'If I let you,' she gave a sniff and tossed her hair over her shoulder, 'which I'm not going to do. So you don't need to worry.'

Well that told him. But what if she broke his?

A few more songs and a third highball later, Fiona was as ready as she was ever going to be. Gabe had been quite intrigued when, after the German couple had come off the stage, she'd signed up for a turn. That was the first whisky talking.

Stage fright was a real kicker. Even the thought of mounting those steps filled her stomach with rocks and the whisky hadn't helped the way she'd hoped it would but something inside her drove her on; she wanted to impress Gabe for once. He was always so competent, so self-assured. She wanted to show him that she was good at something.

A group of Japanese girls were doing terrible things to the Spice Girls 'Wannabe' and quite literally having a 'wail' of a time doing it. Not that the crowd cared; they were going wild. She was the act after the next one and prayed that the next act wouldn't be as high octane because they would be a tough act to follow.

'You sure you want to do this?' asked Gabe as she drained the last of the third highball.

'Yes,' she gave him what she hoped was a confident smile, doing her best to squash the squirmy wriggling running wild in her stomach. *Come on Fiona, you can do this.* You're planning to sleep with him! This will be much easier. There, she'd admitted it to herself, she was going to sleep with him. Maybe like being on stage, once you were there, it would all be fine. It was the physical act of stepping onto the stage that made her knees shake so much.

'Are you going to tell me what you're going to sing?' asked Gabe for possibly the tenth or maybe it was the eleventh time.

'No, I told you.' She wagged a finger at him. 'You have to wait.'

'Well, the waiting is over,' he nodded as the teenager hit the closing high notes of his song to polite applause.

Fiona got to her feet. Why had she chosen to do this? Why? But it was too late to turn back. She straightened. Ever since she'd known Gabe, she'd felt a like a small child trying to keep up with an adult. Despite her nerves, she knew she could do this. It was her chance to shine, to show him another side of herself. With her back to the audience, she approached the stage and undid a few buttons on her jumpsuit. She could do this.

Four steps to the stage. She counted them. One. Two. Three. Four. Steadied her breathing. Gripped the microphone. Took another breath, a deep breath pushing down on her diaphragm. She could do this.

The first few strums of guitar played and without having to check the words on the screen, on the fifth one, she opened her mouth, the familiar sensation of being right at home filling every cell in her body. Her voice rang out, 'Everybody screamed ...'

She gave Gabe a dazzling smile.

'... when I kissed the teacher.'

She wished she could have taken a picture of his face. And then she pulled her jumpsuit down to bare one shoulder and gave a suggestive shimmy, still focusing her attention on Gabe as she sang the next few lines flashing her eyes at him. As the beat picked up, she began to twirl and dance around the stage and the crowd began to clap and cheer.

Fiona grinned at the audience stage channelling her inner Lily James for all she was worth. *Mamma Mia, Here We Go Again* was one of her favourite films. Copying her moves and singing along had proved positive therapy. And now, under Gabe's astonished gaze, she sang and danced her heart out, revelling in the music and the song. For some bizarre reason she had never managed to fathom, when she was singing, Fiona felt truly at home. Perhaps because she could pretend to be someone else. Singing came naturally to her and she loved it but she'd never had the confidence to do anything with it.

Now the crowd were joining in the refrain, clapping along, and Gabe along with many others was on his feet.

She beckoned to two girls on the front row, who were already having the time of their lives and invited them on stage. Without needing a second invitation, giggling together, they bounded up the steps to join in the chorus and copy her dance steps as she took two steps to the right and kicked up a leg and two steps to the left.

When the song finally came to an end, the whole place erupted clapping, cheering, whooping, and, grinning like a loon, Fiona took her bows and came down the steps, shaking her head as the wolf whistles and shouts of 'more, more' continued. She wended her way back to Gabe and as she came up next to him, he threw his arms around her and kissed her.

'You were awesome.' His eyes danced. 'And seriously hot. The crowd loved you.'

She laughed. 'Thank you.'

'Seriously Fi, you were incredible.'

'Thank you.' Now the shyness and embarrassment started to creep in. She ducked her head, although she couldn't stop smiling.

'Oh no you don't. Don't get all modest and retiring on me now.' He kissed her again and he might have carried on if they hadn't been interrupted by a polite, 'ahem' – or the Japanese equivalent. A waitress with a tray of drinks stood there and spoke in halting English. 'From the house.'

'That's very kind,' said Fiona, her heart still beating at a thousand beats per minute. She was conscious of the flush on her cheeks as the girl put them on the table.

'You were so good!' The waitress smiled and retreated.

'Well, if that's what a couple of whisky does ... I think you might have had enough. I'm not sure I can take any more,' teased Gabe covering the top of the drinks with a protective hand.

Her fuzzy heart, or whatever was wrong with it, beat faster and before she lost her newfound confidence, she lifted a slightly shaky hand to take his and looked at him. 'Let's go back to the hotel.'

Chapter 22

As they got to the hotel – Fiona having sung all the way back, encouraged by Gabe – they collapsed, bent double with giggles in the lift, and any thought about being nervous had completely sailed.

Okay, she was a bit pissed and possibly high on adulation so when they arrived at her hotel room door, she tugged at Gabe's hand, pulling him into the room. Someone had been in and turned down the bed, switching on the bedside lamps which emitted a welcoming glow that softened the edges of the room. Like a looming guardian angel, through the window the outline of Mount Fuji glistened in the silver moonlight.

Gabe pulled her to him and she lifted her mouth to his kisses. Nerves fizzed a little but curiosity and desire beat them back and she began to tug at his jacket, sliding it down his arms, her fingers digging into his biceps, smiling into the kiss as he made short, efficient work of her jacket.

'I like the jumpsuit,' he murmured against her throat, undoing the buttons with slow, careful attention. She shivered as his mouth vibrated against the tender skin, her hands

273

sliding under his shirt and T-shirt before roving over the smooth skin of his muscular back.

He stepped back and in one fluid movement stripped both off, lifting them over his head to expose a tanned chest dusted with dark hair. Something twisted inside her at the sight of his golden skin warmed by the radiance of the lamplit room.

'Nice,' she breathed, reaching out to touch him.

He gave her a crooked smile and skirted the lace of her camisole with one finger, skimming her skin with a barely there touch that sent fireworks shooting downwards.

He pushed the linen fabric off her shoulder and kissed the bare skin, his lips lingering, sending more tingles racing here, there, and everywhere.

'I've been wanting to do that since you gave me that come hither look over your shoulder on stage.'

She swallowed, a little dazed and bemused by the sensations buffeting her body – aching in some places and burning in others. He tracked kisses along the sensitive skin to her throat and then to her mouth. When his tongue touched hers, everything seemed to go from zero to sixty in seconds. Their mouths duelled, danced, and teased and she felt her breath coming faster as the heat between her legs rose. Unable to help herself, and in truth a little shocked by the strength of her need, she ground against him, feeling his hard erection, wanting more. Heat rose and his kiss deepened, one hand behind her head holding her possessively as with his other hand he pushed down her jumpsuit, his fingers finding her breasts with a heartfelt groan. The gentle roving touch that danced around her nipple was a sparkling, fizzing contrast to his hungry lips that made her breathless with frustration and desire. More, she wanted more. She had thought about this for so long.

She kissed him back, unsure at first as he gave way, letting her tongue take dominance, allowing her to lead the dance.

Her hands found the button on his jeans and for a moment she fumbled with the stiff fabric, finding it difficult to concentrate with the delicious sensation drawn by his fingers, now moving to the other breast leaving her nipple tingling with a heady mix of yearning and aching need.

Somehow with his legs still in his jeans, the jumpsuit pushed to her thighs, they stumbled back towards the bed and when it hit the back of her knees, she fell backwards taking him with her. In a clumsy tangle of arms and legs they wriggled out of their clothes, laughing, and he settled on top of her, his weight igniting a flash of desire. Kissing him more deeply, Fiona pressed her hips upwards to squirm against his groin as his hands delved into her hair. The firm, delicious touch of his fingers grazing her scalp made her sigh with pleasure as he peppered her face with kisses, before skimming down her neck and pressing kisses over her nipples through the camisole.

'Mmm,' she squeaked as he lifted up the cami and pushed aside her bra. The touch of his mouth made her hips rise again. 'Oh wow,' she said in a strangled voice as desperation tortured her.

Gabe, it appeared, wasn't in any hurry and things slowed as he took a leisurely trip tasting and sipping at her breasts, bringing her to breathlessness, her hands fisting in the covers as she gave involuntary moans.

'Stop. Stop,' she panted. She felt like she might explode at any second. It was all too much. Every nerve ending was on fire. 'I can't. I can't.' Her hand fluttered and she swallowed, her breath coming in ridiculous pants. He lifted his head and moved his hand up to her face to cup her chin.

'Too fast?'

'Mmm,' she nodded, grateful for his understanding. 'I need ... sorry. I need a minute.' He rolled from her and gathered her in his arms, pressing a gentle kiss to her forehead. She could feel the heave of his chest as it rose and fell.

Immediately she felt bereft but a little less panicky.

'Phew,' wheezed Gabe. 'I think I might have a heart attack.' He picked up her hand and placed it over his heart. The thunderous pace of his pulse made her smile.

'I thought it was just me.'

'Just you what?'

'Feeling crazy out of control.'

He laughed and kissed her firmly on the mouth. 'Nope, I'm in the crazy out-of-control camp too.'

'Good,' she whispered and placed a careful kiss on his neck, the tip of her tongue tasting the skin on his collar bone.

With a groan, he buried his face in her hair and lay still, their harsh breathing puncturing the still air of the dimly lit room.

She tentatively ran a hand across his chest and could tell he was forcing himself to lie still. 'Sorry,' she said again.

'Don't you dare apologise,' he said gruffly. 'This is about two people. Although you're killing me. Just saying.'

She smiled and kissed him, wrapping her arms around him and tugging him on top of her.

'I've caught up with the crazy now,' she whispered.

'Are you sure? We don't have to do this,' he said, his hand skimming down her ribs.

She nodded, certain.

He moved to the edge of the bed and removed something from the wallet in his jeans.

'We'll need to make these count. I didn't exactly come prepared,' he said with a teasing smile.

She gave him a shy smile. 'You're doing fine so far.'

When his body finally slid home, it was an awful lot more than fine.

She woke slowly to a room lit by moonlight, her body tingling all over, warm and satiated, and brought her fingers to her tender mouth, aware of the involuntary smile there. Goodness, she'd been missing out. Gabe certainly knew what he was doing and ... she smiled again, he didn't seem to have had any complaints about what she'd been doing. Her heart did a little jig as she recalled the long groan of pleasure when he'd come ... both times. She could hear Gabe's slow, steady breathing next to her and felt the steady heat radiating from his body.

For a minute she gazed down at him, his rumpled hair spread on the pillow and his face relaxed. Her heart bloomed with love. Yup, she loved him, every last inch of him. Even when he was being an arrogant jerk. Or now when he was spread out in front of her. God, it was so tempting. To reach out and touch – smooth that hair, stroke his collar bone – but instead she studied his face, biting her lip. Gabe Burnett. Gorgeous. Generous in bed. Last night had been a complete and utter revelation. Fiona almost giggled out loud – would have done if the sadness hadn't clamped down hard. Instead she swallowed as she traced the hollows of his throat. She'd slept with him – Gabe Burnett – the real man, not the illusion she'd held for so long. Surprisingly, she'd felt his equal. A woman. Not the naïve schoolgirl who lived inside her always trying to keep up. Tears blurred her vision. Well they could bloody go away. *Man up, Fi*. This was real life, not a rom-com where he'd turn around and declare she was the love of his life. Men like Gabe didn't do that ... well, not with women like her. And she'd known that. No point getting all sad and mopey. This was going to be a treasured memory when she went back to London. As she'd promised herself earlier, she was going to make the most of the next few days.

She lifted herself to her elbows to gaze at Mount Fuji, now with the moon behind it, all mystical and magical. A good picture. She edged carefully out of bed, casting a quick backward glance at Gabe. He didn't stir.

Grabbing her camera, she slid open the doors to the balcony and slipped out, naked in the cool night air, and the chill pricked at her tender, abraded skin. With a smile she relished the shiver of pleasure and memory. Shades of blue, white, and silver dappled the horizon as the moonlight lit the bright snow encasing the top of the peak. It radiated a bluish ethereal light that seemed to pulse in the stillness of the night. A few stray wisps of clouds drifted into the shot. Hoping she'd capture the sense of spirituality, Fiona took several photographs, so absorbed she almost didn't hear the slide of the door behind her.

'A moonlit shot,' whispered Gabe's voice suddenly.

She turned and glanced over her shoulder, smiling as he tucked his warm body behind her, kissing her shoulder.

'It's so beautiful. I was hoping to get the "definitive" shot.'

'And?' he asked putting his arms around her waist, his chin resting on her shoulder, the faint prick of bristles sanding her skin.

With a scrunch of her face, she shook her head. 'Not quite, but those clouds will move in a minute. I'd like to get a shot without them.'

'And we've got tomorrow ... or I think it might be today now.'

She shivered again, aware of her nakedness, realising that he'd had the foresight to pull on his boxers.

'Want me to get you a robe?'

'No, I'll go and get it.'

She moved past him and into the bathroom where she'd seen a complimentary robe hanging on the back of the door earlier. For a moment she stopped as she caught sight of herself in the mirror, her mouth a little swollen, her hair a mussed halo around her face and her eyes glowing with satisfaction. She nodded at herself, pleased with what she saw and slipped on the robe.

Gabe was leaning on the balcony, his outline a dark shadow

and over one broad shoulder the mountain rose, ghostly in the radiance of the moonlight.

With her heart in her mouth, she snapped the picture, taking several quickly before Gabe lazily turned around.

'Better?' he asked, holding out a hand.

'Yes,' she said, her pulse still tripping with excitement, unsure as to whether to share the shot with Gabe. He probably thought she was taking pictures of Mount Fuji over his shoulder, not pictures of him in the foreground and the mountain in the background. She didn't dare take a peep at it; she'd save that for later.

They stayed a little while watching the moon dance in and out of the clouds before Gabe yawned. 'Bedtime.' And then he bent and scooped her up in his arms and carried her back to bed. He stood her up, took off her robe and nudged her down onto the bed, sliding under the covers after her.

'Mmm,' she murmured as he lay his arm across her and slipped one leg between hers.

'Don't get any ideas,' he teased, kissing her shoulder. 'You've worn me out.'

She smiled and stroked the silky hairs on the forearm draped over her waist, savouring the smooth cotton of the sheets, the heavy weight of his limbs, and soft warmth of his slow breaths lifting the wisps of hair around her neck. Before long he'd dropped off and she lay smiling into the darkness listening to his steady breathing before she finally fell asleep too.

Chapter 23

She woke to Gabe's broad smile as sunshine poured in through the window. He was propped up on his pillows, the soft white cotton bedsheets contrasting with his golden skin and dark stubble.

'Morning, Sleeping Beauty.'

'Morning.' Her smile was shy, which was ridiculous given what they'd got up to the previous night, but she wasn't used to waking up with a man beside her, let alone one of all male perfection. It was a little mind-blowing. His arm snaked out and he pulled her to lie on his chest while he pressed a kiss on the top of her head. Her hand caught his nipple and he sucked in a breath.

'You're not going to pester me for sex this morning, are you?' he groaned with a teasing glint in his eye.

'Me?'

He caressed her breast with a lazy hand, nuzzling down her cheek to find her lips.

It was some time before they made it to the shower where he scooted in behind her and insisted on making her very clean.

'Do you think I dare do the walk of shame in my towel?' he asked, surveying the heap of last night's clothes at the foot of the bed.

'You can't! You'll shock the chambermaids.' Or give them a great start to their working day.

He grinned cheerfully at her. 'Why not? It's a few doors down. You can be lookout.' She gave him a prim stare.

'Or I could get dressed and go and get some clean things for you.'

'You're no fun.'

'That's not what you said in the shower.' She lifted her eyebrows with pointed meaning.

Still clad in a towel, he yanked her to him. 'You are ...' He gazed down and then with a quick disbelieving shake of his head, he kissed her so thoroughly that she was left clinging to him because her knees were having a moment.

'Can you grab my phone? I left it charging.'

'Sure. Anything else?' she shot him a teasing smirk.

'Unless you want me to go commando today,' he raised lascivious eyebrows, 'underwear would be good. Top drawer. And I wouldn't mind a clean shirt. I brought two ... you can choose.'

He dug out his key card from his jeans pocket.

His room was the twin of hers with the same picture window view of the mountain. She gathered up pants and socks and took a little while deciding which shirt to take him. The intimacy of this act she would store up and savour as a memory for the future. She chose a pale blue button-down Oxford shirt before checking to see where his phone was.

Focused on the phone charging on the bedside cabinet, she didn't see the pair of running shoes protruding from under the bed and went flying as she tripped over one of them. Her hand caught the phone with an undignified karate chop and the sudden jolt brought it to life, the screen notification telling her Gabe had three missed calls from Yumi. It was an unpleasant reminder that she'd still be in his life long after Fiona had returned to London.

'But you knew what you were getting into,' she told herself, pocketing the phone. 'This was only ever going to be temporary. It finishes when you step on that plane back to Heathrow.'

Thoughts of flights and London were quickly banished when they went down to breakfast and the tone for the day was set. Gabe seemed to like holding her hand a lot and sneaking in kisses whenever there was a quiet corner. After a Western-style breakfast – Fiona couldn't resist the pancakes on offer – they took the train to Kawaguchiko and the staggeringly steep cable car which climbed 200 metres in three minutes up to Tenjozan Park.

'Fancy walking back down to the lake?' asked Gabe after they'd spent nearly forty minutes in the viewing area taking in the view of Mount Fuji to one side and Lake Kawaguchiko on the other.

'Yes. I'm all viewed out and I don't think I can possibly take any more pictures of Mount Fuji. I'm done.' Besides, a sneaky peep at the middle-of-the-night pictures confirmed she'd bagged the shot she wanted. No one but her would ever know it was Gabe, so she felt safe in planning to use it in her exhibition. For all his promises, she couldn't see him flying to London for it and really didn't expect him to.

'Good. Think you might put the camera away for a while and enjoy yourself?'

'Jealous?' she teased, unhooking the strap from her neck and tucking it into the padded bag she carried over her shoulder.

'Hell, yes. I want your undivided attention for the rest of the day.'

She laughed at his mock diva pout. 'OK then. Let's tackle this climb then.' The route down was about five kilometres along paths and steps lined with dense, wide-leaved bushes which Gabe said were hydrangeas.

'This is lovely. I'm not sure I want to go back to the city,' she said as they paused at the top of one flight of stairs, the birdsong around them sweet and pure, with a slight breeze rippling through the canopy of trees above them. In the distance she could see the blue of the lake, almost sapphire today in the brilliant sunshine reflecting the cloudless sky.

'Me neither. Although don't tell Haruka I said that.'

'Why not?'

'She's a great believer in *shinrin-yoku*. Forest bathing. Walking in the forest to recharge your batteries. Apparently it's good for the soul. We should experience the wonder of nature, the blossom, the leaves, as well as the imperfections of nature.'

'She told me about *wabi-sabi*,' said Fiona thoughtfully.

'Forest bathing is another expression of it.' He gave a short mocking laugh. 'And when I'm here, I can almost believe in it.'

Fiona frowned and took Gabe's arm, disturbed by the return

of his characteristic cynicism, guiding him over to a nearby bench.

'I don't like it when you talk like that,' she said softly, surprised by her own boldness.

'Why not?'

'Because you sound ... bored with life. Weary of everything.'

He shrugged, focusing on something in the distance, his head slightly turned away from her. 'Sometimes I am. I've been around longer than you. I'm trying though.'

She nudged his thigh sharply with her knee. 'You're not that much older than me and I'm not completely wet behind the ears. I might not live in London but I've certainly travelled in and out a lot and to plenty of other places. I'm not bored with life. You've stopped looking at things.'

'Ouch,' he said mildly as if he really didn't give a damn, leaning back against the bench, his arms outstretched on either side as if he owned the damn thing.

'Sorry Gabe,' she said fiercely, annoyed by his seeming indifference, 'but I hate it when you act like this. It's not really you.'

Watching his profile, she watched him press his lips tightly together before he said distantly, 'Isn't it?'

'No. It isn't. I think it's an act ... so you don't get caught out by anyone.'

'What's someone going to catch me out at?'

'Having real feelings. Caring about things?'

She'd got to him, she could tell by the clenching of his jaw as he took an annoyed breath.

'Like Haruka. You adore her really but you can't say it. You always have to say things like, "she's a grumpy old woman". And yesterday you said you'd forgotten what a special place Japan is.'

Some of his stiffness receded and one of his hands crept onto her lap where he intertwined his fingers with hers. 'When I'm with you, I remember all that stuff you do to make me see everything through fresh eyes. But ... things have happened that I find hard to forget.'

Fiona winced at the flatness in his tone.

'I understand that,' she said, squeezing his fingers. 'After the bullying at school, I locked myself away from other people for a long time but what helped was coming back to life and finding decent people who cared about me.'

'You volunteering?' he asked.

She shook his hand in exasperation, saying with asperity, 'I'm not the sort of person who would jump into bed with someone if I didn't care.'

He turned to face her, his blue eyes softening. 'No, you're not. Promise me one thing: don't care too much. I'm not much of a catch.' She shook her head but he carried on talking. 'I'm sorry. Maybe it's time I thought about leaving Tokyo instead of chasing memories. In the meantime, you're right and instead of brooding on the past I should be making the most of this glorious sunshine and the gorgeous woman at my side.' He kissed her cheek. 'Come on, let's try some of this forest bathing. And then I'll take you for lunch down by the lake.'

She followed him back to the path, watching his broad back with a sad smile. He turned and took a shot of the skyline behind her as she stared down at him. Good job she hadn't blurted out last night that she loved him. Did that fall into the category of caring too much? Now that really would have been making a dick of herself.

They walked by the lake and for a very late lunch found a charming if expensive restaurant – the prices included the waterside view – although Gabe insisted on paying. 'You don't have to,' she protested. 'We could go halves. Or I can pay for dinner.'

He paused and gave her a piercing stare as if he were seeing her for the first time. She noticed he'd done it a couple of times since they left Tokyo but this time it was as if he was trying to see into her soul. Her skin prickled with awareness as his eyes roved over her face.

'You're a very nice person. That's the first time in a long while that someone else has offered to pay for me. Which makes it all the sweeter and my pleasure to pay for someone who doesn't expect it. But unfortunately, on this occasion, I can't take the credit. This is on the competition prize tab.' He winced. 'You know I am still officially your mentor. I feel like I'm taking the piss slightly. I'm not sure Kaito would approve of my mentoring last night. I'm pretty certain it's not what he had in mind when he set this trip up. Me seducing the competition winner.'

'Seducing makes it sound one sided. I'm a grown-up.'

'You certainly are. And there was nothing one sided about last night.'

With one sentence he had the power to make her blush and remember the flurry of clothes hurriedly shed in a tangle of limbs.

'So,' his mouth quirked, 'dinner tonight. I thought we'd go to a steamboat restaurant.'

'Explain.'

'Wait and see but I think you'll like it.'

She rolled her eyes.

'And after that …' Oh God, he was doing it again. The man was positively wicked and every naughty thought seemed to be etched onto his face. Her cheeks seemed to be in a permanent state of pinkness. 'I have a surprise, although you'll have to get naked.'

'What?'

'You don't have any tattoos I missed, do you?'

She almost choked on her water at the wicked gleam in his eyes.

'No.'

'I didn't think so. I thought I'd been very thorough in the shower.'

'Gabe!' she hissed, her face turning even redder. His wicked smirk was unrepentant.

'Tattoos are banned where we're going. They're associated with the *Yakuza*, the Japanese equivalent of the mafia.'

'I don't have any tattoos,' she said primly, sitting on the edge of her chair and pressing her knees together, trying hard not to think of Gabe's laughing face that morning in the shower and the intimate places he'd kissed which were now throbbing with latent memory.

'Phew, that's a relief. I was worried I might have missed something and was going to have to give you another thorough inspection.'

'Gabe!' she hissed again, glancing round.

He leaned forward. 'You kept saying that last night.'

She kicked him under the table. 'Will you behave?'

'Why, when teasing you is so much fun?'

And that pretty much shaped the rest of the day.

'Will you quit with the sexy feeding thing,' said Fiona when Gabe lifted his chopsticks to her mouth for the third time during dinner that evening.

'You might starve. I don't think I've ever seen anyone quite so inept with a pair of chopsticks.'

'You've had years to practise. How am I supposed to get any better if you don't stop doing that?'

He fished a piece of Iberico pork out of the bubbling broth in the steamboat in front of them.

'Every time I think I've had my favourite meal, something else comes along. This is another amazing dish,' sighed Fiona.

Since they'd arrived she been fascinated by the big silver steamboats on the tables of the other diners and now it was their turn. The ornate, stainless-steel pan sat over a single gas ring which had been brought to their table and held a bubbling chicken broth. The best way Fiona could describe it was like a savoury fondue, where you chose the flavour of your cooking broth from beef, chicken, pork, fish or seafood and then cooked your own delicate slivers of meats, raw prawns and chopped vegetables that of course came beautifully arranged on a circular tray in front of them. Peppers – red, yellow and even purple – had been sliced into fine strips, while the carrots had been carved into cherry blossoms and the broccoli had been cut into tiny, delicate trees, the stems carved with an intricate pattern.

'That's incredible. I'm not sure I should eat it,' she said, marvelling at the detail of the work.

'Then the chef would be offended. The Japanese take hospitality very seriously and vegetable carving is considered a fine art. You've probably realised that they celebrate the seasons, like with *hanami*, but there's also Iris flower season, the autumn foliage; you'll see it in the art but also in other parts of the culture, especially food. Having the first of the season, like the first strawberry, is much prized and they often carve the food to match the seasons. In autumn you'll find the carrots are carved into maple leaves.'

'That's incredible and these are just beautiful.' She held a radish carved into the shape of a lotus flower between her fingers; knowing her, if she'd attempted it with chopsticks, she'd fire the vegetable at Gabe across the table.

'I wish I had my phone. I'd have WhatsApped a picture to Sophie; she's a food writer and she loves to try new things, and insists everyone else does too. Her motto is that it's good for your food education.'

'Eating in Japan is certainly an education in its own right. I still don't know what half this stuff is.'

'I know what these are.' She poked with one end of her chopstick at the clumps of tiny white mushrooms that looked as if they belonged in a fairy glade. '*Enoki*. We had them at an amazing restaurant in Copenhagen. The food was to die for.' She grinned at the memory. 'We all thought Sophie was going to have an orgasm at the table.'

'Now there's an idea. Although wasn't that done in *When Harry Met Sally?*'

She rolled her eyes. He was completely incorrigible and she couldn't remember when she'd last had so much fun with someone.

After dinner they rose and Gabe held open her leather jacket for her.

'Are you going to tell me where we're going yet?'

'Soon.' He tucked his arm through hers and they walked along a few streets, the cool evening breeze ruffling her hair.

'So what exactly do you do in an *onsen?*' she asked once the receptionist at the front desk had handed them the key without so much as batting an eyelid. Surprisingly, at nine o'clock in the evening the place was very busy with families and teen-agers.

'Relax. It's a big thing in Japan. It's basically bathing in spring water. The water comes from hot springs that contain natural minerals, so different *onsens* claim to have different properties. But they're all supposed to be very good for the skin and it's a nice thing to do. This one is renowned because it's got a bath with a view. Come on, we're on the top floor.'

On the fourth floor, the key opened a door which accessed a private outdoor roof terrace. 'Oh, isn't this lovely,' said Fiona as she stared around the beautifully landscaped garden with its very own steaming mini lake which reflected the snow-covered top of Mount Fuji. The sun had gone down several hours ago and the little terrace was lit by tiny lights along the stone-paved paths and buried among the bamboo planting.

'We have to shower first. Here you have to be clean before you get in the hot spring. And you'll have to tie up all that lovely hair.'

As there'd been no mention of swimming costumes, she was guessing that the etiquette was to go naked and despite having seen Gabe up close and personal quite a lot in the last twenty-four hours, she couldn't help the sudden wave of apprehension. It was one thing to strip off in the heat of passion, quite another to coolly undress and parade about in cold blood.

But with his usual sixth sense when it came to her lack of self-confidence Gabe rubbed at the tension in her shoulders. 'Do you want to shower first and hop in. I'll just take in the view.' He nodded towards the wooden fencing at the far side of the terrace offering a perfect view of the mountain.

'That ... that would be great,' she said and with embarrassing speed almost ran to the little changing area which she realised also housed a sauna. She couldn't imagine going in there and lying naked.

She showered quickly, before Gabe changed his mind, taking care to wash thoroughly as per the rather authoritarian instructions on the wall. Feeling all kinds of fool for being such a Victorian prude, she edged out of the door. As promised, Gabe had his back to her and was staring out at the view.

'I'm in,' she called as the silky water enveloped her. She found she could sit on one of the underwater ledges and be submerged up to her neck.

'And how is it?' he asked.

'Heaven,' she sighed and leaned back, stretching her arms out on either side of her to gain some purchase and stop her floating up out of the water. It seemed more buoyant than she was used to.

'All right if I join you?'

She nodded, her throat a little constricted. Why, oh why, couldn't she be more casual about this? Trying her best to relax and not think about Gabe's long, lean body in the shower, she put her head back to gaze up at the sky. As her eyes grew accustomed to the dark, pinpricks of light started to appear, thousands of tiny stars millions of years away. The sight of them and the thought of the size of the universe and how insignificant a human life span was in the scheme of things made her realise that her fears about nudity, about falling in love with Gabe, about not being good enough, were all really quite inconsequential. This time was a gift and she would be daft to waste it worrying about things like the shape of her body and how much it would hurt when she had to say goodbye to him. She'd seized the moment last night and the joy and pleasure would stay with her for a very long time. Surely that was what life should be about, focusing on the good bits rather than the bad bits. Like her mother.

When Gabe sauntered out of the changing room with lean-hipped grace, her breath caught and all her good intentions about looking away went up in smoke. Embarrassingly, she let out a little mouse-like squeak as she tried to breathe normally.

He smiled and shook his head as he stepped into the water with total unconcern.

All she could do was nod, her mouth too darned dry to speak. Life was so unfair – his body looked as if it had been honed in a gym although to her knowledge he didn't work out. But then she remembered the running shoes she'd had a near miss with in his room this morning.

'Do you run or anything?' she blurted out.

As if he knew exactly the tangent of her thoughts, he lifted his eyebrows and one side of his mouth lifted in a twisted wicked smile.

'I run and do a few weights every now and then. Why?'

'Just wondered.' Her attempt at being blasé came out high and squeaky.

Gabe laughed but immediately stepped down into the water, coming to sit opposite her. Now all she could see was the dark hair in the vee of his chest, much to her relief.

They sat in silence for a while and she went back to star-gazing.

'I should do this more often,' observed Gabe idly, lifting his toes out of the water and pushing his shoulders back. 'I'm not sure I want to go back to Tokyo tomorrow.'

Fiona sighed; she definitely didn't want to go back.

'We could ask Kaito if we could have the room for another night.' Gabe looked at her as he said it, a question on his face.

'I'd really like that, but I ought to get back. I still need to take pictures of the tea house and I provisionally agreed tomorrow with Setsuko. I don't want to let her down.'

'You're right, I have work to do too. *The Sunday Times* has suddenly decided I'm flavour of the month; they've offered me a couple more jobs and so has a film studio in LA. I'm hoping I'll be able to coordinate everything so that I'm not flying back and forth all the time. Jet lag to LA's a killer.'

'I wouldn't know,' said Fiona practically. LA sounded glamorous and exciting.

'You could come with me. Be my assistant again.'

Startled, she glanced at his face, surprised by the sincerity she read there.

'I get the impression you can work anywhere.'

'But ... I'm going home soon.'

'They have planes from London.'

At his quietly sincere words, her heart seemed to think it was doubling up as a Mexican jumping bean. The water was probably rippling around her chest.

'They do,' she acknowledged. Expensive planes probably, but that seemed a minor thing to bring up when he ... he was wanting to see her again.

'I'm in London quite often. My agent is always badgering me to spend more time there. I've been asked by a gallery in Dover Street if I'd like to put on an exhibition. They've refurbished the building and have a new space. I'm thinking about it. Been thinking about it for a while, except I didn't think I had any decent material. I was going to do a retrospective.'

Gabe gabbling was cute and she wasn't about to rescue him.

'And of course, I'll come to your exhibition. You could stay at my place if you like. That's if you wanted to ...'

He finally petered out.

'I'd like that,' she said softly. Amused and touched by his

unexpected diffidence, she moved towards him. It only took two short strokes before she stood before him and cupped his face with her wet hands. 'I'd like to see you again.'

His hands reached for her waist and he pulled her forward to kiss her. 'That would be good then,' he said as if everything was all sorted, which she guessed it kind of was when you were dealing with two people who lived in two different countries. It was far more than she'd expected.

Chapter 24

Real life bit hard on the way back. Gabe's phone seemed to be ringing non-stop and he spent most of the journey darting out to the deck between the carriages. Apparently 4pm in Los Angeles was a good time to do business. With a seventeen-hour difference, Gabe explained, it was difficult to find a better time to talk.

Fiona regretted losing her own phone and prayed that it was back at Haruka's because if it wasn't she had no idea where it could be, unless a pick pocket had stolen it, but from what she read before her trip the crime rate in Japan was low – definitely in comparison to Britain.

Having uploaded all of her photographs from her camera she turned on her laptop. She began selecting some of the more recent ones and putting them into her folder marked *Exhibition Possibles*. Once she'd decided on the pictures, she would be handing the file over to Kaito and his team who would be responsible for staging and the final curation of her exhibition. She was hoping to go through her favourites with Gabe before she made the final selection. If he wasn't too busy.

He spent more time on the phone than he did in his seat and even when the train finally drew to a standstill at Shinjuku he was nowhere in sight.

'Thanks. I feel like I've put in a full day's work already,' he said, reappearing at the very last minute as she pulled their bags down from the overhead shelf. 'Sorry for abandoning you.'

'It's fine. You were working and I got quite a bit done.'

'Want to come back to my studio?' He laid a hand on the small of her back and she leaned into it, relieved by the small touch of intimacy. She'd be lying if she didn't feel a sense of loss that they were going back to real life. As if he knew how she was feeling, he pressed a quick kiss on her mouth. 'And that's not a euphemism, although there's a serviceable couch in there.'

'Yes, but I need to pop back to Haruka's and dump my stuff.' And look for her phone; it had to be there somewhere.

'No problem. We could pick up a couple of bento boxes, have a working lunch, and go over your photos.' They walked through the vast Shinjuku station hand in hand and made their way to the Yamanote line. With Gabe holding her hand, resting loosely on his thigh, the journey home on the suburban train felt very different to the one out. By mutual design rather than spoken agreement, Fiona pulled her hand from his when they came in sight of the teashop and Gabe gave her an understanding nod. Whatever their relationship was, it felt too private to share and Fiona wasn't ready to discuss it or let it be discussed by anyone else, especially not by people who knew Gabe so much better than she did.

Setsuko called a cheery hello from the doorway of the

teashop as they wound their way into sight from the local railway station.

'How was Fuji?' she called from the doorway.

'Wonderful,' said Fiona and felt the brief butterfly brush of the back of Gabe's hand against hers. 'Absolutely beautiful.'

'Full of tourists,' said Gabe with his usual teasing grin.

'He loved it really.'

'Did you take lots of pictures?'

'Just a few. I'm going to drop off my things and then we're going to the studio and I'll come back later. Is that okay?'

'Okay, *Haha* is out but the door is open.' Setsuko bowed. 'I must get the shop ready for a tour today. And,' she added with one of her serene smiles, 'for the photographs.'

'Okay, I'll be over later.'

Fiona couldn't imagine what the other woman had to do as the shop was always immaculate.

'It's all about the ritual and the preparation,' murmured Gabe in her ear.

'Sometimes I think you're a mind reader.'

'I'm an observer of faces. Plus it's not difficult – you have a wonderfully expressive face.'

'You mean I'll never play poker and not lose the shirt off my back.'

'That too.' They'd reached Haruka's door. 'Come on over when you're ready.'

'Okay, I won't be long.'

'See you soon.' And before she could take the step up into the *genkan* he looped his hand through her arm. 'Aren't you forgetting something?' He pointed to his lips and puckered up.

She laughed; it was rather sweet. 'No idea what you're on about.'

He swooped in and kissed her firmly on the mouth with a mock growl.

There was no sign of her phone in her room which was odd and slightly perturbing. Fiona racked her brains. Where the hell had she last had it? Mentally she retraced her steps. That morning it had been a rush. She remembered stuffing it into the pocket of her bag thinking she would message her mother on the train. Damn. It was looking increasingly likely that it had been stolen. The other faint hope was that Haruka had found it and put it somewhere safe, but surely that would be Fiona's room?

What a pain. Everything was backed up on the Cloud but the phone was on contract and only half way through the eighteen-month period. Now she was going to have to report it stolen to the police and try and claim on the insurance which she knew she couldn't do anything about without some kind of crime number, and she had no idea how to do any of that. She hoped the thief came out in hives or got worms or something worse.

Her mother would be frantic by now. Had probably called the British embassy and reported her daughter missing. Fiona dropped her head in her hands. She really did need to persuade Gabe to let her use his phone. Surely there was some way of blocking the number when you phoned someone. Or she could lie and say she was calling from a public telephone box – that was a thought.

With her head still buzzing about how to deal with her

mother, she walked around to Gabe's building and climbed the wide-planked steps to his studio. In daylight it was a lovely airy space with clear bright light filtering through the *shoji* doors.

Humming lightly to herself and already picturing the soft smile on his face when she saw him again, she walked through the main studio space into Gabe's work area. Her face went slack and she stopped dead. Gabe was seated at his desk and next to him was Yumi, leaning against the desk massaging one of his shoulders. Her musical voice was saying something that brought a whimsical smile to his face and Fiona was almost felled by the instant surge of jealousy. It punched her in the stomach and she thought she might be sick.

'Hey Fi.' Damn. Gabe had spotted her before she could back out.

Yumi wore a khaki-green wrap-around dress that emphasised her delicate figure and little stiletto ankle boots on her tiny feet. With her porcelain skin and red lipstick she resembled a very pretty china doll.

She pushed herself away from the desk with a lingering smile at Gabe.

'Gabriel says you've been to Mount Fuji.' She made it sound impossibly tedious and as if she had every sympathy for him.

'Yes. It was'—she schooled her face into a polite mask—'interesting.'

Gabe turned away and she felt even more sick. Yumi was examining her with careful disdain and the only thing Fiona could be glad about was that she'd left her hair loose. Gabe had intimated several times that it was her crowning glory and he'd seemed unable to leave it alone, even on the train on the way home this morning he'd pushed a stray strand from her face and stroked along the length of it with a gentle hand.

Yumi was tapping her foot, a little staccato beat that gave away her irritation about something. Gabe was absorbed in something on the screen but looked up as Fiona made an uncertain movement, unsure as to whether to stay or go.

'Have you got your memory card?' he asked, all brisk and business-like, holding out his hand.

'Yes.' She stood, shifting her weight from foot to foot for a second. Stay or go. Make an excuse and leave. Her skin prickled at Yumi's sharp-eyed perusal and the tiny sniff as if she'd been found wanting. Even though inside everything was telling her to retreat, she deliberately lifted her chin, her hair rippling down her back. It was her bed Gabe had shared last night.

Gabe caught the movement and his expression softened, a faint smile playing around his lips as he beckoned her over and patted the seat next to him. 'Come on, let's see what we've got.'

Yumi gave an impatient huff. 'So you're going to work this afternoon.'

'Yes,' said Gabe patiently, 'but only until four.'

'And then you'll take me to Albatross?'

'And then I'll take you to Albatross,' he said with an indulgent smile as if appeasing a child.

Yumi still didn't seem particularly satisfied. 'I suppose I can go and do some shopping until then.' She smoothed the fabric of her dress over her enviably tiny waist. Unless you studied her closely, Fiona decided, you would have thought her face devoid of expression but there was something there that reminded her of the portrait in the photographic museum, the one with Yumi in the white silk dress and the expression of inviolate triumph. It was there now in the tiny twist of her lips, the knowing look in her eyes.

'I will see you later then.' She snatched up her Mulberry bag and stalked out.

Her footsteps rang out on the wooden steps but Gabe gave nothing away. He held out his hand for the memory card. A sense of deflation hit Fiona. He might have said he wanted to see her again in London but he was still tied to Yumi and nothing was going to break that bond.

'Do you want a coffee or anything?' he asked, loading the photos, the thumbnails of which were flicking onto the screen one by one like little soldiers reporting for duty in strict formation.

'Yes, shall I help myself?' she asked, regretting the stiffness in her voice.

He lifted his head from the screen and reached out a hand to pull her nearer. 'Sorry about that. I didn't know she was in Tokyo. She just dropped in.'

'No, of course not.' Although she tried to sound blasé, she knew her smile was wooden. Making a fuss, which wasn't her style anyway, would make her seem petty and demanding.

'It doesn't mean anything, I promise.' He rose and took her into his arms, his fingers rubbing up and down her upper arm which was actually quite irritating, as if she needed placating. 'I'm only taking her out for a drink and I won't be long. You said you wanted to get some more pictures of Setsuko and the teashop. I'll be back before dinner. Her husband's away again and she's lonely. She hasn't got anyone else.' She detected a wariness in his tone as if he was unsure how she was going to react. 'I could text you when we're done and meet you back here.'

She studied his face. He genuinely believed what he was saying, and she wondered if he even heard how it sounded.

Leftovers, she thought. It would always be leftovers with Gabe.

'No, not at all,' she said with false brightness. What was the point in making a fuss? It would be churlish and fruitless. He wasn't hers and never would be. 'If you don't mind, I'd like to do some work here on the album I want to put together for Haruka and Setsuko.'

'That's a lovely idea; you can print the pictures off and I have a couple of presentation albums you can have.' He rose and pulled two from a shelf above his head and laid them on the desk. 'I always keep a stock of them in, as they're sometimes useful for presenting client work.'

'Thank you. That's great.' She went over to the machine and slipped a sidelong glance at him as she went, sceptical of his absorption with the contents of the screen. 'Do you want a coffee?'

'Yes, please.' He pushed his chair over to the other desk and grabbed a notepad. 'Pen and paper still works best when noting down the image numbers.'

With a nod she moved towards the kitchenette and caught her foot in the handle of his overnight back which had been dumped on the floor. Something went spinning across the

304

floor. Damn, his phone. Its rapid flight was stopped by the little fridge in the corner.

'Sorry,' she said, hurrying to retrieve the phone that was now wedged under the fridge, praying she hadn't broken it.

'What?' Gabe was still absorbed in copying something down on the notepad and she crossed her fingers. Please don't let it have broken.

It hadn't, which was just as well, because it wasn't Gabe's phone.

As soon as she picked it up, the familiar wallpaper of the opera house in Copenhagen flashed on the screen.

She looked from the screen to Gabe and back again.

'Gabe?'

'Mmm, you've got some cracking shots here.'

'Gabe!' she said more sharply this time.

He lifted his head and looked at her properly. She held up the phone, her brain clumsily trying to compute the facts. Her phone was in Gabe's bag. Right on the top. He must have known it was here. All the time.

A range of expressions flitted across his face: trapped, caught out, and guilty before settling on consternation.

'This is my phone.'

'Uh-huh,' he said and she could see his Adam's apple dipping. 'Your phone.'

'What was it doing in your bag?'

He grimaced and stood up. As he took a few steps towards her, she held it out in front of her like a sword, albeit a very feeble and pathetic sword, warning him to keep his distance, but he kept coming.

305

She shook her head. 'No, stay there.'

He sighed and held up his hands.

She scowled at him. Did he really think his easy surrender was going to get him out of this?

'I'm sorry but I did it for your own good.'

She raised a scandalised eyebrow, making it clear what she thought of that sorry-arsed line. 'Own good?'

'Sorry. Now I've said that out loud, it sounds a bit dickish.'

'Probably because it's a lot dickish.'

'I wanted you to have a good time and ... not have to worry about your mum every five minutes.'

She let this sink in amid a mass of fury that was radiating through every cell in her brain. If someone could thermo image it right now, it probably looked like the centre of a volcano before it blew.

'So you ... took my phone.'

He nodded, shoving his hands in his back pockets and leaning back slightly. 'Yes. But we did have a good time ...' He paused.

What, he expected her to agree? Her mind clouded by bloody marvellous sex?

Now he added more tentatively. 'And you didn't have to worry about her.'

Her head was surely going to explode. 'And you think that's okay? What if my mum had been seriously ill? What if she needed me?'

'Fi, she could have got hold of you. At any time if it was urgent. You know she could.'

'That's not the point.'

'Yes, it is. She's constantly messaging you. You said yourself there's nothing wrong with her. She manipulates you.'

'Yes.' Fiona drew herself up with all the disdain she could muster, anger battling with disappointment for dominance. 'She does. And I handle it. I'm not a child, you know. I've been dealing with my mother for years. I know exactly how she operates.'

She glared at him and saw him flinch. Good. With icy hauteur, she narrowed her eyes and took a step towards him. 'Did it ever occur to you that my messages to her are reassurance? Her security blanket? A fail safe, like a pressure valve? She knows I'm not going to come running. We've been there, done that. She's a lonely woman who doesn't have much in her life but me.'

'And maybe you like that,' he said standing straighter, folding his arms, suddenly combative.

She stared at him. 'Pardon?'

He screwed up his mouth before speaking, giving her a level assessing gaze. 'We all want to feel needed and essential to someone else's happiness and wellbeing. I'm just pointing out that perhaps it satisfies something in you. Makes you feel a bit better about yourself. A bit less guilty that you don't take her illnesses seriously.'

Outrage took her breath away. 'What! How dare you? You're the last one to talk about manipulation. Yumi's got that leash so tight, one tug and you come running.'

'Don't bring her into this.'

'Why the hell not? You say I'm manipulated but I'm completely aware of what my mother is up to. I manage it.

You, you're absolutely clueless. And you're a complete fool. She's got you dancing to her tune whenever she wants.'

Gabe's fists clenched at his sides and she could see she'd really touched a nerve. His jaw jutted out with all the belligerence of a boxer in the ring.

'You're jealous,' he spat with a touch of spite. It hit bang on target because it was true and in that moment, she knew if she'd ever had him, she'd lost him now. Gabe would always be tied to Yumi.

She lifted her chin, determined to be honest because she had absolutely nothing to lose.

'Yes, I am. She's everything I'm not and you can't let go of her. You're in love with the idea of being in love with her. I think you probably always will be.'

She didn't take any satisfaction in the aghast expression on his face as the words sank in. Instead she pushed her phone into her pocket and walked out without another word.

She didn't go straight back to Haruka's. Instead she stalked around the neighbourhood with stiff-legged strides, trying to burn away her fury, going over and over Gabe's words in her head. He was wrong. He didn't know anything about her or her mother. And he was the last person to ... to say anything. He was still too messed up by Yumi. Well, he deserved her. If he couldn't see how she used him, that was his problem.

Finally, when she was convinced she could act normally rather than like a fire-breathing dragon, she found her way back to Haruka's house, grateful that the Japanese left their doors open and she could slip into her room without having to speak to anyone, although it seemed no one was home. Even so, with burglar-like stealth she crept quietly in and drew the *shoji* doors closed.

Her phone had one percent of battery left, so she plugged it in to charge and scanned the messages. Annoyingly, Gabe had been right. Her mother's messages had ground to a halt once she realised that Fiona wasn't responding.

I was so worried but I phoned the emergency number you gave me and I spoke to a very nice lady who told me you'd gone away to an area where there was no phone signal but that it's very safe in Japan and that I shouldn't worry. She was very reassuring.

Thank you, Haruka. Fiona lay down on the mattress and stared up at the ceiling holding her phone in one hand.

For a moment her finger hovered over the little white conversation box at the bottom of the screen in WhatsApp and then she put her phone down. There was a sense of relief. A burden lifted. She didn't have to message her mother, not right now. The get-out-of-jail-free card was valid for a little while longer. Who knew, maybe it would do her mother good to survive on her own for a bit. Fiona had been out of touch for two days. Hardly a lifetime. And no, she wasn't going to think about Gabe's unkind words, that maybe she liked being needed because that wasn't true ... was it?

And he was one to talk. Their fling, or whatever you wanted to call it, hadn't really meant anything to him. A bit of fun. An interlude. The only person he really cared about was Yumi which, yes, did hurt. She'd never expected Gabe to love her but seeing that he was capable of loving someone who so didn't deserve it, well, that did hurt. It hurt a lot, almost a real physical pain digging in under her ribs with a hollow ache. She clutched her middle, fighting back tears. She'd never stood a chance with Gabe, she always knew that, but having it brought home to her so absolutely made it harder to bear somehow.

She heard a noise downstairs and straightened up, swiping away a stray tear that had the temerity to fight free.

Chapter 25

Setsuko reached up, her pale hand stark against the black matt caddies with their gold calligraphy, and Fiona knew the shot was perfect. Taking a breath, Fiona pressed the button slowly this time, feeling her anger dissipate at the sight of Setsuko's sure, calm grace.

Fury and rage had driven her for the first fifteen minutes and she'd been like a whirling ninja firing shots left, right, and centre, greedily sucking up every image that presented itself of the tourists exploring the tiny shop, lifting and pawing at the *chawan*, cooing and exclaiming over the scents of the teas and their recent tea ceremony experience. To her churning spirit they were like invaders, but now that the tour group had left, the quiet and heavy layers of history and culture began to settle her. Without saying anything, Setsuko made a small pot of tea and put it on a tray with three *matcha* bowls and came to sit at one of the tables.

'Come, sit.' She patted the bench beside her.

Fiona set down her camera and watched as Setsuko poured three jasmine-scented cups of tea and pushed one towards her. The other woman didn't say anything, just sipped at her tea and waited. Next to her, Fiona was aware of her absolute stillness.

Fiona swallowed, trying to down the lump that had wedged itself tight in her throat. She stared at one of the paper lanterns hanging from the roof, the long red tassel dancing in the light breeze that stole through the open window.

Setsuko laid her elegant hand on top of Fiona's and offered her a sad, gentle smile.

'What happened?'

Fiona made a small noise, half laugh, half bunged-up snuffle. 'I fell in love with Gabe again. Stupid, huh?'

'And that does not bring you joy?'

Like a silent wraith, Haruka appeared and slid onto the bench, sandwiching Fiona against Setsuko. Even though she really didn't feel like it, it made her smile. Two bodyguards flanking her. Love for both of them blossomed inside her.

'It did but he's still in love with Yumi.'

Next to her, Haruka actually growled and it drew another small laugh from Fiona. She tucked her arm through the older woman's in a gesture that she couldn't remember ever doing with her own mother. Something about the presence of the older woman soothed and grounded her. Being in the shop made her think more clearly. 'In England, a famous poet, Tennyson, said, "Tis better to have loved and lost than never to have loved at all." Right now I find that difficult to believe.' She pressed a hand against her breast bone.

Haruka nodded. '*Mono no aware*. We would translate it as poignancy, the joy of being in love tempered by the loss of that love. The joy of the cherry blossom and the sadness of knowing it will last only a short time.'

The three of them sat in silence, drinking tea and gazing thoughtfully out of the window at Haruka's garden. Fiona studied the blossom on the weeping cherries drifting like snowflakes and the tracery of acer leaves dancing on the light breezes. Even though her heart felt heavy in her chest, like a solid lump of stone, she could appreciate the beauty of the garden. There was light after dark, laughter after tears and happiness after sadness. Next to her, she felt the body warmth of both Setsuko and Haruka, tiny indomitable women offering her their support.

'The blossom is falling,' said Haruka. 'But we can hold on to the memories.'

Fiona thought about it and almost smiled. She had memories of Gabe. She should cherish those.

Haruka patted her hand. 'Like the cherry blossom, you will love again.'

'I hope so.'

'But if you don't enter the tiger's cave you can't catch its cub.' Haruka turned and gave her of one her now familiar, impassive stares.

'I think that translates as nothing ventured, nothing gained.' She gave both women a rueful grimace. 'I ventured, I gained, but now it's time to go home.'

Haruka shook her head. 'Fall seven times, stand up eight,' she said fiercely.

Fiona took in a deep breath. 'I know my limits but I want to thank you for everything.'

Gabe was only part of this. She'd always known he was out of her league and if she were honest with herself, he was far more suited to the worldly Yumi and her ilk.

She didn't want her memories to be negative ones. 'My stay has been amazing. I've learned so much and there are some things I'll never forget. Your and Setsuko's dignity and grace. Your generosity in inviting me into your home. Teaching me about *wabi-sabi*, *kintsugi*, the peace of nature and so many other things. I'm ready to go home. To put some of those things into practice. To talk to my mother.'

'She called.'

'I know.'

'She's lonely.'

'I know but I can't be the only answer to that. We both need to learn to live our own lives.'

She fumbled for her phone, which she'd tucked inside her pocket. Raising it above her head, she took a selfie of the three of them.

'Where is Gabe now?'

'He's going in to Tokyo to meet Yumi.'

'Foolish man.'

Fiona gave her a tight smile. 'That's what I told him.'

'You didn't.' Setsuko gave her a cartoon-wide stare, while there was an approving smile in Haruka's warm brown eyes.

'I did. I told him he was a complete fool. He didn't like it when I told him he was like a dog on a leash and that he was still in love with her and probably always would be.'

Both women exchanged startled glances. 'And what did he say to that?' asked Haruka with great interest.

'I didn't give him the chance. I walked out.'

'Bravo.' She clapped her hands. 'I have been telling him this but does he listen? Maybe this time he will.'

'Well he might do but I'm done with him. I don't want to see him. I wish I could get an earlier flight.' Was that running away or bringing her trip to a graceful end?

'That's a good idea,' said Haruka, shocking Fiona. 'If you'd like I can ask Kaito to change the flights; he has a good friend at Japan Travel. You could go tomorrow instead of the day after.'

'Er ... um ...' The suggestion took the wind out of her sails for a moment but the more she thought about it, the better that idea was. She'd seen everything she wanted to, taken enough photos to mount ten exhibitions. Things with Gabe, no matter how else she wished it, weren't going to change and it would be better for a swift amputation. Not seeing him again would make life so much easier. She'd gone into things knowing it was always going to be temporary, so there was no point prolonging things.

'I'd like that.' She had a good idea of which photos she wanted to enter into the exhibition and she could send them to Kaito from London. She just needed to retrieve her memory card from Gabe's studio and print off the pictures for Haruka and Setsuko before Gabe got back.

When she came back from Gabe's studio with the two albums clutched under her arms, she felt a sense of triumph. She'd pulled together a lovely selection, a real tribute to their kindness. The first picture in both albums was the one of the two

315

women and their heart-to-heart in Ueno Park, then there were pictures of Haruka in the garden and Setsuko in the teashop as well as the staged shot of the three generations of women. She'd also included pictures of Mayu at the Robot Restaurant but also a more sedate one of a thoughtful young woman gazing up at the cherry blossom.

On impulse, she went up into the teashop rather than the house, drawn to take a few more pictures, hoping to capture the elusive mystery and magic of the place. There was a clatter as she stepped inside the room and Mayu whirled round clutching one of the caddies to her chest.

'You frightened me,' she said, ducking to pick up the lid she'd dropped.

'Sorry ... I just wanted to take some more ...' She indicated her camera. 'What are you doing?'

Mayu's eyes slid past her and it was almost comical to see the girl's attempt to find an excuse. 'Just tidying up, you know.'

The place was immaculate, as always.

'Can I take a picture of you?'

The enthusiasm bounced right back. 'Sure. What do you want?'

Fiona lifted her shoulders. 'You suggest something.'

'Me blending tea,' said Mayu immediately. 'I've watched Mama do it. She knows so much.'

They set up the shot, Fiona smiling at Mayu's quick-fire explanations of what she was doing and why. In fact, the shots she took of Mayu preparing were far better than the posed ones at the end but she didn't tell her that.

'I've got some great stuff here, thanks.'

'Cool.'

'I love this place,' said Fiona, giving it a fond look around. 'There's something ...'

'There is ... but I don't know what it is,' the girl agreed before adding dreamily, 'and one day it will be mine.'

Tears pricked Fiona's eyes at the quiet pride in Mayu's voice.

'And one day I'll be a master of tea like *Jiji*.'

'I'm sure you will.' Fiona gave her a swift hug. 'And your grandmother will very proud of you.'

'After I've been a dancer at the Robot Restaurant first, of course.'

'Well naturally. But master of tea ... that's going to make her very happy.'

'Yeah, just don't tell her yet,' and Mayu winked.

Fiona followed the sound of voices and found Setsuko and Haruka all of a twitter in the kitchen.

'Kaito's friend has found you a flight tomorrow morning. First class.' Haruka beamed proudly.

'Oh. Wow. That's ...' Were they really that desperate to be rid of her? Her consternation must have shown because Setsuko patted her on the shoulder. 'It was the only flight available with Japanese Airlines that he could get upgraded and he thought you would like that. We will be very sad to see you go.'

'But you will come back to see us,' said Haruka as if this was a fact rather than a request.

'Th-thank you. I don't know what to say.' It was all so sudden but now that the offer was there, she was suddenly desperate to go home. Sleep in her own bed and eat toast and Marmite. She'd enjoyed exploring Japanese food and culture but she was dying for a cup of PG Tips, a digestive biscuit, central heating, and sound-proof walls, although she wouldn't mind taking a *kotatsu* table home with her.

'I have something for you both.' She handed them their individual albums.

They both opened the first page. Setsuko sighed and placed a hand over her heart. Haruka simply nodded. And then both of them, in complete accord, and with their usual calm reverence, insisted on going to sit down at the *kotatsu* to give the albums due consideration.

They turned the pages in silence, nodding every now and then. Fiona could feel herself hanging on to her breath waiting for their reaction but she wasn't nervous. This was some of her very best work. The respect and admiration she felt for the Kobashi family was etched into every single picture. Her affection for the two women resonated from the pages of the album. Before they reached the end of their respective albums both of them had reached out a hand and laid it on Fiona's.

'Thank you,' whispered Setsuko, resting her other hand on the album. 'This is beautiful.'

Haruka didn't say a word but a single tear worked its way down her normally impassive face and she gave Fiona a solemn bow. They sat in silence for several minutes more and Fiona couldn't remember a time when she'd felt a greater sense of achievement.

With the kindness that had characterised her whole stay, the two women helped her pack, rolling up her clothes, admiring her leather jacket which she decided to travel in.

'Would you mind getting rid of this for me?' she asked, holding up the hairy coat, threadbare in some places and long overdue for the textile bank.

'Can I have it?' came a sudden yell from another room and Mayu appeared in the opening of the *shoji* doors. Yes, Fiona was definitely looking forward to sturdy walls again.

'I guess.' Fiona laughed while the teenage immediately put it on and modelled it with a prancing walk, a future master of tea but for the time being a rebellious teenager.

'It's cool.'

'It's ugly,' said Haruka, making no apology to Fiona. 'I despair.' She frowned at her granddaughter and shook her head.

'It's had its day,' Fiona said, 'but I'm glad you like it.' It was a symbol of her moving on. Gabe might have broken her heart but in admitting he had found her attractive, he'd also freed her from that awful sense of failure and humiliation that had influenced so many of the decisions that had limited her horizons. His heart might be out of reach, but she had her self-respect and that was worth plenty. She was a leather jacket kind of girl now.

Chapter 26

In the morning his head ached from too much thinking into the night, but he bounded out of bed with fresh purpose. He took the flight of stairs down to the studio and wondered whether to forgo coffee and go to Haruka's straight away. Coffee won and while he was waiting for the machine, he switched on his computer. He stood and studied the photos he'd taken in the last couple of weeks. They were good, more than good. He'd got his mojo back. He'd known the pictures of Ken were good and already the magazine offers were coming thick and fast and he couldn't wait to tackle the new commissions.

Sipping at his coffee he studied the last lot of shots he'd worked on late last night, cropping to make sure they put the subject and compositions centre stage and gave himself a small pat on the back. There was an energy and honesty about his work that had been missing for quite a while. He'd called Fiona Sleeping Beauty, but it had been him that had been sleep walking through the past three years.

He winced. Funny how quickly a scene like that could remove the scales. Yumi didn't really love anyone but herself and with sadness, he reflected, she probably hadn't ever loved him anymore than he'd really loved her. It had suited them both, their careers and their lifestyles, to be together; it had become habit and then when she'd married, pride had made him hang on to a friendship to demonstrate to curious eyes that he was man enough to take her rejection. A friendship that was as empty as it was authentic.

Despite these less than edifying thoughts – and the realisation he'd been a complete arse for a lot of his life – this morning the world appeared so much brighter. The load was lighter. He scanned the surface of the desk. The memory card. It had gone. He sighed. He didn't blame Fiona; he'd said some awful things to her, when she was the person he most wanted to be with. Over the last two weeks he'd woken up. It was time to make amends.

He put down the coffee and saw the studio through fresh eyes, remembering the first time Fiona had stood taking in the pictures of Yumi. Her hair had flamed gold in the light, that wide mouth dropping open in admiration. They were good pictures; he would always be proud of them, but it was time to take them down and make way for new work. Maybe he'd ask Fiona to choose some pictures to replace them. His mouth curved with a smile of anticipation. They could work together. The idea gave him a warm glow and he put down his coffee, kicked off his slippers, and padded down the stairs to pull on his shoes.

'Hello,' he called into the quiet house. There was no answer but the kettle on the gas top was steaming slightly and

Haruka's shoes had been in the *genkan*. He walked through the house to the *engwan* and followed it round to find Haruka leaning on the top wooden rail. Stern and unapproachable, she glanced up at him briefly before turning back to her silent contemplation of the garden.

For once he stopped, taking in all the tiny details, the moss-covered stones around the pond, a touch of verdigris on the bronze pots, the fierce, stalwart shadows of the bonsai fir trees their sturdy shapes untouched by the light wind rippling through the bigger trees. The strength in their small compact shape belied by their size. Haruka had done a beautiful job. His blood sang with the urge to take a picture of her, a close-up of her smooth, impassive face shaded by the cherry blossom, or with the blossom in the background, or in the autumn among the russet and red colours of the exotic trees. He traced her profile, the small nose, the neat chin. Despite her size she was a formidable character with a depth and spirituality to her that he'd yet to find in anyone else.

'Do you know where Fiona is?'

'Yes.' Her tone wasn't exactly forthcoming but it wasn't the first time he'd been on the receiving end of her disapproval.

He waited for her to say more but her mouth was pinned shut. 'Where is she?'

Haruka slowly lifted her wrist and checked her watch. 'Gone to the airport.'

'The airport? Why?' He felt a kick to his pulse.

'To catch a plane.'

He stared at her.

'But her flight's not until tomorrow.' Panic gnawed low in his belly.

'Kaito was able to get her a sooner flight.' Her voice was too innocent, too smooth, and a little bit too satisfied.

'But ...' He glared at her. She'd had a hand in this.

'You let her go,' she said reprovingly.

'I made a mistake.' His voice rose, as the reality of it hit him.

'Even monkeys fall out of trees,' she said with a dismissive lift of her shoulders.

Everyone makes mistakes. It hit like a demolition ball. This wasn't just a mistake, it was ... he couldn't put the panicky, turn-your-stomach-inside-out fears into words.

'I need to speak to Fiona, to see her.'

'Too late,' said Haruka with finality, smug triumph in the way she dusted her hands together.

It couldn't be too late. There was too much he had to say to her. He had to say sorry. He had to tell her ... to tell her things ... all those things jumbled up in his head and he couldn't pluck one particular thing but he knew he needed to see her. When he saw her face, everything would be all right. He'd know the words then. Find them. If not he'd say it in other ways. She'd know. 'I need to speak to her, to tell her ...' He lifted his shoulders to cover the gap.

'You need to show her,' reproved Haruka. 'Go to London. Chase her. Words aren't enough.'

He held up his hands. 'I've been a fool.'

Haruka raised one stately eyebrow of agreement. He eyed her, suspicions stirring. He wasn't fool enough to accuse her of setting this up, but he had a pretty good idea that she had been pulling a few strings.

'She left twenty minutes ago.'

He'd always dismissed those films where the hero makes a mad dash to the airport to stop the love of his life disappearing into the blue yonder and show her how much he cares – the stupid sap should have just told her – but now as he jostled his way through the queue at the barrier from the monorail to Haneda International Airport, he prayed to move faster. He'd also always jeered at the dumb dolt who'd left his phone on the side with the camera doing a meaty close up. Why hadn't he texted her? Told her to wait for him. Irritation at his own dumb-ass stupidity made him jittery and jumpy, hopping from foot to foot to the rampant disapproval of the woman in front of him. When he started to mutter under his breath, she turned and shot him a sharp scowl, but for Pete's sake couldn't she see he was in a hurry? He needed to catch Fiona before she went through security and ... well, he still wasn't sure what he wanted to tell her. His brain had gone into some kind of basic hunter mode where getting to the airport and finding her at check-in was the primary focus. The baseline was that he had to see her.

He hurtled into the airport terminal scanning the departures display for the combination of JAL and Heathrow. Bugger. He hadn't even stopped to get the flight number. Haruka had thought that it left at about twelve-thirty which made the last check-in at ten-thirty and it was ten past ten now.

There, he'd spotted it. Check-in desk G, or it could be N, depending on what class she was flying. Shit, he had no idea. Taking off at a run he headed down to the check-in lines. The one at G was long and so was the one at N. There were too many people, lots of Westerners, so he couldn't even pick out her hair. Her hairy coat. That was individual. No one else had a coat like that. He examined the queue once and then again. No sign of her. He ran to the next queue, for business class. Again he checked the people in the queue. He forced himself to slow down and check again. Where was she? She couldn't have gone through. Not already.

In desperation he scanned the crowd again, one by one. Sweat, real actual sweat, dripped down his back and his hand was shaking. Maybe she wasn't here yet.

He paced. He watched the clock. The queue got shorter and shorter until there were only two people left to check in.

It was now ten-thirty. The girl on the desk rose and the lights above the desk went out.

He stood there and stared at the darkened screen, unable to move.

She'd gone.

With despair clutching at his gut, Gabe turned and then, miraculously, in the distance he spotted the sleeve of a familiar coat. His heart leapt. There was Fiona's hairy coat moving along in a tide of people walking down the concourse. The rush of relief almost pushed his pulse into overdrive. Taking off at a run he belted down the concourse. 'Fiona! Fiona!'

The coat stopped and a figure detached itself from the group.

Disappointment, sharp and jagged, tore through him. 'Mayu?'

'Gabe! What are you doing here?'

'Where's Fiona?'

'Oh, she's gone. Went through ages ago. I like hanging around here; it's kinda cool.'

Unable to say anything, he gestured to the coat.

'Great, isn't it? Fiona gave it to me.' She clutched the lapels and swaggered, twisting her shoulders from side to side.

He grimaced, a sort of yes, from between pinched lips and looked back towards the gates.

'Have you got your phone?'

'Yes.'

'I need it. I need to phone Fiona.'

Mayu smiled cheerfully at him. 'Her phone's dead. No charge. And no cable. It's in her suitcase. She said no worries because she couldn't use it on the plane anyway.'

He pushed his hands through his hair. Even if he bought a plane ticket, he didn't have his passport. He threw his head back and sighed.

'What are you doing here, Gabe?' asked Mayu with a puzzled frown.

'It doesn't matter,' he said.

'Were you going to say goodbye to Fiona? Do you like her? Please tell me you don't like Yumi anymore. Fiona is so much nicer.'

Gabe dredged up a reluctant smile. 'Yes, she is.'

Mayu suddenly stopped and her eyes widened with saucer-like wonder. 'You came to stop her. Like in the films. The big gesture.'

'Grand gesture,' murmured Gabe.

'You have to go to London. On the next plane.'

'I do have to go London. You're right. But not on the next plane.' No, this time he was going to do things properly. He knew exactly how he was going to show her how he felt.

Chapter 27

Fiona put her phone down with a thud on her dressing table and stared out of her bedroom window at the early hawthorn blossom in the hedgerow. She picked up the little *netsuke* and held it tightly, the smooth planes of the rabbit tucked into the centre of her palm. It had been two weeks and she hadn't heard a word from Gabe. Not that she'd expected too. Not really.

Except, her exhibition opened this evening. In a few hours. Inside, she had a tiny desperate hope that he might come. Or at least wish her luck. But there'd been nothing, and why should there be? He was in love with Yumi.

It wasn't supposed to hurt this much. Memories of those two days at the hotel shouldn't have burned their way into her consciousness as much as they had done. She wasn't supposed to have fallen in love with him.

She eyed her phone and right on cue it beeped.

Even though she knew it couldn't possibly be Gabe she snatched it up. A message from Avril.

See you soon. Break a leg. Ax.

Oh God, she felt nervous. Avril had been nagging her about what she was going to wear. In a fit of obstinacy, she'd decided she'd wear the linen jumpsuit but she had bought some navy-blue suede stiletto-heeled boots to dress it up and had abandoned the cami underneath, instead opting to wear a chunky gold signature necklace and show a bit of cleavage.

It didn't take a psychologist to work out that she was hoping Gabe might turn up, or the message she was sending by wearing the damn thing.

Now, standing in her underwear, she reached for it with a tortured mix of emotions. Why hadn't she decided to wear something else? It seemed impossible to erase the image of Gabe opening the buttons or his fingers stroking her skin around the lace of her camisole. With a hitch of her breath she pictured him, his fingers dipping into her cleavage.

'Fiona,' her mother called up the stairs. 'Fiona, are you there?'

She closed her eyes with a sigh and resisted the urge to call back, 'No.'

Luckily her mother hadn't noticed her lack of appetite or propensity to stare out of windows lost in thought. She was actually busy. To Fiona's amazement, she'd joined the WI in the village which was a very brave and unexpected new step. When Fiona had asked what had brought this on, her mother had given her a guileless shrug and said she didn't know what Fiona was talking about.

'Be down in a minute, Mum.' She glanced at her watch, checking the timings again. Four-thirty train. That would get them into Waterloo at twenty past five. Then half an hour to get to Kensington which left half an hour before the official launch party began. She knew the timings because she'd been to the white-walled gallery with its stark black floors and *shoji*-style windows several times to supervise the final arrangement of the pictures and watch them all be hung by the gallery manager, Mr Morimoto, a small dapper man who bowed like a bobbing robin and had twinkling bird-bright eyes. He also had the propensity to worry about every last detail which was reassuring as she was confident he had everything under control. All she had to do was turn up and, thanks to Avril's mile-long contact list, they were guaranteed plenty of attendees including her friends, Kate and Ben, David and his husband Reece, Conrad and Avril's husband Christophe.

'You look nice, Mum,' she said, meeting her mother at the bottom of the stairs. Judy Hanning was always neat and tidy but today in a pale blue shift dress, she looked much younger and prettier than usual. Normally she wore unflattering mid-length skirts and baggy cardigans that made her appear more like an old lady.

'Thank you, dear. And so do you. I do like how you're wearing your hair down. I'd forgotten what a glorious colour it is.' She reached forward and smoothed a curl from Fiona's face.

Fiona swallowed and pressed her lips tightly together, worried she might burst into tears.

'Are you sure you'll be all right walking in those heels though? I've put my flats on because sometimes you have to walk miles from the platform at the station down to the tube.'

She held out a leg and waggled her foot encased in a very sensible black ballet flat.

'I'll be fine. I've done the journey a few times; there's not much walking.' Besides, even if there had been, sheer vanity would carry her through. She liked the way the shoes flattered her legs, making them appear so much longer and slinkier. For once she didn't feel like an awkward stork.

'If you're sure, dear. You don't want to sprain your ankle or anything. Now, do you think I ought to take an umbrella?'

'The forecast is good but if there's room in your handbag I guess you might as well.' Fiona knew that if she said no there'd be a protracted debate about the pros and cons of leaving it behind. 'We need to go in a minute.' It was a five-minute drive to the station but she didn't want to leave anything to chance.

'Yes. I'll leave some food out for Daisy as we'll be out until late. She's had her nose pressed up against the window all day watching the birds nesting in the hedge. I worry about one of those poor babies falling out of the nest and Daisy pouncing on it.'

Fiona didn't laugh, although a wry smile touched her lips. The babies were safe because the cat was the laziest creature alive. Why pounce when dinner was on tap? She waited in the doorway of the kitchen, trying not to feel impatient as her mother took a fresh bowl out of the cupboard, picked up the dirty one and put it in the sink and began to wash it. Why did she have to start fussing with this sort of thing now? But she counted to ten as slowly as she could. They had time.

'Do you want me to check the doors and windows?' Fiona asked, knowing that this might hold them up too.

'No, dear.' Fiona blinked in surprise. That was new.

'Peter says if a burglar really wants to get in, they will. The alarm is a better deterrent.'

'Right.' Peter? The man that lived next door and had done so for the last eighteen months.

Her mother finally took the box of cat biscuits out of the cupboard, giving it a good shake, at which point bat-eared Daisy came streaking into the kitchen, early tea propelling her from her usual slothful indolence. Unfortunately, her speedy entrance coincided with Fiona's mother's sharp turn to fill up the bowl by the cat flap. There was an aggrieved yowl, a shower of cat biscuits and a crash as her mum went down in a crumpled heap and the cat shot out of the cat flap.

'Mum! Are you okay?' Fiona darted to her side.

Blinking back tears, her mother's mouth wobbled as she quavered. 'My ankle. Ouch.'

With a sinking heart, Fiona crouched at her side. 'So much for sensible shoes.'

Her mother managed a small laugh. 'How silly of me.'

'Come on, let's you get up. We need to get that foot elevated.'

Her mother allowed herself to be helped to her feet then hopped to the kitchen table and collapsed with a groan into one of the chairs. Fiona pulled a second chair out and propped her mother's foot up, wincing. It was starting to swell.

'What a stupid thing to happen,' muttered her mother.

'Do you think you twisted it or was there a crack or anything?'

'I went over on it. It's probably just a sprain.' Fiona, a little nonplussed by this uncharacteristically pragmatic response simply nodded. Where were the histrionics? Her mother normally loved a drama.

'We need to ice it.' Elevate, ice and compress, she remembered from First Aid training. She crossed to the freezer to retrieve the cold pack in there. As a fully registered hypochondriac, her mother had kitted the house out with every piece of First Aid equipment she could get her hands on.

The ankle was already swollen and was starting to turn a little blue. It didn't look good at all.

'What do you think?'

Fiona had no idea.

'I think I may have to go to A&E.'

Fiona nodded. She thought so too. Looked as if she was going to miss her own exhibition.

Now she really did want to cry. Although she was nervous, she was still eager to see people's responses. The pictures represented her best work; tonight was supposed to be her triumph. And what if Gabe did turn up?

'I'll make a couple of calls. I need to contact Mr Morimoto at the gallery, let him know I won't be there, and then we'll go.'

'Go? You're not going anywhere, young lady. Well, apart from to London. You've got an exhibition to get to.'

'I can't leave you.'

Her mother huffed. 'Fiona, I'm aware that I've been quite a burden to you.'

Fiona started to object.

'Yes, I have. I realised when I couldn't get hold of you in Japan ... I was all set to call the British Embassy.'

Fiona almost laughed. Hadn't she predicted that very thing?

'And then when I'd spoken to the nice Japanese lady—'

'You mean Haruka?' Fiona smiled. She missed Haruka more than she would have imagined. And Setsuko. And Gabe.

'Is that her name? She was very kind but it was then I realised how ridiculous I was being. And that I didn't need to text and message you all the time. You have your own life to lead.'

Fiona bit her lip. Oh, the irony. Gabe had been right all along.

'And when I talked to Peter about it—'

'Peter?'

'Yes, Peter. He was very supportive while you were in Japan. Made me see things a lot more clearly. I've not been a very good mother.'

'Don't be silly,' Fiona protested. Her mother wasn't that bad. She fussed a bit and was a hypochondriac but as Gabe had pointed out, perhaps Fiona had let her.

'I could have been a lot better. When your dad died, I was so angry with him for leaving me. I put everything into taking care of you but when you got older and more independent, especially these last couple of years, there was nothing for me to do. So I leaned on you ... too much. Anyway, Peter, well, he gave me quite a stern talking to. Said I had a lot of life left in me and I needed to start enjoying it and doing things on my own and to stop acting like a housebound old lady. He dared me to join the WI.'

'I did wonder.' Fiona gave her mother's hand a squeeze.

'Oh, look at the time, you need to go. You'll have missed the first train but there's another one in forty minutes. You'll be a little late.'

'Mum, I can't leave you on your own. You ought to go to the hospital and get it checked out.'

'I'll ask Peter to take me. My mobile's in my hand bag. Can you go and get it for me?'

Chapter 28

Unfortunately, the train was delayed by a points failure at Vauxhall which left Fiona drumming her fingers on her other palm wondering if she should let Mr Morimoto know of the further delay. Poor man had been beside himself when she told him about her mother. By the time she rushed through the doors to her own launch party she was an hour late. She stood in the small lobby for a moment considering turning tail. The next room was full, with people looking at the large framed prints. Excitement fizzed her in stomach. Her photographs. On display. And people were studying them, properly examining them. God, what if they didn't like them? Goosebumps raised on her skin. There were so many people here. She crept forward to the entrance of the room, just hovering in the archway. From just out of sight she scanned the faces, searching for one particular face, her heart in her mouth.

He wasn't here. Everything inside curled a little with disappointment, like the edges of paper burning. He hadn't come. She took a deep dragging breath followed by a half sob. *You can't cry. You can't.* Nor could she turn around and walk away, no matter how much she wanted to – and which she might have done eventually if a woman with long, dark glossy hair hadn't spotted her. With a brilliant, mega-watt beam, she came striding straight over on long legs wearing ridiculously high stilettos and still managing to appear totally graceful.

'Fashionably late, darling,' said Avril, draping an arm around her shoulder and drawing her into the crowd.

'Who are all these people?' whispered Fiona, staring around at the packed room. 'There are loads of them. Is that ... Dan Snow? And Kay Burleigh?'

'Probably,' said Avril with an airy wave of her hand. 'Now get your arse in here and throw some Prosecco down your neck then come and tell us about these fabulous photos. Especially the one of Mount Fuji.' Her fingers dug into Fiona's shoulder and she beckoned a waiter over and snagged Fiona a glass before guiding her to a group standing in front of the picture of the little boy and the *torii* gate.

'Look who's finally made it.' Avril pushed her forward and suddenly she was surrounded by her friends. She grinned at them. The gang were all there, except for Sophie who was all loved up in the States with her decidedly delicious American boyfriend.

There was a quick flurry of hugs and kisses.

'This is a great photo,' said Ben, pointing to the little boy in the red anorak. 'They're all great.'

'I really like the one of the man in the dark in front of Mount Fuji,' said Kate, her eyes gleaming with curiosity.

'You would,' said Ben with a teasing grin. 'I was trying to compliment Fiona on her talent and skill, not the eye candy.'

'Thank you.' Fiona smiled shyly at him; he'd always been kind to her but even though he'd softened since moving in with Katie, she'd always found him a little intimidating, which was weird because Gabe was much more imposing in so many ways.

'Such a great angle of the little boy. What did you do. Stand on your head?' he said and she laughed far too loudly to hide the stab of regret. The memory of Gabe's offer to hold her upside down pinched at her insides.

'I suffered for that one. I lay on the wet grass. But ...' she gave the photo a quick pleased glance. It had turned out well. 'It was worth it.'

'Fiona, you are so talented. These are wonderful. Honestly, it makes me want to get on the next flight and go to Japan.' Katie flung her arms around her.

With her affectionate hug, the lump in Fiona's throat threatened to overwhelm her again.

'That was the intention.' Fiona's smile was brittle but no one seemed to notice. 'I suppose I ought to make myself known to the organisers. I did phone and tell them I was running late but if I don't show my face, Kaito, who was my host in Japan, will be humiliated.'

'They can wait a bit longer,' piped up the older man with greying air dressed in a dapper tweed jacket and a burgundy bow tie. 'You've done an excellent job and if I was in the market for one of these, I'd buy that one of the people looking up at Shibuya Crossing. Bit costly for my purse.' Conrad winked at her.

'I don't think they're for sale. You can have one.'

'That's a very generous offer, young Fiona, but I think you'll find that their value is going to skyrocket. This exhibition is going to put you on the map, mark my words.'

'It will if I have anything to do with it,' said Avril, and Christophe laughed as Conrad whispered to Fiona. 'I'd sit back and enjoy the ride – you know what she's like.'

Motherhood had not slowed Avril down; she was still a dynamo even though her son Dylan was nearly two now.

'They're beautiful pictures, Fi,' said David softly. 'You should be so proud of yourself. You've come a long way.'

'Thank you, David,' she said, nearly undone by his kindness. 'I almost didn't come at all,' she said, attempting to make light of it, hiding the horrible panic that had surfed her emotions before Peter had come to the rescue. 'My mother had an accident and I thought I was going to have to take her to A&E, but luckily the handsome widower next door fancies himself as a knight in shining armour.'

'That's why you're so late,' said Katie. 'It's a shame, there was a gorgeous man here who particularly wanted to speak to you but he had a plane to catch.'

Fiona whirled around, her heart somersaulting in her chest. 'Who?'

Katie's eyes widened and she took a step back. 'Er ... erm. A man?' she said hopefully. 'Very handsome.'

'What did he look like?'

'Hot,' supplied Avril giving her husband's arm a squeeze. 'And familiar, I'm sure I've seen him somewhere before.'

Fiona could have shaken her. 'Hair colour. Eyes.'

'Dark hair. Collar length, swept back from his face. Striking eyes, almost navy blue. Divine suit. Honestly, he was very handsome.'

'Gabe.' Fiona's body sagged.

'Gabe Burnett?' Avril straightened. 'Oh, I'm so stupid. Of course, it was. He's aged well. I knew I knew him.'

'Where did he go?'

'No idea,' she said. 'I got chatting to the features editor on the Radio 4 arts show. She'd like to meet you.' Fiona tried to smile but inside she was dying. Gabe had been here and she'd missed him. Why hadn't he waited?

Reece said very quietly, as if sensing her distress, 'He left about five minutes before you arrived. He did wait for a while, pacing he was, but then he spoke to the woman at the desk and then left ...' Reece winced. 'He was in a bit of a temper by the size of things. He snatched his coat from the rack and stalked out. He seemed pretty angry.'

Fiona lifted her head and narrowed her gaze to the desk where there was a pretty Japanese woman in a black suit handing out programmes for the exhibition.

'Excuse me a minute.' She felt all eyes follow her as she walked over to the woman.

'Hello, can I help you?'

'Yes. I'm Fiona Hanning.'

'Miss Hanning. Does Mr Morimoto know you are here? Everyone loves your pictures. There's been so much excitement here. We're very honoured to have them.' She bowed. 'Very good pictures.'

'Thank you. There was a man here earlier but he had to leave. Dark hair. Blue eyes.'

'Oh yes. He was asking when you would be arriving as he had to catch a flight. Mr Morimoto told him your mother had fallen ill and before he could finish and explain that you were on your way, he bowed, said thank you and that he was going to miss his plane. He left very quickly.'

Fiona winced uncomfortably, reminded of the image of Gabe's furious face the last time she'd seen him. 'Thank you.' Well, that was that then. Gabe had been and she'd missed him. She turned to walk away, her boots like concrete weighing down her steps. 'Oh wait, he left something. It's a bit ...' She held up a crumpled flyer. 'I don't know if it was for you. He screwed it up and left it on the desk.'

The woman handed over the creased leaflet.

Love Letters.
An exhibition by Gabe Burnett.
The Castille Gallery, Dover Street.
April 25th – June 15th

Fiona stuffed it into her pocket. It wasn't for her. He'd talked about a retrospective. She wasn't a glutton for punishment. Those pictures of Yumi were brilliant, clever, and inspiring but she'd seen enough of Yumi to last her a lifetime.

Why had he even come this evening? Because he was in the country? As a courtesy to Haruka and Kaito? They would have expected him to call in, she was sure. And if he were coming to see her, or of his own accord, surely he would have been in touch. To tell her was going to be here. Or that he was even in the country. And if he had a flight to catch, he'd clearly never intended on staying for very long. Why hadn't he texted or phoned her? If he'd wanted to see her, he could have done either.

'Miss Hanning. You are here.' Mr Miromito stepped into her path and bowed. 'Welcome.'

'Hello, I'm so sorry I'm so late.'

He bowed again and with his hands waved away her apology. 'Your mother had an accident. How is she? I was most sorry to hear this.'

'She's fine. It's not serious, I don't think. She had a fall.' That sounded better than that she tripped over the stupid cat. 'She's gone to the hospital with a friend to get it checked out.'

He bowed again. 'I am very pleased to hear that she is being looked after. I hope that she will make a fast and good recovery. May I introduce you to some people?'

The rest of the evening was a blur of bowing, shaking hands and being introduced to so many people whose names she was never going to remember – well, except for the few celebrities that were there. Who would ever forget meeting Bryan Adams and talking photography techniques with him? Or Katie giving her a thumbs up and taking lots of pictures on her phone. She even spotted Brian May with his wife.

Even so, none of it made up for the disappointment squeezing her heart without mercy.

Finally, as the crowd began to thin, she had no more excuses for avoiding Avril and she made her way back to the others.

'Well, I think you've officially got a hit on your hands, young lady,' declared Conrad.

'It seems like it,' said Fiona, a little bemused. She'd been talking to the arts editor of one of the nationals who was going to put it in his guide for the weekend as a must-see show.

'Well done, Fi,' said David.

Avril was putting her phone away. 'Sweetie, I've been speaking to my producer and he's agreed we can film a segment here and interview you. With the Olympics coming up, tourism in Japan has had a huge boost. So we're going to run a story on that and we'll include a little piece on the exhibition and your inspiration. I'll liaise with the crew tomorrow but I'd like to film it the day after tomorrow. Will you be free?'

'Er ... erm, I suppose—'

'The answer is, "yes, Avril I'd love to, you're amazing. Thank you so much." You do realise people would kill to be on my morning programme?'

'Not everyone wants their five minutes of fame,' drawled Ben.

'Yes, they do. And Fiona needs the exposure. This will do wonders for her blog, her influencer profile, and her career as a photographer.'

'You've got it all sussed,' said Ben.

She patted him on the cheek. 'You'd better believe it, babe.' Fiona was starting to relax, thinking she'd got away with it, when Avril pounced.

'So, now. Gabriel Burnett. What's the story there?'

'There's n-no story,' she stammered, giving herself away.

'I knew it. What happened? Did he remember you? Please tell me you made a big joke of it.'

'Yes. He remembered me. And it was fine.'

Avril turned to others. 'Our little Fiona went and planted one on him when she was a teenager. He was her teacher.'

'Seriously?' asked Katie staring at Fiona with astonishment.

'I was young and foolish. And he did remember and he was nice about it.' She blushed under their combined interest.

'How nice?' asked Avril.

'We ...'

'He seemed quite agitated earlier,' said David.

'Apparently he had a plane to catch; he just popped in.'

'Mmm, interesting,' said Avril.

'No, it's not.' She coloured under their combined scrutiny.

'But you didn't know he was coming.' Her smirk was far too knowing.

'No.' *Please stop asking questions*, she prayed. It was as much as she could do to hold it together.

'So he was here to surprise you.'

Fiona closed her eyes, realising that she'd adopted her awkward stork pose. 'I really don't want to talk about it.'

Everyone suddenly shifted on the spot.

'Okay, sweetie,' said Avril, the only one who wasn't the least bit uncomfortable. She tucked her arm through her husband's. 'We need to go home. We promised the babysitter we'd be back by eleven. I'll be in touch tomorrow, Fi.'

Fiona gave her a tight smile, annoyed at giving herself away. Avril would want to know everything now. And telling her would bring all the rawness back up. Katie gave her elbow a discreet squeeze of solidarity.

With a round of kisses, Avril swept her long-suffering

husband away leaving the group in amused but awkward, shuffling silence.

'She doesn't change, does she?' said Conrad.

'She doesn't,' agreed Kate with a smile.

'But heart of gold,' he added. They all nodded. Thanks to her he had a regular monthly TV slot on furniture and interior design which had significantly raised his profile and led to other work – a lifesaver for a man in his sixties who had been living hand-to-mouth for several years.

Fiona smiled at them all. She didn't know where she'd be without their friendship but if she told them about Gabe now, she'd start crying and she didn't know if she'd be able to stop.

'I ought to be going. I need to find out how Mum is.' She waved her phone at them. 'The last message I had from her said she was still waiting to be seen. Hopefully, she hasn't done any serious damage. I ought to give her a call.'

Chapter 29

'That's it,' said Avril two days later as the camera man began packing his up kit. 'All done. And stop fretting you, look gorgeous.' She flicked Fiona's hair over her shoulder. 'This is so much better than the Heidi look and I'm glad you've ditched that hideous bloody orangutan coat. Please tell me it went into a skip.'

Amusement twitched Fiona's mouth. 'It's been passed on to someone whose mother is probably saying much the same.'

'Oh, how could you? The fashion police will lock you up.' She shuddered with typical Avril melodramatics.

Fiona just grinned at her. 'Thank you for the interview. Let's hope I won't put people off their breakfasts.'

'Darling, if I don't, you certainly won't. I'm fed up with telling you, you're gorgeous. You're on your own now.'

The roll of her eyes made Fiona smile and say impulsively, 'I love you Avril.'

'Well of course you do. Now, I'm afraid I can't linger any longer. That'll air tomorrow. And we need to catch up. You still haven't told me all about the handsome Gabe Burnett. In fact, we're off to film a quick segment at The Castille Gallery on

Dover Street. Apparently he's got a limited exhibition and my producer knows him from way back when. Want to come?'

'No. No thanks.' The thought of going to see pictures of Yumi in all her gorgeousness made her feel positively sick. She'd never forget that final flare of triumph in the other woman's eyes. I've won, you've lost.

'Okay. How's your mum by the way?'

'Just a bad sprain ... although Peter next door is insisting on chauffeuring her everywhere. I've never known her need to go to Tesco so often. Twice yesterday.'

'Ooh, do I detect romance?'

'I'll keep you posted.' Fiona had never seen her mother so happy.

'Right. What are you up to now?'

'I'm meeting someone here who wants to talk about a photography project.'

'That's exciting.'

'We'll see. Lots of people have approached me in the last twenty-four hours wanting me to take pictures except they don't have any money. They want pictures for free.'

'Don't do it. Don't you dare sell yourself short. Talk to me before you agree anything. In fact, why don't you tell people I'm your manager. Or Christophe could be.' Her eyes lit up with the idea. 'Gotta go. The nanny finishes at one. But call me.' And with that Avril had gone, making Fiona relieved that Avril was on the clock.

She was surprised when just half an hour later her phone rang and Avril's name popped up on the screen.

'Sorry, I should have switched that off. I do apologise.' Fiona pressed the red button to ignore the call as her meeting was just wrapping up.

Now she had no excuse – all of a sudden it seemed she was surplus to her mother's requirements whereas once she would have kept her phone on in case her mother called.

'No problem,' said the woman who represented an environmental charity who wanted to stage an exhibition to raise awareness of plastic pollution in British rivers and waterways. The charity, she'd already explained, did have a limited budget but Fiona would have been interested in the project anyway.

Fiona listened as the woman began to talk again, explaining more about the brief.

Almost immediately her phone rang again. She apologised and deleted the call but before she could switch it off, which is what she should have done the first time, it rang for a third time.

'Sounds like it might be urgent,' said the woman. 'We're about done – I don't mind if you answer it.'

'Thank you. I think it must be, although I've no idea what she wants. She was here half an hour ago.'

She picked up the call. 'Hi Avril.'

'You have to come here. Dover Street. The exhibition. Now. Today.'

'What?'

'Gabriel Burnett's exhibition. You have to see it.'

'Why?'

'You'll know when you get here. Trust me. Wish I could hang around. Call me later.'

349

Fiona stared at her phone, bemused.

The woman did her best to hide her curiosity but she'd clearly heard both sides of the conversation.

'I have no idea what that's about.'

'No, but she sounds insistent.'

Fiona laughed. 'She's that sort of person.'

'Well, good luck and I'll send you an email confirming some of the details.'

They wrapped up the meeting, although Fiona's curiosity was so piqued, she could barely concentrat e.

Tapping her foot, she waited at South Ken for a Piccadilly train anxiously anticipating the familiar rattle of the rails. Upon arrival the tube train was packed, although nothing compared to Tokyo standards. Everyone on the platform swarmed in the through the inadequate sized doors, pushing and shoving and she ended up with her nose pressed to a grey wool coat that smelled of takeaways and damp dog. It reminded her of when she'd been squished up against Gabe, so close she could see the individual bristles of stubble. She closed her eyes, fighting against the dull, ever-present pain that she couldn't quite pinpoint.

When she was disgorged at Green Park, agitation and uncertainty made her fidgety and impatient, especially with the sheep-like horde of tourists that dithered outside the Ritz indecisively. Why did Avril want her to go to the gallery? It didn't make sense.

'Move,' she snarled, which came out far more loudly than she'd meant, but for God's sake what was wrong with them cluttering up the pavement. Why couldn't they stand at the side under the pillars like sensible people?

A horn blared and a taxi just missed her as she nipped across the road, ignoring the rapidly diminishing countdown of the crossing sign. There it was. Dover Street.

She tracked the numbers on the building, searching for the gallery sign and nerves slowed her furious pace. What was she going to find? Why had Avril been so insistent? She shouldn't have come.

Spotting the building, she walked across the road and without breaking her stride, she pushed the door open.

There was a reception desk manned by a young man in a sharp suit with an equally sharp haircut and an impressive hipster beard.

'Can I help ...?' his voice trailed off and he stared at her, his mouth actually dropping open.

'I'm looking for—'

'The Gabe Burnett exhibition,' he interjected recovering quickly, 'of course you are. Through the gallery to your left.'

'Thank you.'

His sombre face suddenly broke into a broad smile. 'My pleasure.'

What? Was she covered in fairy dust or something? The world had gone mad today. Puzzled, she cast a backward glance to find him staring after her, still smiling.

Following his directions, she walked along the highly polished wooden floor, her feet echoing within the high-ceilinged space of the old Regency building which had been sympathetically modernised with discreet contemporary fixtures. There was a quiet, hushed library-air to the space and she was aware of a couple of people examining some pictures at the opposite end of the gallery. She turned left and her feet skittered to a halt as she stopped dead.

Shock and surprise flashed over her like an April shower.

It felt as if she'd run into a wall. Her runaway, racing heart came to a thudding halt.

She stared. And stared. And stared. Then her pulse burst back into action, thundering through her veins so hard she thought she might faint.

Opposite her, hanging on a partition wall, her own face stared back at her. Lips slightly parted, her hair loose, rippling and shimmering with gold in the slanting sunlight and her eyes glowing with a secretive smile.

Her mouth moved with unintelligible words. How? What? Why? Again she took in all the details, her hand clasped over her mouth as it dawned on her. Oh my God.

The subtext was unmistakable, blown up for the whole world to see. A woman in love. And if that wasn't bad enough, there was a small title card beneath the picture saying exactly that.

She blinked as if that might change things. There was no mistaking what this woman was thinking or feeling and Fiona had to swallow back the sudden tears.

It was the picture Gabe had taken in the Kyoto suite, the moment she realised she'd fallen in love with him again.

Stunned, she began to move forward, transfixed by the image. As she neared it, she realised there was a small square room beyond with a simple wooden bench situated right in the middle. On the walls were six more pictures. Her heart pitched again as she sucked in a gasp.

They were all of her.

Hardly daring to breathe, she moved to the first one. Her face was blown up to poster size.

Lying on the sofa with her hair spilling over the arm like a molten golden waterfall dappled by the sunshine, her face was serene and happy, her mouth curved in a satisfied smile.

Then, still dumbstruck, she moved to the next.

Her, under the cherry blossom at Churito Pagoda, laughing up at the photographer, warmth and tenderness in her eyes.

One by one, she took each one in.

Wet and triumphant at the Meji Shrine, chin lifted.

Leggy and impossibly glamorous, caught mid-stride at the Shibuya crossing, her skirt whipping up around her thighs.

Wide-eyed with enthusiasm and passion on the train, the moving background a blur.

Perched on the top of the vendor's cart at Shibuya, excited and animated. He'd called that one 'Surprise at Shibuya'.

Overwhelmed, she sank onto the bench opposite the final image and her heart almost burst.

Gabe had taken it at Tenjozan Park, the morning after they'd first slept together, when he'd asked her not to care too much. She was looking down at him, sadness in her eyes but her chin lifted and a determined set to her mouth.

Her heart contracted; it was picture of such piercing tenderness it made her cry.

With blurred vision she stared at the picture, amazed and touched by how much he'd seen. By his sheer talent and the depth of emotion he'd revealed in each and every one photo. He'd seen into her soul.

And played it back to her.

Love Letters. The name of the exhibition, it clicked. Each one was a love letter. To her.

Silent tears ran down her face, her heart filling with so much joy she would surely burst with it.

She was aware of someone sitting down beside her, sliding closer, thigh to thigh, taking her hand and lacing his fingers through hers.

'They're beautiful,' she whispered.

He squeezed her hand.

'They're not supposed to make you cry.' His voice was gruff.

And then she did, small hiccupping sobs and he put his arm around her, pulling her into his chest, holding her so tightly with both arms as if he couldn't bear to let her go.

Finally, she dared lift her face up to his. She blinked as his familiar, handsome face came into focus and lifted a hand to his cheek. Those blue eyes softened as he searched her face. 'I missed you.'

She managed a small smile. 'Me too.'

And then he kissed her.

A tender kiss full of pent-up longing, as his hands roved over her face as if trying to reacquaint himself with every dip and plane. The tenderness of it brought more tears spilling out and he kissed each one.

'Please don't cry. I'm sorry I didn't come before.'

'Why didn't you?' She thought of the bleak emptiness of the last two weeks.

'Oh God, I'm sorry.' His smile was gentle but worried as his eyes searched hers. 'I wanted to. I ... I went to the airport but you'd already gone through.'

'You were there? I didn't know.' But if she had, would it have stopped her getting on the plane? Probably not.

'I nearly caught the first plane after yours back to London. But ...'

She took pity on him. He deserved her honesty. 'I might not have listened ... or believed.'

With a half laugh, he took her hand in his again, lacing his fingers through hers. 'Good old Haruka. She tried to tell me as much. Interfering old bat.' His dark eyes twinkled as he said it, reminding her of the conversation they'd had when he'd taken this very picture. That gorgeous day in the shadow of Fuji on the edge of the lake.

'I did wonder why she was suddenly so keen for me to leave.'

'Testing me. And punishing me, a little. For being such an idiot for such a long time.'

Fiona lifted her chin with a touch of impish mischief. 'You don't expect me to defend you, do you? I'm with Haruka on that one. you were. What changed?'

He winced. 'You, making me see what had been there all the time.'

She saw the chagrin in his rueful slow blink and didn't need to know the details. She shook her head but squeezed his hand in understanding. 'You were the only person that couldn't see it.'

'I'm sorry. I realised that night that I didn't love her. I'm not sure if I ever really did. Not real love. Not like ...' He cupped her chin and placed a kiss on her mouth. 'I came to find you in the morning but you'd gone. And that's when I realised I needed to show you. To show you the you that I see. The you that I fell in love with before I even knew it.'

He nodded towards the picture. 'I was worried words weren't enough.'

'A picture is worth a thousand words,' she said, gazing up at the picture, still not quite believing what he'd done. Each of the images were stunning. 'You are brilliant.'

'Thanks to you.'

'I don't think so. You have an extraordinary talent. I'm glad you're using it again.'

'So am I.'

For a moment they both stared at the picture, each lost in their own thoughts.

'When did you know?' she asked softly.

'When did I know what?'

'That I was in love with you. Before or after you saw the pictures.'

'Then,' he pointed to the final picture, the one from Tenjozan. 'When I asked you not to care too much and you lifted your chin as if you'd go into battle for me. And I fell a little bit in love right back because you cared even though I told you not to.'

They lapsed into silence.

'Can I ask a question?' she suddenly said.

'Mmm.'

'Why did you call the train picture "Tupperware"?'

Now his eyes danced with amusement. 'Do you know something about Tupperware?'

She frowned, completely lost. 'The proper stuff doesn't leak and it lasts for ever.' Perplexed, she raised her palms. 'What does that have to do with—'

'My parents' marriage is the kind I'd like one day; their relationship is durable and reliable ... like Tupperware. Everything that my relationships have not been. During the tea ceremony I was thinking about my values and where I'd gone wrong.'

She glanced back at the picture and he squeezed her hand. 'Not very romantic I'm afraid but in that moment, you reminded me of what I'd lost along the way. That I'd been chasing the wrong things and how different I'd been when I first came to Japan. And the enthusiasm and wonder in your eyes made me start to see things differently.' He grinned. 'Tupperware somehow seemed appropriate.'

She rolled her eyes.

'I know it's not very romantic but there's a Japanese word, *shinbui*, the aesthetic of simple, subtle, beauty. You could say Tupperware is like that; there's a simple, subtle beauty in its durability and reliability.'

With a giggle – as much born of the silliness as the effervescent happiness bubbling away inside – she remembered that Setsuko had said she had *shinbui*. She'd tell Gabe later, and in the meantime said, 'I'll never look at it in quite the same way.'

'Well, hopefully when you do, you'll realise ...' He took her face in his hands and rubbed his nose against hers before pulling back to say, '... how much I love you.'

With a heartfelt smile, she kissed him on the mouth, savouring the feel of his lips. God she'd missed him. Things might have started to get out of hand from that moment if it wasn't for the discreet cough behind them. They both turned to find the man from the front desk.

'Just checking everything is all right.' Behind him two more members of staff peeped over his shoulder, their faces bright with curiosity as they whispered to each other. In the hushed echoey space, she heard them say, 'It is her.'

'Everything is perfect, thanks Jay.'

'Okay, well, let us know if you need anything.' He backed away, taking the two young women with him.

Fiona swung round to Gabe, frowning in puzzlement. 'How did you know I was here?'

Gabe laughed again. 'I've been staking out the coffee bar across the road every day. And the staff all had strict instructions to call me if you turned up.'

'What if I hadn't come?'

'Then I'd have come to you but I knew you would.'

'How?'

'Because you face things. No matter how difficult, you try. You do new things. You challenge yourself, even though you don't think of yourself as bold. You are my *kintsugi*, the golden glue that healed this jaded, cynical idiot and made him believe in love again.'

She put a hand up to her hair. 'Haruka said something similar to me.'

'Haruka is a very wise woman.'

358

'She is.'

'I need to send her a WhatsApp. Let her know that all is well.'

With that he held up his phone, put his arm around her and took a selfie and they agreed it didn't need a message because, after all, a picture is worth a thousand words.

THE END

Acknowledgements

You could probably spend a lifetime exploring Japan and still find there's more to learn about the culture, the history and the people. It is a truly fascinating place and I am indebted to a number of people who helped broaden my research by sharing their experiences of living, working and visiting there. Harley Cyster-White, who helped with the day to day living details on houses, pubs and transport. My dear friend, Alison Cyster-White, who told me all about the digital museum and negotiating the train system to travel around the country (and snow monkeys, even though I couldn't get them in). Also Alan Garner, who helped me navigate my way around Tokyo with invaluable advice on the Yamanote line, and Claire Doherty, a veteran of the Japanese Embassy, who gave me brilliant insight into Japanese customs and food as well as some highly entertaining anecdotes too libellous to include!

Thanks to my fab editor, Charlotte Ledger, whose love of Japan was so infectious she inspired this book, and to my ever patient agent, Broo Doherty, whose unfailing support and brilliant guidance kept me going when I was convinced

361

that this was the second worst book I'd ever written. (The worst book I ever wrote ended up being nominated for a Romantic Novel of the Year award which just goes to show, I know nothing!)

And no book would ever be finished without my writing pals, Donna Ashcroft, Phillipa Ashley, Sarah Bennett, Darcie Boleyn and Bella Osborne, who cheer me on and keep me focussed when the going gets tough. Special thanks also go to my friend Paulene Le Floche for her proofreading help and unfailing support.

Last but not least a huge shout out to all the lovely readers and bloggers who still amaze me by being so supportive and bring me joy when they send wonderful messages. I'm so grateful to you all.

Ozone layer An atmospheric layer between ten and twenty miles above the earth that contains a large amount of ozone, which absorbs most of the harmful radiation from space.

Phytoplankton Plankton consisting of microscopic plants floating in bodies of water.

Plastic An artificial substance made from a range of chemicals that can be moulded into shape while soft, and then set into a rigid or slightly elastic form e.g. single-use plastic bottles.

Pod A group of whales or dolphins.

Pollution The presence in or introduction into the environment of a substance which has harmful or poisonous effects.

Plastic pollution The accumulation of plastic objects and particles in the Earth's environment that affects humans, wildlife, and their habitat.

Sandpipers A wading bird with a long bill and typically long legs that nests on the ground by water and visits coastal areas.

Single-use plastic Products that are used once, or for a short period of time before being thrown away and cause harm to the environment. They are more likely to end up in our seas than reusable options.

Spyhopping A vertical half-rise out of the water performed by a whale in order to view their surroundings.

Synthetic Typically a material made with chemicals in a lab to imitate a natural product, such as clothes and accessories.

Tail fluke A whale's tail is known as a fluke.

Wagtails A slender Eurasian and African songbird with a long tail that is frequently wagged up and down, typically living by water and sometimes found in the hills of Scotland and Wales.

Waste A material eliminated or discarded as no longer useful or required after the completion of a process. Also known as rubbish.

Whale breach A whale's jump where most of its body rises out of the water.